CUT & RUN

Cut & Run Series Book 1

By Abigail Roux

RIPTIDE PUBLISHING

Riptide Publishing
PO Box 1537
Burnsville, NC 28714
www.riptidepublishing.com

This is a work of fiction. Names, characters, places, and incidents are either the product of the author's imagination or are used fictitiously. Any resemblance to actual persons living or dead, business establishments, events, or locales is entirely coincidental. All person(s) depicted on the cover are model(s) used for illustrative purposes only.

Cut & Run
Copyright © 2008, 2024 by Abigail Roux

Cover art: L.C. Chase, lcchase.com
Layout: L.C. Chase

All rights reserved. No part of this book may be reproduced or transmitted in any form or by any means, electronic or mechanical, including photocopying, recording, or by any information storage and retrieval system without the written permission of the publisher, and where permitted by law. Reviewers may quote brief passages in a review. To request permission and all other inquiries, contact Riptide Publishing at the mailing address above, at Riptidepublishing.com, or at marketing@riptidepublishing.com.

ISBN: 978-1-963773-02-6

Second edition
June, 2024

Also available in ebook:
ISBN: 978-1-963773-01-9

Cut & Run

Cut & Run Series Book 1

By Abigail Roux

RIPTIDE PUBLISHING

To everyone in my life who isn't afraid to tell it like it is. Right to my face. As many times as it takes.

Table of Contents

Chapter 1 1
Chapter 2 35
Chapter 3 63
Chapter 4 89
Chapter 5 119
Chapter 6 165
Chapter 7 177
Chapter 8 189
Chapter 9 211
Chapter 10 245
Chapter 11 271
Chapter 12 297
Chapter 13 313
Chapter 14 331
Chapter 15 353
Chapter 16 379

Chapter One

Allison McFadden walked slowly in the cool night air, her arms tightly wrapped around her slim body to keep the wind from whipping at her coat. The man with her saw her shiver and gently put his arm around her, sending an electric jolt of anticipation through her.

She laughed softly, slightly giddy from the dirty martinis he had bought for her all night. He'd actually taken her to Bemelmans Bar in the Carlyle Hotel; it was possibly the most romantic place she had ever been, complete with live piano music and a sophisticated, old-fashioned ambiance that had seduced her just as completely as he had.

He was witty and charming, and he was good-looking and chivalrous almost to a fault. He hadn't even stolen a kiss yet.

Allison smiled as she remembered how he'd taken her up to the murals that lined the walls of Bemelmans and told her about them; how some writer who had lived in the hotel had painted them and they'd been part of some children's books. She had tried to listen, but she had only been able to concentrate on his hand, resting just a little lower on her back than it had been earlier in the evening, and his lips moving next to her cheek as he spoke. She only remembered that the paintings were of animals in Central Park. There had been an elephant skating. And he had pointed out an armed rabbit stalking its fellow bunnies with an automatic weapon in one of the cartoon-like murals.

They'd both laughed at the morbid humor of it, and Allison loved the way he laughed.

Now, he was walking her home, like a true gentleman. He had asked the cab driver to stop several blocks away from her building to have the privilege of doing so. It was only their first date, and Allison couldn't believe that she was going to do what she was planning.

"Do you . . . Would you . . . I mean, would you like to come up? For coffee, or . . ."

He smiled, and Allison was lost in the way it made his eyes warmer. He reached up and ran his hands through her hair, watching the way the blonde strands glimmered in the artificial light of the streetlamps.

"Is your roommate home?" he asked her softly, his intimate voice cutting through the chilly wind and right into her.

She licked her lips and nodded. "But she won't bother us," she insisted quickly, her words almost breathless as she reached out and smoothed her hand over his lapel, feeling his badge under the material.

"Then lead the way," he murmured with a smile.

It would have been the perfect time for him to kiss her, she thought, as she took his hand and led him into the building. It would have been just as ridiculously romantic as the rest of the night. But, she supposed, nothing could be perfect.

Hours later, as Allison struggled for her last breath, she couldn't help but wonder if he'd never kissed her because it would leave his DNA behind.

The phone call could not have come at a worse time. FBI Special Agent Ty Grady was still pissed off and cursing about its unfortunate timing two days later as he sat alone in his living room.

Four weeks of undercover work—round-the-clock surveillance, phone taps, wires, bribing informants, and some high-speed tailing— all shot to shit because some rookie hotshot forgot to leave his cell phone at home. Bums begging on the street do not ring to the tune of a Mozart orchestra, and unfortunately for the team of tired undercover FBI agents tailing Antonio de la Vega, their target was aware of that particular bit of random information. He'd disappeared just as quickly as the rats on the New York sidewalks as Ty and his team had scrambled.

The operation had been blown, their target was now in some other country where they had no jurisdiction, and all their evidence would be bagged, tagged, and stuffed in a box in a basement, never to be seen again. The fact that most of what they'd done had been under Ty's direction and slightly irregular, depending on a high-profile collar in order to keep them from getting their asses fired and thrown in jail, was not helping Ty's mental state.

He sprawled on his sofa, still covered in sweat from his attempts to work out his frustration at the Bureau's Baltimore gym, and stared out at the city through the large windows on either side of the television. He could see his own reflection in the black screen of the plasma TV on the opposite wall, and he looked even more exhausted than he felt. He needed a shave; most of his handsome face was covered in three days' worth of beard, and his dark hair could probably use a trim. He was a large man, nearly three inches over six feet, and he usually carried his frame like a large cat, lithe and easy. Tonight, though, there was a slump to his broad shoulders as he sprawled. He had no intention of moving anytime soon.

Not until his cell phone began to trill demandingly. With a heavy sigh, he snapped it off his waistband and flipped it open. "Grady," he answered curtly, his West Virginia drawl still pronounced after all the years he'd spent away from home.

"Special Agent Grady, Assistant Director Burns would like to see you," a clipped, professional voice informed him.

"When?" Ty asked flatly.

"Special Agent Grady, the Assistant Director of the Criminal Investigations Branch does not call to make appointments. He expects you in thirty minutes."

"Thirty minutes!" Ty blurted. "Do you have any idea where I am?"

"In your dirty underwear, no doubt. Be here in thirty," the voice answered in the same flat, businesslike tone before hanging up.

Ty closed his eyes and mentally kicked something. Thirty minutes to get into DC was going to require the flashy blue lights. Ty fucking hated the flashy blue lights.

"Great job, Special Agent Garrett. You are a credit to the Bureau," the Division Director said as he shook the man's hand. "A commendation will go in your file for your work, of course."

"Thank you, sir," FBI Special Agent Zane Garrett answered curtly as the other agents murmured quiet, slightly reluctant congratulations.

"And I get to reward you for your work well-done," the Director continued smoothly. "You're being promoted out of the division. I'm very sad to see you go," he said smoothly, still pumping Zane's hand vigorously.

Zane shook his hand somberly, his face a mask of pure professionalism that covered the brutally honest thoughts he harbored beneath it. "I've enjoyed working for you, sir. But you know me; always looking to be where I can do the most for the Bureau."

"That's a good man. Say goodbye and get yourself upstairs. Assistant Director Burns wants to see you in ten."

Showing no hint of a smile—or the disdain for the praise over doing his boring-ass desk job—Zane turned and walked through the other agents he'd worked with in the division that pursued cybercrimes. He'd gotten along with them fairly well, considering he did his job, and sometimes theirs as well, with complete and utter focus. Zane knew many of his co-workers were just as happy to see him go as stay; his strict adherence to the rules and logical, single-minded work to achieve his goals were often tiring to those around him. He had goals, several of them, and they were all that mattered. None of them included working with this division any longer than necessary.

Looking around the open office, Zane knew with complete certainty he wouldn't miss it. While his obsessive attention to detail had steered him perfectly while on these assignments, he knew he was worth far more to the Bureau than serving on this mind-numbing, numbers-crunching detail. Now he would get his chance to prove it.

Shaking some hands and enduring a few "so sorry to see you go" back slaps, he waved off his soon-to-be-former co-workers, told the office administrator he would be back later to clear out his desk, and walked out the door. He looked forward to seeing what the Assistant Director of the Criminal Investigative Branch had in store for him. He had worked damn hard for this promotion. It had to be good, since the man wanted to see him immediately.

Zane stopped into the bathroom to straighten his tie and check to make sure his close-cropped brown hair lay down neatly. The suit he wore was sharply tailored to his six-foot five-inch frame, but it didn't hide the bulky muscles that moved under the fabric. His was not a body you'd expect to see riding a desk, a fact he was reminded of daily, looking at the slightly pudgy agents who worked around him. He frowned slightly, surveying the crow's-feet at the corners of his eyes and the ridges of his twice-broken nose. With a displeased twitch, he ran his hands over his close-shaven cheeks and dismissed his image before buttoning his suit jacket and heading upstairs.

The secretary gave Ty Grady a look over her glasses that clearly said she disapproved of the air he breathed. She lifted her chin and looked him up and down, wrinkling her nose at his appearance. "You're early," she announced with a touch of surprise to her voice.

Ty looked her up and down in return and cocked his head to the side. "I used the flashy blue lights," he told her with a helicopter motion of his finger.

She sniffed as she glanced over his unshaven face, scuffed leather jacket, jeans, and dirty cowboy boots. His T-shirt seemed to be particularly appalling to her sensibilities, even though it was clean. It was black and had the words Cocke County FBI in large white print on the front. Upon closer inspection, there were smaller words between the larger ones, and when she squinted, she was able to read the entire shirt: I was probed in Cocke County by the FBI. She made a small, insulted noise as she looked back up at him. Ty ignored her, leaving her looking slightly scandalized as he headed for the Assistant Director's door.

"You can't go in there yet!" she hissed as she stood from her desk and pointed at him.

He stopped at the door and turned around to look at her, blatantly putting his hand on the door handle and pushing it down with a smirk. Her mouth worked soundlessly, and she turned and scrambled for her intercom to announce him before he could get inside.

Assistant Director Richard Burns looked up at him in surprise and annoyance as Ty stepped into the office and closed the door behind him. "You wanted to see me, sir," Ty greeted, the words perfectly professional, but the tone somehow just as insolent as it always was.

"Sit down," the man ordered with a jab of his pen at one of the seats across from his desk. "We're waiting for one more person."

Ty moved to the seat and sat, his leather jacket sending up a tiny little cloud of dust as he flopped into the seat. He did a fairly good job of concealing his surprise. "Someone else?" he inquired evenly. "Am I being lynched?"

"If you keep your mouth shut for the next thirty minutes, you may not spend the night in jail. How about that?" Burns answered seriously without looking up from the papers he was signing.

Ty cleared his throat and shifted uncomfortably in his seat.

Zane Garrett entered the wide outer office to see the Assistant Director's secretary scurrying around her desk, obviously flustered. He paused, folding his hands behind his back. "Ma'am?" he asked politely when she didn't notice his entrance.

She looked up at him in surprise. "Special Agent Garrett, thank you for being prompt," she said, looking him up and down and nodding in approval of the tailored blue suit and silk tie. "You may go in now."

"Thank you, ma'am," he said evenly, proceeding to the door as she announced him through the intercom.

Burns looked up from the papers he was shuffling and gestured him in. "Come in, Special Agent Garrett. We've got some things to thrash out," he said to Zane, with a narrow-eyed look at the man sitting slumped in a chair in front of the desk.

"Yes, sir," Zane answered, moving to sit as the Director gestured. His eyes followed Burns's gaze. Only a blink betrayed Zane's surprise. The unkempt man sitting opposite Burns was a complete mess. Zane barely restrained the urge to sneer at him. Maybe he was an informant of some sort. He had that burnt-out, fidgety look to him.

Focusing on Burns again, Zane waited, composed and attentive, ready to start jumping through the next set of hoops.

Ty shifted in his seat, slouching further down and glancing over at the new man. God, the guy looked like he had just come off a printing press or something. "What are you doing, a how-to manual?" Ty asked the Assistant Director sarcastically. "Before and after?" he suggested wryly with a gesture at himself and then at the other man.

"Yes. You are sitting here before you get fired," Burns answered studiously. "And he is taking your job after you leave."

Ty pressed his lips tightly together and looked down at the shiny desktop sedately. Zane shifted his eyes between the man and Burns before narrowing them. He wondered why he had been asked to sit in on this meeting when the guy was obviously being fired. It seemed overly cruel. He clamped down hard on any further reaction and waited to see what would happen.

Ty licked his lips and looked up again to meet his superior's eyes almost defiantly.

"Fortunately for you, Grady, you have more lives than a cat," the man said to him with a small frown. "And you're getting another chance to prove to us that you can do this job without blowing shit up. I won't say one more, because God knows I'll just keep giving you more until you get yourself killed. Meet your new partner, Special Agent Zane Z. Garrett."

Zane couldn't have been more appalled, and it showed clearly in his reaction. This wreck of an agent was his new partner? "Director Burns," he started impulsively, but he caught his tongue and tightened his grip on the chair. What kind of reward was this?

"The hell he is!" Ty interrupted as he sat up straight. "I can't do my job with a . . . a . . . poster-boy partner," he practically stuttered angrily as he flopped his hand toward the squeaky-clean man next to him.

"And you can't do it without a partner, either, Special Agent Grady," Burns responded with a hard glare.

"Sir, it seems obvious," Zane said, not bothering to keep any edge of disapproval out of his voice, "that this agent needs more than I can possibly provide to help him. Frankly, it will take a miracle to make him even remotely professional. No one will take him seriously."

"Take me seriously?" Ty echoed in disbelief. "Christ, have those shoes ever even seen pavement? Shit," he exclaimed in a sudden panic as he gripped the arms of his chair and leaned forward. "Are you sending me to Cyber?" he asked Burns, who was sitting behind the desk and grinning like a small child at Christmas.

"Your tone of voice implies that investigating technological crime and terrorism might be below you," Zane said to him coldly as he leveled an even gaze on the other agent. "Perhaps you should consider requesting a transfer to professional staff. Or submitting your resignation altogether."

"Hey, fuck you, candy-ass," Ty snarled without looking over at him.

"Quiet, both of you!" Burns barked suddenly. "Grady, you're staying in Criminal until you get your ass killed or do something so illegal even I can't cover for you, understand? Garrett, you're to make certain he doesn't do either of those things. Is that clear? And you will both like it."

Ty's eyes widened as he realized he was being assigned a bookkeeping babysitter, and there wasn't a damned thing he could do about it. His stomach turned at the thought, but he supposed it was better than being fired. Or being in jail.

The thought of being attached to this troublemaking loose cannon was nearly enough to make Zane lose his composure. After all he'd done, all he'd worked for, this was all he was going to get. Despair threatened for a moment, and he had to take a deep breath to push it aside. He wanted to rail at Burns, but it wasn't his place to object. He'd make the best of this clusterfuck, and then leave this agent behind, just as he had the Cyber Division. That or go down in spectacular flames.

"Yes, sir," he acknowledged through clenched teeth.

"I expect you to learn from each other," Burns instructed, his heart going out to Zane Garrett. It was a shitty thing to do to him, sticking him with a man like Ty Grady after he'd worked his way back up from hell to be Cyber's top performing agent. But for this particular case, these two men were unusually qualified. "And the Bureau expects you to perform efficiently on your next assignment," he added as he tossed a file across the desk at Ty.

"Respectfully, sir, I understand you need someone riding herd on this . . . agent," Zane gritted out. "But what am I supposed to learn from him?" he asked, slanting a disbelieving look Grady's way.

Burns gave Ty a dubious glance and then shrugged apologetically in answer to Zane's query. He was well-acquainted with Garrett's past, but the man was resourceful. He'd had to be. He'd find a way to make this work.

"You can learn to kiss my ass," Ty shot back as he fumbled with the file his boss had chucked at him. "Just like you do everyone else's," he muttered.

Zane's temper lightened in the face of Grady's ridiculous assertions, leaving behind more than a trace of resentment. He would have rolled his eyes if he weren't aware of how it might be construed. The man's language was complete and purposeful insubordination. It looked like his new partner was a real prize, one that had somehow gained the favor of the Assistant Director of his new division—just as he himself was the focus of Burns's ire.

"Sir, if I may ask, who is this delightful new person I'll be calling my partner?" he asked, the sarcasm thinly veiled.

"Special Agent B. Tyler Grady," Burns answered as Ty scanned the file he had flipped open, ignoring them both as he looked through it. "Despite his appearance, he is unfortunately very good at his job."

"You're putting us on the Tri-State case?" Ty asked suddenly, utter disbelief coloring his words as he looked up at Burns.

Zane stiffened and inhaled sharply. He knew all about the Tri-State case. Hell, everyone in the Bureau knew all about the Tri-State case, even though they had only been working it for a few weeks. A really messy, really conniving, really frightening serial killer kept popping up and going to ground every few weeks—for almost two months now—in New York City. Two bodies were found just across state lines, near the Tri-State marker, and most involved seemed to think the killer deliberately left them there to involve the FBI. Most recently, just days ago, the man took out two of their own agents, so the Bureau was now more personally invested.

Zane's eyes shifted back to Grady. "Very good at his job," Burns had said. Zane decided it must have been undercover work. Drugs or organized crime, maybe import/export. Somewhere that rough-and-tumble image would fit in. His mind started to buzz, calculating how their skill sets might complement each other. Or not.

"That's right," Burns answered with a tap of his pen on his desk. "And you will report to the New York field office—appropriately attired, Grady—at 1100 Monday. Is that clear?"

Recognizing the dismissal and standing, Zane nodded. "Yes, sir," he said curtly. Zane's most recent tour may have been spent in a high-tech computer lab, but that wasn't all he could do. He was a damn good agent, and he knew it. But he couldn't help thinking of Tyler Grady as a snake that might strike at a critical moment and poison his fragile job security. He could already tell this wasn't going to be easy. Actually, he could already tell it was going to be beyond hard as hell. But while there was the chance that one whiff of the bat could collapse his carefully reconstructed career like a house of cards, he also had a prime opportunity here. If he could make this work, it would send him a long way. And he wouldn't let any scruffy agent who fancied himself a badass get in his way.

Ty sat and stared at Burns for a long moment before standing and stepping toward the desk. He put two hands on the desk and leaned over, crumpling the file in his hand as he glared down at his boss. "You know me better than this, Dick," he murmured. "My partners don't last long."

"This one had better," Burns responded without blinking at the insubordinate tone.

"You promised me," Ty murmured accusingly.

"Consider it recanted," Burns replied unapologetically. "Go home and shower, Ty. You fucking stink."

The voices were low, but Zane heard enough. Burns's parting shot was clear, and Zane's lips twitched as he turned to lead the way. This Ty Grady must be some kind of special superstar for the Assistant Director to put up with that behavior. That or he was blowing someone further up the chain, Zane thought uncharitably. He allowed himself a slight grimace when he stopped in the outer office. He'd heard the same rumors about himself at one time. More than a few times.

Ty followed him and glared at Zane for a long moment as the secretary sniffed disapprovingly at him. "Sooner we get this over with, sooner we can go back to how it was. Got it?" he finally said to his new partner.

Zane didn't dignify the utterance with a reply. "May I see the case file, please?" he asked civilly.

"Get your own," Ty answered as he turned and stalked out of the office.

Zane stood there for a moment, mouth slightly agape. Ty Grady was a rude, insufferable, egotistical, stinking son of a bitch, and Zane was going to need to figure out how to tune him out. Otherwise, he just might give in to the pressure and kill the bastard, for the good of humanity.

Ty sat at the all-night diner near his apartment and read the file for the fourteenth time as he poked at his bacon and eggs. The papers had greasy fingerprints on them, and a few smudges that weren't identifiable, but Ty didn't notice. What he was seeing were the facts of the case. It was one of the most fascinating cases he'd ever read about, much less been involved in. The killer seemed to pick his targets at random; there was no victim type at all. He had no MO to speak of, and he left little to no evidence behind. The current belief was that the little evidence that had been collected was left intentionally, and the scenes where the bodies were found were certainly staged.

Eight murders and counting. The only two that hadn't been positioned after death (or "killed creatively," as Ty thought of it) were the two FBI agents who had been investigating the murders. Two trained agents, both with military backgrounds, shot point-blank in their hotel room before either man could even fire a weapon. And the only reason the Bureau attributed their deaths to the killer was because they were working on his case, and the FBI didn't believe in coincidences.

Ty shook his head and sighed, glancing at his watch with a blink. "Fuck," he groaned, digging in his pocket for money to leave on the table as he gathered his highly classified information and unceremoniously stuffed it under his jacket. He had things to do tomorrow—today, really—before he had to fly out early Monday morning.

Zane sat at his dining room table, a whole stack of copied files spread out in front of him. Case details, reports, autopsy recalls, scene photographs, forensic evidence... there was so much to read through, so many details. Details that caught and filtered through Zane's analytical mind. He'd been sifting through notes for hours trying to identify patterns, not in the case itself, but in the standard structure of investigation: where it was followed precisely, where it differed, where there were gaps in the investigation, where there was too much useless information. There'd been so many people on this job that it was already a mess.

All of that, he thought, as he shifted to take a bite of a late Sunday dinner of chicken and grape salad, was easy enough to track. He'd already decided to give a few specialty agents a call to ask questions; maybe Serena Scott in New York's Behavior Analysis Unit could help. She looked at murders all the time, and although this case was driving them crazy, she could explain some things for Zane. Murder wasn't exactly his forte. Plus, she owed him a favor.

A man didn't work at the FBI for nearly twenty years and not collect favors.

Sighing, he pushed away the coroner's reports comparison chart he'd made and carried his bowl to the kitchen sink, washing it out carefully before wiping the counter down. He glanced at the clock on the wall, straightened his shoulders, and cracked his neck. He'd have to leave extra early to get from Arlington to Dulles by 0530 to catch the plane. And he'd need every bit of patience and fortitude he could scrape up to get through what he knew was coming.

It was a commercial flight, and the tickets were waiting for them at the airline's front desk. Ty rolled his head from side to side and loosened his tie, grumbling unhappily as he walked in the hazy predawn through the parking lot. He had his suit jacket over one arm and two duffel bags of clothing and gear slung over his shoulder. He carried a beaten and scarred leather satchel by a strap across his chest as he walked. He was running just a little late, but he wasn't exactly worried about it. When he got inside, his tie askew and his suit coat wrinkled, he finally pulled the satchel over his head and plunked everything down to shrug into the jacket. He then hefted everything again, repositioned the bags, and made his way to the check-in desk.

"I knew you'd be late," Zane commented as Ty walked past him.

"And I knew you'd still have that stick up your ass," Ty responded with a shake of his head, not slowing as Zane spoke to him.

Ty's smart-ass response didn't rate a reply. Zane waited for him to get his ticket and check his bags before falling in beside him to walk to security. They'd met a total of two times now, and Zane had the same fleeting impression: Ty was an asshole who'd been lucky enough in the red zone to make it this far. And the Bureau wanted him to be lucky some more, but they didn't want to risk anything going wrong (because Ty was so very obviously insane), and that was why the very efficient Zane Garrett was charged with holding his leash.

It made Zane tired just thinking about it.

They showed their identification and were waved through security after a brief check. Still thinking about Ty's shit-for-attitude, Zane amused himself by thinking about what Ty must have had to do to pass muster. All agents went through the academy's sixteen-week New Agents Training Unit, and then they were farmed out and specialized. Because of his background, Zane excelled in the finer points of the law. Layers of information. Patterns. Details. Puzzles. It surprised people that Zane had a brain to go with his brawn, and he'd used it to his benefit many times.

Way back when, the Bureau assigned him to the Criminal Investigation Division of the Criminal Investigations Branch, working on financial crime. As he got more cases under his belt, he shifted to organized crime and informant matters, which put him into a brief stint in undercover work. Several personal and professional swerves and wild dives later, he was moved out of the CID and into the Cyber Division, digging up and dusting off those old pattern and detail skills to reestablish himself and hopefully polish his very tarnished reputation. He tried not to think about that tarnish often.

He was starting to suspect Ty Grady possessed a completely different set of specializations, and Zane was absolutely sure that they wouldn't mesh with his own. Looking over his new partner, Zane decided immediately that Ty obviously wouldn't have any trouble with the physical side of the job. He was an inch or two shorter than Zane, but his muscle weight probably equaled Zane's own. He was physically impressive, no doubt, and together they were clearly intimidating as they walked through the terminal.

It was the mental aspects of Ty's abilities that Zane pondered almost gleefully as they moved. Zane wondered if Ty would even be able to handle any of it, or if that was why Zane had been partnered with the guy; to be the brains of the operation, so to speak.

"Listen up, 'cause I'm only gonna say this once," Ty muttered as they walked to their gate. "I don't talk when I fly. I sleep. And I don't listen when I eat, understand? I don't wanna be buddies. I don't wanna chat," he said with a sarcastic lilt to the word. "I don't wanna know about your childhood or how your momma whipped you with a rubber glove or how much therapy you had to go through 'cause you flunked out of preschool. I don't wanna hear about how you want to be Director someday or how many collars you got chasin' those Internet freaks or how proud you are of your bowel movements. I don't wanna go shopping at Barneys with you, and I'm not gonna help you pick out your ties to match your socks and, I swear to God, if you get me shot, I'll kill you."

As he followed the other agent onto the plane and found his seat, stoic demeanor in place, Zane couldn't decide whether to be offended, upset, or just sad. Punching his new partner would likely not be condoned, and he wasn't sure Grady wouldn't give as good as he got just to cause a scene. But what a miserable life the man must have. Well, he wasn't the only one who had had it hard. Zane tried hard to sublimate the anger that line of thought caused, but so far, Ty just made him want to reach out and throttle the shit out of him. Wouldn't the Bureau just love that?

He decided it was best—for all parties involved—to ignore the man beside him. He went ahead and pulled out the comparative chart he'd made of the coroner's information with notes all over it in his tiny, crablike handwriting. At least some of the time could be well-spent.

Ty sighed heavily as he flopped into his seat and shook his head as he dug out the seat belt. His brand-new partner had failed the first test. Anyone who would quietly take the vitriol he had just spewed without so much as a "fuck you" in return was nothing but a brown-nosing ladder-climber who should have been riding a desk or working in the civilian market. At least his last partner had given as good as he got, he thought with a wince.

Zane heard the annoyed exhalation and ignored it. He gritted his teeth and wished there was some way to get out of this assignment. It was going to be an utter debacle, and he likely wouldn't be able to do anything about it. He wondered what ninth level of clerking hell he would be demoted to if this went wrong, or what type of civilian job he could get after he was kicked out of the Bureau. That upset him more than anything, thinking of all the years going to waste.

The flight was only about an hour long, and Ty planned to sit there and sleep the entire fucking way. The kid kicking the seat behind him was the only thing keeping him awake as the plane taxied down the runway. He turned around and peered through the coach seats, his hazel eyes piercing the kid as he narrowed them.

"Kick it one more time, and I'll rip your toes off and eat 'em," he promised.

"Have some decency," Zane chastised as his head turned to the side to check the situation. "He's gotta be three. He doesn't know any better."

"He does now," Ty countered as he turned back around and settled into his seat contentedly. Behind him a horrified young mother was holding her son's toes and gaping, wide-eyed and speechless.

"You have absolutely no people skills," Zane muttered, shaking his head. "No wonder you're sinking fast in the Bureau."

"Yeah, I'm a real anchor," Ty drawled as he leaned his head back and smiled. "I hear no one else will work with you."

Zane's lips pressed together slightly and he didn't look up from his paperwork. "You should have your hearing checked," he said flatly.

"My hearing's just fine, Skippy. You were 'promoted,' right?" Ty asked sarcastically, giving the word quotations with his fingers without opening his eyes. "Hate to tell you, Sport, but being transferred to another division in the same level ain't a promotion. It's called shuffling the unwanted."

"Reliable information, I'm sure, from someone on a landslide down the ladder."

"We both seem to be on the slip 'n' slide to the gutter, Shuffleboard," Ty observed happily. "Difference is, I don't give a shit," he offered as he reached up and turned off the overhead light and adjusted the cool air blowing down on him.

Zane didn't reply, instead closing his eyes for a moment to swallow down on the flare of annoyance. It was true. Ty didn't give a shit. But Zane did, which meant they were destined to be at each other's throats the whole time they were forced to work together.

Ty merely snickered quietly, knowing he had hit a chord. This could provide some amusement after all, he decided, even if they did end up killing each other.

Zane focused again on the notes. The rest of the flight passed in silence. Details about the deaths bounced around in his head, not really settling into any sort of pattern yet. He would dig the photos out and study them once they got settled. Maybe he could get a feeling for each victim.

He glanced up when the seat-belt light went on, and he looked over at Ty unhappily. The other man had dozed lightly in expectation of the long day ahead, and Zane decided that Ty sleeping was him at his most charming. But now he had to wake him up.

"Grady," he muttered, voice clipped.

"Not again, sugar, m'tired," Ty muttered as he flopped onto his side and jostled them both in the cramped seats.

Unamused, Zane pushed against the other man. "Grady," he said more insistently. "Wake up."

Ty huffed and opened his eyes slowly, looking around sleepily. "Hmm?"

Zane looked down at him, mildly surprised by the momentary drop in the rough attitude. "We're getting ready to land," he murmured.

Ty groaned softly and rolled onto his back again. He stretched his arms high over his head, yawning as he turned his body slightly and reached one arm way out into the aisle. The air hostess who was making her last check down the aisle walked right into his hand and gasped as he grabbed her. Ty dropped his arms and twisted to look up at her. "Sorry, sweetheart," he offered with a small, unrepentant smile.

She huffed slightly and gave him a wry smile as she turned in the aisle. "I've had worse," she murmured in response as she bent and slowly buckled his seat belt for him. "Put yourself in the upright position, please," she said to him softly before moving away. Ty raised his seat obediently and grinned, watching her with a contented smirk as she turned and continued on down the aisle.

While Zane silently envied Ty's free attitude and behavior, in the end, he just couldn't believe the man's gall. "How did you become such a total ass?" he asked, morbidly curious.

Ty cocked his head and watched the woman until she took her seat, then turned to look at Zane. "I didn't mean to," he insisted innocently. "C cups can get in the way."

Zane's look was patently disbelieving. "I think you decide what a perfectly polite person would do and then do the absolute opposite. It's like it's your life's goal to be the Antichrist."

"The Antichrist," Ty echoed, laughing as he shook his head. "Yeah. I bet you were head of the Drama Club in school, weren't you?"

"You didn't deny it."

"And Lord knows I mean everything I say," Ty responded with mock sincerity, pressing his hand to his heart and leaning closer to Zane earnestly.

"You just have that look," Zane confirmed, face stilled to passivity.

Ty chuckled and turned to look back at the front of the plane as the wheels squealed on the tarmac and the plane decelerated rapidly. "You're gonna have to dislodge that stick up your ass pretty damn quick if we're going to be working together," he added as the plane taxied to their gate. He unbuckled before the seat-belt light went off and rolled his neck.

"What's the matter? Afraid it's catching?" Zane asked. His patience was already wearing thin. He didn't have the time or the luxury to deal with Ty's antics.

"No, I'm not afraid of turning into you," Ty answered wryly, laughing softly as he shook his head. He leaned closer to Zane, almost close enough to touch his cheek with his nose. "You smell like Feeb," he explained in a low, serious voice. He was probably one of the only FBI agents who would actually utter the derogatory term other agencies used when talking about them.

When Zane turned his gaze on the other agent, his eyes glinted dangerously. His voice was frigid. "I bet you get off on it."

Ty smiled slowly, his eyes glittering mischievously. "If I did, would you change?" he asked.

Zane merely shook his head as if he felt sorry for the other man, deciding not to comment as he stood. The words on his tongue were certainly ungracious and unbecoming, and he couldn't afford it being reported. Not that his would rival Ty's behavior.

Ty shrugged and stretched to retrieve his satchel from the overhead bin. He didn't say another word as he followed the short line to the front of the plane and the exit. The stewardess stood there, smiling and saying goodbye to each passenger, and when Ty came up to her, he grinned widely and nodded at her cheekily.

"You have a nice stay in New York, sir," she said to him as she reached out and took his hand, discreetly pressing a piece of paper into his palm.

"Oh, it's getting nicer already," Ty responded brightly as he lingered there for a moment, looking her over rakishly, and then moved on to the exit.

"And just how is your image supposed to represent the Bureau better than mine?" Zane asked under his breath as they walked toward the concourse.

"It's not," Ty answered over his shoulder. "That's the whole damn point, Shuffleboard."

With his long legs, Zane easily caught up to walk alongside him. "So why the hell work for the Bureau at all if you don't give a damn?"

"'Cause I ain't in it for the status," Ty answered blithely.

Zane stopped in his tracks, looking at Ty's back with real hatred. The implication that the glory was Zane's reason for working at the Bureau was way the hell over the line. He watched him walk away and seriously, seriously considered calling Burns and accepting whatever fucking demotion it would take to not have to deal with this bastard. His temper was already roiling, and that was not good. Not good at all. His hand clenched on his briefcase for a long moment as he stamped down on the anger, watching Ty walk toward the exit.

Ty knew Zane had fallen away, but he didn't stop walking. If the dickhead wanted to sulk his way into being late for their meeting, that was his business. Ty was looking out for Number One. As always.

He also had a slightly more personal interest in this particular case.

Zane finally exited the main terminal and stepped out into the cool air as Ty was climbing into a black government Tahoe. Within a minute, he was seated inside as well, and the truck left the curb and pulled out into the airport traffic.

Ty slumped in the back seat, trying to shake off the grogginess and think up new ways to annoy his new partner. He looked at the driver in the rearview mirror, seeing brown eyes and high cheekbones and short, curly hair. This guy was too pretty to be an agent. And he looked like he was about fifteen. The light-haired man in the passenger seat looked even younger. "What are you two, the Hardy Boys?" he asked them with a huff.

Eyes flickering forward, Zane took in the two agents in front of them and frowned.

"That's very clever of you, sir," the driver responded dryly without taking his eyes off the road. "I could point out that we're too young to know who the Hardy Boys are and make you feel very old," he added as his brown eyes glanced to the rearview mirror and looked back at Ty. "But I would never do that, sir."

Zane's lips twitched, but he didn't comment. His eyes displayed his amusement as he glanced a little more carefully over the two young men. They were both very young, but Zane knew that experienced agents were practically being churned out of preschools these days.

"Welcome to New York, Special Agent Garrett, Special Agent Grady," the passenger greeted as he turned slightly in his seat. "I'm Agent Mark Morrison, this is Agent Tim Henninger," he went on. His voice changed slightly to add a hint of sarcasm. "We're the lollipop boys sent to take care of you."

Ty narrowed his eyes and examined Morrison and then Henninger slowly. He turned his head and glanced at Zane critically. "I think that was supposed to be a cultural reference of some sort," he explained to his partner. "I don't get it," he huffed.

Zane snorted. "Big surprise," he murmured, almost under his breath.

Morrison leaned around the seat to look back at them. "We'll be your escorts and New York Field Office contacts while you're here. We're on the way to the office now to meet the Assistant Director in Charge. Can we stop anywhere on the way? Food? Drink?"

"What, you didn't pack your lunch?" Ty asked sarcastically as he shifted around in the seat and wedged himself against the door. He kicked a foot up and propped it on the console between the two front seats.

"Sure, in my SpongeBob SquarePants lunch box. I have the thermos too," Morrison shot right back.

Zane kept his mouth shut, eyes moving between the two men, and occasionally back to the driver, who was casually paying attention.

Ty stared at the kid and narrowed his eyes further. "Sponge-what?" he asked flatly.

Zane didn't even try to hold back the chuckle when Morrison looked at Ty like he'd lost his mind.

"Sponge-wha . . . you're yanking my chain, aren't you?" Morrison said. "Henny, he's yanking my chain."

"Yeah, well, that's what you getting for waving it in his face," the driver answered reasonably.

"What the hell is a SpongeBob?" Ty asked Zane quietly in the back seat.

Zane turned his chin, taking a moment to gauge if Ty was serious and if he'd slam Zane for answering. "It's a cartoon character popular recently," he answered, voice low. He could see the driver's eyes in the rearview mirror again, watching them. Examining them.

Ty stared at Zane incredulously for a moment and then looked away with a shake of his head.

"Perhaps you prefer Scooby-Doo?" Henninger offered politely.

"More like the Dark Knight," Zane muttered without thinking first.

Ty smirked and glanced over at the man. "Does that mean I can call you Robin from now on?" he asked with an amused glint in his eyes.

"That's Boy Wonder to you," Zane answered flatly, turning to look out the window as Morrison stared at them both.

"Ugh," Ty grunted as he looked away again and propped his other foot up on the center console. "You're too easy," he grumbled disconsolately.

Zane barely restrained a snicker as Morrison blinked. The young agent looked at his partner. "Well, we got the right two guys," he said grimly. He turned to look back at the two older men suspiciously. "They told us this was your first time working together, and that you'd probably not be too fond of each other."

"They were right," Ty and Zane both answered, practically in unison.

"Shut up," Ty huffed at him.

"Gentlemen, so glad you made it. Assistant Director in Charge George McCarty. Nice to meet you both. Let's get on with this, shall we?" the head of the New York Field Office greeted hurriedly without giving either of them a chance to respond in kind. He dropped a few files onto the table and adjusted his tie. "I trust you're both familiar with the case? Good, then we can get on to your arrangements and right into it."

Ty raised an eyebrow at the whirlwind tour and glanced at Zane. Zane flipped open his file where he had a list of notes and questions, waiting for McCarty to continue.

"As we all know, this case has claimed two of our own," McCarty continued as he bent over the table and looked down at his file. "Which has made it of the highest priority. You'll be working alongside the other leads, Special Agents Sears and Ross. They couldn't be here this morning; they're still in the process of interviewing the staff from the hotel where Special Agents Sanchez and Reilly were found," he said tightly. He sighed briefly, as if the little speech were taking a lot out of him. "You'll be given a car and a driver, if you want one. We have booked you two adjoining rooms at the Tribeca Grand. It's within walking distance of the office here and has the highest security. All our records and resources are open to you, although I will tell you right now cooperation from your new teammates will likely be at a minimum despite my orders to work with you," he told them candidly, making no secret of the field office's bitter feelings toward anyone from outside being sent in to handle their cases. "Any questions?"

"You provided the contact list, right?" Zane asked.

"It's all in the file," McCarty answered with a nod. "Anything you need during the course of your investigation is at your disposal, including the team Special Agents Reilly and Sanchez were using. Anything else?"

"Have you found out how the killer knew where the agents were staying?" Ty asked as he turned in his seat and propped his feet up on the chair next to him.

McCarty turned to one of the men at his side. "No," Morrison answered. He was the shorter of the Hardy Boys, but wiry, with spiked blond hair and bright blue eyes. "We don't believe it was an inside thing, though. We speculate he may have tailed them from one of the scenes."

"Is Serena Scott in town? I'd like her opinions on the crime scenes," Zane asked in reference to New York's head profiler.

"We've not brought her in on this one. Yet," Henninger answered. Zane could now see the young agent was tall and lanky, and his short haircut couldn't restrain the dark curls that had to be natural. "Did you want to meet with her personally?" he asked with an indiscernible look at Ty.

"Absolutely," Zane answered firmly. "Her insight is invaluable, and some things just don't translate from paper."

"We'll arrange the meeting ASAP," the man assured him, looking again at Ty almost questioningly.

Zane glanced at Ty to see if he had anything to add. His new partner was kicked back in his chair and staring up at the ceiling idly, a slight curl of distaste on his lip.

"We won't need the driver. Thank you, sir," Zane said as he closed his file and stood.

"You need anything else, you just go through Agents Henninger or Morrison, here," McCarty said with a gesture of his thumb over his shoulder at no one in particular. "They'll get you anything you need," he assured them as the Hardy Boys nodded.

There was a discreet knock on the boardroom door, and McCarty straightened up and called out a curt "Enter!"

The receptionist cracked open the door and stuck her head through. "Sir, Assistant Director Burns on line four for you and Special Agents Grady and Garrett. He says it's urgent."

"Thank you, Denise," McCarty grunted, and she withdrew silently. McCarty watched the door until it clicked closed, and then he leaned forward and pressed a button on one of the units in the middle of the large boardroom table. "Richard," he greeted.

"Good morning, George," Dick Burns's voice said clearly over the speakerphone. "I trust Grady and Garrett are there and already causing problems?"

"You always did take the safe bet," McCarty responded wryly. "I must repeat my disapproval of this little operation, Richard. I just don't believe one of my staff here is responsible for this madness."

"I understand how difficult your position is, George," Burns responded easily. "But unfortunately, Director Radshaw and I disagree."

Behind McCarty, Henninger and Morrison both shifted uneasily and shared an indiscernible glance. Ty cocked his head, frowning slightly at the speakerphone. He wasn't liking the sound of this conversation, but he thought maybe he understood why they were here now. His sharp gaze traveled up to observe McCarty curiously as the two men spoke over the phone.

McCarty sighed and looked up at Ty and Zane with narrowed eyes. "They look slightly confused, Dick," he told Burns with a hint of amusement.

"Gentlemen," Burns said loudly over the phone. "I do apologize for not filling you in more completely while you were here, but the finer points were still being ironed out."

"Finer points?" Zane asked, a bit peevish at being left out of the loop.

Ty rubbed his nose and squeezed his eyes closed. "Why do you always do this to me?" he asked plaintively.

"Because I dislike you quite a lot," Burns told him in amusement. "You will be working the Tri-State case," he went on without waiting for a response. "You will appear, to the members of the New York team, to be inexperienced, inept, and lackadaisical. If you happen to stumble across any leads, then good for you."

Ty glanced over at Zane and smirked, restraining himself from commenting. Zane was hard-pressed not to sneer back at him.

"On the periphery, and more importantly to your own assignment, you will be concentrating not on the serial murders, but on the deaths of Special Agents Reilly and Sanchez."

"Because you suspect an inside job?" Zane inquired quietly.

"Precisely. We believe if we can uncover how the killer got to them, we'll have him."

"And our parameters for operating?" Ty asked eagerly as he sat forward, closer to the speakerphone.

"Don't kill each other," Burns ordered with a smile in his voice. "Any future questions, you come directly to me. George is to be left out of the loop on the off chance he needs to deny knowledge of your operations," he added.

Ty and Zane both looked up at McCarty. The man did not look pleased, but it was obvious that he'd already had words with Burns regarding the plan.

"That will be all, gentlemen. Good luck," Burns told them. "George, give my love to your girls," he added before the line went dead.

McCarty looked at the two agents sitting across from him and snorted. "Anything else?" he asked them with a raised eyebrow.

"No, sir," Zane answered with a shake of his head.

McCarty merely nodded. "Now, if you'll excuse me, I have a meeting with the mayor." He grunted unhappily and swept out of the office, leaving Morrison and Henninger behind.

Ty sat twirling his pen idly, unmoving as he looked at the two younger men in amusement. "How'd you get stuck with this shit?" he asked them finally.

"We're just errand boys, sir," Henninger answered in a low voice, a hint of amusement in his dark eyes as he looked at Ty.

Ty grinned crookedly and nodded. "So are we," he responded wryly. Henninger fought hard not to smile.

Zane glanced at the two agents and back to Ty. "Any miraculous sparks of insight, Grady?" he asked.

"Yeah," Ty answered as he stood and removed his suit jacket. He yanked off his tie and threw it onto the table. "I need to find me a Batgirl," he drawled thoughtfully.

"I'm sure the Bat-Signal's upstairs," Zane answered absently as he paged through the folder, checking to see if there were materials he wanted to request. Morrison and Henninger exchanged dubious looks.

"You have way too many of these comments stored up," Ty told Zane disapprovingly. He turned to Morrison and Henninger and gave them a sweeping gesture of his hand. "Take us to the Batcave!" he ordered with a straight face.

Morrison's jaw dropped as he stared at Ty, obviously thinking he was insane. His partner looked at him and rolled his eyes. "C'mon, Mark," he muttered. "He's still yanking your chain." The two younger agents led the way out, muttering to each other.

"You know it's more likely they're taking us to Wayne Manor," Zane said as they followed along, both to make his point and to get a jab in at Ty while he could. "Hide in plain sight and spare no expense account." Sad, but true. It was a good thing they weren't supposed to be completely undercover, or they'd already be spoiled.

"That doesn't even make any sense. Shut it, sidekick," Ty muttered to him.

Zane allowed himself a small smile before he remembered how much he actively disliked this man.

"You two want breakfast before the hotel?" Morrison asked. He seemed to be the talker of the matched set.

"The Batcave isn't the hotel," Ty protested in annoyance with a few snaps of his fingers. "Get on board the metaphor, kiddies."

"Where the hell is the Batcave, then?" Henninger asked with a long-suffering sigh.

"The lab, man. Take us down to the lab," Ty ordered in exasperation. Zane glanced over the Hardy Boys, struck again by how young they seemed. Surely, they'd seen some version of Batman. This was making him feel old.

"Well, how the hell are we supposed to know that? You old guys saw all that original crap. The new stuff's a lot better, and the Batcave is not a lab," Morrison blustered.

Zane blinked. Old guys? He glanced to Ty, wondering what sort of fireworks that little comment would set off.

"Do I look like I saw the original anything, SpongeBob?" Ty asked with a smirk and a point to his own chest. "What are you doing reading comics anyway? When I was your age I was in the Gulf, man," he continued.

"The Gulf of what?" Morrison responded, a blank look in his eyes.

"The Persian Gulf," Zane answered sharply, not at all amused. He noticed Henninger closing his eyes in exasperation and shaking his head.

Ty didn't know whether to be more shocked at Morrison's idiocy or at Zane's sudden apparent support. He just stared at Morrison for a minute, all joking aside, then glanced at Zane, who met his eyes for a moment, and sighed. "Kids these days," he muttered as he stepped between the two younger agents and punched the button on the elevator.

The elevator ride was a short one, and when the car jerked to a stop, Henninger led the way out. "The team has been a little scattered since the deaths of Special Agents Reilly and Sanchez," he said quietly as they walked down the hall. "We all knew them. I'm afraid we're not really organized right now."

"Has the team had any off time?" Ty asked.

Henninger glanced at him defensively as if expecting a jeer. "No," he answered curtly as he opened the door to the main laboratory.

"Give it to them while we get ourselves acquainted with the case," Ty ordered.

Zane frowned. He had no problem with giving the overworked team a day or two off, but how were they supposed to do any of the things Burns ordered if none of the team was around to observe? "We should have access to all the subsidiary case material," he said slowly, not arguing openly. "I'd like to spend some time with the photos."

"I'll have them pulled," Morrison responded diligently, obviously knowing he'd insulted the two older agents and hoping to make up for it.

"Are any of the crime scenes still intact?" Ty asked.

"Uh . . . I believe the most recent one is," Morrison answered uncertainly. "May I ask why?"

"I'd like to visit it," Ty answered.

"Me too," Zane added. He wondered if Serena Scott would mind going along and seeing the site in person. He'd have to ask her—unless Ty got it into his head to go right this minute.

That thought made him realize that he really had no idea what Ty was trained to do or how he would behave on an actual case. The other man at least knew what department Zane came from, although that certainly didn't expose his training. Some research to learn a little more about his asshole of a partner might not be a bad idea. It was obvious from the fact that he had been stationed in the Gulf that he had been military of some sort, and when Zane pondered that, it didn't really come as much of a surprise. It wouldn't take long to request a file on Grady.

"When would you like to go?" Morrison asked.

"As soon as we're done down here," Ty answered with a nod to the lab doors as they approached.

"That may be a bit of a problem," Morrison answered nervously as Henninger slid his key card through the security slot.

"Then fix the problem," Ty said to him coldly.

"The NYPD detectives assigned to the case haven't returned our calls for two days. They don't know you're here," Morrison told him.

"So, what's the problem?" Zane asked, stopping at the security desk.

"Technically it's still a joint case. The site was left in NYPD custody," Morrison answered with a grateful look at Zane as Ty sighed in exasperation. "We'll have to notify them of the changes to the case and give them—"

"Then get on it," Ty interrupted before stalking through the security door Henninger held open for him.

"Go on," Zane said quietly. "Let us know when it's set up."

Morrison fled, followed by his quieter partner, and Zane turned and followed Ty, wondering if this would be the pattern for the job: Hurricane Grady sweeps in, tosses everything askew, and sweeps right back out, leaving Zane to clean up the mess.

He hadn't worked his ass off the past two years to be a goddamn janitor.

Four hours after entering the lab, Ty sat amid a flurry of papers and untidy stacks of reports. He leaned his elbows on the table, scowling heavily and staring at the shiny stainless-steel top.

On the other side of the table, Zane was busily working on his charts. He just happened to glance up, the look on Ty's face giving him pause. "What's wrong?"

Ty didn't look up. His eyes were slightly glazed and his brow furrowed. "There's no pattern," he muttered. "The only things connecting these cases are the little tokens the dude leaves with the bodies and the fact they all end up dead. Other than that, there's no common victim type, there's no common MO. Weapon, cause of death, even the way he stages them. All different."

He finally focused his eyes and glared at the files accusingly, as if it was their fault.

"Victim Number One: Kyle Walters," he recited suddenly. "Wealthy Wall Street type, found in his bedroom, still alive, half-insane, suffering from severe hypersensitivity to light, sound, smell, you name it. Dies in the hospital without ever saying a coherent word. Cause of death is ruled a meth overdose. Hell, the only reason we even know this guy was a victim was the maid finding the token from the killer a week later. Serial killers tend to get their kicks from watching their victims die or from the power to kill. Why would he leave him alive and risk being identified?"

"Maybe they get their kicks just as much from watching the suffering," Zane suggested quietly, not looking up from his paper. His fingers moved over the charts, still making notes from the case files. "The best developing pattern is the fact that the victims are so different. Like he's choosing specifically based on some reasoning. A majority of serial killers fixate on a particular style of victim—young blonde women or rich gay men, for instance."

"Yes, dear, I'm aware of that. That's my point. We have a thirty-seven-year-old male stockbroker; overdosed with shitty-quality meth," Ty said as he closed his eyes and rested his head back against his chair. He shook his head, reciting everything from memory. "Next, Susan Harris, a twentysomething hooker found in nothing but a six-hundred-count white sheet in the most exclusive cemetery in the state, all her teeth gone and no apparent cause of death. Then a double murder. Two young women: Allison McFadden and Theresa Escobar. Roommates, both suffocated, positioned in their beds as if they were sleeping. The only notable thing about them is that their hair had been dyed postmortem. Then we have the infamous set of twins who got the Bureau involved, Ryan and Russell Stevens. Killed at the Tri-State marker, one man in each of the bordering states, shot dead. Late fifties, an apparent double-suicide, if not for the token left by the killer."

He rolled his neck and shook his head, trying to make sense of it. "The first guy was a brunet, the hooker was a bottle blonde but a natural brunette, the second and third were blonde and black-haired, then dyed the opposite, and the twins were both redheads. Both sexes, no common body type. Brown eyes, green eyes, blue eyes . . . hell, he doesn't even leave the same tokens! Fuck it!" he spat. "All serials have patterns. It's got to be there," he muttered to himself.

"Not having a pattern can be a pattern." The patient distraction was clear in Zane's voice. "If he's intelligent and not quite insane, he may be deliberately toying with us. It's a game to him." While Ty was getting frustrated, Zane kept himself removed, focusing on the numbers and the data. "I want to plot the locations of the bodies to get an idea of the territory we're looking at." He looked up to see Ty frowning, and Zane's curiosity got the best of him. "Tell me, Grady, why the hell are you here? Why did Burns put you on this case?"

"I understand that there is a pattern," Ty responded slowly, ignoring the question momentarily. "I want to know what the fuck it is," he ground out patiently. He leaned back and rolled his neck. "And he put me on it because he knows me. I'm good at sneaking around and I'm good at mind games," he said curtly, not choosing to elaborate.

Zane nodded slowly. He was starting to see why they'd been paired up for this freak show. Ty was good at mind games, Zane was good at details and patterns. And they so obviously didn't work well together that they didn't even need to make a show of it for the New York team.

"I've got enough here," he announced, closing his file and notebook. "Tomorrow we'll talk with the NYPD detectives, and Serena Scott should return my call. Henninger and Morrison will either get us access to the scene, or we'll get access on our own." He pushed back from the table. "You have anything else?" His voice was neutral.

"No," Ty muttered without moving. He was still staring at the files and frowning.

Zane watched him silently for a long moment before saying, "Ready to head over to the hotel? I don't know about you, but I'm ready for dinner and a drink."

"You drink on duty?" Ty asked incredulously as he finally tore his eyes away from the files.

"Doesn't everyone?" Zane headed for the hall. "I have a new smart-ass partner to deal with, so certainly I can't be blamed," he muttered under his breath while he walked to the door and out of the lab. A few beers with dinner wouldn't even register on a Breathalyzer with his body mass and would go a long way to new brainstorms, but he didn't dare. That didn't mean he didn't dream otherwise, though.

"You've never been a field agent before, have you?" Ty asked with disdain, calling out the question as he remained at the table, staring at the files and crime-scene photos.

Zane stopped at the door, taking a moment to order his thoughts and push away the ghosts of his constant nightmares. "A drink now and then is not going to end the world. I'm guessing that you came from deep cover, which means you were always looking over your shoulder, living the part every minute, knowing one mistake would send you to the morgue." Zane knew the situation very well. "While it's admirable, and arguably the most difficult job the Bureau does, you're going to have to figure out how to downshift, or the people we work with are going to strangle you. You can't work around the clock and stay sharp enough to crunch this much data and get inside a madman's head."

Ty tore his eyes away from the papers again and looked up at Zane seriously. "You think those boys down in the morgue downshifted before he killed 'em?" he asked flatly.

"I think they were locked down as securely as they could get, with no reason to think they'd be found, much less attacked. Which means one of two things," Zane responded, brown eyes hard and unflinching. "They'd either already screwed up and exposed themselves or someone who knew where they were gave them up, either by mistake or not. Either way, letting down their guard made no difference. They were already dead."

Ty just shook his head and snorted derisively. He knew he was damned if he was going to let himself be shot in the chest as he slept. You never thought you were safe. Feeling safe got you killed.

Zane could almost see the tension pouring off Ty in waves. "Are you going to the hotel or are you planning on staying here all day?" he asked.

"I'm going to a hotel," Ty answered as he stood and gathered his coat and satchel. "A different hotel. And you're coming with me."

Zane simply leveled a gaze at him, waiting for explanation. It was the first time the other man had even remotely indicated that he wanted Zane anywhere around him.

"I don't plan on losing another agent to this shit, got it?" Ty responded sharply as he stuffed several of the files in his bag and glared back at Zane. "Even if it is you."

Zane supposed he should feel all warm and fuzzy about Ty at least not wanting him gruesomely murdered and left to bleed out in his shower or something. Somehow, the sentiment didn't really inspire much camaraderie, though. "So where are we going?"

"Holiday Inn, man," Ty answered. "If I'm footin' the bill, I ain't paying no damn five hundred bucks a night."

Zane shrugged. A room was a room. He'd stayed in better and he'd stayed in worse. He followed Ty out of the lab and back down the hall to the elevator. "And then?" He wanted to know if Ty's sudden concern for his well-being included staying in close proximity; he'd planned to come back after dinner to study the maps and evidence notes.

Ty shrugged as he punched the elevator button. "Then we see what's brewing," he answered carelessly.

Zane looked over at his partner in exasperation. First, complete and total focus on the case, a case that wasn't even their main focus, and now, this. "Do you do anything like a normal person?" he asked, although the question was wholly rhetorical. And not at all complimentary.

Ty turned around and looked at him in slight surprise once they were in the elevator. "Only the fun things," he answered finally after a moment of looking at him thoughtfully.

"Fun things," Zane echoed, not looking away from Ty once he was pinned by the man's hazel eyes.

"You remember those, don't you?" Ty questioned with a smirk as he let his eyes travel up and down Zane thoughtfully. "Maybe you don't," he decided with a sigh.

Zane knew with absolute certainty that he did not want this conversation to continue. "How many strikes have I got left?" he asked abruptly. He knew Ty had been taking his measure, in more ways than one.

"None," Ty answered immediately, though he was somewhat surprised Zane even knew to ask the question.

A ghost of a self-deprecating smile crossed Zane's lips. He knew Ty had no respect for him. Frankly, Zane didn't care. He didn't plan for this joke of a partnership to last long. He just wondered who higher up in the Bureau had decided to take him out along with Ty. "So why hasn't the ump thrown me out of the game?"

"'Cause there ain't no umps in this particular game," Ty answered seriously as the doors whooshed open on the ground floor. "And there ain't no rules."

Zane walked out ahead of the other man. "So we do without." He could live with that. Better than working under someone else's thumb like the past two years. "Or we make up our own."

"Yeah, you seem the type to need rules," Ty responded with a derogatory sneer.

Zane didn't answer as they walked through the parking garage. He drew back into his stony silence, focusing on thinking about the next steps of the investigation instead of the insolence of his jackass of a partner.

Chapter Two

After checking in to a hotel just a block or two from the swanky establishment where they were supposed to be staying, Ty Grady immediately fell into the shower and went about washing the frustration of the day away. He had been a little surprised when his new partner had paid for his own room, but it suited him just fine. He didn't want to be within ten feet of the fucker if he didn't have to be. Arrogant priss. God, the man probably slept in his tie.

Having separate rooms would work well if Ty intended to start into this the way he usually did. He wasn't used to the normal channels and he did far better working a case from the underbelly rather than in conventional ways. He doubted Zane would go with him tonight, and he'd just as soon go on his own, anyway. He'd always been more comfortable slinking around in the shadows than waving his authority around.

In a room down the hall, Zane Garrett sighed as he threw down his duffel bags and briefcase. He ran his hands through his hair and then stretched. He and Ty ended up several doors down from each other, but it wasn't far enough as far as Zane was concerned.

A hot shower sounded good, so he started stripping down. Next order of business was food, and then he'd go back to the office. He reminded himself that he'd at least need to call Ty and tell him where he was going. If they were real partners, they'd have stayed in the same room, but Zane sure as hell wasn't going to suggest it. He wasn't that masochistic.

Pulling on comfortable worn jeans and a rust-red V-neck sweater after cleaning up, Zane picked up his holster, checking it all over before settling it comfortably on his shoulders and buckling it down.

He checked the thin sheaths he wore just inside his wrists, then knelt down and strapped another sheath around his ankle. Completely armed, he felt better than he had all day. He hated airplanes. The security tended to get a little strident when you tried to take knives through checkpoints, even if you were a federal agent who always carried a gun.

His canvas jacket went over that, and with a look in the mirror, he rolled his eyes. Ty would probably think he was trying to copy him, looking less stuffy and more street-worthy. Zane sighed at the mirror, then grabbed his wallet, cigarettes, lighter, and key card and headed down the hall to the other agent's door for a quick check-in.

Ty answered the curt knock in a towel, body still dripping wet and steam roiling out of the bathroom door behind him.

Zane raised an eyebrow as his stomach flip-flopped in reaction. "Yeah. That's real safe," he commented, forcing his voice to sound wry.

"What?" Ty asked with a tilt of his head.

Zane looked significantly up and down Ty's barely covered body.

Ty looked down at himself and then back up at Zane with a sniff as he realized what Zane was blathering about. "I'm a lethal weapon, man," he grunted. He turned and gave a wave over his shoulder, gesturing for him to come in.

Zane would have snorted except he figured Ty wasn't overstating all that much. There was no telling what Ty's background was (although Zane had already discerned he was military of some sort) but he did indeed look capable. And fit. Very fit. Zane swallowed as he stepped inside and pushed the door shut behind him, leaving the odd feelings in the hall and withdrawing back into his professional persona for safety.

"I figured you'd want to know if I wasn't going to be home by curfew," he said, sliding a hand into his jacket pocket.

"I'm not your fucking keeper," Ty grunted as he shucked the towel and reached for his briefs. He glanced back to see Zane's hand in his pocket and tensed instinctively.

Zane's eyes narrowed, and he slowly pulled his hand free to let it fall limp at his side. His partner was obviously tenser than he let on. "I remind you of the 'You're coming with me, I don't plan on losing another agent' comment," he said mildly, once more strongly scolding himself inside for wanting to ogle—and grope—when he got a free show. He sighed inwardly. He always behaved these days. Maybe he was a pansy ass now, just like Ty said. The thought made him slightly ill.

"What you do in your free time is none of my concern," Ty was saying as he pulled up the briefs and then toweled off his wet shoulders and arms. The towel passed over a tattoo on Ty's right bicep, but Zane was too far away to discern the details other than the fact that it was a face of something. He fought back the urge to squint in order to make it out.

"Are we even going to attempt to work together, or shall we just agree to meet every few days to compare notes?" Zane asked, voice cool. "I'd rather know now than waste more of our precious time."

"You think this case is gonna be easy for one man?" Ty asked in response as he grabbed his jeans. He turned around to look at Zane again as he stepped into them. "Awful big leap, thinking you're smarter'n the killer."

"You've yet to act like you want me around, Grady. Don't start now," Zane snapped.

"I don't act. And I didn't say I wanted you around," Ty responded calmly. "I implied that I needed you."

"Well, mark my lucky stars, I'm flattered," Zane drawled in annoyance. Ty didn't seem to care if he was unprofessional, so Zane took the opportunity to be just that. Too bad Ty was so determined to be a bastard. Off the clock, they might have gotten along. Over a bottle of whiskey. Zane gritted his teeth.

"You look a little tense," Ty observed wryly.

Zane didn't mention his line of thought. "You implied, so what do you need?" he asked instead of responding to Ty's comment.

"It's okay to be tense. I'm tense," Ty told him with a careless shrug. "You going back to Federal Plaza?" he asked in answer to Zane's question as he pulled on a black T-shirt that had writing in white block letters that said I'M UNDERCOVER.

Zane blinked at the shirt before shaking his head slowly. "Yes. Why?"

"When you get back, will you come check on me?" Ty asked, unembarrassed by the request as he sat on the edge of the bed and pulled his socks on.

"You going to do something that may make you not be here?"

"Hopefully not," Ty answered wryly as he stomped his foot down into one beat-up cowboy boot. "A few blocks from here is pretty close to where that hooker reportedly worked. I'm going to go talk to the ladies."

"Several responses come to mind."

"And I'm sure all of them are wildly clever," Ty responded sarcastically as he stomped into his second boot and then stood and stretched.

Zane deliberately looked away from the wiry body stretching out in front of him. "A couple," he acknowledged. "You want me to come along?"

Ty raised an eyebrow and gave Zane a slow once-over. He cleared his throat and licked his lips as he stretched his arms over his head, then flopped them back down to his sides. "Have you ever, umm . . . picked up a hooker?" he asked with a straight face.

"Yes." Both on and off the job, but that wasn't necessarily germane to the discussion. Zane tilted his head as Ty's eyebrows climbed in surprise. "So, yes or no? Either way, I'm eating first."

Ty tilted his head, thinking it over. This could be a good chance to see how Zane would handle himself on an investigation without hurting much of anything as far as their current one went. "Yeah, okay," he agreed finally as he reached for his military surplus green canvas jacket. He picked it up and looked at it, then cut his gaze to look Zane over with narrowed eyes, taking in the way he was dressed. "Yeah, okay," he grumbled again as he threw the jacket down and went to rummage through his things for his other jacket to wear. He didn't want them looking like fucking twins.

He stripped his T-shirt back off as Zane waited, picking up a clean white dress shirt instead. He was very conscious, as he changed, of the fact that the little round scar on his lower back was probably visible, still new and pink on his tanned skin. He glanced over at Zane and cleared his throat self-consciously, turning toward him again as he slid into the shirt. He wasn't sure why it bothered him that Zane could see the scar, but it did. Perhaps because he hadn't been the only one that particular bullet had gone through.

The other agent just caught sight of the scar, recognizing it for what it most likely was. While Zane had been lucky enough to avoid being shot, he had plenty of other scars, inside and out. He made no comment and pretended not to have noticed.

"So where we going for dinner, garçon?" Ty asked as he grabbed his wallet and stuck it in his back pocket.

Dragging his eyes away from Ty's body again, Zane ignored yet another new nickname and answered, "Morrison told me about a barbecue place down several blocks. Family-owned, original recipes."

"Mmm, New York barbeque," Ty responded sarcastically with a wrinkle of his nose. "No go. I need... fish."

"Fish." Zane shrugged. "Okay, we can find a place. Unless you already have something in mind?" He really didn't care. He'd eat anything. It was just the cocktails that got him in trouble.

"We'll walk," Ty suggested as he attached an ankle holster and checked that his backup was loaded. He dragged out his shoulder holster and did the same, then slipped his beaten leather jacket on and flexed his shoulders experimentally with a frown.

"Strap's twisted," Zane offered. He walked over and reached up under the jacket to flip the buckle so the strap laid flat along the back of Ty's shoulder. Ty turned his head wordlessly and raised his eyebrows as Zane stepped into his space and fucked around with his weaponry.

Now, Zane wasn't a stupid man. He'd seen Ty tense earlier at a slightly perceived threat. It wasn't ignorance on Zane's part, getting so close without being invited. But he wanted his new partner to know that he wasn't afraid of him. That he wasn't quite the paper-pusher he made himself out to be.

Zane straightened the length of strap and pulled Ty's jacket back down to cover it. "Let's go. I could eat a whale," he said absently, already warring within himself. Had he truly wanted to telegraph a message? Or had he simply taken advantage of the chance to touch the hard muscles he'd been seeing? Danger zone, Garrett.

Ty cleared his throat and followed silently. Not many people had the nerve to step into his reach and touch him without his permission or some sort of forewarning. Either Zane really didn't give a shit—which was contrary to his demeanor and actions—or he had no clue how dangerous Ty really was. The third option was the most frightening; that he knew what Ty could do to him and he wasn't concerned. Either way, it left Ty slightly unsettled as they went in search of food.

Their hotel was located just a block or two from Little Italy, and they had no trouble finding a restaurant there, which seemed to suit Ty just fine. Zane followed along as they were led to the table, eyeing the bar across the room with an internal sigh. He sat down at the table and immediately opened the menu.

Ty, however, left the menu in front of him and turned to the waitress with a grin. He went about ordering his Guinness and dinner with a series of well-honed innuendo and rakish grins that had the girl giggling at him as she moved away.

Zane ignored what was becoming his partner's customary behavior. Sitting back, he reflected that maybe they should have kept looking for a different restaurant. One with televisions. Here, there was nothing to do but look at each other.

As he sat, Ty was observing the other patrons in the restaurant idly, noticing things about them that most people didn't notice. His training forced him to take in who looked anxious, who seemed to be waiting for someone, who was wearing a coat too large for them that might conceal a weapon, who looked out of place. The list went on and on. "So," he huffed as he looked back at Zane. "What now?"

"As opposed to what then?" Zane said, leaning back in his chair. "You had the plan, remember?"

"You hijacked it with dinner," Ty pointed out as the little waitress came back and slid Ty's drink onto the table. "Thank you, darlin'," he drawled as she passed by. He took one long draw from the bottle, then glanced around and placed his palm flat on the opening of the bottle before turning it upside down. He patted himself down with the beer like someone would have done with a bottle of cologne, taking another gulp every now and then as he smeared some on his neck and chest and finally rubbed his hands together and patted down his scruffy face.

Zane just watched, stirring lemon into his tea, shaking his head. "That's a waste of good beer. You should have ordered some shit like Bud Light."

"Do I look like I drink Bud Light?" Ty sneered before downing what was left of the beer. He raised his hand and called over the waitress again.

"You think the girls are going to be able to tell the difference?"

"You underestimate their prowess." Ty laughed as he leaned back and stretched his hands over his head. The waitress sidled over and Ty smiled at her. "Bring my irritating friend here a Bud Light, would you, sweetheart?"

She repressed a snort and gave Zane a nod before turning away again. "No," Zane said sharply, voice quite firm. "That's not necessary."

She turned around and raised her eyebrows in question. Ty pursed his lips and then smiled, shaking his head and gesturing for her to bring it anyway.

"Your irritating friend has no interest in a beer, Grady," Zane ground out.

"It's not to drink," Ty responded with an easy smile.

Zane relaxed slightly, though he was still frowning. "Then what do you plan to do with it?" he asked suspiciously. Ty merely waved a hand at himself in answer. Zane rolled his eyes before he could stop himself and really wished Ty had waited until after dinner to "freshen up." It would be bad enough walking around with him without smelling it all through dinner too.

The waitress brought the ordered beer and smiled at Ty flirtatiously as she passed by. Zane watched her thoughtfully and wondered if Ty really was charming or if he was just good-looking enough to pull it off. Either way, it irritated Zane already.

Ty slid the bottle across the table and waved a hand. "You can wait till after we eat, if you like," he offered charitably.

Eyes narrowing, Zane looked at Ty, then the bottle, then back at Ty. "Oh, hell no. One of us smelling like a drunk is plenty."

Ty merely shrugged. The man wasn't going with him without playing the part. Whether he did it voluntarily was not Ty's concern. It might even be fun to douse him down, Ty pondered with a smile.

"So." He leered as he leaned his elbows on the table again. "Tell me about your hookers. You don't seem the type," he said with a pointed look at the wedding band on Zane's finger.

Zane willfully ignored the beer bottle. "And what is my type?" he asked in a clipped voice, his left hand curling into a loose fist before he pulled it off the table and settled it out of sight, hiding the ring. He wondered how many new insults Ty could come up with. It really was a game to him, apparently, and it made it more difficult for Zane to maintain his stony reserve.

Ty snorted in response. "Yeah, okay," he responded in amusement. "I guess you would need to pay someone to tolerate you."

Letting the insult pass, for more reasons than the truth of it, Zane prodded back instead. "I'm sure you have a very well-formed and detailed profile ready to throw out there, proving how lacking I am."

Ty's eyebrow rose and he leaned forward. "Have you read my file?" he inquired curiously.

"In what time, since we've been together practically the entire past thirty-six hours?" Zane asked sarcastically. "That's not to say I didn't think about having it pulled."

Ty narrowed his eyes, then let it go as a coincidence. "Profile of you, huh?" he drawled with a smirk instead.

"Despite your insistence on being an utter asshole, you are undeniably educated and highly trained," Zane said, drawing on the minute clues and data he'd been gathering about Ty to make a strong guess. Number-crunching, as it were. "So, I'm betting you've assessed for threat, judged for education, gauged strengths and weaknesses . . . yes. A profile."

"Your logic is irrefutable," Ty complimented, still grinning. "I do have one," he answered with a matter-of-fact nod. "I'm still waiting for you to change it."

Zane's interest in the line of conversation dissipated, as did any life or spark in his dark eyes as his expression went hard again. People were always expecting him to change. "Very charitable of you," he said curtly.

Ty shrugged. "You want me continuing to think you're a candy-ass content to ride a desk, that's fine with me. Don't say I didn't give you a chance, though," he warned as he leaned back in his seat again and glanced to his right as someone moved too quickly in his peripheral vision. He watched them suspiciously for a moment in silence, the sudden tenseness filtering through his entire body.

"There's nothing I can do to change your opinion," Zane said sourly, not even noticing the change in Ty's demeanor. "Besides, it's not too far off." His tone had turned decidedly bitter, and Zane took a long drink of his iced tea to get the annoyance back under control.

"Ah, I hear a past bubbling forth," Ty responded with a point at Zane as he pulled his attention away from their fellow diners. "There's another thing I don't wanna talk about."

"I've got no desire to hear violins wailing, anyway," Zane snapped.

Ty laughed joyously and nodded. "That's better," he said approvingly.

Zane's nose wrinkled as he reined in his temper yet again. Something about Ty brought out the parts of him he tried to hide from the light of day. Surely, this was headed for disaster. "There were four," he muttered before thinking better of it.

"Four what?" Ty asked in apparent confusion.

Zane cleared his throat in annoyance and glanced around them. "Hookers," he said through gritted teeth.

"All at once?" Ty asked with a mocking sort of wide-eyed innocence.

"Not all four, no," Zane said under his breath.

"Shame," Ty drawled with a smirk. "Why?"

Zane sighed inwardly. "One of them was busy with a john in the other bed," he said as he lifted his glass to call for a refill. That had been one hell of a night—what he remembered of it.

"That's fascinatingly kinky," Ty drawled flatly. "But I meant why hookers," he corrected with an impish grin. "Paying for it usually means you're doing it to get out frustrations, not enjoy it."

"Or being too drunk off your ass to know otherwise," Zane pointed out, taking another sip of tea.

Ty raised his eyebrows and inclined his head in interest. "Are you a drunk?" he asked directly.

Zane's lips twisted in wry amusement, and he took a drink of tea rather than answering.

"Well, that should make any firefights we get into interesting," Ty drawled sarcastically. "Sorry, boss, I aimed for the middle one!" he cried softly as he squinted and raised his hand and waved it in front of him, mimicking a man who was seeing double as he tried to aim.

Zane's eyes were flat and emotionless. "I don't drink anymore," he said after a long pause.

"Meaning?" Ty prodded slowly. "What, you're a recovering alcoholic?" he asked with sarcasm lacing the words.

Trying very hard to push down a sudden desire to commit homicide, Zane's eyes narrowed and began to glitter with anger. He should have known Ty would disrespect even this. "Alcoholics don't recover," he said sharply as he pushed out of his chair. "I'll be back," he muttered, heading to the front door.

"I know they don't," Ty called after him without getting up. "They must not have a sarcasm translator in Cyber," he muttered to himself with a roll of his eyes.

Zane heard him but was too angry to turn around. He had to calm down or he'd lose his grip on his well-practiced control. He pushed out the doors and onto the sidewalk, walked a few yards away, pulled out a pack of cigarettes, and lit up, watching the foot traffic go by as he cooled off.

Left behind in the restaurant with several patrons glancing at him curiously, Ty simply shrugged and reached for a breadstick to gnaw on. The alcoholism thing didn't mesh with the mental profile he'd created of his new partner. He'd have to reconsider after his task tonight.

Taking his time with the cigarette, Zane jammed the butt out when he was done and tossed it in a trash can outside the restaurant before heading back in. The salads were on the table, and he sat down and started eating without saying a word.

"Bit of a temper, huh?" Ty greeted as he chewed. "That's a good idea," commented the man who was notorious for losing his temper in explosive ways. "To walk away like that."

Zane grunted in answer as he ate a few bites of salad, deciding if he wanted to answer. "Had to learn," he finally said as he nabbed a breadstick.

"Were you a cop?" Ty asked him in return, his mind making leaps and bounds of logic as he continued to chew.

"Are we playing twenty questions now?" Zane asked. "No. I was never a cop."

"I ask 'cause big city cops are usually plagued by drinking and anger problems," Ty informed him. "And I assume they started and were taken care of before you were in the Bureau because you wouldn't have stayed in after developing them. Military?" he asked dubiously.

Zane had to smile a little as he looked up and saw the wheels turning. "Not military. You get two more guesses."

"Funny, I had you pegged for Air Force," Ty drawled with a shake of his head and a smirk.

A sharp bark of laughter escaped Zane before he could repress it. "Unfortunately, my candy-ass image is only recently cultivated. I'm pleased that it's so convincing," he said, not at all brightly. He still wanted a drink, and his itchy hands and parched throat were getting worse. "You're military, of course."

"Marines," Ty offered as he looked up at Zane without moving his head, his fork stopping as he smiled slowly. "Force Recon."

Zane's shoulders stiffened. So Ty was a highly specialized warrior, trained to take the worst of a hostile environment. To be there and be invisible. To be there and be deadly. The knowledge made something inside Zane go cold. "Makes sense," he said tightly. "Anyone who could be so insubordinate could only have been the total opposite at some point in time," he observed. Zane pushed the salad bowl away and strongly contemplated another cigarette.

Ty snorted and shook his head in amusement. "Insubordinate," he echoed with a little snicker.

Glancing up, Zane was already resigned to being insulted. Modus operandi for Ty. "What?"

"If I were really all that much of a liability, do you think I'd still be around?" Ty inquired curiously. "I mean, I'm good, but I ain't that good."

Zane didn't even have to think up his answer. "Incorrect. It means you're so good that you can be as insubordinate as you like and get away with it. We both know there's a difference between being a liability in the field and an asshole in the office."

"We certainly do," Ty agreed with a shit-eating grin. "Asshole."

"Coming from you, I'll take that as a compliment."

Ty merely shrugged and went about eating his salad happily. Zane seemed to have a higher opinion of his abilities than he did of Zane's. Which was how it should be, as far as Ty could tell. Soon, the main dishes were brought out and Ty gave the waitress a wink for her trouble. "So, what'd you do?" he asked Zane finally.

Zane knew what Ty was asking. His lips lifted into a small smile. "The hookers were informants."

"Oh, yeah?" Ty asked, his tone of voice that of a patient parent entertaining a child.

The anger flared again, and tamping it down took serious effort. "I don't need another goddamn priest. You want to know or not? Because if you're just going to humor me, then I'm shutting up," Zane growled.

"Temper, temper," Ty tutted with a wave of his fork in Zane's face. "What sort of cybercrimes informants are hookers?" he asked, completely changing the direction.

"I didn't always work in the Cyber Division," Zane told Ty tightly.

"Huh," Ty commented disinterestedly. "And you were fucking your informants too?"

Zane shrugged one shoulder. What was it about Ty that made him want to fly off the handle?

Ty gave a low whistle, shaking his head. "No fucking wonder you got busted down."

Zane gave him a hateful look. "Didn't think when they put you on a leash it would be to a damn anchor, did you?" he asked testily.

"I was expecting an anvil with a little pink slip attached," Ty admitted. "Call me Wile E. Coyote."

Surprised by the candor, Zane leaned back when the waitress refilled his tea pitcher, waiting until she was gone. "So what'd you do to piss them off?"

Ty actually winced as he took a sip of his water and shrugged. "That's still classified," he answered honestly.

"Ouch." Still classified usually meant the shit hit the fan, and then some. "So the bricks, the anvil, and the ACME explosives."

"You got ACME written on your forehead," Ty muttered. He leaned back and cocked his head with an audible sigh. "I was in charge of the op," he explained, completely unashamed of what he knew probably should have gotten him fired . . . and possibly arrested. "We skirted some corners and whited out some of the rule book; then it all went to hell."

"From what little I know of you, it should have worked, though, huh?" Zane said as their dinners were delivered. "It would have been worth it."

"Yes," Ty answered succinctly. "It would have been worth it."

Zane raised his eyes to study the other man. "So what went wrong?" Ty looked up and met his eyes seriously, hazel eyes glinting angrily at just the memory. "That's classified," he murmured finally before looking back down.

The clipped heat of Ty's voice and the snap in his eyes gave him away. "Sounds like you've got your own anger issues."

"Only when I'm pissed off," Ty answered with a forced smirk. Snorting, Zane shook his head. "And that's what . . . only seventy-five percent of the time?" he asked seriously.

"I'm very easygoing," Ty huffed with a pious inclination of his head. "Mm-hmm," he hummed contentedly as he picked at his food.

Zane shook his head, stifling something nearly resembling a snicker. "You're not right in the head, Grady. And I mean that in the most respectful way possible."

"What the hell?" Ty responded with a gesture of his hands.

"Easygoing, my ass. You go out of your way to make people's lives hell. But now, I wonder if it's because you enjoy it or if it's because you honestly don't care about anything but the job anymore." He'd seen it before. Hell, Zane had lived it before.

"Does it matter?"

Zane lowered his fork and looked across the table, eyes focusing on something over Ty's shoulder. "I didn't use to think so," he admitted.

Ty watched him with one expressive eyebrow raised. "And?" he invited with a wave of his hand.

Dark eyes refocused and zeroed in on Ty's face. "The threat of castration, unemployment, and hard jail time made me rethink things," Zane supplied.

"Yeah, well, hang out with hookers and you get into some kinky shit," Ty offered with a straight face.

The corners of Zane's mouth turned up slightly. "Everyone has their hobbies," he replied smoothly.

"Whatever floats your boat, man." Ty shrugged dismissively, obviously having lost interest in the conversation.

Zane went back to finishing his dinner. Ty wasn't just good at figuring out games, he was good at playing them. It was tiring trying to keep up with his banter, but it was also almost fun. Zane was reminded that this "partnership" might not last so long, and now he couldn't decide if he felt ambivalent about it, or worse, disappointed. There was the slight possibility that they could have been a formidable team. But it was clear that Ty's obvious disdain wouldn't allow that to happen.

They ate in silence for a while, and as soon as he was done with his dinner, Ty wiped his hands on the linen napkin and nodded at Zane. "So, tell me about the case," he said without preamble.

The other agent's brain snapped back to its gathered data without further prompting. "Eight murders, different locations, nothing to tie them together. No pattern of victim choice, cause of death, time of death, or other establishable MO. Just the tokens left at the scenes, none of them the same. He's taunting us," Zane rattled off, pushing his empty plate away.

Ty closed his eyes and nodded impatiently. "Does anything ring any bells?" he asked pointedly.

Zane slowly stirred his tea, eyes distant as he reviewed lists and lists of details in his head. "I don't have anything concrete, but the state of the victims really catches my interest. He's being creative. That's unusual."

"Aside from the tokens, the dye job is what's getting me," Ty returned with a nod. "I feel like I should know why he did it. Why dye a natural blonde jet-black, then take her dark-haired roommate and bleach her blonde?"

"Could be he was trying to switch them before he killed them, but they weren't raped," Zane said. "I'll have to give it some thought. Chew on the details."

"That's what you're doing now, genius," Ty huffed.

"No, right now I'm just tossing stuff out. Working the details requires more concentration and less distraction." Zane looked at him significantly.

Ty rolled his eyes and leaned back in his chair. "You wanted to work together," he reminded.

"When did I say that?" Zane asked quietly.

"It's in the silent pleading in your eyes," Ty answered sarcastically.

"What's it going to be, Grady?" Zane asked, feeling very tired. "Decide now, so we can get to work. Together or not?"

Ty looked at him thoughtfully and then smiled slowly. "Well, I'm quite enjoying you so far."

Zane studied that smile for a long moment before scooting his chair back. "Ready to go?"

Ty reached for the empty bottle of Guinness and the flat Bud Light and tucked them under his jacket. "Ready," he said cheerfully.

Frowning at the concealed beer, Zane stood and flipped a large bill from his wallet onto the table. He figured the rest of the night would be interesting. Ty was enjoying him so far. Well, whoop-dee-doo.

As soon as they hit the street, Ty extracted the beer and reached out and took hold of Zane's elbow, pulling him to a halt. The taller man stopped and looked back at him, eyebrow raised in question. Ty raised the full bottle and sloshed the beer around, the scent wafting on the cool night breeze.

Zane blinked, and then he raised his chin sharply. "Hell, no."

"You do it or I will," Ty told him matter-of-factly.

Zane's lips pressed together firmly on the simmering anger. There was no doubt in his mind that Ty would follow through. "Asshole," he muttered, snatching the bottle from Ty's hand. He knew why Ty wanted this; if they looked like cops they wouldn't get close enough to ask a question. But that didn't mean he liked it one little bit. Pouring the beer messily out into his left hand, he smeared the liquid on his shirt and throat, and up under his chin, like where a drunk would have dregs trailing. Wiping his hand off on his jeans, he stalked over to the nearest bin and threw the bottle into it so hard it shattered as it hit bottom. "Let's go."

Ty would never let the man know it, but the sacrifice earned him just a little bit of respect. He nodded and fell in beside Zane, beginning to whistle as he walked. As they got closer to the working girls, he began to sing softly, the words slightly slurred and off-key as he swung his empty beer bottle happily at his side.

After the fifth street corner, Zane and Ty found a girl who knew the second victim. It took a couple of C-notes to get her to talk in the alley where she usually worked, and they came out with nothing more than finding out that the victim had been from Oklahoma and had run from her abusive husband.

"Any reason she'd have some expensive sheets at home?" Ty asked the girl as she glanced around nervously.

"She ain't made the money to buy things like that," the girl answered as she kicked her platform heel against the pavement. "She ain't nearly made the money to feed herself," she added with a shrug.

Ty just nodded and looked her over carefully. She looked back at him defiantly, seeming to think he was contemplating taking her up on her services after all. Instead, he reached into his back pocket and took out three more bills and handed them to her. "Buy yourself a couple days off, huh? Safer," he grunted as he turned around and began making his way back down the alleyway.

Zane turned silently away as the girl stared at the money in her hands. Stalking after Ty, he lit a cigarette and pulled the collar up on his jacket as the wind picked up. It just made him crankier, blowing the stale smell of the beer off his shirt into his face.

He nearly ran into Ty, who was standing and watching a couple walk slowly down the sidewalk, scowling impressively as they neared him.

"Looking for a date, sugar?" the woman asked Ty. The man with her snorted and shook his head, looking away and sighing.

"You look a little too official to be throwing out hooks," Ty responded wryly. The woman smirked and nodded, tossing her blonde hair over her shoulder. "They tailed us," Ty muttered as he turned to Zane and sneered.

Zane grimaced, his mood going even further south with yet more trampling on his nerves. He should have known the Bureau would go looking for them when they didn't show up at their prearranged hotel room. Annoyed, he turned to the side, watching the area around them, leaving Ty to talk to the newcomers.

"Special Agent Marian Sears," the woman introduced herself, showing her badge to them. Ty reached out and snagged it quickly, taking the woman's arm and none too gently escorting her away from the alley. "And that's Special Agent Gary Ross," the woman continued, unfazed by the rude and slightly violent handling.

"Do you have any concept of how much you stand out?" Ty asked the woman conversationally, not even acknowledging the introductions. "Or how very much I hate you both already?"

"My feelings are hurt, they really are," Ross muttered as he followed along.

Sears extricated herself from Ty's grip and stopped, turning to face him. "We understand the need for secrecy in certain circumstances, Special Agent Grady," she said in clipped tones. "But when the new detail on a case that just lost two agents to a serial killer doesn't show up when and where they're supposed to, we tend to get concerned."

"Next time I'll have Momma write a note," Ty drawled. She narrowed her eyes at him.

"You two are outside orders," Ross sneered in response to their rude welcome.

"Your assignment does not include going undercover amongst the working girls," Sears added.

"If you're even working the case out here," Ross muttered as he looked down the alley and shook his head in disgust.

Sears looked at her partner in apparent disapproval. Ross shrugged at her and then looked past Ty to glower at Zane.

"Public drunkenness, huh?" Ross snapped at him. "I can smell the beer on you from here."

"So arrest me," Zane growled.

"Wiseass," Ross grumbled.

"We're working this case beside you, not under you," Ty snarled to them both, losing the good-humored glint in his eyes as he interrupted the sniping. "Don't go tailing us when you've got more important shit to do. You want us, you fucking call us on the phone."

"Got a card?" Sears asked with a little smile, still completely unintimidated.

Ty's lips twitched in slight amusement again, and he reached out and took her hand. He reached under his jacket with the other, finding a pen in one of the inner pockets as Ross bristled angrily. Ty ignored him and held the woman's hand in his, writing a number on the palm of her hand and then sliding the pen back into place slowly without releasing her.

She smirked at him, looking him over in amusement and just a hint of interest, before she slid her hand out of his and took her partner's arm to pull him physically away as Ty smirked after them.

Zane took the few steps to stop beside Ty and watched them go, simmering. "They're going to be trouble," he muttered.

"No, they're not." Ty grinned as he watched them walk away. Ross's hand now gripped Sears's elbow rather than the other way around, preventing her from looking over her shoulder at them as he griped about sexual harassment. "They don't think much of us, which is just how we want it. They'll want to work this case on their own, keep us out of the loop. Plus, see how possessive he is? He won't let her near us again," Ty chuckled darkly as he cocked his head to admire the sway of her hips.

Zane looked after her. "He won't, huh? What did you do? Cop a feel?"

"Might need me a Sears catalog when we get home," Ty drawled out with a sly smile.

"Bastard," Zane murmured. He dropped the cigarette butt to the concrete and ground it out under his heel.

Ty sighed and looked around at the empty street corners. "Looks like our quarry has gone to ground." He growled in annoyance, beginning to walk slowly in the direction from which they'd come. "Did you happen to look at the report on that sheet the body was wrapped in?"

"Bleached Egyptian cotton, six-hundred-count king-size flat sheet, only sold at two places in New York: Bloomingdale's and Henri Bendel. Retail cost four hundred fifty dollars. No catches, no pulls, no tears, no stains besides blood, still smelled like plastic, thought to be fresh out of the package," Zane rattled off as he lit up another cigarette.

"Did anyone follow that up?" Ty asked before they crossed the street at a jog.

"I'll call Morrison and ask him to have someone call the stores. All the report says is that neither had them in stock for a five-day span around the discovery of the body. Bendel's had a linen sale the weekend before," he said. "I'm sure they were flying off the shelves."

"Great," Ty groaned. "We'll go by tomorrow and talk to whoever. What else? Were the sheets changed with the two dye girls? Was it in the report?"

"Nothing in the report said they were."

"Goddamn it," Ty muttered. There had to be a connecting factor. "We'll find the damn thing," he muttered to himself.

Zane stopped for traffic, working his way through the cigarette. "I still want to go back to the office."

Ty exhaled heavily. "Do you understand what we were doing tonight?" he asked softly.

Zane looked at him, not sure if he should be offended, but still irritated merely on principle. Ty looked over at him and raised a questioning eyebrow. "Enlighten me," Zane invited tightly.

"If it's an insider that got Reilly and Sanchez, then he may already be tailing us," Ty explained quietly. "I wanted to see if I could spot anyone."

"You're using yourself as bait?" Zane asked disbelievingly.

"Are you getting hysterical?" Ty asked eagerly. "Can I smack you?"

Zane merely sighed and looked away before he could give an acerbic response.

Ty grunted in mock disappointment. "Anyway, if you do go back to Federal Plaza, make sure you're not alone, and keep an eye on your six. I'm crashing," he admitted.

"I can take care of myself," Zane said curtly. He ground his teeth as Ty snorted, and they each loped across the street to come to the front of their hotel. "I usually get going about seven in the morning," Zane told Ty. "You?"

"Nights," Ty grunted as he headed toward the lobby doors. "I've been working nights. I'm on hour thirtysomething trying to right them, so I really couldn't say."

Zane nodded, stubbing out the cigarette on the brick wall outside the doors and tossing it in an ashtray sitting outside the doors. "Just come bang on the door when you're ready in the morning. I've got plenty to keep me busy." He walked toward the parking garage, hands in his jacket pockets.

Ty just grunted in return as they parted ways.

Zane stopped and turned to watch Ty stalk the last several feet into the hotel. Pondering the puzzle of Ty Grady, Zane made his way to the car. He was infuriating at best. An absolute bastard at worst. And Zane had to grudgingly admit that he might just be good at his job.

Zane sat at the table, feet propped on the air conditioner unit, notepad in hand as he looked through reams of reports. Paperwork was spread out all over the desk, the small round table, the floor, the second bed, the dresser . . . even on top of the television. He'd taped maps to the wall and stuck up photos from the crime scenes. Right now, they were in dated order, but he'd move them around as he formed ideas about how they fit together. Their concentration might be on the two agents who were killed, but the serial itself was just too fascinating and frustrating to leave alone.

He mulled over the ideas about the bodies, the idea Ty had prodded him about last night. He'd made a simple list of how they were found, and he couldn't help but feel that the killer was following a script of some kind. Dropping his heels, he reached over to the bed to snag the photos of the tokens left behind at each scene.

There was a gilded mirror found with the twins. A pair of linked plastic rings like the type found in princess costume kits for little girls left with the dyed roommates. A pair of dog tags, complete with rabies licenses, were discovered by the first victim's maid after the man had died of the meth overdose. The hooker, left in her sheet in the middle of a graveyard, had been left with a small, empty wooden box.

Zane knew they all made sense somehow. He just wasn't seeing it yet.

The slow rapping on the door interrupted him, and he glanced up, immediately on guard. In theory, he should be fine; if someone was there to kill him, they likely wouldn't knock. Still . . . he picked his gun up from the tabletop and held it slightly behind him as he walked to the door and checked the peephole.

Ty stood in the distorted little circle of Zane's view with his head tilted back and his eyes closed, swaying slightly on his feet as he waited. Zane pulled his head back and blinked, then removed the chain and opened the door, shoving his gun into his waistband at the small of his back.

"I'm awake," Ty muttered to him in greeting.

Zane tilted his head and pulled the door open further, amused by how out of it Ty looked. "You sure about that?"

"No," Ty grumbled. "I didn't sleep for shit. You?"

"Not really. Too much reading before bed. My head's swimming. You coming in? I've got coffee."

"I don't drink coffee," Ty grunted as he remained in the hallway. "Any epiphanies?"

"Other than thinking this guy may be some kind of creative freak show genius? No." Zane shook his head. "Give me a minute to get myself together."

He turned and walked back into the room, stopping at the dresser to grab his wallet and push it into the back pocket of his jeans. They weren't going with the usual suits and ties for this job in order to further the inept façade, so he wore just a thin cotton Henley and jeans. It brought back memories of his assignments before he'd been dumped in Cyber. He noticed with some amusement that Ty wore faded jeans that were losing the denim at their knees and a camouflage T-shirt that read, You Can't See Me and I'm Right in Front of You in small yellow print. Over it he wore the green canvas jacket he had passed over the night before. Zane wondered if he coordinated his outfits to look like a slob or if he just really was one.

"I think until we figure out what the hell the connection is, we need to concentrate on the agents," Ty was saying as he stepped into the room and let the door fall shut. He looked around at Zane's piles of files with a sleepy frown and ran his hand through his short hair.

Zane lifted his shoulder holster from the bed and shook it out. "At least with them we can backtrack. According to the notes, the team was having trouble . . . building . . ." His words trailed off as his eyes unfocused in thought.

"Huh?" Ty asked flatly, still too tired to be confused yet.

Zane just stood there for another long moment, then raised a hand to make a wait motion. He turned slowly in a circle, looking at the paperwork, trying to nudge what caught his attention. Then his eyes fell upon the timelines he had tacked up next to the photos.

"Backtracking. The team is having trouble figuring out where the victims were that night. That day. Even the day before," Zane mumbled. Then he turned sharply on his heel and looked down at a particular stack of papers.

"You think he's nabbing them and keeping them? There wasn't much evidence of restraining or struggle," Ty pointed out doubtfully.

Zane's brow furrowed, and he pulled the straps of the holster through his fingers idly as he skimmed the reports. "No. But I think he's watching them. Studying their patterns, then taking them when they're detached from attention."

"Makes sense." Ty nodded as he watched Zane with one eyebrow cocked. "You're not, like . . . going into a trance, are you?" he asked dubiously as he observed the distant look in Zane's eyes.

Zane blinked out of it. "You try sifting through several thousand bits and pieces of data and see how aware you can be," he said shortly.

Ty snorted in a derogatory manner and shook his head. "Whatever, man. I'm always aware," Ty drawled through a yawn.

"I'm sure," Zane muttered, pulling his gun out of his waistband, checking it and sliding it home. "We're going out to the scene, right? Out on the street too?"

"Which scene?" Ty asked as he leaned against the door.

"The last site. The one that's still intact," Zane answered as he moved his jacket to reach for two small black sheaths.

"Did you ever hear from whats-his-face about whether they were ready?" Ty asked as he watched Zane with a small smirk. "Did the terrorists attack while I was asleep?" he asked sarcastically, nodding at the vast array of weaponry.

"Always be prepared, right?" Zane prodded as he pushed up his sleeves, slid on the sheaths, then covered them and pulled on his jacket, sparing a silent thank-you to God that it was October and he didn't have to get creative to hide the armament. "Yes, Morrison set it up; we'll head over after we meet Detectives Holleman and Pierce at two. So we have three hours, and I'm eating first. We'll probably miss lunch. And Scott's coming in to meet us at six."

"Oh, goody," Ty responded flatly, clapping his hands together in a mock display of excitement.

Zane picked up the keys and turned to face Ty, inclining his head. "Of course, if you have a hot date lined up, feel free. It'll be dry, boring stuff, I'm sure." He felt fairly sure his patronizing tone would get just as enthusiastic a response.

"I dislike that woman," Ty returned easily. "A lot."

"Why? She's very good at her job."

"She's also a raging bitch," Ty answered flatly.

Zane's lips quirked. "Yeah, so?"

Ty merely shrugged negligently. "We have history. Why do you care?"

"If you're not going to be able to work with her, then you need to skip the meeting," Zane said. "No point in butting heads." He paused. "Of course, you seem to enjoy that sort of thing..."

"Go fuck yourself, man," Ty huffed.

Zane actually let a smile escape, and the light brightened his dark eyes. He studied Ty for a few moments, undeniably amused. "Fair enough." He swung the keys on his fingers. "Is the feeling mutual?"

"God, I hope so," Ty muttered.

Zane's smile grew and he felt the urge to snicker. "Well," he drew out, "maybe she's utterly charmed by you—being that she's a raging bitch, and all. Like drawn to like, you know?" he said as he walked to the door.

"Logic doesn't mesh with the fact that you're a raging bitch too, and you hate me," Ty pointed out drolly.

Zane glanced back at Ty, not fazed by anything Ty said anymore. "Fair enough."

"How'd your night go after you left me?" Ty asked as he followed.

"Quietly. Henninger was still in the office so he got me the maps I wanted, tracked down pictures of the tokens left at each scene," Zane said, pulling the door shut behind them. "Then I got coffee and came back here."

"Thanks for the itinerary, man," Ty muttered sarcastically. "I was referring more to the anyone following you, trying to kill you, getting laid aspect of it."

"If I could have been so lucky for the latter," Zane said, his voice dry. "No. No one followed me, no one tried to kill me, and no one propositioned me."

"Shame," Ty sighed sadly. "Anything bother you at all?"

"Except for Henninger around the office, no. He's so eager it even makes me wince. Morrison's even worse. I imagine you wanted to kill them right off."

"Maybe," Ty affirmed with a nod.

Zane snickered. "And you accused me of being a candy-ass brown-noser." They walked across the lobby toward the parking garage elevator. "I think Burns must have put us together figuring we'd strangle each other and do his job for him."

"You're really on the chopping block?" Ty asked in some surprise.

Going quiet for a long minute as they entered the elevator and it started moving down, Zane finally shrugged, emotionless mask sliding back into place. "I don't know. Maybe. Probably. I've been told several times that I'm on thin ice, no matter how stellar a job I do. I guess it depends on who's jonesing for an example that week."

"Example of what?"

Zane looked over at him significantly. "An example of what not to do. How not to behave. Who not to be. To show others what happens when you fuck up royally. I'm sure you're familiar with the feeling."

"I couldn't possibly know what you mean." Ty sniffed daintily as the elevator doors opened. He stepped out and started toward the car.

Zane snorted, clicking the key fob and unlocking the car.

"So, what, you're a reformed version of me?" Ty asked with a derisive snort as he went around to the passenger side.

Zane got in the car and pulled on his seat belt, all the while wondering why he allowed this conversation to continue. "I am not reformed. I just want to keep my job," he said curtly as he started the car. "If that means acting like a yes-man in the office, wearing a damn suit, keeping my opinions to myself, and kowtowing to the directors, that's what I'll do."

Ty snorted again as he shook his head. "Forgive me if I don't buy it."

"Don't buy what?"

"You," Ty answered bluntly.

"What's that supposed to mean, Grady?" Zane asked as he started the car and put it in reverse. "It's not all that difficult to understand."

"You seem to have carefully created yourself," Ty told him candidly. "This whole overly reformed bright and shiny image you want to project. It's all very bad cop movie. And I don't buy it."

"What of it?" Why should he care what Ty thought about how he dealt with life now? There was nothing wrong with what he was doing to stay in the Bureau.

"I'm talking about the fact that you want to project it," Ty answered with a soft laugh. He shook his head again in amusement. "If you were truly reformed from any state of less than perfect, you'd keep your mouth shut about your past. You're doing a lot of telling and not enough showing."

"So help me God, I am going to thrash you to within an inch of your life someday," Zane gritted out, simmering. Possibly because Ty was right, in a way; Zane had reformed, but he wasn't proud of it. On some level maybe he did want people to know this wasn't the real him. "You drive me absolutely insane. And I'm almost sure you do it on purpose."

"I like you better when you're angry," Ty responded absently as he looked out the window at the passing scenery. "It's more natural to you."

Zane shook his head. "You like me better when you're making fun of me," he muttered.

"I've never made fun of you," Ty responded instantly. "Making fun of you would imply that something about you is fun."

Zane's hand shot out to smack Ty's chest with the backs of his knuckles. "Asshole," he muttered. "You're no fun yourself."

"Ow!" Ty cried out in surprise, rubbing his chest and scowling. "Damn it," he muttered in protest. "Don't you know you're supposed to wait at least a week before you physically assault your new partners?" Ty asked plaintively as he rubbed his chest where Zane's class ring had thumped against his sternum.

"I must be out of practice. You're the first partner I've had in a long time," Zane said, trying not to think about the last one. A real partner. Not an assigned one.

"Pft," Ty responded with a roll of his eyes and another yawn he tried and failed to repress.

Zane halted the car at a stoplight and turned his chin, eyes glancing over Ty. His eyes were sunken and dull, and he still looked exhausted. "You need some more rest?" he asked. "Won't be able to concentrate for shit if you're tired."

"You worry about your own self," Ty griped.

He thought some of the sharpness hadn't returned to Ty's voice, so Zane didn't push. Seeing a sign for a diner, he turned the corner and parked in a Police Only space on the side of the street. "Food," he said happily.

"What the hell?" Ty muttered as he stared out at the diner. "Can't you eat stale bagels and shit like normal people?"

"We all have our vices. You want to eat a stale bagel and brighten your oh-so-lovely disposition with constipation, be my guest," Zane invited as he got out of the car.

"Kiss my ass," Ty shot back as he sat in the seat and huffed.

"Maybe after breakfast," Zane answered with saccharine sweetness as he shut the door and walked toward the diner, lighting up and pausing just around the corner to smoke.

After a couple minutes, Ty got his holster redone correctly and his jacket collar straightened, and he trudged after Zane into the greasy spoon. "I think I just got heartburn by osmosis," he grumbled as he sat down opposite Zane. He didn't trust New York eateries as far as he could fling one.

Zane ignored him, looking over the menu with a content expression. "Mmm. Waffles," he murmured, giving them proper consideration.

Ty rolled his eyes and waved his hand at the waitress. "Eggs, bacon," he ordered. "And my idiot friend here would like a stale bagel," he said with a wave of his hand at Zane.

The waitress raised her eyebrow and looked over at Zane questioningly, who just rolled his eyes. "Waffles and sausage links. And orange juice." The waitress nodded, chewing her gum, and took off after making note of their orders.

"I appear to be moving up in the world," Zane pointed out, deliberately prodding at Ty all he could while the man was tired and not as snappy with the comeback as yesterday.

"By being an idiot?" Ty asked with a tilt of his head. "Yeah, I suppose that is a step up from your usual state."

"Better than a prickly ass," Zane commented, turning his head to look out the window.

"Other than the little bit of buckshot still left in it, my ass is perfectly smooth, I'll have you know," Ty replied easily.

"I hope so, since I'm supposed to kiss it after breakfast," Zane said facetiously as the waitress arrived with his drink.

"I don't do that before lunch," Ty cautioned. "Can I have an orange juice, please?" he asked the waitress with a brilliant smile that fell back into a tired frown immediately after she turned away.

Seeing the wide-spectrum mood shift on Ty's face, Zane let the odd moment of teasing die and instead watched MSNBC on the television over Ty's shoulder.

"See? I can be nice," Ty pointed out as they sat there.

Zane's eyes shifted to Ty, and he nodded. "Yeah. I'm only a little suspicious of what you're going to want, but nice is good. For a change. Occasionally."

Ty sat there looking at him for a long moment, face expressionless. "Shut up," he finally muttered.

Lips twitching, Zane did, until the waitress came over with their food. He thanked her politely.

"So, aside from being annoying and shaving every four hours, what is it you do, exactly?" Ty asked Zane as he picked up a piece of bacon and crunched into it.

"I just finished six months in a stock market brokerage's computers," Zane answered evenly.

"Is that a euphemism for Hell?" Ty asked seriously.

"Very nearly," Zane said, voice dark. "I have new respect for the nice, plain insanity of terrorists after those cyber freak bastards."

Ty hummed noncommittally and crunched another piece of bacon, finally waking up some more and shaking off the last of the exhaustion. "What'd you come up with last night, anyway?" he asked finally. "Did I ask you that?"

Zane smiled a little. "Yeah. And the answer was noth—" The smile fell off his face as his eyes focused totally over Ty's shoulder, and without warning he was up, tossing a twenty on the table. "Time to go," he said sharply, pulling out his cell phone as he stalked past the television and out the door.

Ty cursed quietly and gathered his bacon in a napkin haphazardly as he got up to follow, glancing up at the lurid red letters scrolling across the television screen: NYPD reports Tri-State killer strikes again.

Chapter Three

"Bird flu," Ty repeated in disbelief as the medical examiner gave them the autopsy report. He held a white mask to his face, refusing to put the little elastic bands over his ears. "What the hell?"

The woman nodded and shrugged as she handed Special Agent Ross the file. "'What the hell' is not my job," she answered with a small smile that showed in her eyes. The white mask she wore over her nose and face covered the rest of the expression.

"Isn't bird flu pretty rare?" Ty asked her in a mystified voice. "How would he get it?"

"Well, more than two hundred confirmed cases of human infection with avian influenza A viruses have been reported since 2004," the ME answered, sounding to Ty as if she were reciting facts she'd just recently looked up.

She flipped her hair over her shoulder and frowned. "The virus isn't easily sustained from human-to-human transmission, but it can mutate to be highly contagious. Still," she went on with a shake of her head, "the most likely source would have been from handling dead birds that were infected. And, to my knowledge, there haven't been any reported cases in the Tri-State area in at least three years."

"So . . ." Ty prodded as he leaned closer expectantly.

"Unless he was traveling in East Asia or the Middle East, Special Agent Grady, I don't believe he would have been able to contract it by natural means."

"He was intentionally infected," Ross concluded with a frown.

"How?" Zane demanded before the ME could even answer.

"I'd rather wait to get the preliminary reports before speculating too much," she answered hesitantly. "But the easiest way to do it—and safest for the person who did it—would have been an injection."

"How long would it take for an injection like that to infect someone?" Special Agent Sears asked, looking up from her notes. Sears and Ross hovered near the exam table. Ross merely held his mask to his face like Ty did and looked down at the body in distaste. He handed the file to Zane absently without looking up.

"Incubation period would be about the same as if he were infected in more typical ways," the ME answered. "I can tell you that bird flu does not have to be lethal. Most cases, in fact, if treated promptly, there's a full recovery. That's pretty much the extent of my knowledge."

"So what you're saying is, either he didn't know he was sick, didn't care that he was sick, or wasn't able to get to a doctor?" Ty asked with a deeper frown.

"Pretty much," the woman nodded.

"For two weeks?" Zane asked. "Were there any signs of restraint or struggle?"

"None," she answered with a shake of her head. "Is there anything else?" she asked as Zane flipped open the folder and started reading. "I've got more in the morgue."

Zane closed the file and looked back up at her. "Thank you, Karen. I hope we won't be seeing you again while we're still breathing," he said. She gave him a little laugh.

Ty rolled his eyes and looked away. She shook their hands and went back to work, and Zane turned to look at Ty. "We need to talk to the cops. Number one, why didn't they call us first—before the damn press got hold of it? And number two, see if they're having any luck connecting the victims."

"That's their job," Ty responded pointedly as he nodded his head at Sears and Ross. They both gave him disgusted looks as Zane glanced over at them and raised an expectant eyebrow.

"We'll get right on that," Sears said to them in annoyance as she jerked her head at her partner and they both stalked out of the room.

Ty looked down at the body, still on the table and covered mostly by a sheet. "Bird flu," he murmured in a slightly mystified voice.

Sighing, Zane tapped the file against his hand. "And another token."

"What is it this time?" Ty asked dejectedly.

"A black feather," Zane answered with a frown. "It's the first one that's made any sense when you consider the method of killing."

"Hmm," Ty responded distractedly, still frowning as they made their way out of the morgue. "I need . . . I need to go somewhere and just look," he finally said in frustration as he took his mask and tossed it into a nearby waste container.

Zane stopped and looked at his partner as he removed his own mask, tilting his head. "Where do you want to go? Crime scene?"

Ty shook his head. "Somewhere empty," he answered with a wince. "Maybe they have a meeting room at the field office with a whiteboard we can use," he suggested.

"There are classrooms at Federal Plaza. Most times they're empty, if there's not a team in training," Zane offered. "Henninger told me about them last night."

"Oh, yeah? What else did the kid tell you?" Ty asked sarcastically.

"He suggested putting you out of your misery," Zane answered pleasantly.

"Your gun ain't big enough, son," Ty drawled with a smirk.

"At the risk of sounding clichéd, I've never had that complaint before," Zane answered, turning to lead the way toward the car.

Ty remained where he was and tilted his head to watch Zane as he walked down the hall. "I'll believe that when I see it," he scoffed finally, smirking as he followed.

"Somehow I just don't believe you're remotely serious about that," Zane replied without looking back or breaking stride.

"Your loss, Brutus," Ty laughed as they came up to the elevators and he punched the button.

Zane's brow furrowed. "Brutus?" he asked. "As in Brutus and Cassius?"

"Sure, man, if you say so," Ty laughed.

Rolling his eyes, Zane got on the elevator once the door opened. "You know, at first I was insulted by the way you treat me. Then I realized it's not personal; you treat everyone like shit. I find it doesn't bother me all too much anymore," he said.

"Usually I only don't bother people I want to see naked," Ty told him seriously as the elevator rose. "So stop it. You're freaking me out."

Zane watched his partner curiously as several people filed into the elevator from the hallway. "I'll keep it in mind," he said under his breath as they walked out. The slightly suggestive tones of Ty's words freaked him out too.

The walk and drive to the office were quiet, and his mind wandered back to the case. They made it into the office and secured one of the empty classrooms with a minimum of fuss, mainly because Ty didn't request one—he just took one over.

"Okay," Ty grunted as soon as they had settled in. "So, what do we know about the latest victim?" he asked as he thunked the stack of paperwork down on the table in the middle of the room and went to the wall where a whiteboard was bolted up. He grabbed the dry-erase marker and began scribbling the names of the victims. "The new victim," he started. "Prison tat on his arm was pretty clear, so he's not squeaky clean."

"File says he was paroled two years ago. Clean record since then," Zane said.

"Uh-huh," Ty muttered as he began writing in the physical characteristics of each victim, excluding the two FBI agents. Age, race, height, weight, hair color, eye color. "Well," he said as he stepped back and cocked his head. "They're all Caucasian?" he offered weakly.

"Actually, no, the stock broker was biracial and the roommate was Latino."

"Goddamn it," Ty cussed as he made the corrections. "They're too random to be random," he muttered, neither noticing nor caring that the statement would make little sense outside of his own mind.

Zane raised his brow. "Didn't I say that yesterday?" he asked, forcing himself to be patient. Somehow.

"You say that like you think I listen to you," Ty responded instantly, a smile pulling at his lips.

Zane snorted in irritation, scooted his chair back, and crossed his legs restlessly.

"Maybe it's not the victims at all," Ty went on as he sat on the edge of the table. "Maybe they're just wrong place, wrong time."

"Possibly," Zane allowed. "But what's been done to them is very specific."

"Mm-hmm," Ty nodded. "So that's where we look for the trigger. Either the way the scenes are staged or the method of killing."

Zane nodded slowly. "Yes, I think so."

"I don't want a goddamned yes-man for a partner, damn it," Ty snapped.

"Stuff the attitude, asshole," Zane snarled.

Ty turned his head to look back at Zane and grinned. "Better," he said approvingly.

Zane closed his eyes for a moment and then looked up at the ceiling, shook his head, and forced himself to take a deep breath before looking back down at the papers.

Ty continued to watch him, narrowing his eyes as he did so. "You should do that more often," he told him. "Let go and tell someone to fuck off, I mean. Makes you look less like you're about to have a coronary."

"I don't look like I'm going to have a coronary," Zane objected stiffly.

"Sure, you don't," Ty responded placatingly. "Have you had your blood pressure checked lately?"

Zane narrowed his eyes. "Not recently. Are you insinuating I ought to?"

Ty shrugged noncommittally and smiled crookedly. "That or unclench your ass a little."

"Gee, thanks," Zane muttered. "Any other advice you want to bestow?"

"Just some friendly counsel," Ty shrugged as he turned to look back at the white-board.

Zane watched his back, wondering why the conversation had turned semiserious. He didn't like it. "What do you care?"

Ty looked down and to the side slightly, not moving otherwise as he watched Zane in the periphery of his vision. "What makes you think I do, Hot Shot?" he countered in amusement.

"I'm thinking a 'fuck off' would fit really well about now, so, fuck off."

"Why does it bother you so much?" Ty asked in amusement as he turned slightly and looked at his partner. "What do you care what I say or do?"

"I already told you, I don't do violins. So back to your whiteboard," Zane said crankily. He wasn't going to open himself up for more criticism. "I don't care if you insult me," he claimed, looking like he'd bit into something sour.

Ty grinned widely and turned back around. He enjoyed irritating Zane more than he had others in the past. He wasn't sure why, but he did. "They never ran a check of the phone calls made to and from Sanchez's hotel room," he said abruptly. "We should look into that."

"Reilly and Sanchez's," Zane muttered, not feeling all that charitable.

"Hmm?" Ty asked distractedly.

"They shared a room," Zane reminded. "They were partners. There were two of them?"

Ty stared at the man for a moment and then curled his lip before looking back at the board. "Whatever," he finally grunted. "I'd also like to look at their belongings," he said after a moment. "Maybe there was a token left and the investigators just didn't recognize it. Might give us something."

Zane's brow furrowed. "They didn't recognize it, but you think you will?" he inquired with a small sneer.

"You never know," Ty answered vaguely.

Zane shrugged and made a note. "As good as anything else we've got." He slid his finger down another column of notes. He sighed quietly, trying to remember what he'd been reading the night before. "Why am I not seeing lab reports for skin and nail scrapings?"

Ty looked up with a frown, then back down at the report in his hands. "I don't know," he said as he picked up another and paged through it. "Maybe they're not in yet?" he suggested doubtfully.

"It's been almost two weeks," Zane said as he continued to flip through sheets. "They should have been in with all the other lab work." He pushed out of the chair. "I'm going over to the lab. Maybe they're just stuck in with the ME's notes. You want to come?"

Ty groaned slightly. "Not really," he answered honestly as he looked back up at the board.

"I think you're taking this inept and lazy objective a little too far," Zane complained.

"Shut the fuck up," Ty murmured with a serious glance up at Zane. Zane met his gaze for a long moment before turning his back and walking out of the room. He'd hit a nerve of some kind, and Zane wasn't about to go poking a Recon Marine. Not without at least two guns in hand. Storing the tidbit away, he headed down the quiet corridor, and his footsteps echoed on the worn floor.

When he entered the records room off the lab, there was no one at the desk, so he leaned over it, calling out a hello. He heard movement back in the stacks of files, but didn't see anyone. He skirted around the desk and peered into the well-lit recess, but there was no one there.

"Can I help you with something, Special Agent Garrett?" Henninger asked from behind Zane with a tinge of amusement in his low voice. Zane glanced over his shoulder, concealing a small jolt of surprise. The young agent leaned against the desk Zane had just passed, seemingly having appeared out of nowhere. "It's lunch break. No one down here," he said softly.

Zane recovered from his surprise quickly and gave the young agent a small smile. "If you don't mind my interrupting whatever you're doing for a bit, maybe you can help me find some records?"

"What are you looking for?" Henninger asked as he gestured for Zane to follow him.

"Some of the medical examiner files from the third and fourth victims, about two weeks ago. There would have been routine skin and nail scrapings and hair clippings, that sort of thing. They're not in the resource file," Zane explained.

"Third and fourth," Henninger replied with a nod. "Those were the girls with the dyed hair, right?" he asked Zane.

"Yeah," Zane answered as they walked between the stacks. "Where's your partner?" he asked curiously. He hadn't seen Morrison since yesterday afternoon.

"Taking a long lunch," Henninger answered haltingly. "Girlfriend thing," he explained with a glance back at Zane.

Zane's lips curled slightly. Henninger was obviously covering for his partner. That, at least, was admirable in a way. It made him wonder what it would be like to actually like his own partner enough to even consider covering his indiscretions. "Here's the file number," he offered, politely leaving off the questions as he handed Henninger a piece of notepaper.

"You've already got the file, though, right? The hard copy?" Henninger asked. "I'll look it up on the computer, see if the sheets got misplaced," he offered as he turned down a long row of shelves and toward a nook in the side of the room that housed three computers. The FBI logo turned lazily on two of the screens, while the third sat black and dormant.

"Yeah, I checked the hard copy out with the others last night," Zane said, flipping through the file of his own notes he'd brought with him.

Henninger sat down at the computer on the far left and began tapping at the keys rapidly, entering his badge number and pass code and then steering through a number of pages as he tried to locate the correct file. They navigated the electronic stacks unsuccessfully for some time before there was a sudden pop and a hiss from the machine that was sitting dark.

Zane glanced over at it with a flinch as it popped again, and without any other warning the computer and monitor exploded in a blast of glass, metal, and singed plastic.

Henninger cried out and covered his face, ducking away from the mini-explosion and thumping to the ground to cover his head as the muted sound and crack of shattering glass bounced hollowly through the large room. Zane was less fortunate. He only had time to turn his back and take half a step away, cursing a blue streak as glass, plastic, and heated air whooshed toward him to slam into his back, debris cutting through his jacket, shirt, and skin. The heat made him stumble forward, and he fell roughly to his knees into the glass and metal shards that littered the floor as pain seared through him.

The computer—or what was left of it—sizzled angrily in the alcove. There were no sprinklers in the stacks to put out the small fire the explosion caused. In the hallway there was shouting and running feet; agents coming to investigate and give aid.

Zane groaned and reached up to touch the back of his neck. It felt like it had been cut to pieces, and that feeling was pretty much confirmed as his hand came away bloody. "Goddamn it," he hissed. At least he still had on his thick canvas jacket. It had probably saved him from being seriously sliced up.

The crunch of heavy feet on glass warned Zane that someone was walking up behind him, slowly and calmly through the chaos.

"You touch my back and I will beat the fucking hell out of you," Zane growled to whoever it was. He could feel the glass moving with his jacket, some of it through the canvas and into him. Ouch. Ouch.

"Don't move," Ty murmured in his ear as a gentle hand came to rest on the back of Zane's head.

Zane hissed at even that light touch. The exposed skin was inlaid with glass fragments and starting to well with blood that trailed in rivulets down into his collar.

"What the hell happened?" Ty asked as more footsteps pounded on the concrete floor. "Call an ambulance!" he barked at the first men who came in. They scrambled to do so.

"Computer blew the fuck up. Where's Henninger? He was sitting here . . ." Zane tried to push off his hands to sit back on his heels.

"I said don't fucking move," Ty hissed angrily as he held Zane down and looked around. "Kid's moving; he's all right."

Trying to stay in one spot, Zane set his hand back down on the floor littered with debris. "Monitor was dark when we came in," he said. "The others had screensavers." He flinched as he felt the blood run from the back of his neck over and around to drip down the curve of his throat.

Ty frowned as he listened, reaching down and plucking bits of glass out of Zane's jacket. "No way whoever set it could have known when it'd be used," he answered, picking bits of glass out of the jacket like a chimp grooming its mate. "We need to move."

Zane winced as Ty freed a particularly jagged chunk of glass. "You think someone did this on purpose?"

"No, I think everyone likes to randomly blow shit up," Ty answered sarcastically. "Where else are you hurt? Anything internal?"

"Where else? You don't see enough?" Zane asked sharply. He took a slow, deep breath despite the prickling pain. "Nothing inside. My neck. Feels like I've been hit with needles all over my back and down my legs too. I'm bleeding under the jacket." He could feel the warm ooze spreading and wending down to his waistline.

"Oh, yeah?" Ty asked as he lifted the jacket gently and peered under it. The jacket itself was ruined, but it looked like a lot of the smaller pieces had been stuck in it. It was just the large, mean pieces that had made it into skin. "You'll live," he declared in a careless voice.

Zane's language degenerated as he muttered to himself. "Damn it, I want a cigarette."

"Shit'll kill you," Ty chastised, trying to keep the concern out of his voice as he bent to help Zane to his feet.

Zane grimaced as his muscles flexed instinctively and pain shot through him. He hissed as an agent scooted past, jostling him and making him arch his back to keep his balance.

"Come on," Ty muttered as he reached under Zane's arms to lift him. He had assured himself that no arteries had been nicked, and now he wanted to get the hell out of there.

Zane climbed awkwardly to his feet, trying not to shift too quickly. Once he stood, a good amount of the glass and plastic dropped to the floor, leaving only the pieces that were embedded too deeply to fall out. He kept his head bowed. Straightening his neck felt like it pushed the tiny glass bits in deeper.

"There," Ty said with a pleased smile as he plucked one last larger glass fragment out of the back of Zane's neck. "Walk it off, man," he suggested with a smirk as he began leading him by the elbow out of the chaos of the stacks and toward the hallway.

"Bastard," Zane hissed. He admitted, silently, that this was practically nothing compared to the last time he'd been caught by an explosion. It was just the shock of it happening that had thrown him. And it hurt like a bitch. "You'd probably say that if I lost a leg."

"Nah," Ty scoffed as they got out into the hall. He looked left and right, then moved Zane to the far wall, out of the way of the people scurrying by, and stepped behind him, running his fingers gently through the back of his partner's hair and removing loose glass pieces. "I'd probably say hop it off," he corrected with a barely restrained snicker.

Zane didn't even try to hold back the snort, his eyes fluttering shut as he felt Ty's fingers brush his scalp gently. "That's a good one," he admitted wryly, moving his arm and dripping blood onto the carpet.

"Quit it," Ty chastised with another brush through Zane's hair and another glass shard removed. "You wanna wait for the EMT crew to get here?" he asked. "Or do you want me back at the hotel with a pair of tweezers and some peroxide so we can avoid the possibility of being yanked off this case?"

"Throw in a shower with the last bit and you've got a deal. I hate EMTs. 'Breathe evenly, Special Agent Garrett.' 'Don't move, Special Agent Garrett.' 'Don't worry, Special Agent Garrett, it only feels like we're removing your arm with a dull hacksaw.'"

"Shake a leg then, Special Agent Garrett, before they see you covered in blood and detain you," Ty said as he took Zane's elbow and began pulling him down the hallway toward the elevator. The sentiment gave Zane enough motivation to move, despite the painful prickling and sharp jabs, and they made it before any medical personnel made an appearance on the scene. As the elevator doors closed, Zane set his hand against the wall to lean against it and hissed instead, jerking back his hand to pick at a piece of twisted plastic embedded in his palm.

Ty merely watched silently, inwardly wincing in sympathy. "At least you had your back to it," he offered finally.

"Reflex," Zane answered. "I actually had my side to it." He lifted his hand to his mouth as a trickle of blood seeped from the abused skin just under the curve of his chin.

"Eh. Ass, face, same difference," Ty muttered with a shrug.

Zane's good hand flashed out and smacked Ty upside the back of the head.

"Ow! What the hell?" Ty cried as he rubbed his head and huffed. "You're lucky I repress the Instakill for you," he muttered.

Zane sniffed and pried at a piece of glass in the heel of his hand. "My lucky streak is about played out."

"Want a little cheese with that whine, maestro?" Ty drawled.

"Never mind," Zane replied tightly, not even wanting to think about wine. The pain was worse moving, and he was not looking forward to sitting in the car. "Let's just get to the hotel. I feel like a pincushion."

"Look like one too," Ty observed dryly as the elevator doors opened. "After you, Oh Injured One," Ty invited with a sweeping gesture of his hand. "Want me to commandeer a van?" he asked with a bit of gleeful anticipation in his voice.

Zane looked at Ty sideways. "Why do you have that 'I'm up to something ever-so-wrong' sound in your voice?" he asked suspiciously as they got outside and approached the car.

"I don't," Ty answered defensively. "Don't bleed on the seats," he added with a huff as he slid into the driver's seat. "God, I hate driving in the city," he muttered under his breath.

Closing his eyes as he sat carefully and felt glass chunks dig into the backs of his thighs, Zane's face went very still as he gritted his teeth. "I'm not wearing the damn seat belt," he said as he gripped the door handle to keep himself from leaning back.

"You could try not sitting on the parts that got hit," Ty suggested.

"Just get us out of here."

"You got it." Ty grinned as he tore out of the parking place and out of the parking deck in record time. He hit the lights as they got to the street. "I love the flashy blue lights," he told Zane almost gleefully.

Groaning, Zane braced one hand on the seat behind him. Despite Ty's reckless driving, they got to the hotel quickly and in one piece without leaving carnage behind, so he didn't say a single word. By the time they got upstairs, Zane seriously wanted several stiff drinks. Hell. A bottle.

"Strip," Ty ordered as soon as the door was closed. "And face down on the bed," he added as he took off his jacket and tossed it onto the back of a chair, then began rolling up his sleeves.

Zane walked over to the corner of the room and carefully shrugged out of the jacket, seeing glass chunks scatter on the carpet as he dropped it. Instead of trying to pull the holster off, he pulled at the straps to totally unfasten it, and he carefully set it and the gun on the stacks of files covering the small round table. It was followed by the sheaths, but for one knife that he pulled and used to handily slice open his Henley from collar to waist, not willing to try pulling it over his head. The back of the shirt was matted with blood, and he let it drop too, hissing as the fabric pulled debris fragments loose as he peeled it off.

He unfastened his jeans and shoved them over his hips with another hiss, leaving his legs mostly free of glass. He toed out of his shoes and socks, leaving them under the jeans, and stepped free to the foot of the bed. He crawled onto the mattress in nothing but his boxer briefs and settled on his belly with several winces.

Ty watched him with a furrowed brow, his face unreadable as his eyes followed the bits of bloody clothing to the floor. He snapped open his KA-BAR folding knife with a distinctive metallic clink as he stepped closer to the bed.

Pressing his lips together hard, Zane closed his eyes. It occurred to him that he just might need to be worried, but he made himself dismiss the thought. He wasn't all that sure he trusted Ty, but he did trust him enough to think he wouldn't maim or kill him, given the chance. Grady had already had those chances.

Ty knelt on the bed beside him, surprisingly gentle as he tried not to jostle Zane too much, and he leaned to his side, putting his head beside Zane's ear to get a better look at the glass fragments. "Going to have to dig for some of 'em," he told Zane with that same gleefully anticipatory tone of voice he had used earlier.

"Go on," Zane murmured tightly, not moving. It would hurt like hell, but it all had to come out. At least the damage wouldn't require surgery this time. He would have sighed at Ty's seeming enjoyment, but it would have required him to move.

Ty didn't touch him for several moments, just hovered next to him on the bed peering over the wounds quietly. Finally, he moved, the rustle of his clothing and the slight dip in the bed the only indication that he was even still there. A moment later cold steel touched the skin of Zane's nape. Once, twice, three times in rapid succession, merely brushing over the skin as if Ty were touching the side of the blade to his skin experimentally and then raising it again. The movement was repeated several more times, the only sound a swish of cotton and the tinkle of glass shards being deposited into Ty's hand after every three or four flicks of the knife.

Zane's eyes squeezed shut and his fingers curled in the bedspread, but otherwise he didn't move or make a sound. He was breathing shallowly to keep his back still, and he thought after this a good, angry fit was in order. Some of the glass felt like pins being removed as Ty scraped, just little pricks. Other times he felt the knife cut in, and his breathing stilled as he felt the glass pry loose, leaving a tiny gouge behind.

"When I was in the service they had us testing this stuff," Ty told him in a conversational manner as he saw the muscles in Zane's back bunch with tension. "It was called Dragon Skin Body Armor. They wanted us to see how far it could go, you know, before it would give in. Put it through the wringer. And since we were these crazy-ass Recon boys with a bit of a reputation for destroying government property, they figured we'd be perfect to do it. Well, we took that shit everywhere with us. Threw it out of planes, planted landmines under it, tossed grenades at it, ran over it with a Humvee. My buddy and I even set it up on this pole once and launched a ground-to-air missile at it. God, that was funny as hell," he mused with obvious fondness.

"Only damage we ever did to it was tear the cover fabric," he told Zane in a tone that could have been respect. "But the Bureau don't allow it. You tell me why that is, hmm?"

"Because they don't want us to turn into pansy asses?"

"Natural selection, maybe," Ty responded with a snicker. "You ain't smart enough to run away from the grenade, you get weeded out."

Zane chuckled and winced. "Fuck, don't make me laugh," he practically begged.

"Hold still," Ty warned with a hand pressed to the back of Zane's head. He laughed suddenly, nearly snorting as he said, "I've had dates like this."

"Christ. Now, he develops a sense of humor," Zane complained. "Please leave some skin intact? I'll need it to match the other scars back there."

"I could just connect them all," Ty responded with a brush of his finger over the mess of thin white scars covered with blood. He didn't ask what had happened. For someone who had seen combat, wounds from a car bomb or something similar were fairly obvious. What he did want to ask was how Zane would come by such mementos. He refrained, though. Mainly because he didn't really care all that much.

"I'd look like a spiderweb," Zane said, muscles shifting under Ty's fingertips.

"We'll just call you Spider-Man," Ty offered with a smirk. "I don't know enough about him to make jokes," he added with sincere disappointment.

Zane snorted and the muscles in his back involuntarily clenched and shifted, catching against the knife. Ty jerked the knife back and immediately whapped Zane on the head for moving. "Shit," he huffed as blood welled where his knife had cut into Zane's skin. "Asshole. That ain't my fault."

"Get back to work," Zane ordered curtly. "I need to bleed some more before I can have my afternoon bender."

"Yeah, I've definitely had dates like this," Ty responded with a small smirk.

""You mean you actually date? You must pick some real winners. I need to meet one of them," Zane said with obvious snark in his voice.

"Good luck with that," Ty answered sarcastically.

"Damn," Zane muttered, setting his chin back on his crossed hands. Then he shifted uncomfortably. "There's a chunk below my right shoulder blade."

"I know," Ty responded testily. "Stop moving," he cautioned again as he pressed his hand down on the back of Zane's head. Zane stilled, but the smile still pulled at the corners of his mouth between grimaces. Ty had to lean closer, bracing his free hand on Zane's other side as he peered across the plane of Zane's back. "That might be metal," he observed in a detached sort of manner. "It's gonna hurt like a bitch."

"Lovely," Zane said drolly, curling his fingers into the bedspread and laying his forehead against his wrists. "Glad I've had my tetanus shot."

"I know you can't drink, but what about some painkillers?" Ty offered.

Zane pressed his lips together. "I don't take them," he said quietly.

"Okay," Ty said with a nod. "So . . . want a stick to bite?" he offered.

"Is it gonna be that bad?"

"I don't know," Ty answered honestly. He shook his head and finally just gripped the piece of jagged plastic-covered metal and yanked it.

The pain was so sudden and sharp that Zane didn't even get to inhale before it streaked through him. His neck and back went rigid and his face went white, and by the time he gasped a breath in he was unable to do anything but just lie there, trembling. After several heartbeats he spoke, voice low, clipped, and heartfelt. "Fuck."

"Yeah, it's gonna hurt," Ty murmured as he put his hand on the back of Zane's head again and rested it there. "That's all," he said with a little pat of his hand.

The muscles in Zane's back slowly started to flex as he cautiously moved to check for what he could feel. "Thanks," he said quietly, as he started to push himself up.

"Why don't you just stay down?" Ty suggested seriously.

Zane turned his chin to look at Ty, studying his face and not seeing any sign of teasing or disgust. He sighed, letting his shoulders slump and his mask crack. The pain and exhaustion showed more fully upon his face as he lowered himself back down onto the bed, still moving very cautiously and stiffly. What a bitch of a day, and it was only half over. He shifted his eyes to Ty, but he didn't have anything else to say to the man. He didn't want to insult or tease right now, and that was about the extent of their relationship, besides having the same employer.

Ty nodded in satisfaction and hefted himself up from the bed. "I'm going to clean some of that off, okay? Got to go get some things from my room; I'll be right back."

"I'll be here," Zane murmured, not droll at all. His patience, his energy, and his pain threshold were all tapped. If he'd let himself joke about it, it might help, but he didn't want to let go of what little reserve and dignity he had left.

"Don't move," Ty ordered yet again as he headed for the door. He left the room with the latch pulled so he could get back in, and he jogged down to his room and moved as quickly as he could to gather his small medical kit, not even bothering with the lights. After a brief glance around the dark room he realized that something felt off. The curtains were drawn and there was barely any light for him to see. The stench of Zane's blood on his hands and shirt was beginning to hit him; he hadn't stopped to wash it off. The hair on the back of his neck began to rise, and he gathered his bags and left the room as quickly as possible, promising himself he'd come back to investigate when he hadn't left his partner helpless and injured in an unlocked room.

When he got back to Zane's room, his pulse was a little higher than he would have liked. Zane hadn't moved. He was still sprawled on the bed on his belly, cheek pillowed on one hand, the other curled in the bedspread as he breathed carefully. His eyes opened and looked right at the door when Ty entered, and then he relaxed again.

"How ya doin'?" Ty asked in a slightly tense voice. He wondered if it was something legitimate that had caused his alarm or if he had just been on the edge for too long and was finally losing his grip. Finally he decided that he was just tense. And not willing to leave Zane alone in this state.

Zane tried to shift slightly, but stopped abruptly with a wince. "Fine," he answered quietly, staring at the wall as he tried to pull together enough strength to get up and get in the shower as soon as Ty was done cleaning him up. "Once you're done, I'll hop in the shower so we can get back to it," he said. He figured Ty would be chomping at the bit soon, if he wasn't already, and Zane really, really didn't want to give the man another reason to razz him.

"I'd say you've earned the day off," Ty replied as he came closer.

"Day off?" Zane echoed in surprise, craning his head to look at Ty and flinching as his neck pinched.

"Someone tried to maim you today, Zane," Ty responded evenly. "Probably me too, but they didn't know how lazy I am. That someone, in case it's gone under your radar, has access to restricted Bureau areas in a federal building and was close enough to know when to detonate that bomb. We pretty much confirmed Burnsie's suspicions. I'm thinking spontaneously exploding federal property is a long way toward proof that this guy is a Fed."

Zane set his forehead back against the pillow, straightening his neck to relieve the slicing ache. He'd noticed Ty had called him by his first name. It sounded odd coming from his new partner. He sighed softly. "So it really is one of us," he said sadly.

"At least he isn't trying to kill us, yet," Ty muttered and frowned as he glanced over Zane's nearly nude, bloody body worriedly. "Unless you'd been sitting on the damn thing, a blast that small wouldn't kill you. It was just enough to take you off the case." He continued to stare at the man for a long, thoughtful moment. With a sigh, he decided to go all out and treat Zane like the partner he was going to have to be. For a minute, at least. "My room made me nervous," he admitted.

Zane shifted his chin, and his slightly narrowed eyes tracked over to Ty. "Think someone was in there?" he asked. Zane knew Ty wouldn't say something like that unless it was for real. One good thing about all that trash he talked was that you knew when he was serious.

"Could have been Housekeeping," Ty hedged with a shrug. "Could have been me being paranoid 'cause I'm fucking covered in your blood. I didn't see anything out of place. Just... felt it. Probably nothing. But I'm going to sleep here tonight, if you have no objections."

Zane didn't reply immediately. After a short pause he spoke quietly. "I'll warn you, I'm going to be grouchy as my back really starts hurting."

"And I'll be on the lookout for that major change of attitude," Ty responded sarcastically.

Zane rolled his eyes and quashed the impulse to respond in kind. "You probably ought to put stuff on my back after the shower instead of before," he said regretfully instead, shifting slowly to climb to his knees.

"Do you need help?" Ty asked as he watched without moving.

Stopping once he was on his knees, Zane drew a shaky breath as the abused skin shifted and stretched. He cursed under his breath. "Is there glass on the floor?" he asked. "I'd really rather not walk in it."

"Why don't you stay there, and I'll clean you off?" Ty answered. "There's no reason for you to have to get up. The bed's already bloody."

Zane turned his head to study Ty, wondering where this solicitous side had come from. Did he just bury it under so much attitude that you couldn't normally notice? "I'm going to take you up on that offer," he murmured, slowly shifting to stretch out sideways.

"Good." Ty nodded with a slight smirk. "We're making progress. Now you know I'm always right," he said over his shoulder as he headed into the bathroom to spread out the contents of his medical kit.

Zane sighed. He should have known Ty would have some kind of angle, the bastard. Zane reached for one of the pillows and pulled it over, stuffing it under his chest to lie on, his arms wrapped around it as he waited.

In his medical kit, Ty had iodine and gauze, a tin of Rawleigh's salve, some tape and bandages, and in keeping with his always prepared mantra, a flask of peach-flavored moonshine all the way from home.

None of it was worthy of being called a proper medical kit, but it got the job done. He extracted most of it and laid it out on the long counter. He filled the ice bucket with water, grabbed the stack of hand towels, and headed back out into the outer room. Zane was draped over the pillow, long, bare legs extended out over the bed.

Ty licked his lips and for the first time took a moment to really look at his new partner. It had been hidden under the suit, but there was no denying that he was impressively muscled, at least. And kind of hot, in a stuffed-shirt, stick-up-his-ass sort of way. When he wasn't covered in blood.

He shrugged that thought off and moved closer, kneeling beside the bed and setting the water down next to him. "All I've got to disinfect with is iodine," he told him as he looked up and examined the wounds. "Gonna burn."

"Sure, what's a little more pain?" Zane bit off tightly, squeezing the pillow tighter.

Ty was silent as he carefully wedged several towels under Zane's body to catch the mess the water was going to make. "Takes a lot of strength to say no when you don't have to," he finally murmured as he began cleaning the blood with a moistened cloth. "I respect that, if that matters to you."

Zane was quiet for a long minute as the cool rag wiped carefully over his back. "Thank you," he finally said quietly. Wouldn't a glass of whiskey or a handful of Vicodin be great right about now? Hell, even some ibuprofen.

Maybe he'd think a little more seriously about taking the ibuprofen. There were other things he said no to, as well . . . most of the time. Things he'd do better not to think about at all. Like the man behind him. Zane could feel the heat coming off him.

He fell silent for a bit before speaking again. His voice wasn't self-deprecating or self-sympathetic; if anything it was a little cold and clinical. "There's a lot of things I say no to," Zane murmured without thinking about Ty's reaction. "But there's certainly no one to care."

"You saying you don't care?" Ty asked curiously.

Sighing, Zane pressed his cheek to the pillow. "I do care. But it's the bare minimum of motivation. Like I won't pick up a bottle because I want to keep a job I love. That doesn't necessarily translate to caring if I pickle my brains or not. I guess I've gotten a bit self-concerned since my youth."

"Nothing wrong with self-concern," Ty said as he wiped one last time at Zane's back, then set the cloth aside and reached for the iodine. "I could just do salve," he offered as he looked at the iodine doubtfully.

"Compromise," Zane said. "Put iodine on the worst ones so they won't get infected. Salve on the rest ought to be fine."

"All righty," Ty rumbled, then he quickly spread iodine on the deeper gashes. "Why'd you drink?" he asked suddenly.

Zane's shoulders tightened in response.

"Don't have to answer," Ty went on with a careless shrug. "Just curious."

Zane pressed his lips together tightly. "My wife was killed in a car accident," he said tonelessly. "I was across the country at the time. Had been for a month."

Ty pursed his lips and continued with the iodine, his eyes drifting to the ring on Zane's finger. "My condolences."

Zane let out a pent-up breath. "I kind of got . . . a little out of control. Clichéd, I know, but there it is."

"Happens," Ty responded with another emotionless shrug.

"So here I am: widower, alcoholic, addict, all-around asshole turned squeaky clean by force of will, threat of jail, and sheer terror. I suppose it's no wonder your 'pansy ass' comments get in my craw," Zane muttered.

"I wouldn't think much of you if they didn't," Ty answered, frankly a little surprised at Zane's self-description. "And we all have our sob stories. Nothing to be ashamed over. Being a pansy ass, that's something to be ashamed over."

"I'm not a real pansy ass," Zane objected. "I just act like one sometimes."

That caused Ty to laugh. Hard. "If you say so, man," he practically giggled after he'd gotten control of himself.

Zane thwapped his knuckles back against Ty's ribs. Hard. "Asshole," he said, in a vaguely fond fashion.

"I'm not an asshole," Ty objected officiously. "I just act like one sometimes," he added slyly.

Zane chuckled tiredly and laid his head back down. "I can live with that," he murmured after a short pause.

"Oh yeah?" Ty asked in slight surprise.

Zane wondered why Ty sounded like he didn't believe him. "Yeah," he said simply as he lay still under Ty's hand, which was spreading some sort of awful-smelling salve over the myriad nicks and cuts. Now that he knew what to expect—mostly—from Ty, he could ignore the worst of it. "You got a problem with that?"

"Maybe," Ty drawled with a smirk as he dipped more of the salve out onto Zane's back.

Zane's lips twitched. "Like what?"

"Give me a minute, I'll think of something," Ty answered as he finished up with the Rawleigh's.

Zane's expression was torn between a slight frown and an amused smile, and something glittered in his eyes for a change.

"There," Ty huffed finally as he stood up and looked Zane's back over. "Don't roll over; you'll never stop. That shit's worse than Astroglide," he warned. "I might take a shower," he added musingly as he looked down at his hands, still covered in blood and now salve that wouldn't come off without serious scrubbing.

"Help yourself. My clothes should fit you if you don't want to go back to your room," Zane murmured, eyes tracking the other man.

Ty merely nodded, not admitting that he was hesitant to leave Zane alone. "Your clothes would fit me like a burlap sack. I brought my bag," he muttered as he wiped his hands off on the towel at Zane's side. "I'm going to go get you some ice first. I'll be back," he added as he picked up the key card to Zane's room. He'd rather not leave the door open again.

"Hey, give me my gun, would you?" Zane asked as he shifted, only to wince as the skin pulled.

"Why, you planning on shooting me in the ass when I turn around?" Ty asked sarcastically as he reached for the holster.

"Tempting, but you'd probably get off on it," Zane said, holding out his hand.

"Maybe so," Ty drawled again, grinning widely as he placed the gun in Zane's hand.

Zane's palm covered the gun, and his fingers curled firmly around Ty's hand. His eyes had gone serious when he looked up at the other agent. "Why did you help me?"

Ty looked down at their hands and then up at Zane with open confusion. "Why wouldn't I?" he asked.

That certainly wasn't the answer Zane expected. He figured he'd get yet another smart-ass remark. His face softened slightly, and he nodded slowly, letting go of Ty's hand. "Thanks."

"Don't thank me," Ty responded with a smirk. "Just don't get your prissy ass hurt again."

"Better watch it, Grady, I might get to thinking you're taking a liking to my prissy ass," Zane said, sliding the gun under the pillow.

"I'm sure I'd like parts of it," Ty shot back as he headed for the door. "Be right back."

Zane grinned and pushed his face into the pillow to muffle his chuckle. Maybe Ty wasn't quite so bad as he'd thought. Still an asshole, though.

Ty was gone for perhaps five minutes, quickly filling the ice bucket and grabbing himself a drink from one of the machines. He couldn't shake the feeling of being watched, no matter how many times he assured himself that he was alone. When he returned to the room, his entire body was tense again.

Zane slid the gun in his hand back under the pillow once he saw Ty. "Everything okay?" he asked.

"Yup," Ty answered succinctly as he set the ice down and reached for his bags. "How's it feeling?"

"Annoying as hell," Zane said frankly. "It's not killing me, but I'm certainly feeling it. It's not too bad if I don't move a lot."

"Well, I would suggest not moving, then," Ty drawled as he set his bags on the other bed and began stripping off his clothing.

Zane just raised an eyebrow in wry acknowledgment, watching idly. Ty yanked off his shirt and tossed it to the floor. He toed off his boots and kicked out of his jeans, sighing with the realization that they'd have to frequent a laundromat if they expected to stay smelling decent.

He bent and began rummaging through his bag for clean clothing. His body bore the evidence of a life lived in the trenches, and it was easier to see now in the afternoon light streaming through the sheer curtains. Zane got a closer look at the tattoo and realized that it was a drawing of a bulldog wearing the distinctive white cover of a Marine. Two guns crossed behind the dog, the smoke from their barrels forming the letters USMC. It wasn't possible to make out the finer details. Zane would need to get closer to appreciate the artwork. A lot closer.

The rest of Ty's body was covered with battle scars. There were wounds that Zane recognized as gunshots and knife gashes, and several older, more interesting patterns along his side that might have been caused by barbed wire. The one that was most recent was the one he had noticed before, low on Ty's belly. Zane knew it went all the way through to the back.

None of it detracted from his physique. Not in Zane's eyes. Zane had his share of "mementos" from the job. But to him, the Bureau was just a job, albeit one he loved. Ty lived it. Ty did the job because he believed in it, though Zane suspected Ty would never admit it. It was a stark difference, and Zane lowered his chin to the pillow to mull silently over his own choices.

Ty pulled out a new T-shirt from his seemingly endless supply, one with ExFed written across the front in purple and green letters, and he slid into it as he turned around and looked over Zane. "Sure you're all right?" he asked, sounding almost self-conscious as he covered up.

Zane refocused on the man in front of him, blinking a few times. Ty looked uncomfortable suddenly. Worried his partner wouldn't be up to the task? He spent a short minute thinking of what he wanted to say. This slightly different side of Ty—the man who'd tended his wounds—made Zane feel like he could be a little more open. But the man now in front of him looked uneasy.

"I will be," he answered quietly.

Ty raised an eyebrow dubiously and pursed his lips. He finally nodded and then looked back down at himself. "I was going to shower," he muttered, almost talking to himself as he pulled the clean T-shirt off again and flushed slightly in embarrassment. He wasn't used to being flustered.

Raising an eyebrow, Zane watched the slight blush cross Ty's cheeks. Seeing such a soft look on the other man stirred something inside Zane, something warm he had to swallow on. "Okay," he murmured. "I'll hold down the fort."

Ty nodded and picked up a battered leather toiletry bag on his way to the bathroom. He couldn't even produce a snappy response. Zane watched him disappear into the bathroom, still a little mystified. He certainly hadn't said anything he thought could be construed as embarrassing. Sighing, he shook his head just slightly, winced as the back of his neck screamed, and tried to relax, eyes shuttering.

Taking the minimum amount of time in the shower, Ty washed the blood off and made sure he was reasonably clean. He stepped out of the steamy bathroom with nothing but a towel around his waist, and he peered at Zane closely, trying to determine if he'd gone to sleep. He moved closer and knelt beside the bed, resting his chin on the mattress and looking into Zane's face.

Dimly, Zane sensed his partner close. "What?" he murmured softly.

"Nothin'," Ty answered in the same soft tone. "Just making sure you weren't dead."

The corner of Zane's mouth curled up. "Would you miss me?" he asked sleepily, the drowsiness lulling him into the odd question.

"Sure," Ty answered in a gently placating tone as he reached up and petted Zane on the head to humor him.

Zane's soft chuckle was mostly muffled by the pillow. "Sure you would," he said as he went to sleep, trusting Ty to keep watch.

Ty squatted by the side of the bed for a long time, frowning at Zane's sleeping face. Thinking hard about it, he realized that he just might miss the guy. Even if it was just because he was so fun to annoy. "Damn you," he muttered softly.

"Hey, Henny," Mark Morrison greeted from the opening in the curtain around the emergency room cubicle. "Are you maimed for life?" He smirked at his fellow agent.

Tim Henninger glared up at him and curled his lip into a sneer as the nurse finished his stitches. "I'm not in the mood for humor right now," he warned seriously. "I almost lost my fucking eyes, man."

"Aww. Those puppy-dog eyes you blink at the girls to get your way," Morrison teased.

Henninger glared at him balefully, wincing with the last of the stitches.

Morrison rolled his eyes. "Geez." He glanced around. "So where's Garrett?"

Henninger blinked at him and stiffened. "What, he's not here?" he asked in concern.

The other agent's eyes shifted from side to side before he stepped out of the small curtained area. A couple minutes later he rejoined Henninger. "I don't see him. Could he have been released already?"

"No fucking way; he was hit harder than I was," Henninger answered, trying not to frown because it pulled at the stitches. "Was he killed?" he asked in a near whisper.

Morrison stared at him for a moment, and his lips tightened. "I haven't heard anything. The coroner wasn't there," he offered flatly. "Why wouldn't he come to the hospital if he was hurt?" His eyes narrowed as he thought it over.

"Maybe he's got something to hide? I remember Grady being there awfully fast," Henninger told Morrison in a hushed voice.

"I don't remember seeing Grady at all," Morrison murmured. "But I got there after the medics. Was that before or after the thing blew up?"

"After," Henninger answered with a scowl. His eyes glazed over slightly as he tried to remember the events in sequence. He and Garrett had approached the computers, and he had sat down and typed in the pass code. Then he'd had time to do several short searches before the bomb inside the computer had gone off. He remembered he was still wallowing on the ground and bleeding, yelling for help, when Garrett's asshole partner appeared out of nowhere and started barking orders. He'd been forced to sit through hours of doctoring and interviews while Garrett got away, damn him. Quietly Henninger related what he remembered to his partner.

Morrison frowned as well. "If Grady got Garrett out, he couldn't have been hurt that bad," he said.

"He was," Henninger murmured. "Trust me."

"So what are they hiding? Something's off."

"You're saying you think they're dirty?" Henninger asked dubiously.

"I haven't said anything," Morrison objected sharply. He looked around them again. "But it looks bad, you know? Oversight is coming in to interview us. We'll have to tell them what we saw."

Henninger pursed his lips and glanced at the dividing curtain with a sigh. "I fucking hate Oversight," he muttered.

"Shit, Henny. You about got your face taken off. Don't you want to know who did it?" Morrison asked, crossing his arms.

Henninger looked up and narrowed his eyes. "Oversight is highly unlikely to make that discovery, wouldn't you say?" he asked softly. "Besides, that's supposed to be what Grady and Garrett are looking into."

"You saying we should keep our mouths shut?" Morrison asked quietly.

Henninger stared up at him for a long, silent moment, mulling over the decision. "Yeah," he finally said with a slow nod. "If they find out Garrett was there, it won't have come from us, got it?"

"Yeah," Morrison agreed softly. He stared at him for a long moment before turning his eyes away and shifting uncomfortably. "I hate Oversight too," he muttered. "Always picking around in your personal business."

"Yeah, you should," Henninger spat. "I swear to God, Mark, if I have to cover for you when you go missing one more time, I'm going to shoot you. In a fun place. One that bleeds a lot."

"Christ, Henny, fine. I'll be more careful with my fucking lunch dates. That work for you?" Morrison asked, looking a little put out.

Henninger rolled his eyes and shook his head. "You could wait till you're off the clock like normal people," he grumbled in annoyance. "It's so unprofessional, it's—"

"Enough! Jesus! You're on your damn soapbox again. How come you have to be such a Goody Two-shoes?" Morrison muttered.

"It's called doing your job, man," Henninger snapped. "Where the hell did that doctor go?" he asked with a near growl as he resisted the urge to poke at the stitches. "I want to get the fuck out of here."

Chapter Four

Ty wasn't sure when he'd fallen asleep, but he woke with a little gasp and a flail of his arms, still sitting in the chair he'd dragged in front of Zane's map of the crime scenes that was pinned to the wall. When he checked, he saw that Zane was still asleep, having shifted only slightly, perhaps stopped from moving by pain when his back flexed. Ty looked around the room with a frown. He'd been dreaming, but he couldn't remember anything save for the waking. Had he heard a sound? He grunted and pushed himself out of the chair, walking over silently to kneel next to Zane again.

The agent's face was softened as he slept, a little flushed, despite being totally uncovered in the room's cool air. He slept silently, one arm curled around the pillow against his chest, the other under the pillow that was under his head—most likely wrapped around his gun, Ty figured. His short brown hair was mussed, and he was scruffy, a day's and night's worth of whiskers growing out. He looked like a different man.

Ty reached up to feel the side of his face with the backs of his fingers. He didn't feel fevered, at least.

He had just pulled his hand back when the vibration at his hip caused him to jump guiltily, and he stood quickly and paced away from the bed as he answered his phone.

"What?" he snapped in a low voice.

"Special Agent Grady? What is your status?"

"My status?" Ty asked, feigning confusion.

"There was an explosion at Federal Plaza today. Several witnesses claim you and Special Agent Garrett were present and possibly injured in the—"

"No, we're both fine," Ty answered, cutting the voice off. He resisted the urge to ask how Henninger was doing. "Special Agent Garrett and I were in the reading room when the explosion occurred," he said firmly instead. "We left to follow a lead and get out of the way of the EMTs."

"That's not the information we were given, sir. We were told by several bystanders that Special Agent Garrett was present with an Agent Tim Henninger at the time of the incident, and that he sustained serious injuries."

"Your information is wrong," Ty answered matter-of-factly.

There was a short silence and a rustling in the background. Ty assumed this desk jockey wasn't accustomed to bald-faced lies, and she didn't quite know what to do with it. "Very well, Special Agent Grady," she finally said curtly. "We request that you submit observation reports as soon as possible, as we are, of course, investigating the incident. May we speak with Special Agent Garrett, please?"

Ty turned to look down at Zane and raised an eyebrow. "I'll have him call you as soon as he's out of the bathroom," he answered before hanging up.

Zane woke while Ty was talking, and he'd figured out what it was about pretty quickly. When Ty ended the call, he opened his eyes to see the other man watching him. "Bathroom?" he asked, amusement in his sleep-laden rasp.

"I could have said a number of other things that came to mind," Ty pointed out. "If they know you were hurt, they'll yank you."

Zane scrunched up his nose as he slowly pushed himself up, only wincing a little. "Yeah, probably."

"I figured you didn't want that," Ty added pointedly.

"You figured right," Zane answered, sliding to sit on the end of the bed, carefully shifting his shoulder and back, checking his range of motion. He was stiff at first, but soon was moving fairly fluidly, the pain a mere annoyance.

"You're moving better, anyway," Ty observed. "Guess that stick up your ass helps posture, huh?"

Reaching his arms up behind him to stretch, Zane yawned, still mostly asleep. "You'd be surprised what that stick up my ass helps with." He stood up, twisted a little and flinched, then started toward the bathroom, rubbing at his eyes.

"Do I even want to know?" Ty called after him.

Zane laughed as he shut the door behind him, but it died off quickly, and he leaned on the sink looking at himself. "Probably not," he murmured before turning on the water. He stretched again carefully, grimacing, and looked over his shoulder at his back. While most of it looked okay, a couple of the deeper chunks were red and swollen-looking. He pulled open the door and stepped halfway out. "Hey, would you put some more of that stuff on my back? There's a few..." Zane let the words trail off as he realized Ty was looking at the wall intently like he had heard something. "What?" he asked.

"Nothing," Ty answered with a shrug, his expression unreadable as he turned his head to look at Zane. He sat on the end of the bed, one eyebrow cocked curiously as he waited for Zane to continue what he had been saying.

Zane tilted his head, frowning a little. "Help me out?" he asked, pointing his thumb over his own shoulder.

"Sure thing," Ty muttered as he stood and strolled over to grab the ointment. "Does it still hurt?"

"If I move too quick or twist side to side, it's sharp. Otherwise just a dull ache, a few spikes here and there," Zane said.

"Pansy," Ty offered with a smirk.

Zane sighed. "I'll have to lose a limb before I get any respect from you, won't I?" he said, deadpan.

"Maybe not a whole limb," Ty answered thoughtfully as he made a dainty little turn around gesture with his finger.

Shaking his head, Zane spun slowly in place, presenting Ty with his back. He closed his eyes at the first touch of Ty's fingers, telling himself to ignore the yank in his gut.

"Relax," Ty muttered as he placed his hands on Zane's tight muscles. "You're so damn tense, no wonder you still hurt." He huffed as he prodded at some of the tender spots gently. He dipped his fingers into the tin of salve and began dabbing it onto the open wounds, then massaging it into the areas around them carefully.

"You try taking a sheet of glass in the back and not be tense," Zane objected, though he had to admit to himself it was more than that.

Something about Ty was digging at him: the attitude, the bullshit, the hard-ass style—none of it fit with the gentle touches of his fingers. Zane's body was noticing.

"No, thanks," Ty responded wryly. "I prefer not to be a moron."

"I'm flattered. I've moved up from idiot to moron," Zane said. "And you have moved up from utterly reprehensible asshole to only moderately annoying asshole."

"Only?" Ty repeated with a huff. "It takes effort to be this abrasive, I hope you realize."

"Yeah, I guess so. But you just make it look so easy."

"I make everything look easy," Ty responded with a smirk that Zane couldn't see.

"I can't judge that till I see it," Zane said with an apologetic shake of his head as he rolled his shoulders under Ty's fingers.

"See what, everything?" Ty asked in amusement.

Zane bit his lip on a smile. "You. Being easy."

"I am easy," Ty replied with a laugh.

"Now see here, you've already proven the opposite. You're not easy to get along with, you're not easy to understand, you're not easy to keep from getting under my skin," Zane ticked off on his fingers.

"I think the glass is what got under your skin. And I am perfectly understandable," Ty said as he let his heavy Appalachian accent take over. "I enunciate," he replied with special drawling emphasis on the last word.

Zane chuckled, almost against his will. "I was thinking of you more as a thorn, actually."

"Ouch," Ty objected with false sincerity.

Zane sighed and tilted his neck to each side as he felt the texture of Ty's rubbing fingers change. The salve was sinking in and the skin was catching on skin. "We should get back to work," he said quietly.

"We have the rest of the day off," Ty replied firmly as he continued to doctor.

Looking over his shoulder, Zane raised an eyebrow. "What are you and I going to do with a day off?" he asked. Was the other agent saying they were going to spend time together? Off the clock?

"I don't know about you, but a few hours' real sleep would do me wonders. And we can get plenty done right here in the room. Quite frankly, I'd prefer to stay away from Federal Plaza till I can figure out more about who and how."

Zane nodded slowly. "All right. I agree with all that." Suddenly, he felt awkward, standing there with Ty still touching his back, especially because Zane didn't want to move. Not at all. He found that a bit frightening. He could be partners with Ty. He could, someday, maybe, be friends with Ty.

But anything beyond that was simply dangerous. Zane raised a hand and swiped it over his face, noticing the prickles. "I should shave," he murmured.

"Why?" Ty asked, genuinely curious as he finished smoothing the salve over the bloody spots.

"Why? Why shave?" Zane asked. "Uh." He blinked, trying to think. "I don't suppose I have a reason," he answered with a slight shrug. "Habit. Have to be clean-cut, you know. Don't want to attract negative attention."

"Yeah, man, that negative attention, pffft," Ty responded sarcastically as he stepped away, then pushed Zane slightly to the side so he could step through the bathroom door and to the sink to wash his hands. "You have to sleep in the bloody bed."

"It's just the spread that's bloody," Zane said mildly, still rubbing his chin as he walked out of the bathroom and toward the bed. "Food later?" he asked hopefully as he yanked the spread and sheets down.

"No, we're fasting till we catch the guy," Ty answered with a curl of his lip as he came out of the bathroom with a hand towel in his hands.

With an annoyed grunt, Zane snagged one of his pillows and whacked Ty upside the head with it.

"Bastard!" Ty barked as he swatted at the pillow with the damp towel. Zane laughed and bapped him again. "Now who's got a stick up his ass?"

"Shove it," Ty huffed as he pulled back the sheets on his own bed.

Collapsing onto his bed, Zane was careful to stay on his side and keep an eye on Ty just in case he launched a counterattack. "You're just a big softy," he taunted.

"The last person said that to me got Viagra in his coffee next morning," Ty warned seriously.

Zane buried his face in the pillow to try to muffle the sounds of his laughter. "Oh, God. You would too." His eyes were wide and dancing when he looked back up.

"Of course I would. He had to question a guy," Ty told him with the beginnings of a laugh in his voice. "Three hours he was in there, trying to hide this raging hard-on. I've never seen a suspect more terrified in my life." He snickered with the memory.

Zane pulled the pillow over his face, stifling the continuing laughter as he tried to get himself under control. Finally he sighed and looked back at Ty, shaking his head. "All right, I'm warned." He kept a straight face for a long moment, but ruined it when his lips twitched.

"Shut up." Ty groaned as he flopped onto his side, turning away from Zane, and pulled the covers up over his head.

Chuckling, Zane shifted the pillow back under his chest and lay against it, settling where he could gaze at Ty's figure under the sheets. As he watched, Ty lifted his head up again and reached for his pillow, then burrowed his head under it. Zane couldn't help but smile at how innocent and almost childish the action seemed. He recognized it as a habit of someone who was accustomed to sleeping in the daylight hours, and the thought charmed him.

Who would have thought they'd play off each other like this? He'd not wanted a drink or a cigarette all afternoon. Being in pain and keeping up with Ty was absorbing. One minute Zane hated him. The next, he thought he just might be able to like him. Conflicted, he sighed, closed his eyes, and let sleep overtake him.

Ty had barely managed to find the state of unawareness that came just before sleep when Zane's phone began to trill demandingly. He jerked and hopped from the bed, still half-asleep and tangled in his sheets when his feet hit the floor.

Zane lifted his head and squinted at the bedside table where his phone almost bounced around. "Great," he muttered. He sat up carefully, reached for the phone, picked it up, and looked at the number. He glanced at Ty, who was still standing and blinking blearily at him as he flipped open the phone. "Hello, Serena."

Ty opened his eyes wide and shook his head, reaching up to rub at his eyes like a tired toddler as he looked around the room. He had been out of the service for almost seven years, and he still got out of bed before he woke up. At Zane's mention of the caller's name he growled wordlessly and thumped down on the side of the bed with a grunt. They'd forgotten about their dinner appointment with the profiler.

Watching Ty carefully, Zane made agreeable noises as Serena talked. Then she said something that got his attention. "Yeah?" Zane asked. "You heard that?" Ty merely glared at him as he listened. "I didn't know that," Zane finally answered as the profiler on the phone kept talking. "So, dinner?" He listened again and nodded. "All right. I'll be there." Another pause, and Zane's eyes flicked to Ty.

Ty practically snarled at him, but gestured to him that he would be included in the meeting.

"Yeah, he's coming," Zane said quietly. Then after listening for another few seconds, a soft smile curled his lips.

"Bitch," Ty muttered under his breath as he pushed to his feet and padded over to his bag to begin rifling through his clothing.

"Yes, Serena. Okay. See you in a bit." Zane thumbed off the call. He watched Ty silently as the other man moved. He was rummaging through his duffel bag and apparently trying to find something he wasn't able to get his hands on.

When the silence stretched on, he looked over his shoulder at Zane. "What'd she have to say?" he asked flatly.

Zane watched him, the mask in place. "She's glad you're coming to dinner."

"Oh, yeah?" Ty asked, feigning interest. "Why, could you hear her loading her gun?" he asked as he pulled free a flat, folded bag and frowned at it.

"Sharpening a knife, actually," Zane said lowly as he got out of bed. Ty grumbled disconsolately as he unzipped the bag in his hand and extracted a perfectly pressed black dress shirt.

"What did she really have to say?" he questioned as he laid it carefully on the bed and then reached behind him to yank his T-shirt over his head.

Zane blinked at the shirt as he walked over to his own bag. He pressed his lips together, trying to decide how or if to answer. "She said you're dangerous," he finally said.

Ty pulled the shirt over his head and peered over at Zane with a raised eyebrow. "What?" he asked incredulously.

Zane looked over his shoulder to see Ty's reaction. "So? You're dangerous." It would be interesting to hear Ty's reply.

"I am not," Ty protested in an insulted voice.

"Bullshit," Zane said, pulling a clean dark red shirt out of his bag. "What's your problem with Serena?"

"She's a raging bitch," Ty answered as if that should be obvious.

"So?"

"Shut up," Ty huffed in annoyance as he picked up his shirt and slid into it fluidly. He shrugged his shoulders, flexing unconsciously against the soft, tight material to make certain he didn't pull at the seams, and then he glanced around for his boots.

Zane studied him closely. "She's good at her job. One of the best," he said, slowly and carefully pulling the shirt over his head, but his eyes returned immediately to Ty.

"Doesn't mean I have to like her," Ty grumbled as he flopped down on the end of the bed to pull his boots on.

"Apparently, she feels the same." Zane fell silent as they finished getting dressed. "She said I shouldn't trust you," he finally stated. "That you're trouble. That you only look out for yourself."

"She's right," Ty agreed in a clipped voice as he finished buttoning his shirt and carefully smoothed it down. "Where are we meeting her?"

Zane slid into his holster with a wince and a grimace. "Chinatown. We should be able to hoof it."

"Fucking great."

"Zane Garrett," the tall, svelte woman said as she stood from the small table in the Chinese restaurant. "Almost a year is too long."

He easily accepted her embrace, barely keeping himself from flinching. "Gorgeous as always, Serena," he greeted before kissing her cheek lightly. She was too, with the face of an angel and blonde hair to match. Too bad it didn't fit her innate personality. Because Ty was right; she really was a raging bitch if you didn't live up to her standards.

Serena smiled brilliantly. "Flatterer." She turned to sit back down. "Grady," she greeted curtly in the barest acknowledgment of Ty's presence.

"Miss Scott," Ty responded as he pulled out the chair opposite her and slid into it. His tone was surprisingly more civil than it usually was.

Zane's eyes flickered between them as he sat down, wondering about the past between them Ty had mentioned. "I wish we could have met under better circumstances, Serena," he said to the woman.

"Yes, well, if you'd come to New York more often, it wouldn't be such a problem," she said, propping her elegant chin on one palm. "It's been too long without a visit."

Zane's lips quirked into a smile. "What can you tell me about the murders?"

Serena sighed. "Straight to business, huh? I miss the old you, Zane," she said, glancing at Ty. "Did you read up on the serial?"

Ty rolled his eyes and glanced around for a server. He raised his hand and got the attention of a woman passing by as the other two talked. She came over, smiling at him, and he gestured for her to come closer. When she bent over next to him he turned his head and whispered into her ear, "I'm going to need something highly alcoholic that looks like water."

She remained motionless for a moment, then she straightened back up and smiled at him again. "Wednesday Night Special, yes, sir," she said to him softly before turning away. Ty watched her walk away, smiling in appreciation of her discretion and then returned his attention to the table.

"We've formed some opinions of our own," Zane was telling Serena, though he watched Ty's exchange with the waitress distractedly. "We'd like to hear yours, though."

"You show me yours," Serena invited with a flirtatious smirk.

"You first, dear," Zane responded in the same tone.

Serena smiled warmly at Zane before giving Ty another unsavory glance.

"Look, we'll get business out of the way, then I'll leave you two to it. Deal?" Ty offered as he met her eyes.

"Why Special Agent Grady, I didn't realize you had the ability to be reasonable and gracious," Serena observed sarcastically.

"I don't," Ty grunted. "Call it self-preservation," he offered.

"Fair enough," Serena said in her liquid-honey voice as she favored Zane with another look. "What is it exactly that you want to know?"

"Well, first of all, why is the NYPD being such a pain in the ass?" Zane asked.

"Turf wars, of course," Serena said, rolling her eyes. "You know all about that . . . don't you, Ty?"

Ty looked up from the empty water glass he had been examining and stared at her, not responding otherwise.

Zane looked between them and wondered if this had been such a good idea after all. "Serena, behave," he said lowly. She turned light, calculating eyes on him for a long moment, and Zane knew what she was doing. A day ago he would have almost looked forward to Serena and Ty going at it like he knew they were about to do.

She waited another long moment and then smiled. "Since you asked nicely," she said finally.

"Give us a basic profile on the serial, please," Zane requested, noting that Ty was still holding his tongue.

Ty glanced at Zane and narrowed his eyes. He didn't know why they were here, and he didn't think they needed to be dealing with this woman. She couldn't tell them anything they didn't already know, and she was a pain in the ass to be around. Ty and Serena could go back and forth at each other all night, twisting knives in old wounds and making new ones until they were both curled up in their respective corners and crying. They'd done it before. The part she enjoyed most was watching Ty losing his temper and shouting at her. And the only way he could avoid doing that was to keep biting his tongue or drink. Or both. He preferred both.

"I believe he's sane and sending a message of some kind. He's an organized killer, probably plans the murders far in advance. Likely follows the victim for days, maybe weeks before he takes them," Serena shared. "Odds are he's got his next victim, or possibly next two, already picked out."

"Do you think he's watching the investigations?" Ty asked in a low voice, curious to see if she agreed with them in that respect as well.

"Closely," she answered with a smug look at Ty, as if gloating about the fact that he had asked her opinion.

"And not just in the media," Ty murmured, letting her know what they had been thinking.

"Agreed," she responded easily, still looking at Ty and seeming to measure him.

Zane got the very distinct feeling that Serena knew a lot about Ty and his past that Zane didn't, and he wondered if he could learn anything about his new partner from what was obviously a biased source. He might have to get Serena alone later just to pump her for information. He couldn't force himself to stoop to reading Ty's file yet. It just didn't seem right.

"It's possible he has a peripheral role in the investigation that allows him access," she went on as Ty nodded silently. "You think it's someone internal," she said to him with a small smile. "Is that why they brought you two in?" she asked as she turned her calculating gaze back to Zane. "To run around in the dark and cause internal trouble? Tyler here is very good at that sort of thing."

Zane cleared his throat and sat back as the waitress returned with Ty's drink and took their orders. Once that was taken care of, he blatantly ignored her last comment and continued on. "It is possible that it's someone in the Bureau or NYPD," he acquiesced. "I've flagged a list of items missing from the reports. Different pieces, all small and somewhat inconsequential. It may all be chance... but I doubt it. So I went looking."

Serena glanced between the two men, eyes lingering on Ty suspiciously. "What did you find out?" she asked Zane.

"Nothing," Zane answered with a shrug. "I'll need to talk to the handling agents in each case, and frankly, the details are so minor they don't rank being worried over, other than the fact they're missing."

The woman nodded. "If you need assistance with the ME, let me know. Karen and I go way back."

Zane's face transformed as he smiled openly, eyes bright. "I love it when you're so helpful."

"You know you'll pay for it later," Serena cooed as she glanced at Ty again, almost as if the continuing flirtation were a challenge to him. "So. Ty," she said suddenly. "I won't say it's nice to see you. But at least you've got a good man to work with on this case."

"Yeah, he's a real Boy Scout," Ty answered flatly as he met her eyes unerringly.

Though she smiled at him, her eyes were utterly frigid. "Don't fuck him over like you did your last partner."

"Serena," Zane said sharply.

She didn't turn her chin to look at him. "What's wrong, Zane? Surely you don't think I'll hurt his feelings. He doesn't have any."

"I see you're still spending more time on your colleagues than your cases," Ty responded calmly. "How's that workin' out?"

"I've still got the highest successful profiling record in the region, so it's working out pretty well, thanks," the woman answered.

"Easy to be a success when you hand off the hard ones," Ty drawled. "Can't figure it out, so you hand it off on an overworked Feeb, let him take the fall if he fails."

She narrowed her eyes, but continued to smile. "Sometimes the white flag is all you can do for a case. You didn't fail, though, did you, Tyler? Made quite the case out of it."

"After four more people died, sure," Ty answered without flinching.

"That's enough, Serena," Zane broke in, voice low and serious. "I called you for information, not so you could pick a fight with my partner."

"But picking fights with your partner is so entertaining, Zane," Serena drawled. "Surely you've found that out by now?"

"I wouldn't know," Zane responded coldly.

Serena sniffed and turned a disappointed moue on Zane. "You're no fun anymore, you know? I liked you a lot better when you still drank." She reached over and picked up Ty's glass, taking a dainty sip and nodding in approval.

Ty narrowed his eyes slightly, experiencing an odd feeling of possessiveness as the woman spoke. It seemed that he could bitch at Zane about his problems all he wanted, but no one else could without ruffling his feathers. "See?" he asked Zane conversationally. "Raging bitch."

"A raging bitch who used to care more about solving murders than picking fights," Zane said pointedly, and Serena shifted her eyes to him.

The woman went totally still, and her cold gaze would have struck many men dead on the spot. "Don't cross me, Zane," she warned suddenly.

"How's your husband?" Zane asked pleasantly. "Still no pre-nup?"

"Fucker," she hissed in response. "Don't call for my help again; you can figure this shit out all by yourselves," she snapped as she stood abruptly and looked between the two men. "You know, Zane, I would never have thought to say this, but you've turned into a real bastard."

"Ha!" Ty responded in gleeful surprise. He looked from the offended woman to Zane in amusement and then threw his head back and laughed.

"You're not officially on the case, but I know you have notes," Zane responded seriously. "Send them to us," he said in a tone that brooked no argument. "You owe me."

She was so angry that high spots of red peaked on her cheeks and the hand on her purse was curled tightly like a claw. "This makes us even, Garrett," she spit out. "And don't think I won't remember this."

"Great to see you again, Serena. Let's not make it so long next time," Zane drew out as sincerely as possible.

She gave him another dark stare and turned her back on them, flouncing out the door. Once the glass shut behind her, Zane leaned back and scowled. Ty was still laughing heartily, possibly the first time he had truly done so since their partnership had begun, and he was beginning to have trouble catching his breath. Patrons were turning to look at them, some smiling and giggling as Ty laughed contagiously.

Zane shook his head as he watched Ty. "I'm glad you're amused," he muttered. "She could have helped us."

"I've never seen her huff off like that!" Ty laughed breathlessly. "Oh, my God, I think I can die happy now."

"She's a spitfire, that's for sure." As long as she didn't turn on them, Zane figured they'd be okay. He wouldn't put it past her to cause them trouble just to spite him, though. "That's one good contact I ruined for you, partner," he said.

Ty's laughter trailed off, and he shook his head, still smiling slightly. "I suppose I owe you a thank-you for putting up the Big Blue Shield," he said to Zane sarcastically. "Thanks," he offered sincerely.

Zane nodded slowly and sighed, finally relaxing again. "I didn't want to pay her off anyway," he murmured. His back hurt enough without more scratches.

"Eh. We don't need her," Ty responded dismissively as he took another sip of his drink.

"And why is that, All-Knowing One?" Zane asked as the waitress came by with drinks for Zane and the now-departed Serena. After a quick explanation, the waitress headed off to cancel the meals and get the check.

"She didn't tell us anything we didn't already know," Ty pointed out logically. "Besides. We already got a profiler," he added with a small smile as soon as the waitress had left.

"Who?"

Ty raised one eyebrow mockingly and then raised one finger with a little smirk.

Zane narrowed his eyes. "You," he said flatly. "You're trained to profile."

"I am, indeed," Ty answered with another small sip. "How did you think I knew her?" he asked with a cock of his head as he gestured toward the door. "I was put here in New York my first year out. Any case she couldn't handle got shuffled over to me," he said with a sniff. "We certainly never fucked," he continued pointedly.

Zane's eyes sparkled. "You missed a hell of a ride, then."

Ty groaned with feeling and actually shivered in distaste. "I'd rather fuck you than her," he muttered thoughtlessly as he looked over at the door she had stomped through.

Snorting, Zane lifted his glass for a drink. But his eyes stayed on Ty, and his gut cramped uncomfortably as he watched him.

Zane's stomach woke him a couple hours after they crashed in the hotel room. It was dark outside, and he was contemplating getting up and yanking Ty out of bed to go and find food since they had skipped dinner. When he heard Ty shift and mumble, Zane sat up with a wince and turned on the lamp between the two beds. He tilted his chin to look at the other man.

Ty rolled onto his back, body tangling in the sheets around him, and he stretched and growled and grumbled noisily. He looked different asleep: softer, somehow, which Zane supposed made sense. Younger too. He wouldn't have thought it before, but it was pretty clear now that Ty was younger than he was, and not by just a little.

Ty made a few more sleepy growling noises and stretched until his muscles shook with the tension. Then he flopped back down into the bed and rolled onto his side, snuggling his head against the pillow and finally cracking one eye open. "Hmm?" he hummed questioningly when he found Zane looking at him.

"Evening," Zane greeted quietly, voice still dark with sleep. He yawned and ran his hand through his hair. The short curls were riotous. "I'm hungry."

"Ugh," Ty groaned sleepily. "God, you're worse than a date," he muttered. "I have to feed you too?"

"Hell, we sleep together, and you won't spring for dinner? What kind of guy are you?" Zane climbed gingerly out of the bed and flopped his pillow over Ty's face as he walked by to the bathroom.

"The kind who slept through the getting laid part!" Ty called after him as he grabbed the pillow and immediately confiscated it, tucking it under the covers and wrapping around it like a child with a teddy bear.

Zane leaned out the door after turning on the light. "Bad planning on your part," he chastised before ducking back inside and pushing the door shut.

Ty gave a loud, slightly squeaky huff and snuggled back down into the bed. The mattress was hard as a rock, but he'd had worse. "You want room service?" he called.

Stretching carefully, Zane looked over his shoulder at his back in the mirror. "Yeah, that's fine," he answered, raising his voice. "I'll eat pretty much anything."

"I'm sure you will," Ty muttered grumpily from his warm cocoon of pillows.

Zane turned on the shower, ready to risk washing down his back. The hot water would feel good, at least. He pushed his briefs to the floor and climbed in, standing facing the showerhead (which was actually tall enough for him for once) before turning slightly to see how it would feel on his damaged skin.

Ty climbed out of bed when he heard the water turn on and hopped to the bathroom door, sticking his head inside the bathroom with wide, disbelieving eyes. "You're gonna wet it?" he asked incredulously without even giving a thought to Zane's privacy.

Jerking his shoulder out of the water and stepping back as the door pushed open, Zane swallowed against the surprise and tried to calm his pulse. "What the hell are you talking about? I'm in the damn shower; it's wet by default."

"It's gonna hurt," Ty protested almost childishly.

Zane leaned back and pulled the curtain aside just enough to look at Ty. "Well, yeah?" he said, face displaying patent disbelief at Ty's objections. "Won't hurt worse than the getting hurt in the first place," he said as he pointed at Ty, catching the curtain just in time as it fell away and yanking it shut, blocking the flow of cool air. He felt like a fucking idiot, standing naked in the shower while he held the curtain between the two of them.

Taking an even breath, he turned in place immediately, standing far enough away that the hot water just sprayed on his ass and thighs. Then he took small steps backward, and as the hot water started raining on his lower back he let out a low, unconscious moan of pleasure.

"It's gonna hurt," Ty crooned as he leaned against the door, waiting almost gleefully for the howl.

Ignoring him, Zane stepped backward again, inhaling sharply as the hot water splattered across the cuts and slices and gouges. It did hurt, but it was all a heated flush that tingled and buzzed rather than actually causing blinding pain. He sighed and relaxed and moved further back so the water sluiced over his shoulders, and he groaned at how good it felt, the mélange of little prickles and bites of hurt mixing with the hot raps that jarred and soothed his tensed muscles.

"Like pain, huh?" Ty laughed as he listened. "I'll leave you to it, then." He snickered as he turned to go.

"Pansy ass," Zane murmured with a smile, just loud enough to be heard.

"Masochist," Ty shot back.

Zane chuckled. "Lightweight."

Ty stepped outside the bathroom again without bothering to respond. The groan from Zane had sent an odd jolt through his body, and he wasn't sure he liked it. He needed . . . to shoot something, maybe.

He stalked out into the room to pick up the phone.

Zane took his time showering, staying in the hot water until the steam in the room was making it difficult to breathe. With a sigh, he bent over and turned off the water, pleased by how much easier he could move now. He stepped out of the tub, grabbing a towel to wipe his face, and he flicked on the fan.

If he could get Ty to put more of that salve on the wounds, he might just be ready for action again.

In the outer room, Ty was on hold, desperately trying not to think as he waited. He didn't need to be thinking about Zane Garrett in any form other than as an annoying partner. He glanced up at Zane when the man came out of the bathroom and snorted heavily through his nose in annoyance. "What do you want to eat?" he asked him, letting his eyes take in Zane's toned muscles and then turning off that instinctive reaction willfully.

"You haven't ordered yet?" Zane asked as he came out from under the towel he had been using to dry his hair. Another was wrapped around his lean hips.

Ty growled at him.

Zane ignored him. "I don't care. Burger, steak, chicken, pizza. Whatever." He shrugged and walked over to his duffel bag and started digging through it. Ty seemed to be back to his normal twitchy self, he thought, as he dug out clean briefs and a pair of jeans.

"Make a damn decision," Ty huffed just before someone finally answered his call.

"Bacon cheeseburger, dressed, and fries. And a couple cans of Coke." Zane walked back toward the bathroom with his clothes and kit.

Ty repeated the order into the phone and then added his own order to it. The man on the other end took the order and politely ended the call, and Ty replaced the receiver slowly as he listened to Zane's movements. After a moment he let out a long, slow breath and flopped back into his bed. "How's it feeling?" he asked as he squeezed his eyes shut.

"Better," Zane called out before making quick use of his toothbrush and then looking unsuccessfully for his comb. He slid into his clean briefs and pulled on the jeans, but he was still distractedly fastening them up as he padded back out into the main room and over to his duffel bag. "Will you put more of that shit on my back?" he asked as he searched.

"You're going to smell like a racehorse," Ty observed from inside his cocoon.

Zane looked up from digging in his duffel, brow furrowed in confusion.

Ty laughed softly and buried his head under the pillow again, burrowing tiredly. Zane smiled at him as he looked him over, letting his eyes slide up and down the lean body just once before shaking his head and pushing the thoughts away. "Have you seen my damn comb?" he muttered.

"Yes, I've been keeping close tabs on all your personal items, Special Agent Garrett," Ty answered officiously, his voice comically muffled by the pillow.

"Thank you, Special Agent Grady, I appreciate that," Zane answered before pushing away the duffel and running his fingers through his hair instead. He glanced back at Ty and tilted his head. "How can you breathe like that?"

"Like what?" Ty asked from under the pillow. "Breathing and thinking at the same time, while difficult to master, comes pretty natural after you've practiced for a while. I'm sure you'll get the hang of it soon enough."

Zane rolled his eyes. "At least I think with my head and not my ass," he muttered as he buttoned his jeans and zipped up.

"Your ass is more fun to look at," Ty shot back from under the pillow.

Stopping in place, Zane boggled at the pillow. "You did not just say you've looked at my ass." Dear God. The tease of that was fucking inflammatory. He didn't need this kind of torture.

"You show it often enough," Ty countered in a sly tone, still muffled.

"You don't mean that literally," Zane muttered as he started stacking folders on the table, trying to make room for food.

Ty finally pulled his head out from under the pillow and rose up onto his elbows to look over his shoulder at Zane. "I mean everything I say literally. Literally," he said with wry emphasis.

Zane sighed and rubbed his eyes with one hand. "I think you do it deliberately," he grumbled. "Say whatever you can think of to drive me up the fucking wall." And Lord, his imagination was now in overdrive. Zane moved his hand, turned, and looked at Ty with narrowed eyes. "And how am I showing off my ass, pray tell?"

"You're breathing," Ty said as he laid his head back down.

Zane sighed, whether in relief or exasperation, he didn't want to have to figure out. Ty was just razzing him. A cigarette was starting to sound appealing, and the knock at the door was a godsend.

Ty peered out from under his pillow and watched Zane go to answer the door. "Now you're wondering if I'm looking at your ass, aren't you?" he teased.

Zane flipped him the bird as he passed by, gun in the other hand.

"Mm-hmm," Ty murmured with a self-satisfied grin.

After a minimum of fuss, Zane carried the room service tray back into the room, his gun shoved into the back of his jeans. And damn it, if Ty wasn't right, the smug bastard. As soon as he walked past him, he wondered if he was feeling Ty's eyes on his back or his ass.

"It's not you, it's the food," Ty offered as if he was reading Zane's mind.

"You keep telling yourself that," Zane drawled, uncovering the plates.

"You know it," Ty drawled as he stretched again. "Give me food, bitch," he ordered with relish.

Zane snorted. "I ought to make you get off your lazy ass and get it yourself. But you were kind enough to help me out, so . . ." He carried

Ty's plate and drink over and set them on the nightstand between the beds.

"Thank you," Ty said primly as he sat up and placed a pillow in his lap to serve as a tray.

Zane sketched a bow. "I hope it's to your satisfaction, Your Majesty," he drawled before going back to his own food and sitting at the table.

"I'm glad to see you're so easy to train," Ty responded happily. Raising a brow, Zane chucked a fry at him, hitting him in the chest. "Hey! A little respect for the cleaning ladies, huh?" Ty chided.

Zane grinned and threw another one, this time landing it on Ty's plate. He held up both arms in a touchdown sign. "You know, I'm starting to get this whole bug-the-hell-out-of- somebody thing."

"You're a natural," Ty responded flatly as he stared at the vagrant fry in distaste.

Zane sighed and shook his head, going back to his food. It seemed Ty would only tolerate so much of his own medicine. A moment later a fry hit him in the nose and bounced off into his lap. Zane's jaw dropped, but he grinned before plucking the fry up from his thigh and popping it in his mouth.

"Mm-hmm," Ty hummed again with a smirk from his side of the room.

Considering the other man as he took a bite of his burger, Zane wondered if this Ty was more like his normal self. He seemed younger right now, not as jaded. "What's your story?" he asked impulsively.

"Which one?" Ty asked between bites, with a cock of his head.

"The one about why you have a chip on your shoulder the size of Manhattan?" Zane asked mildly. "About why when you sleep you look about five years younger than me, and when you're awake and pissed off you look five older."

Ty cocked an eyebrow. "You were watching me while I slept?" he asked incredulously.

"You watched me," Zane pointed out. "And don't avoid the question."

"I wasn't," Ty protested in amusement. "That's just . . . really fucking weird, man," he observed with a snicker. "And I told you my story. I was Marine Force Recon. After the last mission we were supposed to run went tits up, they deemed all of us stricken with PTSD. We were all discharged with big-ass pensions before we could get upset. Full honors. It was all complete bullshit, and everyone knew it, but we were all tired and slightly traumatized from the bureaucracy of it all," he said bitterly. "They needed to plant us all somewhere nice and safe and keep us from Idle Hands Syndrome, know what I mean? Me, I got sent to Quantico as a 'civilian aid' sort of thing until Burns found me and convinced me the Bureau might be entertaining. I was a Marine, in it for the long haul, and I miss it. But that's life and here I am. No chip," he insisted with a shake of his head.

"So why be such a bullshit artist? Amusement factor? Mask to avoid questions? You're just a prick at heart?" Zane asked after another bite.

"All of the above," Ty answered readily through a mouthful of food, grinning and chewing as he watched Zane.

Nodding, Zane took a few more bites. "You know, when I was fucked up, I got real familiar with medical regulations and treatment regimens. Did you know they won't clear agents for field work if they're being treated for depression or mood disorders?"

"Yep," Ty answered succinctly.

"Post-traumatic stress disorder falls into that category. If it was in your file as a reason for discharge, you'd have been parked at a desk and never let out into public," Zane commented neutrally.

"Yep," Ty responded again as he looked up at Zane and smiled crookedly.

"So, you're lying to me," Zane said, just as neutrally as before. "Any particular reason you don't care to share? Other than the fact that I'm just your partner who might have to bail your ass out of something someday."

"My file is classified for a reason," Ty responded readily, as if he had known the cover story wouldn't pass muster with Zane. "Parts of that story are true, though," he assured Zane seriously. "And nothing in my past is going to come up and bite you or me on the ass," he added with a shake of his head. "I've got no mysteries. Only thing I've got back there is some broken hearts and a whole lot of red tape."

Zane studied him for a long moment. "All right," he murmured, going back to his fries.

Ty watched him, narrowing his eyes. Finally, he sighed loudly and looked around the room, then back at Zane in annoyance. "Special Agent Sanchez," he announced with a huff. "He was on my Recon team."

Raising his eyes to look at Ty again, Zane thought he was beginning to understand. Understand why Ty was so determined to stay on this case no matter what exploded. And why he was such an ass to keep people from getting too close. It was a similar defense mechanism to what he himself had, albeit for a different reason. Ty and his companions had lived a dangerous life. They expected to lose one another. Just not to serial killers. "That's hard," he said quietly.

"What's hard is figuring out how some punk serial killed him. He slept with an arsenal under his pillow and one eye open," Ty told him seriously. "And if anyone looked at the files close enough and saw that we were colleagues before the Bureau, they'd yank me off the case," he added.

"That's why you were surprised when Burns handed you this case—and why you're so keen to solve it. Beyond keen," Zane said as it all clicked.

"Burns knows me," Ty said as a form of answering. "And he knew Sanchez. He recruited us out of the dregs of desk work we were being forced to do at Quantico, personally pushed us both into the Academy. He knows I'm not supposed to be here. Meaning he wanted me here for a reason. I just can't figure out what the fuck it is, other than to be sneaky."

"Okay, then why stick you with me? I'd been up in Cybercrimes over two years, mostly off field work. I've not been out like this in nearly four years. Why would he try to weigh you down?"

Ty looked up at him thoughtfully and tilted his head inquisitively. "Are you going to weigh me down?"

"I know I won't. But Burns, he's the one that threw my ass out of action, sent me into detox on threat of jail. He's not liked me since. Why give me this chance?" Zane asked rhetorically.

"Why would he care enough to put you in detox and then reinstate you if he didn't like you?" Ty countered quietly.

Zane didn't have an answer for that. It was a question he'd asked himself over and over.

Ty just shrugged as he watched Zane think it over. "We got one thing in common, though, Garrett," he finally pointed out. "Neither one of us belongs here. And they don't expect us to play by no rules anyway."

"Do you ever play by the rules, Special Agent Grady?" Zane asked.

"Can't think of a for-instance," Ty answered with a flippant shrug.

Zane peered at him for a long moment. "How old are you, anyway?"

Ty raised his head and looked over at the other man. "Why?" he asked suspiciously.

"Just wondering. Thought you were about my age or older until I saw you sleeping," Zane answered.

Ty frowned at that. "I'm thirty-four," he answered grudgingly.

Zane nodded slowly and went back to eating his now lukewarm fries with no comment. He would never have guessed that Ty was that young.

"Why?" Ty prodded.

Shrugging slightly, Zane looked up at him. "Sometimes you look older than that. You sure as hell act older than that. Jaded."

Ty blinked at him, slightly nonplussed, and looked back down at his food with a purse of his lips. Zane watched him, observed him, seeing a glimpse of the more ordered and disciplined man Ty hid under the brash asshole. He wore a mask, just like Zane did. It was somehow reassuring. It was beginning to become clear that Ty actually expended energy to be as abrasive as he was. The calmer former Marine that was beginning to show through seemed much more natural to him.

"How old are you?" Ty finally asked in return.

Zane smiled slowly, still watching. Ty hadn't looked up at him. "You mean you've not checked up on me yet?"

Ty slid his eyes sideways to look at Zane seriously, the rest of his body unmoving.

Zane shook his head, smile pulling at his lips. "I'm forty-two," he admitted.

"Yeah, you look it," Ty drawled with a grin that was slightly more teasing than his usual smirk.

Zane snorted. "I suppose I've been ridden hard and put away wet a few too many times."

Ty rolled his eyes and poked at his food. "Where you from?" he asked without looking up. "I mean, since we're bonding and all."

"Texas. Austin, to be specific."

"I'm sorry," Ty offered sympathetically, the smirk playing at his lips again.

"Where are you from, asshole?" Zane retorted.

"Bluefield, West Virginia," Ty answered, letting his words roll with his pronounced accent.

Zane grinned. "West by-God Virginia," he said. "Fits you."

Ty glanced up and smirked again, jabbing at his ketchup with a fry. "Wild and Wonderful," he quoted with a barely restrained snicker.

"Wild and Wonderful," Zane echoed with a short chuckle. "All that mountain climbing got you in shape for the Marine Corps."

"More like spelunking, but it's all about rocks in the end." Ty shrugged with a smile. "Son of a miner ain't got much in the way of career options," he added. "It was either the Marines or going into the family business."

Zane tilted his head. "Somehow, I don't see you as a coal miner."

Ty glanced back up at him and narrowed his eyes. The urge to take exception to the statement was clearly written on his face, but finally he gave his head a shake and bit the tip off his fry. "Just add dirt," he finally responded with a gesture to himself, even though the industry of coal mining had left Bluefield in the 1960s.

Zane saw the look on Ty's face before the other man shook it off. "Did you want to be a coal miner?" he asked.

"Nobody wants to be a coal miner," Ty answered evenly. He looked up at Zane and studied him, pondering the rest of the answer. "But then, nobody wants to get shot at, neither," he added thoughtfully. "I wouldn't have been a coal miner. They don't mine coal in Bluefield anymore. But my daddy minded the abandoned mines. He was a caretaker after they were shut down. Meant he was still in those damn mines all the time, making sure no one got down there and lost or trapped. Monitoring collapses. And I would have been doing it too. Or off in another town doing the real thing. I had to choose between a fear of bullets and a fear of small spaces," he admitted. "Turns out bullets ain't that scary, after all."

Nodding, Zane finished off his burger. He studied the other man as he chewed, putting together the details he'd crowbarred out. The little bit of his history made Ty much more human.

Ty returned his attention to his food, feeling eyes on him and just letting Zane stare for a while. "So what else was there, Serpico?" he finally asked after a tense moment of silence. "Need my blood type? SAT scores?"

Zane's brow wrinkled. "Did you go to college or just join the Marines?"

That question did rankle, but Ty visibly repressed his initial reaction. He exhaled loudly and pushed his plate away.

"You did say SAT scores," Zane reminded.

"I went to college," Ty gritted, acknowledging that he had indeed opened up that door. "Government paid for it."

Zane nodded slowly, feeling as well as seeing the tension back in the other man. "Nothing wrong with that," he said. "You earned it."

Ty cut his gaze up to look at Zane from under lowered brows. "You humoring me, Lone Star?"

Zane set his plate on the table with a clunk. "If you served our country in the armed forces, you deserve it." He was dead serious; it showed clearly in his eyes.

Ty glared at the man for a brief moment longer and then looked back down. "Thirteen ten," he finally answered with a nod.

Raising a brow, Zane sat back with a nod. "Well-done," he complimented.

"Bite me," Ty muttered as he poked at his chicken and frowned.

"National average is eleven fifty," Zane said, a small smile curling his lips. Tough guy obviously didn't take compliments well. It was almost endearing.

"I find it disturbing that you know that offhand," Ty informed his partner flatly.

Zane shrugged. "Numbers stick with me."

"I find that disturbing too," Ty deadpanned.

"Disturbing, huh? Maybe I'll take that as a compliment."

"Whatever helps your ego," Ty muttered with a shake of his head. "How'd you fall into this, anyway?" he asked, ready to change the subject.

Zane considered what to share, figuring Ty would rag him about anything he gave up. "I jumped."

"And then the rope broke?" Ty supplied.

"More like they cut it and let me fall," Zane muttered, turning back to the files and starting to shift them. "I was totally unprepared for the academy."

"Wait wait, let me guess," Ty said as he held out his hand toward Zane. "Psychology major with a . . ." He narrowed his eyes and cocked his head ". . . political science minor," he guessed.

"Statistics and Spanish. Before law school," Zane admitted, not looking over at the other man.

"Don't tell me you're a lawyer," Ty groaned in response. "I was starting to almost not hate you."

Zane snorted and glanced up. "No, I'm not a lawyer. I was saved from that gruesome fate by an academy recruiter."

"Send that man flowers," Ty ordered.

Zane actually laughed. "I agree . . . now. Then? I wanted to skin him. Slowly."

"Why? Were you the mascot being tortured in your academy class?" Ty asked.

Eyes narrowing, Zane's good humor faded. Bad memories did that. "I bet you were top of the class at climbing that damn rope," he muttered crankily. "For me, it was only four months of utter hell. Then I got to go through it again. How lucky is that?"

Ty frowned and cocked his head, looking Zane over critically. "You got recycled?" he asked incredulously.

Zane looked over at him and could tell right away why Ty was asking. "Out of grad school I was six five and one seventy. Not a scrap of muscle on me."

Ty's eyebrows climbed in surprise, but he shook his head and shrugged. "Must have been hell on wheels with the mental parts of it," he ventured.

The answer was a wry smile. "Fifteen eighty."

"What happened with the other twenty, spell your name wrong?" Ty asked with a teasing smile.

The smile warmed a little. "Thanks," Zane said deadpan.

"What's the Z stand for?" Ty asked abruptly. "Zane Z. Garrett," he mused with a slight wince. "Momma didn't like you much, huh?" he inquired in amusement.

"Family name," Zane said with a shrug. "Zachary. Nothing really scary. And in Texas, Zane is fairly common." He squinted at Ty. "I remember Burns said your name. Something Tyler Grady. An initial for your first name. I was too busy being horrified about being paired up with you to catch it."

"Probably better for it," Ty told him with a shrug, obviously having no intention of answering or meeting Zane's eyes while he had his mind on it.

Zane raised one eyebrow and considered pushing, but since they were finally actually talking, he didn't want to ruin it. So he opted for humor. "You were right about the name."

"Of course I was," Ty responded almost immediately. He looked up and narrowed his eyes. "Right about what?" he asked.

Zane sighed. "About my name. And the other twenty points?"

Ty stared at him blankly for several long moments. Finally, he closed his eyes and shook his head. "You spelled your name wrong on the SATs?" he asked in exasperation.

"No," Zane said, smiling slightly. "I left out my middle initial." His eyes sparkled and he was hard put not to smile.

"Jackass," Ty muttered under his breath.

The grin broke free and Zane chuckled before leaning back and looking up at the ceiling, drawing in an even breath and relaxing. "It was embarrassing," he tacked on, just for effect.

"Yeah, well. I'm sure you're used to that," Ty muttered. "What the hell," he added with a sigh. "We can't all be perfect," he offered as he looked back down at his uneaten food in distaste. His foot was bouncing slightly as he sat cross-legged on the bed. He was beginning to get edgy again. All the training in the world couldn't rectify a natural nervous twitch.

Zane sighed quietly and turned back to the files. "Long way from perfect," he murmured.

Ty rolled his eyes and banged his head back against the headboard.

"Don't jar loose the few you've got," Zane advised, eyes on the papers he'd pulled out.

"Well, get done with your little pity party, then," Ty huffed.

"Party, great, where's the drinks?" Zane sniped.

"And I was almost starting to like you," Ty sighed under his breath as he twisted and swung his legs over the side of the bed.

"God forbid."

Ty nodded and glanced back down at his food. He had lost his appetite along with the desire to spend any more time with his self-pitying partner. "I need a break from this fucking room," he muttered as he pushed to stand and stretch.

Zane glanced up from where he'd been staring blankly at the reports. Ty was patting down his jeans as he searched for his wallet. Finally, he located it and pulled it out, retrieving a little piece of paper and unfolding it with a frown.

Zane didn't say a word. He just made himself keep his eyes on the paperwork. He remembered when Ty had been handed that piece of paper, and he knew the implications. He fought hard not to be slightly jealous.

Ty reached for the phone and dialed, eyes straying to Zane and glinting in the low light. "Want me to see if she has a friend?" he asked with a smirk.

"I'll pass, thanks," Zane murmured, not even looking up.

Ty nodded, watching his partner as the pretty little stewardess answered her phone. Ty didn't take his eyes off Zane as he set up the illicit rendezvous that he knew would rid him of some of the frustration his new partner had been creating.

The hair on the back of Zane's neck rose. Ty was watching him. Waiting another minute, Zane turned his chin to look toward him, a brow rising lazily. Hmm. Ty shouldn't be the only one to vent his frustrations.

Maybe he'd go find someone to pass the time with too, now that he thought about it.

Ty smirked as he watched Zane look up at him, grinning at the slightly breathless voice of the woman as she said goodbye. He hung up and looked at Zane. "Going to be okay on your own for an hour or two?" he asked rakishly.

"Me and my right hand will be just peachy, thanks," Zane said down at the papers.

"Won't get no sympathy from me, Lone Star," Ty told him as he slid into his boots. "I served my time with you," he said with a shake of his head. "I'll call you if I spot a tail," he added as an afterthought.

"Have a good time," Zane offered sincerely, finally looking up.

Ty just laughed as he walked out the door, waving his cell phone over his shoulder to let Zane know how to contact him as he went.

The other agent watched the door for a bit before shifting in the chair. He stood up and paced a little before making a decision. He walked over to the desk and uncovered the area directory the hotel provided in each room. Laying it open on the papers, he found a list of bars and nightclubs in the area. There was even a little map of the ten-block area. Zane decided he might as well take a break while he could. He walked over to his duffel and pulled out a change of clothes. After getting dressed, he stuck his wallet into his back pocket and strapped on his holster, though he winced a few times. Then he pulled on his boots and a heavy button-up shirt to cover the gun, and he was ready.

Before he walked out, he shoved a couple condoms in his hip pocket, and the door shut behind him.

He stood on the busy street corner outside the hotel Special Agents Grady and Garrett had moved their operations to. He had, of course, been keeping tabs on their location from the moment they'd stepped off the plane. When they'd declined the Bureau accommodations and moved to another hotel without telling anyone, he'd known he was in trouble. It meant they either suspected someone with inside resources or they were overly paranoid. Either scenario meant more work for him. It had taken a while to find their hotel, but they hadn't been paranoid enough to check in under false names and he had finally tracked them down.

The new FBI team was a nuisance, but so far they weren't proving to be as much of a threat as he had expected. When he'd gotten word that Washington was sending a crack team, it had very nearly scared him. So much so that he'd set up the computer in the FBI archives for them and removed vital bits of the files as bait before they even landed. These two, however, had turned out to be anything but a threat.

Still, it was better to be rid of them sooner rather than later.

The exploding rig he had set up in the computer of the archives had worked perfectly. Exactly to plan. The only problem with his plans to this point was the fact that Special Agents Grady and Garrett didn't seem to give a shit about each other or about working with each other. They were both supposed to have been in that room. Even if Garrett was maimed to the point they had to replace him, it still left Grady for him to deal with, and Grady was the real threat. He didn't follow any rules, and that made him hard to keep ahead of. He had specialized training too. Garrett just seemed to be a pushover trailing along behind him.

He took a deep drag of his cigarette as he waited. They had to come up for air soon, and when they did, he would take care of things.

CHAPTER FIVE

Ty slid the room key into the electronic lock and winced as the lights blinked red. He tried it again, looking up at the door number to make certain it was the right room as the lights blinked red again. He sighed and banged on the door with his fist. Waiting a few moments and hearing no movement inside, he banged again, harder. "Garrett!" he called out, trying to keep his voice down. It was late, after all, and they didn't want to attract any undue attention to themselves. He glanced up and down the hallway and grumbled to himself.

He looked at his card in annoyance, realizing that he'd put it in his wallet with his credit cards and probably demagnetized the damn thing. He muttered to himself as he tried it one last time to no avail. He turned on his heel, intending on going to his own room, but before he got even a step he remembered that his own room key was inside Zane's room with the rest of his stuff.

He growled to himself and glanced down the hall at his own room, frowning at the Do Not Disturb sign on it. What if someone had been in there earlier? What if someone knew where they were? With that thought, a sudden cold swelled in his chest. What if his erstwhile partner was hurt? What if Ty had gone to get laid and someone attacked Zane? He had very little confidence in his new partner's ability to protect himself when he was healthy, much less injured and relatively defenseless.

Ty hurried toward the elevators and jabbed the button for the lobby, but when it took too long he headed for the stairwell and began jogging down the eight flights of stairs. He muttered to himself impatiently, dread rising as he thought about the myriad of things that could have gone wrong. He tried to tell himself he was merely being paranoid and feeling guilty. No one knew where they were, right?

Except for Sears and Ross, who had been tailing them earlier, and probably every other agent in the New York office, including whoever they were after. He pushed through the stairwell doors and stalked across the lobby, trying to get a hold on his irrational panic.

Moments later, he stood at the lobby desk. He had some difficulty at the front desk in getting Zane's spare key reprogrammed, mainly because he wasn't exactly Zane. Finally, he had to flash his FBI identification and growl at the woman to get it done. By the time he got back to Zane's room, he was tense and almost shaking with dread.

"You better be fucking taking a bubble bath or something," he muttered as he swiped the card and the lights blinked green.

He was further dismayed to find the hotel room empty. He stood in the entryway, calming himself before walking around the room in search of some clue as to where Zane had gone. There were no signs of struggle or a hasty departure. Everything was ordered and in its place, insofar as order went amidst the chaos of their files.

Finally, he spotted the hotel directory, open and sitting on the dresser. He stepped over to it and placed his hand gently on the laminated pages, peering down at the small map and the list of nightclubs and bars.

With a groan, Ty realized that Zane had merely gone out to get his drink on.

"Fucker," he snarled to the empty room.

Zane walked along the busy street, looking idly in shop and restaurant windows, just letting his mind wander. Thinking about anything but the case was a relief. He stopped on a corner, waiting for the light to change, and lit up. He rolled his shoulders, winced just a little, and sighed. He felt pretty decent after relieving some of the tension that sparked between him and Ty. A hot grapple in the dark bathroom of a club would do that.

He glanced at his watch: 10:10. He figured Ty would take every bit of his mentioned two hours and then some, not that Zane really cared. He'd needed this break more than he'd thought.

Ty sat on one of the beds, reading a faxed list he had received earlier while he waited for the telltale slide of a key card in the door lock. When it came he lowered the fax and looked toward the door, eyes hard and angry as Zane came strolling in. The other agent glanced up and stopped short when he spotted Ty. He was obviously surprised that Ty had come back early.

"Hey," Zane said. "Have a good time?"

Ty didn't answer immediately, instead trying desperately to gain control of his temper. "Did you?" he finally asked curtly.

"Yeah, I did." Zane shrugged out of the thin shirt and looked over Ty again. "I'm guessing you didn't?"

"I'll give you three guesses what went through my head when I found you gone," Ty replied calmly, simmering just beneath the surface.

Zane's eyes narrowed. Some of the tension started rebuilding between his shoulder blades again. "You're not my keeper. I didn't ask where the hell you were going, did I?"

"You knew I wasn't off getting drunk off my fucking ass," Ty snarled as he held up the hotel directory accusingly and tossed it to the end of the bed.

It took some willpower to swallow on the flare of anger. "I told you," Zane said sharply. "I don't drink anymore."

"Sure, Garrett. And I don't fuck strangers 'cause I'm bored," Ty replied sarcastically.

Quite a bit more willpower was required as Zane stared at him. "I can take care of myself, Grady. I'm not fresh out of the academy, and I don't need my hand held," he bit off.

Ty practically trembled with anger, the kind of anger that could only stem from a bad scare and quite a bit of guilt. He glared at Zane and then looked away, taking a long, calming breath as he stared at the map of crime scenes on the wall. "Just . . . leave a damn note next time, okay?" he finally requested softly.

Zane studied him for a long moment. Ty was truly upset, though Zane had no clue why. It was also clear that Ty was exerting quite a lot of effort trying to remain calm. "Yeah, okay," Zane agreed, not wanting to rock the boat any further. He took off his gun, grabbed the television remote, and sat on the end of Ty's bed since there was paperwork all over his.

"If you're gonna sit there, go take a fucking shower first," Ty griped. "You smell like smoke."

Looking over his shoulder in annoyance, Zane wrinkled his nose. "You smell like perfume and spunk. What's a little smoke?"

"Smoke is unpleasant," Ty retorted. He gave a sniff and realized that, yeah, he probably did smell like sex. He found himself wondering if Zane had enjoyed the same sort of distraction that he had, then shook that thought off immediately.

Zane raised a questioning eyebrow at the look on Ty's face, earning a defensive "What?" from the man.

Zane's lips twitched. "Sorry to have ruined your relaxing fuck," he drawled out.

Ty gave a derogatory snort and stretched his arms over his head. "You should be," he declared haughtily.

Zane shook his head, but he was smiling. "At least I'm not stressed anymore," he said as he turned back to flip through the channels.

"Well, praise be," Ty muttered as he stood and headed for the shower. He was tired of smelling like a woman he'd never see again.

⚔

Isabelle St. Claire had just gotten out of the shower. Her next flight didn't leave for another four hours, a cross-country to Los Angeles that would no doubt be full of drunk businessmen who would enjoy grabbing her ass as she passed by them. At least she would have some good memories to get her through this particular flight.

She ran the towel through her long hair again, biting her lip against the guilty smile that tried to bubble up as she looked at the tussled sheets of the bed and her clothing strewn across the hotel room floor. It all belonged to her. He hadn't left a thing behind.

An FBI agent, he had said. His badge had looked awfully official, anyway, and Ty Grady hadn't struck her as the type to lie just to impress her. Get her into bed and never call again, yes. But lie? No.

Isabelle knew the man would never call her again. It was just as well, because he was the type that girls like her fell hard and fast for, and he was definitely not the type she could take home to meet Daddy.

She allowed herself another little smile and wrapped the towel around her damp hair. It had been fun, anyway. She didn't bother dealing with the mess they had made of the bed, instead beginning to bundle up her clothing into neat little rolls, the kind that you could stuff in a small suitcase easily and wouldn't leave fold or wrinkle marks.

Finished packing and already wearing her uniform skirt, she was shrugging into her white blouse when the knock at the door came. She looked over at it in surprise. Not many people would be knocking on her door. It was either Tina or Sylvia, her fellow air hostesses on the LA flight, wanting to get a bite to eat before they caught a cab, probably. Or it could be him again.

She bit her lip, unable to restrain a hopeful grin as she padded over to the door and peered out the little peephole.

An FBI badge was all she could see, held up so close that it was obscured other than the big blue letters on the card.

She laughed quietly and shook her head as she stepped back. She could really fall for this guy if he let her. She looked down and unbuttoned the one button she had managed on her blouse, biting her tongue in anticipation. When he had showed up before he'd merely grabbed her, dipped her backward like they had been waltzing, and kissed her. She wondered how he would greet her now that they actually knew each other's names.

"Back for another round so soon?" she called as she unlatched the door and swung it open to let him in.

She gave a little gasp of surprise when she realized that the agent in the hallway wasn't Ty.

"I—I'm sorry, I thought you were someone else," she stuttered as she blushed furiously and began buttoning her blouse hastily.

"I get that a lot, ma'am," the man said before he produced a small white handkerchief and grabbed her roughly, pressing it over her mouth and nose and pushing her back into her hotel room. She flailed and tried to scream, but his hand covered the noise she made and her attempts at hitting and kicking him seemed to go unnoticed.

He kicked the door shut behind him, and Isabelle struggled as her world faded to black.

Zane worked deep into the files, sifting through details, muttering about the missing reports he'd been looking for when the monitor exploded. He'd also found other smaller bits and pieces missing, likely the result of overworked agents and the number of departments information filtered through in the Bureau. But it didn't make him happy, not one bit.

Ty sat cross-legged on his own bed and stared at the map on the wall. He'd tacked crime-scene photos near each location where bodies were found, and beside them pictures of the accompanying tokens, trying to make sense of them. At first, he'd hummed slightly every now and then and murmured to himself, and he'd been perfectly still as he looked over the wall and took notes. But now, he rocked slightly back and forth and seemed to merely be staring mindlessly. If there was brain activity going on, his eyes didn't betray it.

Disgusted, Zane tossed down the files. "I need a cigarette," he muttered, standing up. "You game for a walk?" he asked as he reached for his holster.

Ty turned his head slowly, pulling at his ear with a frown. "Is my brain leaking out my ears yet?" he asked grumpily in return.

"Is that what that gray stuff is?" Zane asked, poking at the side of Ty's head. Ty growled and flopped onto his back to stare blankly up at the ceiling. Zane grinned down at him. The past several hours of work had successfully cooled their tempers, and they were almost getting along again. "C'mon. Stretch of the legs will do you good since we're short on other forms of entertainment. I think we exhausted those options earlier this evening."

"I'm never short on entertainment," Ty grumbled.

"But you're not particularly entertaining. So come on. Maybe we can find an ice cream place or something." Zane nudged Ty's arm with his knee from where he stood next to the bed.

"Ice cream?" Ty repeated flatly as he sat up. "Seriously?" he asked dubiously.

"Yeah," Zane drew out. "Why? What's wrong with ice cream?"

"Nothin'," Ty grumbled. "Hurts my teeth," he added with a slight blush as he sat back up, his head lowered.

Zane frowned. "You can stay here, you know," he said. "I just figured you might want a break too."

"I'm coming," Ty muttered. "I hate this feeling," he told his partner as he sat on the end of the bed and pushed his feet into his boots. "I hate knowing I'm missing something and not being able to place it."

That, Zane could identify with. He nodded and adjusted the straps of his holster once it was over his shoulders, grimacing as it rubbed over sore spots.

"Before we get you ice cream, let's go over to the hotel room," Ty suggested suddenly.

"What hotel room?" Zane asked with a frown.

"The last crime scene, where Sanchez and Reilly were staying," Ty answered as he picked up the fax he had been studying earlier. "This is the list of phone calls made from their room the last few days they were alive. I highlighted everything that's not delivery," he said wryly as he waved it in the air.

Zane took the fax and looked it over with a slight grimace. There weren't many calls at all, and there were only two lines highlighted.

"The first is Tim Henninger," Ty said with a nod at the paper. "He was their liaison, just like us. The second is somewhere at Federal Plaza, but we'll need to go there to figure out the specifics of the routing. My guess is they used their cells most of the time, so really the whole list is a big waste of paper," he went on bitterly.

"What about cell phone records?" Zane asked as he handed the fax back to Ty.

"Another day out, they tell me," Ty grumbled unhappily. "That's why I'd like to go to the room, poke around," he went on.

"'Cause you think something was missed," Zane inferred.

Ty shrugged uncomfortably and sighed, not looking up at Zane as he stared at the paper. "I'd just like to see it," he answered distantly, his voice suddenly softer and almost sad.

Zane watched him carefully, remembering that Ty and Special Agent Elias Sanchez must have been pretty close once upon a time.

He nodded silently and turned away to pull on his jacket, leaving the other man to his thoughts.

Ty looked up and flushed slightly, letting the fax flutter to the end of his bed as he reached for his holster.

"So, crime scene, then ice cream," Zane said in a voice that was slightly louder than necessary.

Ty merely nodded and went about arming himself slowly, and then they headed out without another word.

When they got to the hotel room in the Tribeca Grand that had been provided for the two dead agents, they found crime-scene tape still plastered over the door, sealing it. Ty flipped open his KA-BAR and sliced neatly through the tape, and both men pulled on gloves as they entered. It wasn't really an active scene any longer; it had been kept open simply at their request. Ty knew the manager would appreciate being able to take down the garish yellow tape that caused murmurs and furtive glances when anyone passed by.

The room was dark and almost uncomfortably warm, the curtains drawn tightly and the air vents all closed up. Dry blood still caked one of the beds, and there was another spot on the carpet near the table, where the second agent had fallen. Ty stood in the center of the room, looking around and getting a feel for the scene. He looked back at Zane, where his partner stood near the entry.

"You're the killer," he told the man with a point of his finger. "Okay? Stand right there where the tag is," he requested, pointing to where the ballistics forensics personnel had pinpointed the killer fired from.

Zane gave Ty a measuring look, but moved to stand just over the little yellow placard that marked the spot. Ty moved to stand near the dried blood on the floor, turning to face Zane.

He cocked his head at him. "Reilly's in bed," he said with a gesture to the bed. "And I'm standing here, talking with you about what the fuck ever. Who do you kill first to minimize chances of being maimed in the process?"

Zane gave the bed a cursory examination, noting the belt holster that still rested on the table beside it. He glanced back at Ty, then around the room briefly. "Sanchez was wearing his gun," he answered, not seeing the man's weapon in the room, which meant when they wheeled him out of the room, it had still been on him.

Ty nodded but remained silent.

"So I'd take you out first," Zane answered without hesitation. He held his finger up like it was a gun and mimicked shooting Ty with it. Then he turned and fired another fake shot at the bed.

"Four shots were heard," Ty murmured as he turned and looked down at the floor behind him. The blood on the floor wasn't just a pool, it was a smear. One shot hadn't killed Sanchez. He had moved, possibly drawing his weapon to return fire as he tried to find cover on the floor. But there were two more bullet holes in the carpet amidst the blood. "He never got off a round," Ty murmured to himself.

He closed his eyes, feeling slightly ill. He could see the action as if he had been there. He could see Sanchez, knowing he was going to die even as he pulled his gun and tried to save his partner.

He shook his head and jerked himself away from the visual before he could fall further into it, and he moved around the room restlessly, flipping through the things on the desk, going through drawers, even heading into the bathroom to look at the toiletries the agents had left behind.

Zane still stood waiting patiently when he returned and grunted unhappily.

"They went over this room with a fine-toothed comb, Grady," Zane said to him gently. "Tell me what you're looking for; maybe I can help."

"I don't know what I'm looking for," Ty answered in frustration. He looked around the room and sighed. "I was sure there'd be a token, or..."

"Maybe no token is a clue to the killer in itself," Zane suggested thoughtfully.

Ty glanced at him with narrowed eyes, obviously not following.

"I mean, the tokens have meaning to the murders, we know that. But we also know he killed these two men, and didn't find the deed worthy of leaving a token," Zane explained slowly, thinking it through even as he spoke. "They didn't fit into his pattern, and so they didn't get special treatment like the others."

"Makes sense," Ty agreed grudgingly. "But where does that get us?" he asked.

Zane shrugged and shook his head. "Nowhere, really."

Ty nodded in agreement, looking around the room in disappointment. Rarely did a crime scene not speak to him in some way. This room, though, was telling him nothing.

"Yeah," Ty muttered finally as he jerked his thumb at the door. "Let's go get your freaking ice cream," he grumbled.

Half an hour, two cigarettes, and some walking later, Zane had his ice cream as they sat in the restaurant. Running his spoon through the classic hot fudge sundae, he looked up at Ty. "Now, this is the way to convalesce," he said.

Ty gave him a disgusted sneer and a roll of his eyes. Zane sat back with a shrug, dropping the attempt at conversation. A soft chuckle caught his attention, and he looked discreetly to the side to see two men sitting in another booth with a sundae, sharing it.

Zane smiled slightly before turning back to his treat. While it was great to see that, it just made him feel lonelier, just like any happy couple did.

The smile faded and he stabbed at the ice cream. Two co-eds walked by, whispering as they looked at the two men. They shifted their attention to Ty and Zane as they passed by. "God, why are all the hot ones gay?" one asked her friend plaintively, and then they were out of earshot.

Wincing, Zane sighed, finished the sundae, and scooted away from the table without another word, walking to throw away the plastic bowl and spoon. Ty was sure to be pissed off about that, and Zane didn't want to be in the line of fire. Time for a strategic retreat. Besides, any thoughts combining Ty Grady and the prickling attraction he felt toward him were doomed from the start. It was bad enough being attracted to the asshole, and indulging the idea would just make it worse.

Ty's shoulders began to tense again as he sat alone at the little table, and he forced himself not to watch Zane move away. When he was younger, Ty had allowed himself to enjoy the company of both men and women, whichever struck his fancy at the time. But all his time in the don't-ask-don't-tell environment of the Marine Corps had forced him to suppress many of those feelings. It had left him confused and angry at the world in general for quite a while, but he'd managed to set that aside in order to concentrate on his job. Now, though, the job was easier and so was hiding something like that. After getting out of the service, he'd tried to convince himself that he was free again, but he'd spent too long pretending to be a person he wasn't in order to blend into his environment, and he couldn't shake the habit easily.

The fact that he found himself slightly attracted to Zane Garrett added to the frustration of the situation. It was confusing him again and making him seriously cranky. He hunched his shoulders a little more and crossed his arms over his chest, scowling at anything that moved as he waited for Zane to return.

"Let's go," Zane murmured when he got back to the table, still chewing on his own emotions.

"Thank Christ," Ty muttered grumpily as he stood. Zane didn't answer, just leading the way out the door and heading back to the hotel silently, long legs eating up the concrete.

After several episodes of having to actually jog to keep up, Ty finally huffed loudly and asked, "What the hell, man? You get your hot fudge and suddenly it's all hurry up and wait?"

"We've got work to do," Zane answered shortly. He knew he was overreacting, but he needed to get back to who he was supposed to be and forget about who he used to be—who he wanted to be. A man who wouldn't be afraid to do something about the flickering attraction. That man couldn't exist anymore. He needed to go back to being the straitlaced paper-pusher Ty first met and insulted. That was safe, and it would get the job done. Christ, was he ever fucked up. Zane wondered if he ought to go see that damn lady headshrinker again. Ty had thrown him for a goddamn loop.

Ty grumbled and jogged again to catch up. "You're never getting ice cream again," he muttered.

Zane didn't object. He needed something to get his mind back on track. Immediately. "One of us needs to go back to the office and find those files I was looking for," he said as they walked. "I never did call the investigators back about the explosion, and I should check on Henninger and tell him to keep his mouth shut." His voice was back to the monotone he used in the office.

Ty sighed as he listened. It had been brief and pleasant, but the tolerable partner stint appeared to be over. "You know what?" he hissed finally as he grabbed at Zane's arm to halt him. "I'm getting pretty fucking tired of the Jekyll-and-Hyde deal you have going." He narrowed his eyes and leaned closer to Zane, looking at him intently. "You're not still using, are you?"

Face tightening, Zane jerked his arm away. "You have any idea what deep shit I would get in if I was still using? Fuck, no. Although you may drive me to it!"

"Do you really care what kind of deep shit you get into?" Ty asked as he bristled instinctively.

"Most of the time, yeah, I do. So get off my back," Zane retorted, trying really hard to keep angry from sliding into livid. He turned into a narrow service alley and pulled out his pack of cigarettes in agitation.

"I'll stay on your fucking back until I'm convinced you're not going to get me killed," Ty growled as he stalked after him.

"I'm not the one who fucked over my last partner, now am I?" Zane snapped back as he crushed the unlit cigarette between his fingers and swung around to face Ty.

Ty's entire façade changed, as if someone had flipped a switch inside him. His body tensed and his eyes grew hard and dark. "That's got nothin' to do with you," he growled.

Zane advanced on him, having already lost too much of his cool to be careful. He got into Ty's face, both insulted and outraged that the man who was supposed to be his partner could really care less about being so. "Yes, it does, because unfortunately, I am your partner now because the last one apparently couldn't stand you. And you're not exactly inspiring any trust," Zane snarled.

Ty's impressive control over his volatile temper snapped, and he moved automatically, catching Zane on the chin with a quick left hook. Unprepared, Zane was only able to turn his face away from the impact to lessen the blow, and he stumbled back. He dropped his ruined cigarette as Ty came at him again, and finally reacting, he managed to spin with the next swing and awkwardly jab his elbow against Ty's side. He connected with the gun Ty had in the holster under his arm and both men grunted in pain.

Ty staggered to the side, but moved again so quickly that Zane wasn't ready before he was on him. He took hold of Zane's shoulder, pulled him closer, rammed his knee up into Zane's midsection, and shoved him toward the ground.

Zane whuffed and stumbled back, but he managed to keep his feet as his hard-won reflexes kicked in. He took a deep breath and rushed the few feet into the other man, plowing into him before Ty could dance out of his reach. Zane used his own weight to shove the former Marine and send him hard into the brick wall of the alley, and then he backed away, fists up and ready, gasping as adrenaline pumped through him.

Ty hit the wall hard with his shoulder, and pain shot through him like lightning as something crunched in the joint, but he neither registered it nor reacted to it. Instead, he reached out to the dumpster a couple feet away and grabbed the neck of an old beer bottle. He smashed it against the wall and turned to face Zane with something almost like enjoyment in his eyes. He never gave a thought to the guns under his arms, or to the number of ways he knew how to kill a man with merely his hand. His goal now was to maim and humiliate, not to kill.

Eyes narrowing on the new weapon, Zane focused his attention solely on Ty as they started to circle each other. He could feel the nerves cramping in his gut, and he struggled to keep his breathing even and his face blank.

He would not be drawn out. His hardest lesson when learning to fight had been to wait, although his first lesson had been to run. He realized in a sudden moment of clarity as they sized each other up that if he had any sense of self-preservation he would run now, because Ty was obviously way out of his league. But his pride just wouldn't let him do it. If he buckled under now, Ty would never have an ounce of respect for him. And Zane just couldn't live with that.

He felt his knives heavy at his wrists as he kept his fists curled. Those knives had been another lesson, one suited to his fighting style once the academy instructors had whipped some muscle onto his tall frame. Zane hoped to God he wouldn't have to draw one, because it was far too likely that Ty would take it away and use it against him.

With no warning, Ty lunged at him, feinting with the broken glass in his right hand and swiping at Zane with his left. Zane got his arm up to block the swipe of the bottle, using the metal bulk of the knife against his wrist to jar the other man's hold and send the bottle sailing and crashing into the dumpster. But the left hook caught him in the temple and he went reeling backward, seeing stars even as he grabbed hold of Ty's wrist and used the other man's body to hold himself upright.

Ty latched onto Zane's wrist in return and spun, pulling Zane's arm over his shoulder and jamming his body into the bigger man to send him head over heels to the ground. Zane went crashing down, but Ty lost his balance under the weight and the pain in his shoulder and collapsed to one knee beside him.

Despite the painful impact on the concrete and the spots dancing in his vision, Zane pulled his knees to his chest and used the momentum to spring into a modified kip, getting himself to his feet, albeit shakily. He immediately shifted and kicked out at Ty's side, the bottom of his boot aimed at the other man's ribs. He wasn't a classically trained fighter by any stretch of the imagination. Zane was a street fighter, a scrapper, accustomed to using his greater weight and reach to defend himself. Unfortunately, Ty was too close to him in size for those options to do Zane any good.

Ty rolled in the muck of the alley and the ever-present puddle of dirty water just in time to miss the brunt of the kick. Instead, Zane's toe landed at the tender spot under his rib cage as he moved, narrowly missing the gun in his holster again. Ty rolled up into a crouch and then spun out with a retaliatory kick to Zane's ankles.

Zane's feet slid out from under him before he even knew what had happened, and he found himself once more on his back. He managed to get himself up pretty quickly, just to have Ty aim another spinning kick at his ankles as soon as he was upright.

He tried to jump out of the way but hissed in anger as Ty's boot caught his calf and sent him staggering. "Goddamn it!" he shouted as he righted himself.

Ty was still on his knees, doubled over and laughing at him as he held his bruised ribs. This was just a game to him, apparently, and the thought made Zane see red. Too mad to back away, Zane lunged forward to haul Ty to his feet by the back of his jacket. Ty threw his arms behind him as if he were doing a backstroke and slid out of the jacket easily, leaving it in Zane's hands as he spun away, slightly off-balance and still laughing breathlessly.

Throwing the jacket aside, Zane pushed Ty against the bricks of the nearby wall, face first, grabbing for his arm to try to pull it behind him and restrain him. He realized that Ty wasn't laughing anymore just a moment too late.

He gripped Zane's wrist with practiced ease, squeezing the pressure point there that would send blinding pain shooting up Zane's arm.

"Goddamn it!" Zane howled again as he lost feeling in his arm. He retaliated by pulling Ty back with the other hand and slamming him against the wall again, this time with his forearm across the back of Ty's neck as his other arm hung limp and useless. "Stop it," he growled.

"Got no idea what you're doing, son," Ty murmured calmly, though his body was tense and coiled as he gave Zane one last chance to stop this before he really hurt him.

The hair on the back of Zane's neck stood up, and he shoved himself off the other man and began backing out of reach. He sure as hell didn't trust Ty not to turn around and take another swing. Not now.

Ty turned around slowly and glared at him, but he didn't strike out. He pointed to the ground and snarled, "Give me my damn jacket."

"You're the one who came out of it, asshole," Zane spat back harshly. He wasn't backing down; not now. This was one fight he'd see through to the finish. It would probably end up with him facedown in the alley, but at least he could still look himself in the mirror afterward.

Ty stepped away from the wall angrily and shoved him. Having expected some sort of physical answer, Zane immediately lashed out his right fist, hitting Ty square in the jaw. It hurt like hell and echoed up through his elbow, but he knew he'd made solid contact. Ty staggered back a step but came right back at him with blinding speed, lashing out with two hard cuts to Zane's midsection and then kicking at the inside of his knee as he reached up to find a hold on Zane's shoulder or neck. The speed and ferocity of the motions made it very clear that Ty had merely been toying with him before. Zane didn't have even the slightest chance of protecting himself now, much less retaliating.

Grunting heavily, Zane bent over as he took the two shots in the gut. When his knee went out, he felt Ty's hand close tightly on the back of his neck, and he knew what was coming. Ty was about to break his nose over his knee. Zane had seen it too many times not to know what it would look or feel like. With another grunt, Zane grabbed Ty's calf and yanked the man's foot forward, trying desperately to disrupt his balance.

Ty pulled down on the back of Zane's neck and raised his knee into the man's face, fully intending to smash his nose and hopefully leave him bleeding and unconscious in the alley. But Zane upended him just enough, and as Ty fell, his knee didn't hit Zane's face with enough force to do anything but hurt like a son of a bitch.

Ty landed on his back with a gasp and lay momentarily stunned as the air rushed out of his lungs and the back of his head cracked against the pavement. Zane shuffled back hurriedly and fell on his ass, sprawled and panting as he tried to get a solid breath. He shook his head, trying to clear it, and pushed himself up, trying unsuccessfully to stand. He dabbed at something wet on his face and the back of his hand came away from his upper lip bloody. Holding his still-tingling and nearly numb arm, he looked over at Ty warily, waiting for the man's next move as he tried to steady himself. Zane was sure he wouldn't be able to do anything to help himself if Ty came at him again. But he'd sure as hell try.

Ty was still on his back, motionless save for one slightly bent knee that was slowly flattening out as he remained where he had fallen in the shallow puddle of standing water. He was either stunned or plotting how next to attack.

"Ow," he finally groaned plaintively.

Zane grimaced and straightened, feeling his already abused back object loudly. He braced one hand on his knee and pushed himself to his feet. He tried to even out his breathing as he stepped back a couple more times to put most of the tiny alley between them, just in case. He opened and closed his fist, fingers itching for a knife that he didn't want to draw, the knuckles screaming from the impact of his punch to Ty's jaw. His entire face felt like it was on fire and his arm was just then beginning to regain some of the feeling, sending painful little prickles all up and down the limb.

Ty began moving slowly, rolling to his side and pushing himself up carefully. He brushed himself off as he stood, then looked up at Zane coldly as he reached under his arm, shifting the gun at his ribs and wincing at the bruise already forming under it. "You done?" he asked emotionlessly.

Zane rubbed his wrist and flexed his hand, wincing. His body was still taut with anger and tension. But what was really, truly pissing him off was that he had an incredible hard-on. He hadn't noticed until he'd pushed Ty against the bricks and held him there, using his entire body. What the hell was wrong with him, to be turned on by a vicious fight with a man who could easily kill him?

"Stay off my back about the drugs," he warned in a rasp, shaking off his other thoughts. "You'll kick my ass up and down this alley in the end, but I won't give up without a hell of a fight."

"It was a legitimate fucking question," Ty spat out.

"I'd already given you the fucking answer," Zane snapped. "I don't lie about it."

"I don't care if you lie, cheat, steal, and fuck everything that moves!" Ty shouted angrily. "You stay out of the bars while we're working this fucking case! And stay out of my past!" he shouted in a pained voice.

"What's your fucking problem, Grady? You're jackassing around in my past. You know damn well Burns wouldn't have put me back on the streets if I wasn't clean," Zane grated. "No wonder your partner was reassigned, if you were this fucking suspicious!"

"He wasn't reassigned," Ty ground out as he tried to calm himself. The pain of the memories was taking over the anger, now, and he was deflating fast.

Zane flinched back, stared at Ty for a long moment, then closed his eyes as the heat drained out of him, leaving him cold. Fuck all. He should have known Serena Scott wouldn't consider the death of a partner sacred ground. It was just like her to poke that kind of wound. Zane would never have intentionally sunk that low. He turned sideways restlessly and ran a hand over his close-cropped hair before leaning back against the wall.

Ty took a few steps and bent to gingerly pick up his leather jacket and brush it off. "You bury a friend," he said to Zane as he did so, his voice hoarse and strained, "and then tell his wife and baby girl you got him killed. See how well you work with others after that," he challenged softly before folding the jacket over his arm and turning to head for the opening of the alleyway.

"Ty." Zane's voice was low, no longer throbbing with anger.

Ty slowed and finally stopped, his head lowered and his shoulders tense as he waited.

Any arousal had drained away with Ty's clipped explanation, and now Zane just felt hollow and ill. He knew how much it hurt to lose someone and think it was your fault.

"I apologize," he said quietly. "I didn't know."

Ty turned his head slightly as if listening over his shoulder, then he returned his eyes forward, raising his chin and squaring his shoulders, not responding. Zane drew a slow breath and started walking, each step jarring something physically or emotionally painful, passing Ty after several steps.

Ty watched him, head down and eyes hard. Finally he closed his eyes, trying to regain his calm. "You still plan to go back to the office?" he asked flatly.

Zane glanced at his watch and winced. "It's too late tonight. It'll have to wait until morning," he answered, not turning back to look at him.

Ty began walking again, gesturing to the alley's entrance. "After you," he muttered.

"Better we get some more rest and start early tomorrow," Zane told him as he moved toward the corner of the building. He wasn't sure what else to say.

"Sure," Ty agreed moodily while they finished the length of the city block. "Maybe something'll hit us in the night," he said pointedly as they rounded the corner of the hotel's building.

"Not literally, I hope," Zane said under his breath, wiping away the blood from his nose and lip as they approached the front doors. They got several astonished glances from people inside the lobby. Both men were dirty and bleeding. Ty's back was wet and covered with tiny bits of gravel, and his guns were clearly visible as he held his jacket in his hand. Zane watched him flash his identification to a hotel employee who was hurriedly picking up a phone as they stalked through the lobby, and the woman slowly set down the receiver after seeing his badge. People whispered and watched as he passed, and Zane couldn't help but admire the way Ty could turn on that dreaded "Air of Authority" when he needed it. Zane, absolutely wrung out, kept his head down and followed quietly.

On the way upstairs, he wondered if Ty would go back to his own room. They weren't exactly getting along famously. In fact, they had basically just tried to kill each other, and Zane had no illusions as to who would have come out on top. He squeezed his eyes shut as they rode in the elevator, trying not to think at all.

But Ty didn't even seem to hesitate as he led Zane to his room. Odd. Maybe Ty just wanted him in the room to throttle him quietly. Or he wanted to get his things and then go back to his own room. Still, Zane's shoulders relaxed a little, and he let the death grip on his thoughts and actions ease just a bit as he opened up the room's door. Ty'd had the chance to shoot him. More than once. He hadn't, but Zane still didn't trust the crazy bastard.

"I think, tomorrow, we need to start with a fresh canvass," Ty was saying as he trudged to his bed and held his jacket up to examine it critically before tossing it down in disgust. He began unstrapping all his weaponry as he spoke, looking down at the bed and trying desperately to sink back into the case instead of the pain of old memories and new bruises. "So far, he's made only one mistake, and that was going after Sanchez and his partner. Why would he kill them if they had so little on him? Why would he tip his ace and let us know he was aware of the Bureau's movements?"

Zane watched Ty as he talked. Apparently he planned on staying. Shaking his head, Zane wondered what the hell the whole point of the damn fight had been, and how the hell Grady was already getting his brain in gear. The short fight had certainly shown him that Ty was more than a handful and more than capable of taking care of himself. It had also shown him that he himself could still scrap after some years of soft work.

Ty was anything but soft.

Sighing, Zane wiped one hand over his face, dropping a slightly bloody hand; he obviously had something other than work on his brain, and he consciously pushed it away. It was not the time to be unfocused.

He shook himself and let his jacket slide off his shoulders. His back screamed all the way down, and Zane hissed as the weight caught on his sore wrist. "If I were undercover, I'd kill them if they found out who I was. Depending," he murmured.

"Right. If they found out who you were," Ty responded as he stripped off his sodden shirt and tossed it at the corner. "But they obviously weren't close to finding that, or they would have let someone in on it. Sanchez wasn't the type to play without a net."

"Unless they hadn't made the connection yet," Zane answered quietly, dropping his sheaths on the table and sitting down to pull off his boots. Damn, this was awkward. And everything hurt, no matter how gingerly he moved. He glanced up at Ty, trying to gauge if the other man had walked away with any damage.

"So, what connection did they make but not make that caused him to move on them?" Ty asked wryly as he placed his hands on his hips and watched Zane idly. It bothered him that even now he couldn't quite find it in himself to despise the man or not be slightly attracted to him. It wasn't fair. Not even the recently earned aches and pains could make those things happen.

Bent over to unlace the Timberlands, Zane's brow furrowed. "A lead on who had the missing files?" he put out there, since that was something he wanted to pursue. "Maybe someone was somewhere they didn't need to be. Or shouldn't have been. Or couldn't have known about. And the agents thought it was odd. He got scared."

"Do we know how long the files were missing, though?" Ty countered doubtfully. "Maybe they were removed to lure us to the records room and the spontaneous exploding computer."

Sitting up and sprawling back with his legs spread out, Zane frowned as he chewed on that idea, shrugging off the discomfort of the situation and the throbbing pain of nearly his entire body. "That means some sort of detonation, then. Something to make it go on purpose. So he either had to be there, or he was watching."

"Who else was there? Did you see anyone else in the room?" Ty asked with a frown as he sat opposite Zane.

"Just Henninger," Zane answered, rolling his eyes and pinching the bridge of his nose. "It was lunch time. No clerks."

"And he was hurt almost as bad as you," Ty said dejectedly. Grimacing, Zane shrugged again and winced as he moved his shoulders. He looked up at the photos stuck all over the walls. "It strikes me as unusual just how clean it all is."

"How do you mean?" Ty asked distractedly as he turned and looked up at the pictures. His immersion in the case was working, the lingering tension and the aftereffects of the fight cast aside for the moment.

"No scrapings. No DNA. No fibers. No fingerprints. No trace of foreign substances. No pattern of injuries. No rhyme or reason. No way to track him. Not at any of the scenes at all. Everything has come back totally clean of anything useful. He knows what we look for," Zane murmured as he became very aware of Ty's proximity.

"Yeah. But that's not hard in this day and age," Ty grumbled as he reached up to rub at his side. He didn't know if it was the kick he had caught or the gun pressing into him when he hit the wall and the ground, but his fucking ribs hurt all the same. "He's an organized perp. They tend to be cleaner and smarter than disorganized ones. He may even stage the killing field before he takes the victim. Ten years ago the sterility might point to a cop or forensics expert," he sighed. "Now, it could just point to someone who watches too much CSI or bought a Forensics for Dummies book."

Zane sighed, dropping his jaw to work it a little. Ty had an incredible left jab. "God. Sometimes I hate modern technology."

"Yeah, well," Ty offered with a small, slightly vacant smile. He cleared his throat and looked down at his scraped, slowly bruising knuckles, pursing his lips as he flexed his fingers. He felt the sudden urge to apologize to Zane for sucker-punching him, but he just couldn't find it in himself to do it.

"There's got to be something." Zane carefully twisted in the chair and reached back behind him to the far edge of the table. It meant he had to stretch to put his hand on the bag of notes he wanted, and he hitched and flinched again along the way as his back complained. He frowned as he turned around and looked at his notes.

Ty found himself watching the movement thoughtfully. He sighed heavily when he suddenly realized what he was thinking—again—and he shook his head and looked away with a little snarl at himself. He would have thought the several instances of fighting and fucking recently would have soothed that particular urge.

He glanced back at Zane and cleared his throat. "I'm sorry I hit you," he offered grudgingly.

Zane looked up, surprised to hear it, and he nodded slowly, carefully considering what to say. "I'm thankful you didn't just snap my neck," he finally said, looking down at the bag in his hands.

"I wouldn't do that," Ty responded as he watched Zane, enjoying his discomfort with a small smirk. "Got a bum shoulder; it would hurt like a bitch."

Zane made a face and looked back up at him. "Gee, thanks. Feeling the love. Really." Ty just raised an eyebrow at the response, and Zane shook his head. "You could have killed me, Grady. Probably with one hand. I know that. Just leave me my delusions of lasting a handful of minutes in a real fight with you, would you?"

"If you say so, Hoss," Ty responded, leaning back in his chair and propping his booted feet up on the bed.

Zane glanced up at the former Marine, a little furrow between his eyes. Was Ty saying Zane had been a decent match? No way.

Ty looked him up and down slowly and cocked his head. "You got the size advantage."

Sighing, Zane leaned over, elbows on his knees. "Not that much. You're close to the same size. I'm just bulkier, is all. There have been times it's been more a hindrance than a help."

Ty snorted and shook his head. "Whatever, man," he muttered.

Zane narrowed his eyes. "What? You'd rather be a beast like me?" he asked, disbelief clear. While he knew there were disadvantages to his size and bulk, after years of training, he wouldn't give it up. He'd gone through hell in the academy to develop it, and despite the desk jobs of years past, he'd kept himself up with weights and a workout regimen.

"No." Ty laughed softly. "But I've been thrown across rooms by brutes like you," he said as he unconsciously rubbed his side again and his brow furrowed. "Hurts," he added, as if he needed to clarify that being tossed over someone's shoulder in a dive in New Orleans and splatting against a dartboard like a bug hurt.

"Yeah," Zane muttered, rubbing at his jaw while he carefully rotated his wrist, thinking about what Ty did to him in such a short time with very little effort. The concept that his partner hadn't even been trying to hurt him was both impressive and frightening.

Ty noticed the movement and pursed his lips. "Might want to put ice on that," he suggested with a gesture to Zane's wrist. "It'll hurt worse 'fore it gets better."

Zane looked down at his wrist where Ty had squeezed that pressure point. There was no mark, other than perhaps a reddening of the area where Zane rubbed. But it hurt like hell. He knew he'd left bruises on Ty, although the man showed no signs of it bothering him. "Yeah," he said, and he walked over to the low dresser where the ice bucket was buried, digging it out from under a few stacks of folders.

Ty smirked as he watched him. "If you lose feeling in it again, don't worry too much. I only know one guy who ever lost a limb from it."

Zane flipped him off before picking up the key card and heading to the door.

"Hey!" Ty called after him in slight alarm, moving his feet and letting the legs of his chair clunk down loudly.

Zane turned back, his hand on the door latch. "What?"

Ty frowned and pressed his lips into a thin line. "Watch yourself," he cautioned quietly.

Zane looked at him for a long moment, then nodded once and left the room, pulling the door firmly shut behind him. Ty cursed disgustedly and slumped back into his chair, covering his eyes with a hand as he kicked his feet back up onto the bed and muttered to himself. He would not let that priss get to him. He wouldn't.

Rubbing at his eyes as he walked down the hall to the ice machine, Zane thought about the roller coaster of the last hour. More days like this, and he wouldn't need the drink or the drugs to drive him over the edge. Laughing wryly, he stuck the bucket into the machine. When he tripped the switch, it made a loud, grinding noise that tried to drown out his thoughts, and he looked over his shoulder instinctively as if someone might try to sneak up on him from behind while he couldn't hear them. But the only other thing in the little alcove was the ice machine, and it couldn't drown out what stuck with him the most; what he wanted to forget was the feel of Ty's body under his, if even just for a few seconds. He squeezed his eyes shut and told himself again to forget it. That was one territory that would have to remain unexplored.

Left alone in the room that wasn't actually his, Ty stood up quickly and decided to take the opportunity to change. He didn't think it was a good idea to stay in this room tonight, for several reasons, but he would be damned if he suggested they split up. He was getting more and more nervous about the man they were after, and neither of them needed to be alone. He thought about his new partner and frowned as he moved. Zane had lasted longer in a semi-fair almost-fight than Ty would have given him credit for. He had upended Ty not once, but twice. And that was damned hard to do, even when Ty was hurt and laughing uncontrollably.

As Ty slid his damp jeans down, he realized that for the first time since meeting his partner, he was genuinely curious about him. He was also beginning to grudgingly respect the man's abilities—and the sheer nerve it took to stand up to a Marine in a dark alley. He cursed quietly to himself and tossed his jeans and briefs into the corner with the rest of his dirty clothing as the electronic lock clicked.

Zane walked in to see the absolute last thing that would help him forget what was on his mind: a lean, wiry, nude Ty Grady, muscles shifting under tanned and scarred skin as he shifted to grab his clean clothes off the bed. Zane blinked a couple times as the door shut behind him and changed direction to retreat into the bathroom, where he grabbed a hand towel for wrapping some ice. If he was breathing a little harder, who would know other than him?

Ty pulled up a fresh pair of briefs and reached for the thin white T-shirt he scrounged out of his bag. "You okay?" he called out evenly.

Zane swallowed. "Yeah," he answered, voice amazingly steady as he looked at himself in the mirror. "No problem. Besides these goddamn bruises you gave me. And my hand fucking hurts." He tried to make himself focus on the ice. He pulled out the plastic bag, dumped half back into the bucket, and tied up the bag before covering his whole hand with the towel.

"Whine about it some, it'll make it go away," Ty suggested.

"Bite me, asshole," Zane replied. But there was no heat in his voice. He had worked any anger out in that alley, for the moment. He took a deep breath and walked out, free hand holding the ice, and he stopped to lean one shoulder against the wall.

Ty sat on the end of the bed, pulling on a new pair of socks, looking up at Zane expectantly. "Did you bring me any?" he asked finally as he held out his bruised and bloodied left hand. When he moved, the words on his T-shirt were more visible. It was a plain white shirt with brown print on it. It read, You Have the Right to Remain Silent... SO SHUT UP.

Zane glanced at Ty's hand and shifted his own jaw back and forth. He held out the ice he had prepared. He could make himself another if Ty accepted it.

Ty snorted and smiled slightly. "Fuck it," he sighed as he waved Zane off.

"You want to be able to use that hand later?" Zane asked reasonably.

"You gonna make me hit you again?" Ty countered.

"But you seemed to enjoy it so much," Zane answered sweetly.

"True," Ty allowed as he reached out and snagged the bag of ice.

Zane let Ty take the cold pack and turned on his heel without comment, returning to the bathroom to make another one. He glanced in the mirror and saw another black smudge coming up on the side of his jaw, extending up nearly to his cheekbone. "Motherfucker," he muttered, prodding at it.

"What was that?" Ty called from the outer room.

"You got me good," Zane answered, thinking that not shaving another couple days wasn't a bad idea.

"Yeah," Ty sighed contentedly.

Zane rolled his eyes and walked back out, hand wrapped up again. He felt the need to defend himself. "I got in a few good hits, remember?"

"Yeah," Ty repeated with a frown as he pressed the ice in his hand to his ribs, icing both sore spots at the same time.

Holding his tongue, Zane decided to be content with that knowledge. He slowly turned his chin to look at Ty, and he really looked at him. Looked at his heart-shaped face disguised by scruff, full lips, forehead between dark brows scrunched in concentration, sharp nose, all crowned by sparkling hazel eyes that seemed to change colors as he watched. Zane's mouth compressed ever so slightly, and he blinked slowly, breaking the moment before he turned his eyes away and headed back to the files. He would have shivered if he'd let himself. As it was, his shoulders tensed as he tried to quash that damn itch.

"You really worried about the bruises?" Ty asked as he looked up at Zane. "We can stick a needle in 'em and they'll fade," he offered seriously. When Zane didn't respond, Ty cocked his head and watched him with a raised eyebrow and a small frown. "You okay?" he asked neutrally.

Zane's nostrils flared as he mulled over his thoughts, and he pushed away from the table again abruptly, suddenly antsy and needing some room. He stalked over to the window, moving the drapes to look out on the city, keeping the ice on his wrist.

Ty watched him, still trying to figure out the sudden mood changes his new partner suffered. Maybe Zane didn't drink anymore, but he'd definitely killed off some brain cells along the way. "Want me to leave?" Ty asked in the same neutral tone.

Forgetting about the dark window that would mirror his reflection, Zane closed his eyes as he grimaced like he was in pain. He cradled his wrist against the ice. If Ty left, he might be able to relax more. He just couldn't get the image of that lean, muscled body out of his head. He might be able to get some sleep, to think without the frustration gnawing at him ... after he got off, probably. Damn it. His escapade earlier hadn't done anything but take the edge off. He shook his head in answer to Ty's question, regardless.

"Good," Ty responded seriously. "'Cause all my shit's here now and I'm too damn lazy to move it. Why don't you get some more sleep?" he suggested softly. If he wasn't mistaken, he was witnessing the beginnings of a burnout. He'd seen plenty of them. Even had a few himself.

Zane took a deep breath and forced himself to relax. "Yeah. Yeah, that sounds good," he said softly. He turned away from the window, closing the curtain before he crossed the room for the bathroom, intending to get rid of the ice. His hand was numb enough. He shut the door and sat down on the toilet, threw the towel and bag in the sink, and covered his face with both hands.

Fuck, Garrett, get hold of yourself, he thought morosely. His hard-as-nails partner was going to think he was falling apart. He craved the calm a cigarette would give him and briefly considered going out to get one and smoking it right there in the damn room.

Ty remained where he was, trying to decide on a course of action. Finally, he got up slowly, pulled a clean pair of jeans on, then walked silently on bare feet to the bathroom door and knocked softly. "Hey, Garrett?" he called gently just before his voice turned sarcastic and teasing. "Do you need a hug?"

Stifling a laugh, Zane looked up at the door, raising an eyebrow. Leave it to Ty to snap him out of a funk with five simple words. "Fuck you, Grady," he answered, amusement clear in his voice. He pushed himself up and turned on the water at the sink to fill up a glass.

"I won't tell anyone," Ty continued in a mockingly sincere voice, plastered against the door like a parody of an overeager psychologist, trying to talk someone off a ledge. "You can cry if you need to!"

Zane swallowed the water and rolled his eyes. "You're an ass, you know that?" But he had to admit: it was breaking the shitty mood and distracting him from the curl of arousal in his gut. Sort of.

"It won't make you any less of a man!" Ty insisted as he called through the door. "Much . . . Well, it will, but . . ."

Snorting, Zane set down the glass. "Well, I guess I should feel honored you consider me a man to start with," he said wryly as he looked at himself in the mirror.

"You're definitely more like one now than you were in Burns's office," Ty offered, his voice serious once more as he leaned against the door. "I'll take credit for that."

Zane raised a brow. Typical Grady ego. He looked in the mirror again. It had been a while since he'd had two days of beard. He looked slightly rakish, with the dark clothes and the whiskers . . . and the growing bruise. "Don't go for the clean-cut professional look, do you?" he asked as he grabbed a washcloth.

"Doesn't suit you," Ty responded carefully as he realized the territory he'd stumbled into again. He didn't want to think about what did or didn't suit Zane. Ty had already crossed a mental line where his partner was concerned.

Turning on the water long enough to wet down the cloth, Zane sighed and ran it carefully over the back of his neck as he shut off the faucet, then wiped carefully on his upper lip to get the dried blood off. "Yeah, I know," he said, a hint of resignation in his voice.

"I could help, you know," Ty offered, hearing the water and guessing that Zane was probably messing with his wounds again. He leaned more against the door, forcibly relaxing himself. He desperately needed to change the subject, for his own sanity if nothing else.

It took Zane a long moment to decide what Ty was talking about. With a sigh, he decided Ty probably wasn't offering to help him with his "manhood." Tossing down the rag, he pulled his T-shirt over his head and turned to look at his back. Parts of it didn't look great. There were new scrapes and his wrist and chin were both killing him. He could certainly blame his crankiness on that; it was Ty's fault, after all. He leaned over and pulled the door open.

Ty nearly fell into the bathroom as the door collapsed beneath his shoulder without warning. Reacting instinctively, Zane slid his arms around Ty and caught him up against his chest, stopping his potential sideways pitch. Ty tried not to grab him, knowing Zane's entire back was sore and tender, but it was either that or hit the marble floor. And he really didn't want to hit the floor again tonight. Considering he'd been ready to kick the living shit out of the other man earlier, he didn't feel all too guilty about it.

He offered a grunted curse as he wrapped an arm around Zane's neck and flailed to try to stay upright. He thought he would have been able to keep his feet if Zane hadn't grabbed him and tried to help. As it was, he was pulled off-balance and practically cuddled as he struggled to get away.

"I've got you," Zane said as he pulled Ty against him, one arm encircling his waist and holding tight, easily supporting the other man's weight until Ty could find his feet.

Ty's only response was stunned silence. He looked up and met Zane's eyes as they stayed locked in the clumsy embrace. "Shit," he finally muttered.

Zane's eyes widened as his gut reacted to the proximity, and he stopped breathing when Ty didn't immediately pull back. It registered how Ty felt against him, somehow fitting perfectly against his slightly taller and broader frame—just like before. And his body reacted again. Seconds passed, and he couldn't look away. Oh, he was so going to get the shit beat out of him for this. Again.

Ty's thoughts were running along a remarkably similar line. Beating the shit out of Zane sounded like the ticket. He could feel Zane's physical reaction to the close proximity and he cleared his throat and straightened, pushing gently against Zane's chest to back him away. "Uhh..."

Slowly squaring his shoulders, Zane literally had to force himself to shift back, pulling away from Ty entirely. "You okay?" he rasped. His pulse was elevated, among other things.

"Maybe," Ty answered as he stepped back and cocked his head, looking away from Zane's dark eyes and frowning in confusion. He found himself uncharacteristically unable to think of anything else to say as he fought down his own reaction to the incident.

Zane's hands fell to his sides, and he shifted his stance. "Maybe?" he asked, brow furrowing. It wasn't like Ty not to have a snappy remark. Nerves began to bubble in his gut as he waited.

Ty closed his eyes and lifted his head, turning it the other way like a dog trying to hear a distant sound. "I've forgotten what I was making fun of you for," he mumbled.

Confused, Zane just watched him. He seemed almost nervous. Embarrassed, maybe? For being caught enough unawares to fall over when he opened the door? Or had he felt Zane's very inappropriate arousal? Jaw tightening, Zane swallowed and backed another step away. This wasn't a good thing. He should shut the door again and take a shower. Showers were always a good idea for relaxing. Shit shit shit.

"I think you were calling me a pansy ass again," he murmured, turning slightly away.

"Right," Ty huffed as he turned on his heel and headed back out into the outer room. "'Cause you went and got yourself exploded," he called as casually as possible as he grabbed his pack and walked slowly back toward the bathroom, trying to calm himself.

Zane leaned over, bracing himself on the sink as his fingers curled against the porcelain. There was no way he'd be sleeping well anytime soon.

Shower. That was the ticket. Cold shower, then sleep. He heard Ty coming back and cursed mentally. He couldn't take a shower after Ty tended those cuts. He hung his head and tried to breathe evenly. Every once in a while he met someone who did this to him, who made him crazy. God, why did it have to be Ty Grady? Why now?

Ty stood in the doorway and watched Zane for a moment. He licked his lips thoughtfully and frowned. He had noticed a lot of small things adding up about Zane's behavior, not the least of which was his being aroused by their close proximity. He didn't think Zane was fucking with him. Ty knew his own sexual preferences weren't so obvious that after four days a complete stranger would realize he went both ways. Maybe it was just a series of morbid coincidences that made it seem like Zane might do the same.

Yes, because coincidences were so much more likely than a trained FBI agent figuring something out . . .

He would simply have to tread lightly from now on, just in case Zane had sniffed him out and was planning on using it against him. Or he would have to find out for certain. He really didn't want Zane having any ammunition on him, but his curiosity had always been stronger than his sense of self-preservation.

A shift of weight warned Zane that Ty had returned, and he straightened, looking in the mirror. Without a word, he lowered his head again and pushed the wet washcloth on the counter toward Ty to use when he cleaned his back. Zane resolved that he would work on case details until he fell over exhausted. Or until he could get another night away. He half-wished he could say something, joke about it. The heat next to him was so damn intoxicating, he wished he had the nerve to do something about it. But his nerve was all tapped out after that fight.

Ty wiped his back clean with the washcloth and then covered the wounds on Zane's back liberally with salve, rubbing it in carefully, biting his lip the entire time and careful not to look up into the mirror to meet Zane's eyes. He was still battling with himself, trying to decide what to say. Because an incident like that couldn't be left with nothing said.

Maybe it was the heat and frustration riding him, but Zane thought Ty seemed almost skittish. Christ. At least he wasn't angry. Zane already knew Ty fought dirtier than he did.

Leaning on the counter again, Zane muttered to himself. "This case is going to be the death of me." If the work didn't get him, the attraction to his partner curling inside him certainly would. He shivered slightly as the salve cooled.

Ty removed his fingers from Zane's back as he saw the shiver run through him, and he pressed his lips tightly together, looking up and away in disgust as he resigned himself to what he was about to do. Broaching the subject could possibly cost him his job if Zane went tattling to the higher-ups about sexual harassment or some shit, but Ty was going to do it anyway. "Anything you need to say to me?"

The other man being so calm when Zane was such a mental wreck went a long way toward cooling him down. Ty wasn't interested in working out their frustrations in any other way than a fistfight. Zane kept his eyes on his hands, his fingers clenching. What he would do to Ty, given the chance. And he wasn't thinking about kicks to the ribs.

The visual of Ty's nude body flashed behind Zane's eyelids, and he spoke before he thought better of it. "Nothing you want to hear," he murmured as he faced the mirror, hoping to diffuse the situation. "Thanks for the help," he added, wanting desperately to get away from this tension.

"You sure about that?" Ty asked as his stomach fluttered nervously. His voice finally betrayed the nerves. "Trying to be a real partner to you here, Zane. If you need to tell me something, then here's your chance."

The uncertainty in Ty's voice surprised Zane enough that he looked up at the other man's reflection in the mirror. Four days. It had only taken four days for Ty to get so far under his skin that Zane was losing his grip. It was time to do something about this attraction that had been building. Then, maybe he'd be able to focus again. Another punch from Ty would do the trick.

Zane slowly turned around to face the other man, eyes dark and serious. Ignoring the warning bells going off in his head, he leaned back against the counter and reached out to slide the ends of his fingers into the front of the waistband of Ty's jeans and tug him forward.

The color drained from Ty's face as Zane pulled him closer, and his stomach turned again in a pleasant somersault of nervous butterflies. It only took a moment for him to flush with heat, and he looked into Zane's eyes guardedly as his entire body tensed. If this was anything but completely on the level, Ty was going to knock the bastard on his ass.

The caution that crept back into Ty's gaze was a pretty clear warning. Zane loosened his fingers and almost let go, but Ty didn't pull away. It was now or never. Zane took a slow, deep breath and ducked his chin, tilted his head sideways, and slid his lips firmly against Ty's.

Ty's breath caught, nearly gasping when Zane finally touched their lips together. He shivered and his lips parted tentatively, but his wary eyes never closed. Giving in, Zane pulled him closer and lifted one hand to cup Ty's cheek as he increased the pressure of his lips against Ty's.

Ty groaned softly and finally relaxed against the kiss, returning it tentatively. He knew he'd regret this just as soon as they parted, but he couldn't bring himself to stop it.

Tension cramped Zane's gut as Ty's lips moved, and he deepened the kiss, all the itch and urge heating inside him as he traced Ty's lips with his tongue. Oh, this was going to be an absolute fucking mess, he just knew it. He pulled his fingers out of the waistband and curled that arm around Ty's waist as he leaned into the dangerous kiss. His hand on Ty's cheek trembled.

Ty indulged himself in the deeper kiss for a long, horribly tantalizing moment before he pulled his head back just enough to break the contact and pushed gently at Zane's chest. "That's what I thought," he rasped as his breath gusted against Zane's lips.

Zane slowly opened his eyes as their lips hovered a mere breath apart, and he dropped his hand so both settled on Ty's hips. "Thought?" he asked.

"This . . . but I thought you were fucking with me," Ty gritted out almost angrily as he forced himself not to press their lips together once more.

Zane just barely shook his head, pulling back from Ty's growing ire. "Not about this," he said seriously, already starting to tense and brace himself for a swing.

Ty did kiss him then, breathing in heavily through his nose as if he were about to dive under water as he pulled himself closer to Zane and growled a little. He figured if Zane was fucking with him now, then he seemed to be enjoying it quite a bit.

Tightening his arms, Zane closed them further around Ty as he met the kiss with more strength, dizzy with the surprise and desire blasting through him. This was beyond crazy. Beyond negligent. Just . . . beyond. All the hate and anger was morphing into heat and passion, and he had no idea what to think about it.

Suddenly, Ty yanked away from the increasingly heated kiss again, stepping back and giving Zane's chest a good hard smack with the back of his hand. "Asshole," he gasped as he tried to get himself under control.

"Ow!" Zane yelped as Ty's hand stung against his bare skin. He gasped out a laugh as he leaned back. "Me?" he asked in disbelief, squirming in place where he practically sat against the counter.

Ty grabbed him and pulled him off the counter to kiss him again, forcing himself not to think about the consequences. If he thought about it, he'd cut and run—as far and as fast as he possibly could. Zane grunted as he landed against Ty's chest, his stance spread enough to lower him the couple of inches needed to be at the same height as Ty. Clutching at Ty's shoulders, Zane shifted his weight to push the other man back toward the door.

Ty hit the door with a rush of air from his lungs, his hip barely missing the doorknob as the impact slammed the door closed, but neither man noticed. They were far too distracted by the sudden turn of events. "I had you pegged as trouble from minute one," Ty gasped accusingly between the hurried meetings of their lips.

Zane bit Ty's bottom lip slightly and sucked it between his lips before letting it loose. "Your middle name is trouble," he said as he ran a hand down Ty's side, feeling the hard muscles appreciatively.

Ty hissed with the bite and growled dangerously. He couldn't decide if he was angry or just really fucking turned on. Either way, it was all Zane fucking Garrett's fault . . .

Pulling in a deep breath when his body reacted to the harsh sound, Zane set his forearm against the door over Ty's shoulder, making their chests, hips, and groins rock together. "Now what?" he breathed. "You wanted to know. Now you know."

Ty banged his head back on the door and closed his eyes, huffing through his nose as he tried to regain some control. "I lied," he groaned plaintively. "I didn't wanna know."

Zane couldn't help but smile and snicker. "Too late, hotshot," he said.

"Bastard."

"Coming from you, that's pretty much an endearment." Still grinning, amazed at Ty's pliancy, Zane leaned forward to steal a firm kiss. Ty's lips parted almost against his will, and he groaned slightly. Zane couldn't resist that little sound, and he moved to capture it, sliding his mouth more slowly over Ty's, rubbing, tongue sliding between swollen lips. Ty seemed to melt against him, losing the tension that was always in him, losing the caustic shield he seemed to rarely drop. He merely managed a few incoherent murmurs as he slid a hand into Zane's hair.

Zane wrapped his arms around him when the other man relaxed, not tight, just enough to hold their bodies in constant contact. The tiny sounds and first real touch from the other man rocked Zane's world badly.

"We gotta stop," Ty groaned finally, pulling back as much as he dared. Their lips still touched when he spoke. "Neither of us is up to this," he rasped, breathing still difficult as his body screamed for more contact.

It wasn't the right excuse, Zane knew, but it would have to serve. This could only lead to disaster. He slowly straightened, seeing the desire in Ty's hooded eyes. Somehow he made himself step back, hands sliding on each side of Ty's rib cage until they fell away.

Ty lowered his head, still looking at Zane from under lowered brows, and pressed his lips tightly together. "Fuck," he finally observed flatly.

Zane took another step back, slid one hand into his back pocket to keep it off Ty, and leaned against the counter again. Raising his other hand, he lightly ran a finger over his split lip, feeling the pain return as the tingle and thrill dissipated. He could echo Ty's sentiment, but the urge to touch and taste was still ravaging him, and it was taking all he had not to grab the other man and grind against him. He closed his eyes in a bid to regain some measure of control.

"What the fuck do we do now?" Ty asked in frustration.

After squeezing his eyes shut for a long moment, Zane took step sideways. "You're going back to your room, and I'm taking a cold shower." He turned to yank a towel off the rack.

"Huh-uh," Ty protested stubbornly. "I'd rather completely fuck us both over than separate," he added with a flush that was part embarrassment, part desire to do just what he'd said.

Zane turned back to him, his lack of patience very clear. "Get out of the bathroom or fucked over is what you're going to get," he growled.

Another thrill ran through Ty's body, and he inclined his head slightly—part challenge, part invitation. Fuck it. He had never followed the rules anyway.

Eyes turning sparkling black, Zane reached out, grabbed Ty's arm and yanked him to the side, just enough to get his weight behind him to shove him against the sink, belly first. He was immediately on him, grinding against his ass, and he leaned over to bite the back of Ty's shoulder, hard, before he looked up to meet Ty's eyes in the mirror.

"Is this what you want?" Zane ground out. "Hard and messy in a goddamn hotel bathroom?" He pressed him harder into the sink counter.

Ty looked up to meet Zane's eyes in the reflection of the mirror, and he grinned slowly.

Zane's temper flared, and his stomach plummeted painfully as he realized that Ty was just messing with him. "Son of a bitch," he hissed. He pulled back, yanked open the bathroom door, and then shoved Ty straight out of the room with enough force that the man hit the mirrored closet door on the opposite wall with a rattle. Then he slammed the bathroom door shut between them.

Ty stayed where he'd practically splatted for a long moment, breathing heavily and resting his forehead against the cool surface of the mirror to calm himself. Hard and messy in a hotel bathroom had sounded pretty damn fun, actually. Christ, Zane was a fucking Jekyll-and-Hyde case.

Reaching in the shower to turn the cold water on full blast, Zane kicked out of his jeans and briefs with a growl, the heat of his anger matching the roiling desire for the man he'd just thrown out. "Fucking asshole," he hissed as he climbed full into the shower spray and yanked the curtain shut. How could he have misjudged Ty's reactions? The bastard must have been putting on from the first moment their lips touched.

"Goddamn it all to hell," he growled. The cold water was barely having any effect. He slammed the side of his fist against the tile, only to cuss again colorfully and shake his hand as the pain reverberated through his fingers and up his arm again.

Ty heard the thud from within the bathroom and finally raised his head. He turned to look at the door and narrowed his eyes. So, Rule Number One, apparently, was that he wasn't allowed to crack a smile during foreplay. "Got it," he muttered to himself as he pulled his shirt over his head and tossed it to the side before stepping up to the door and throwing it open.

Zane's head shot up as the door hit the wall. What the hell? Then, and only then, it occurred to him that Ty just might have been serious with that smile. Fuck.

Ty was already half-undressed, so it wouldn't have taken him all that long to finish the job. But instead, he yanked the shower curtain back and stepped into the shower without removing his jeans, and he grabbed Zane and slammed him against the tile along the back side of the shower.

He'd half-expected it, but Zane was still surprised by the other man's vehemence, and he gasped and growled as his back hit the cool wall opposite the curtain painfully.

Ty reached over to the shower knobs and turned the temperature of the water up to something more tolerable, holding his forearm across Zane's chest. "We've really got to work on that temper of yours," he drawled as he pressed himself against Zane's body.

A breath shuddered out of Zane as he spread both hands, palms flat against the tile. The warm water and the press of the other man's body were doing the trick to bring him fully hard again. "Ty," he said harshly.

"Shut up," Ty hissed in response as his entire body turned over into tackle mode and drove all other thoughts from his mind. He ducked his head to lick a trail of water running down Zane's collarbone and then bit him lightly.

Zane groaned and his eyes rolled back as his hands moved without thought to clutch at Ty's hips. "You make me absolutely fucking crazy," he said thickly.

"Hate to break it to you, but I think you were there long before I came along," Ty murmured before he raised his head and kissed Zane slowly.

One hand shifted up to curl around the back of Ty's neck as they kissed, and Zane shifted his feet apart so Ty was right up against his body. His patience and good sense were blown. He didn't want to say no to this. It was so much better than any booze or drugs. His blood thrummed with it; his chest and belly were taut with it.

"You might find it a bit more difficult to toss me out next time," Ty hissed as one hand snaked down Zane's body and between them.

Zane's next breath nearly choked him as Ty's hand slid between their bodies, soft compared to the wet denim that scraped against his bare midsection. No, he didn't imagine he'd be tossing Ty anywhere. His eyes opened. "Next time?" he asked hoarsely.

Ty's hand closed around him, and he nipped at his chin in answer. The back of Zane's head hit the tile, and he held Ty's shoulders tight as he reacted, swelling as a strangled gasp escaped him.

"That's what I thought," Ty cooed to him with a smirk as he stroked him slowly. "When was the last time you fucked someone you didn't pay, Zane?" he asked in an almost conversational tone as the water pounded down on them both.

Dragging his eyes open, Zane met Ty's changeable eyes. His lashes were dotted with water drops. "Too damn long," he said lowly. Ty kissed him again almost before he got the words out, and his hand sped up slightly as he pressed his body into Zane's.

Feeling like he was about to burn to a crisp, Zane shook all over as his hips shifted to move against Ty's hand. Oh, God. He groaned and laid his head back, eyes shut against the water splashing off his shoulder. It didn't matter that he'd gotten off about six hours ago. He was hard and straining. Ty's other hand slid behind his head to cushion his skull from hitting the tiles, and he kissed Zane again demandingly as he continued to stroke relentlessly.

It wasn't going to take much longer, not at all. The hard kiss, the catch and slide of Ty's hand, and the tension all spiraled tighter and tighter as Zane growled into Ty's mouth.

"Come on," Ty urged, not at all concerned with land-speed records or propriety.

Zane gritted his teeth as the electricity of Ty's touch flashed through him. He growled and lowered his chin, then he opened his eyes and reached out to grab Ty for an animalistic kiss as his hips jerked and he slammed into orgasm. Ty pinned him against the wall and kissed him back, enjoying the result of his efforts almost as much as Zane did. Body twitching through the climax, Zane had to gasp against Ty's lips, crying out on an exhale as Ty's hand kept moving while he got more and more sensitive.

Ty finally took pity on him and slid his hand back up Zane's body, wrapping around him and kissing him more slowly as he gave him a chance to recover. Shaky and flushed, Zane relaxed fluidly into Ty's arms and the kiss, anger sloughing off him like the water on its way to the drain.

After a long, leisurely moment, Ty pushed away from the wall and grinned as he licked his lips. "There," he huffed, sounding very pleased with himself. "Now you can stop being so fucking cranky for a while."

Zane snorted and laughed weakly, raising both hands to rub over his face. "Christ," he said with great feeling as he sagged back against the wall.

Ty smiled and gave his characteristic self-satisfied "Mm-hmm" before pulling the curtain back and stepping over the side of the bathtub carefully in his wet socks.

Zane watched him as the water misted over the tub's edge. Ty's jeans were totally soaked and clung to him like a second skin, and

Zane had to swallow hard. Jesus. "Good luck getting out of those gracefully," he rasped with a slight smile, still leaning against the wall.

"Good luck thinking for the next hour," Ty shot back with a smirk.

"Shit," Zane muttered, turning into the spray to wash before leaning and shutting the water off.

Ty stood, silent and dripping in the middle of the bathroom, and watched him intently. When Zane turned around, water still dripped down his neck and wound in rivulets down his shoulders and chest as he stepped out of the shower to stand not six inches from the other man. Ty licked his lips and tilted his head, waiting for Zane's next move. The other man stood there a long moment, then reached forward and unbuttoned Ty's jeans, pulling down the zipper slowly. Ty bit his lip and tilted his head back, his eyes never leaving Zane's even as his body thrummed with the contact.

"Good luck getting me out of these gracefully," he echoed wryly, his voice low even though he was smiling. Zane actually smiled and chuckled as he ducked his chin and slid his hands into the wet denim over Ty's hips, peeling it down over the equally wet briefs underneath. Ty's eyes drifted closed, and he tilted his head into Zane's cheek, groaning softly.

The motion warmed Zane, and he turned his cheek to rub it against Ty's forehead while he slowly worked the wet denim down his hips. The whole thing was disconcertingly tender, but Ty didn't want to make Zane stop by observing this out loud. Without warning, Zane hefted Ty up and sat him on the counter, moving in between his awkwardly spread knees to claim another kiss.

Ty nearly flailed. Christ, he'd never actually been picked up during sex before. He gripped Zane's arms tightly and returned the kiss, but broke it off to warn in a rasping voice, "I don't bottom well."

"Is that so?" Zane drawled uncaringly. "Should I have taken that sultry grin of yours a while ago as an invitation?" he asked, his manner turning more seductive.

"Maybe," Ty answered in a voice that was more of an uncertain whisper.

"It won't make you any less of a man," Zane parroted, bumping Ty's forehead lightly with his own.

"Oh, you bastard," Ty growled, beginning to struggle out of the vulnerable position Zane had set him in.

Zane laughed and pushed further in between Ty's legs as he struggled, wrapping one arm around his waist, grasping the back of his neck with his other hand. "You're stunning when you're angry, you little fuck," he muttered before smashing their mouths together, the odd gentility of the last few minutes obliterated.

Ty did flail then, uttering a muffled exclamation of hatred against Zane's lips. Zane smiled into the kiss as he listened. He used to think he'd be able to quit drinking once he'd had his fill. He was already scared to death it wouldn't work with Ty, either. But the hunger was eating him up, so much so that he was very nearly hard again already.

"Fuck," Ty finally muttered as they broke another heated kiss.

"Is that a comment or a request?" Zane asked breathlessly.

Ty lowered his head to press his lips to Zane's shoulder and closed his eyes. Jacking him off in the shower was one thing. Fucking would be entirely another. But hell, Ty wasn't ever one to stop when he was ahead. "Both," he answered hoarsely.

Zane slid his hands to Ty's hips, gripping them and pulling his body toward him to the edge of the counter.

"Let me get my fucking socks off first," Ty growled as he tried to kick out of the soaking-wet jeans that still clung to his ankles. Zane bent down and tugged them off one leg at a time, then yanked at Ty's socks impatiently before standing and wrapping his arms around him to kiss him again impulsively.

Ty mumbled and put up a token struggle as Zane began dragging him out of the bathroom and to the bed, but the slight resistance in Ty's actions fueled Zane's desire even more.

A handful of stumbling steps later they stood at the foot of the bed Ty had claimed. Ty pulled away and suffered through a brief moment of clarity. "Do you have supplies for this sort of endeavor?" he asked Zane before he got far enough away to meet his eyes.

Zane stalked over to his duffel and dug in it to pull out a small black shaving kit, bringing it back and tossing it on the bed. He stopped a foot away, looking at Ty evenly. The desire ran rampant through him, and he felt like he was dying of thirst. "You're worse than the damn drink," he muttered.

Ty raised his chin and licked his lips. He wasn't sure if that was good or not, but it sure as hell felt good. But then, that pretty much summed up how he felt about the whole situation.

Zane had already made his decision. He wasn't going to be able to concentrate on the case in this state, so he might as well do something about it. And the fact that Ty was ready, willing, and able went a long way toward making it a lot more pleasurable. He moved forward until their chests barely brushed. "What do you want?"

Ty inclined his head even further and tilted it to the side, looking down at Zane's mouth and then up into his eyes. He smiled slowly. "I don't bottom well," he warned again softly.

Heat flared in Zane's eyes. "That's all right," he said in a deceptively light voice just before he grabbed Ty's arm and swung him around, pulling his ass back against him while wrapping his arm around him. Zane knew full well Ty was letting him do it. It made it just that much more tantalizing. His voice was dark and throbbing when he purred, "I'm all for a good, hard fuck."

Ty closed his eyes and let his head rest back on Zane's shoulder, the words sending a dull throb straight to his groin. When he didn't struggle, Zane let his hands roam, getting to know the feel of Ty's skin, and he lowered his head to lick from his collarbone up to his ear. Ty huffed out a breath of air through his nose and shifted back against the hard muscles behind him.

Zane bit down lightly at the juncture of Ty's neck and shoulder as he groped his way down Ty's body. "You going to fight me?" he asked, wanting to know what to expect before throwing Ty to the bed and literally pouncing on his ass.

"Not this time," Ty groaned, surprised by how much he really wanted to be overpowered, a sharp contrast to the painful fight in the alley.

Just like that, Zane was achingly erect, and he rubbed up against Ty's ass as he mouthed along the back of his shoulder. "Another time," he agreed before pushing Ty down onto the bed. He'd enjoy that too. But for now, he just wanted to sink into Ty and wallow there.

Ty hit the mattress on his hands and knees, but almost immediately lowered himself to his stomach. Zane just as quickly crawled over him. His extra height gave him the length he needed to press a heated kiss to the back of Ty's neck and press his groin against Ty's ass as he fumbled for the kit.

For some reason, Ty could no longer do anything but react. His body was reacting, his mind was reacting, and he was greeting each of Zane's actions with a needy, almost desperate reaction of his own. But if he had been needed to act on his own, to actually think, he would have never been able to get off the bed. He wasn't sure if he liked the submissive effect Zane was having on him, but his body certainly did.

On his knees over Ty's thighs, Zane slicked his fingers and trailed down, expecting a man like Ty to tense when he touched him. He actually wished Ty would fight him, although he was incredibly tempting like this. If he'd fought Zane, just enough, Zane would have taken him and fucked him over hard, taking everything he could get out of his tight ass. But this, God, it was incredible and unexpected, feeling Ty writhing and pliable under him.

The intimate touch did make him jerk, but Ty rolled his shoulders and dug his fingers into the sheets, shaking off the tension. He hoped Zane realized just how much effort it took to not buck him off. Zane leaned over to murmur in his ear as he slid his fingers back and forth over where he hoped to soon bury himself. "Ty, for fuck's sake, move," he growled. "You're not going to throw me off so easily."

Ty turned his head to the side, brushing his cheek against Zane's lips. He did move then, but only to push against the bed and raise his body up into Zane's. Groaning, Zane slid his aching cock back and forth against Ty's skin and pushed his lubricated finger inside the other man. It was hard to go slow. Oh, so difficult. But if he did it right now, then soon he could fuck Ty through the damn mattress.

Ty groaned plaintively, tensing involuntarily and squirming.

Zane stilled. "Hurting?" he asked.

"Shut the fuck up and keep going," Ty growled in a strained voice.

"Hell," Zane breathed as he moved his hand again, another few pushes and another finger as he leaned over enough to press his forehead to Ty's shoulder blade while he tried to breathe evenly. Having come once, he'd last awhile. Maybe. With Ty, all bets were off.

Beneath him, Ty arched his back, trying to push up into him and groaning encouragingly. He hurried, unwilling to wait much longer; Ty's body was giving him all the right signals, and he was worried

Ty might suddenly change his mind and kick his ass instead. Zane grabbed up a condom and made short work of it, then lined up, one hand on Ty's right hip, the other on his left shoulder.

Ty lowered his head and raised his hips higher, closing his eyes and breathing out slowly in expectation of what he knew was going to hurt. He wanted it, though. He wanted it badly. His entire body shook with the desire. Zane smoothed his hand over Ty's back and pushed in slowly. He wasn't small and, god damn, Ty was so tight. He pushed in just enough, and then he started rocking gently. Ty groaned and remained still for a brief moment, letting himself deal with the burning pain before he pushed back against the intrusion in a silent demand for more.

Sucking in a shaky breath, Zane answered Ty's movement with a bit more force added to his rocking, sinking slightly deeper each time. He curled over Ty's back, his hand coasting from shoulder to hip and under Ty's belly to slide around the half-hard cock hanging there.

"Garrett," Ty breathed pleadingly. He wasn't even sure what he was asking for. He just knew it felt so fucking good he could barely stand it.

Gasping softly as he turned his cheek against Ty's back, Zane pushed harder, sinking over half in before pulling out, the clamp of Ty's body an irresistible lure. He slid his fist back and forth, feeling Ty's reaction as well as hearing it. It thrilled him. It was so different from the sarcasm, anger, and cold dislike. It went straight to Zane's belly and he shuddered.

Ty trembled under him, and finally he sank back to his stomach, bringing Zane with him and taking the full weight of Zane's body on his to pin him to the mattress. "Come on," he urged, the same words he'd hissed in the shower. He needed this. Needed it.

Zane squeezed his eyes shut, the growl in Ty's voice draining some of his control. The smooth rocking paused as he pulled his hand out from under Ty, and then he snapped his hips forward, hard, burying himself deep with a groan of pleasure.

Ty responded with an involuntary cry. He pushed back again, physically begging for more as jolts of pleasure and hot pain ran through him. Grunting, Zane shifted so he could thrust into Ty's body in a rough motion as he gripped his hips. Even when he pulled back, he was surrounded by the heat of Ty's body, and Zane was steadily losing his mind again as his knees slid on the sheets.

Each thrust was doing the same to Ty, though he tried desperately not to whimper. "Harder," he begged in a hoarse, rasping voice.

Fingers gripping hard, Zane braced one knee and loosed what little control he had left. He truly fucked Ty and then some, jarring them both and the bed enough to shake the pillows to the floor. He grunted with each thrust, a low growl growing deep in his chest, able to let loose when Ty just took more and more, clearly wanting it. Fuck ... had it ever been this way? Zane couldn't remember a time he hadn't been afraid of hurting his bed partner. And it went on and on, both of them struggling for breaths as they strained against each other.

"Ty..." Zane finally managed hoarsely as he felt his body tighten in warning. But Ty couldn't answer, his breath coming in gasps and each thrust forcing a groan out of him as he took the pounding.

Zane gave a hissed curse as he went over the edge, hips losing rhythm and jerking erratically as the heat and press of Ty's body dragged the climax out of him.

Ty moaned long and loud as Zane rode out his orgasm. He tightened every muscle in his already tense body and fisted his hands in the sheets, toes curling involuntarily in sympathy of the pleasure. Zane cried out—a tortured rasp, really—as he was caught by the pressure. The heat washed through him and he shivered, drawing a shaky breath before pulling out and heaving himself up on his knees. Ty remained where he was, face pressed into the mattress and eyes closed as his shoulders shook almost imperceptibly.

Zane shifted to sit heavily at the other man's side. "Ty," he breathed, looking at him, seeing him tremble. He leaned onto his side, tucked his head under Ty's chin and kissed him. "Let me," he whispered against Ty's lips, one hand burrowing under him to reach the straining erection trapped against the bed.

Ty groaned and lifted up, then immediately pushed his hips against Zane's hand as he kissed him hungrily. Zane curled his fingers around Ty's cock and tightened his fist as his mouth gave way to Ty's demand. His sore wrist ached with the motion, but he didn't give a damn just then. Ty jerked into his hand and gave a muffled moan. He raised his arm to pin Zane under him like a large dog would do to capture a cat, and he rocked against him, never breaking the kiss. Several more slow thrusts, and the tight coil of pleasure in Ty's groin snapped. His fingers tightened in Zane's short hair and he groaned plaintively as he came in Zane's hand.

Zane sighed against Ty's lips as he relaxed; the heated slick of Ty's come dripping over his fingers assured him of Ty's pleasure taken. His back stung, his wrist ached, and his bruised fingers hurt like hell, adding a bit of an edge to the overwhelming satiation that threatened to send him to sleep right then and there.

Ty nearly collapsed against him, just barely managing the energy to flop to the side instead of just down on top of him. "Fuck," he offered weakly, eyes closing as he rolled to his back.

"Yeah," Zane agreed. His eyes were blurring, so he just closed them.

"We shoulda done that in your bed," Ty finally grumbled.

"Priss," Zane murmured sleepily.

"Hmph," Ty responded without moving.

"I'm cold," Zane strung together, voice thick.

"Like I care," Ty grunted softly as he finally forced himself to move. He rolled off the edge of the bed and thumped loudly to the floor, then stood and slid liquidly under the covers all in one graceful motion.

Zane grumbled and turned to his hands and knees, backing off the side of the bed and standing up. He disposed of the used condom and cleaned up with one of the dirty towels in the corner. He ran both hands over his face and through his hair, and then looked down at Ty.

"What?" Ty questioned as he burrowed under the covers.

"I want to sleep here with you," Zane admitted petulantly.

"What's stopping you?" Ty challenged with a small smirk, curious as to what Zane would do.

Well, he'd been afraid Ty would stop him. Zane pulled the sheets down on the side to Ty's left and slid into the warm cotton, his legs stretching out easily. He pulled the pillow under his head and rolled to his side, facing Ty. He opened his mouth to say thank you or good night or please touch me again, but instead there was nothing.

Ty lay there looking at him expressionlessly. Finally, his hand slid under the covers and onto Zane's hip, pulling him closer as he gently caressed the skin of his hip and waist. He scooted closer, until finally he had his arm draped around Zane and his other arm under Zane's neck to support his head. He wedged his face between Zane's and the pillow. "This in no way means I don't still hate you," he muttered as he nuzzled his nose and mouth against Zane's temple and closed his eyes.

Zane smiled, his lower arm shifted so he could place his palm over Ty's beating heart, and his top arm curled over his waist. He drifted to sleep, feeling amazingly comfortable, listening to Ty's steady breathing.

Chapter Six

A slim woman in uniform with her dark hair pulled back into a severe bun stopped next to Detective Steve Pierce's desk. "Got some messages for you, Detective," she said, holding out a few pink pieces of paper. Pierce glanced up. "Thanks, Branson. I'm putting in another work order on that voice mail," he promised her.

"Sure thing, sir. It's no problem, unless we're booking," she answered before taking herself back to the front counter across the large squad room.

Detective Steve Holleman glanced up at his partner from across their connected desks and raised an eyebrow at him. Pierce leaned back in the creaky chair and flipped through the pink slips. He scowled at one in particular and stared at it hatefully.

"Care to share?" Holleman finally prodded.

"Goddamn Feebs again," Pierce muttered, tossing the pink slips on his desk. "About the serial."

"What else is new?" Holleman muttered as he went back to the report he was filling out.

"It's from that Henninger guy. There's a new team here," Pierce said, picking up his coffee with one hand and spinning his computer mouse with the other to wake up the monitor.

"Well, yeah," Holleman huffed as if that should be obvious. "The last ones got themselves killed."

Pierce slanted a displeased look at his partner, but didn't tell him off. "I still think they need to check their own house."

"Tell them that. Shit, one of those guys almost went nuclear when one of the uniforms mentioned that at the last crime scene."

"Yeah, I know. We'd probably react the same way, though. I just hate that they can march in and do whatever the hell they want. That's why this thing hasn't been solved yet. Too many fingers in the pot, screwing with the soup."

Holleman plunked his pen down and looked up at his partner with a frown. "You're not starting with the food analogies again, are you?" he asked flatly.

Pierce rolled his eyes. "They got too many people dealing with the details, fucking up the evidence, and then they wonder why the case is so screwed. Then, of course, they call us and expect us to snap to. I'm thinking this time, they can wait."

"Yeah, that won't piss them off," Holleman muttered as he picked up his pen again. "Whatever. I've got too much shit to do as it is."

"I'll call them tomorrow morning. You got that paperwork from Trenton?"

"Somewhere," Holleman answered distractedly. "You got that statement from the chick who didn't like buttoning her shirt?" he asked as he looked back up.

"Yeah, in that stack." Pierce pointed to the corner of his desk. "Singleton put a photo in there too, of course."

Holleman rifled through the stack until he found the folder. He plucked it out of the stack and looked at it with a smirk. Turning it around to show Pierce, he laughed softly and said, "Think we got any of her face?"

Pierce glanced over and did a double take. "Aw, shit. Singleton's gonna get his ass in a sling." He rubbed his hands over his eyes. "The cases keep getting weirder, and then that damn serial pops up again." He sighed and looked up to gaze across the two desks at his partner.

Holleman's tongue was hanging out of his mouth again, stuck to the side like it always did when he was deep in thought. "Wanna go get food?" he finally asked after pondering the universe for a time.

It took a moment for Pierce to blink himself out of his stare. "Ah, yeah. Sure. I could use more coffee."

"Then we can call back those clowns and get it over with," Holleman muttered as he stood and pushed away from the desk.

Pierce followed Holleman out of the office, grumbling to himself disconsolately the whole way.

Ty slid carefully out of the bed and padded around the room, cleaning up and getting dressed almost silently. He risked a few glances at his bedmate and his frown deepened every time he did so. What the hell had they been thinking? They hadn't stopped with just one try. Hours after falling asleep in each other's arms, they had awakened again and gone at it without any thought to the consequences. Ty had taken his turn, giving as good as he'd gotten from Zane. At least they'd both be sore as hell today.

Ty shook his head and went to the window, glancing out at the light rain. His entire body ached, and not altogether in good ways. He frowned even harder as he stood there, waiting for Zane to wake.

The bed growing cool pushed Zane from his sleep and he slowly shifted under the sheet. He made a soft sound deep in his throat when he rolled carefully onto his back. It wasn't just his back that hurt. He opened his eyes to focus on the ceiling before turning his eyes to the other bed. Empty. He turned his chin and saw Ty standing at the window. He looked tired and tense. Zane stifled a sigh. He knew he should have expected something like that.

Ty glanced over his shoulder when he heard the rustling and he cleared his throat. "Hey," he offered lamely.

Zane raised his uninjured hand to rub at his eyes. "What time is it? How long did we sleep?"

"It's nine thirty," Ty answered without glancing at his watch or the clock. He looked away from Zane and back out the window. "How you feelin'?" he asked as he stared at the rain coming down.

"Groggy," Zane said, his voice still thick and warm from sleep. He ran his hand over his hair and yawned, considering turning over and going back to sleep.

Ty lowered his head and considered the pros and cons of admitting how fucking sore he was. Everywhere. It might go to easing some of the awkwardness anyway. "My ass hurts," he finally admitted with a small, wry smile.

Zane reopened his eyes to look at the other man. He had no idea how to respond to that, so he just looked at him. Ty shrugged lopsidedly when Zane didn't respond. The cell phone at his hip began to sing, saving him from having to say anything further. He answered it with a clipped murmur after looking at the number.

Once Ty was distracted, Zane let his eyes slide down the wiry, half-clothed body. Ty's ass hurt. Zane's lips twitched. Not a good idea to laugh, he was sure. But damn... what a boost to the ego. He pushed away the sheet and got out of the bed.

He lifted his arms slowly and started to lengthen his body in a long stretch. He bobbed his head from side to side, and bones popped. He relished the stretch for a moment before heading over to his duffel and digging for clothes.

Ty watched him, listening distractedly to the man on the phone as he did so. He realized with some annoyance that he was pondering the advantages of jumping his partner again. Finally, he looked away and shook his head. When he spoke into the phone after a long time of just listening, it wasn't in English.

Zane glanced over when the lyrical language poured out in Ty's raspy voice. He didn't know which language it was, but something Middle Eastern; it had that sound. Maybe Farsi. Much more melodic than Zane's own rapid-fire Spanish. The sound of it didn't seem to fit Ty's voice—or him—at all.

The conversation didn't last long, and Ty bid the man farewell softly before ending the call and clipping the phone back onto his belt. He turned around and looked at Zane thoughtfully. "You feel up to a little trekking today?" he asked, not even pretending to try and explain who had been on the phone.

"Sure," Zane answered, shrugging off any curiosity. "Moving around will keep my back from getting too stiff." Before he thought better of it, Zane glanced to Ty, then down to Ty's ass, then back up to Ty's eyes. Ty raised an eyebrow and sneered at him. Zane bit back the smile and picked up his clothes. "What do you have in mind?" he asked as he walked toward the bathroom.

"I want to go see a body dump," Ty called in answer, telling himself to let it go. He had offered the information, after all. He knew he risked a little razzing for it. Perhaps he had been looking for a sincere response, something to build up a little trust, instead of what he had gotten. Oh, well.

"Are you going to call Morrison or Henninger to set it up? Or are we still steering clear of the office for now?" Zane got into the bathroom and couldn't hold back the grin any longer. Then he shook his head and started cleaning himself up to go.

"None of them are still cordoned off, so we can just go. I just need to see them," Ty answered as he turned back to the window and frowned at his watery reflection.

Zane stepped around the corner and watched Ty for a long moment. When he spoke, his voice was lower and quieter. More serious. "Crunching profiles?"

Ty cocked his head to the side and cracked his neck with a grimace. "Yeah," he admitted. "I just need to see why he left them where he did."

Considering that response, Zane looked up at the photos tacked on the wall. He hadn't thought about why the bodies were left as they were. "Well, get moving, Marine. We've got work to do." His voice was still quiet, despite the words.

Ty turned around and huffed at him again. "It's raining," he informed the man as he picked up the T-shirt he had pulled out to wear. It was a white camp-style T-shirt with a brown teepee on the front, surrounded by the words Camp Runamuck.

Zane cocked his head to one side as Ty pulled it over his head. "Where do you get these shirts?"

"What do you mean?" Ty asked innocently.

Zane chuckled. "A Marine at Camp Runamuck. Hysterical," he murmured as he started loading up his pockets.

Ty looked down at his chest and smiled slightly. "My former brothers-in-arms send them to me," he answered. "I get a new one about every two or three months."

"Once a Marine, always a Marine," Zane quoted as he pulled on a light jacket.

"I loved being a Marine," Ty responded defensively.

Zane looked at him evenly, seeing the bottom of Ty's tattoo peeking out from under a shirtsleeve. "You still are a Marine," he said.

Ty stopped his movements and cocked his head at Zane, trying to decide whether he was serious or just humoring him.

"My brother-in-law's a Marine," Zane said. "He always said you're one for life." He waited for Ty's response.

Ty's eyes darted over Zane thoughtfully. "He was right," he murmured finally before looking away and grabbing his leather jacket.

Zane kept his eyes on him for a few moments longer before turning to pick up his gun, check it, and slide it into its holster. "Ready?"

Ty merely nodded as he slid his wallet into his back pocket and looked up. His oddly colored eyes met Zane's dark ones. A thousand things to say went through Ty's mind, and he even opened his mouth to speak. He licked his lips and lowered his head before he could, though, and he gestured to the door to cover his discomfort.

Although Zane was fascinated by Ty's behavior, he made himself turn and walk. Maybe it was just that Ty had to work himself up to be such a bastard. Since he'd just had a few rounds of stress relief and a night's sleep, he was calm. Zane sighed and opened the door for the other man, wishing he knew how to build a profile. He'd bet good money Ty's would resemble a Rorschach.

Ty slid his hands into his pockets and kept his head down as they walked to the elevators. He'd lost control with Zane, and he couldn't seem to come to terms with what he'd let happen. Not only had they fucked, but Ty had let Zane fuck him. He'd given up every ounce of control to a man he barely liked. And Ty had enjoyed it immensely.

Zane stabbed the elevator button and waited, Ty silent and nearly brooding alongside him. They both had plenty to think about. At least Zane did, and he resisted the urge to look over at Ty to try to read his face. He watched the elevator numbers change, approaching their floor. "Ty," he said quietly.

Ty glanced at him and frowned slightly.

"My ass hurts too," Zane admitted quietly as the doors opened to other people.

Ty looked from Zane to the several people in the elevator and bit his lip against a smile. Whether they had heard him was hard to tell, but just the fact that Zane had said it lifted a little bit of weight from Ty's shoulders. He couldn't fuck someone without a sense of humor. It just didn't sit right with him. He cleared his throat, trying not to laugh as they entered the elevator. "Okay," was all he managed to say in response.

They said nothing more as they rode down to the lobby and went outside to hail a cab. It wasn't necessarily a comfortable silence. More like a temporary truce.

The taxi dropped them off at the massive Civil War–era gate that marked the main entrance to Green-Wood Cemetery. The rain had lessened some, but it had brought with it a chill that ate through their clothing and nipped at their bare skin. Ty shoved his hands into his pockets and peered up through the falling rain at the stonework with something like reverence. He could already see the appeal of the location as a drop spot.

Zane stood several feet away, looking around. The weather was perfect for the location—cool and dreary, adding to the inherent quiet and sadness in the graveyard. But it didn't take away from the strange beauty of the place. He studied the huge archway with some interest and appreciation before looking to Ty.

Ty was still looking up when he spoke. "Hooker was found wrapped in her sheet at one of the tombs," he told Zane quietly. "No teeth, otherwise untouched."

The other agent's eyes turned toward the monuments that stood further into the graveyard, past the darkening grass and burnt amber leaves that contrasted sharply with the dirty marble stones. Something inside Zane began to ache a little, and he frowned slightly, shoving his hands into his pockets.

Ty glanced over at him when he didn't respond. "You okay?" he asked with a frown.

Zane's eyes flickered, but he nodded right away. "Yeah," he said quietly. He could feel the weight of the place settling around him. He imagined Ty did too. The ambiance was too majestic not to feel and feel deeply. "Lead on."

Ty watched him for a moment and then nodded, bowing his head in the rain as he headed for the gate. Burial grounds had always spoken to Ty in a way not many things did. This one in particular was a beautiful one. It was speaking to him too, telling him about their killer as he walked over the sodden grass toward the older tombstones.

Zane followed along behind him, eyes down. They walked in silence as the rain continued to patter through the trees above them.

The soaked ground was covered with yellow leaves, obscuring grave markers in places, highlighting them in others. Ty stopped under one of the trees and looked around at the aging stone in appreciation. He drew a sheet of paper from his pocket and studied it for a moment, then looked up into the distance, frowning.

When Ty paused, Zane almost ran into him. He was too busy taking in the yard around them; the wide variety of stones, the thoughts behind the monuments. It was very different here . . . different from what he'd expected.

The fall weather had turned the trees into brilliant colors, painting a normally dreary location with streaks of life. It was an odd dichotomy that made his chest ache even more.

Ty finally determined that they were in relatively the right spot, and he folded the paper and slid it back into his pocket. "This is it," he murmured.

They stood on the path that wound through the yard, near a set of family tombs, all lined up in neatly hewn squares. Zane didn't say anything. Instead, he waited to see what insights Ty might have. This side of the search wasn't something Zane had much experience with; he was trained to follow paper trails and details, not pick other people's thoughts and motivations out of thin air.

Ty was silent as Zane waited, walking around the site slowly with his head down. It was an entirely different side of him; a calm, collected one that seemed totally at odds with his usual abrasiveness. Zane could no longer tell which side of him was the real one.

"This has a reverence to it," Ty finally murmured curiously after almost ten minutes of silence and pondering. "Almost . . . romantic. There were no tire or machine marks anywhere, meaning he carried her here from the entrance." He looked back the way they had come. It was a long way to walk with a heavy burden in your arms. He looked back at Zane and frowned. "It feels old. Antiquated," he went on in a voice that sounded slightly confused. "Like something the killer saw in a movie or read in a book and wanted to reenact."

Zane had heard him, but it didn't really sink in at first. As he'd looked around the setting, turning his back to the monuments to look back out at the yard, a grave covered with stacks of fresh flowers had snared his attention. It was impossible not to draw parallels to his last time in a graveyard. Several heartbeats after Ty's words, Zane shook himself. "Yeah, yeah it does," he agreed quietly.

"None of the others seemed to be like that. Left in their own beds, dumped in random places," Ty murmured, talking more to himself than to Zane. "Why was this one special? Was it even special at all or is that just another different element we have to add to this particular murder?"

Blinking a few times, Zane pulled his attention back to his partner. "I'm not sure I'd say it was special. We don't even know if she was killed here or if she was moved here."

Ty glanced around the graveyard, trying to let the setting speak to him. "No," he murmured. "She wasn't killed here," he declared, though he didn't know what made him think that. "But she was left here for a reason, I'm sure of it."

"It would track then that all of them were left where they were . . . as they were . . . for a reason," Zane added, shifting his weight and taking several steps along the path before turning to look around them again.

"Not necessarily," Ty argued stubbornly. "You yourself said that the pattern is in the method. What if part of the method is the placement of the body in one case, but not in another? What if it mattered more where this body was left than how she was killed, but it mattered more that another was killed in a certain way and not where they were left?"

Zane's lips twitched. "You know, I actually understood that," he said, shaking his head. He took a deep breath and let it out slowly. "I guess we'll have to figure it out both ways until we get a lead," he offered.

Ty sneered at him and looked away, pursing his lips thoughtfully as he stared through the rain. It was coming down harder, sliding down the collar of his jacket and making him shiver. He had definitely lived through worse, but it was still uncomfortable.

The start of the rain gave Zane a chill, and his attention was drawn back to the graves. He watched the raindrops plop onto a bare patch of dirt, darkening it drip by drip. Rivulets dappled the colored flowers that were placed along some of the gravestones, and Zane's gaze went soft and unfocused. Rain on flowers. Wet dirt. The ache swelled and he couldn't ignore the memories any longer.

Ty turned back to say more and caught the look on Zane's face. He snapped his mouth shut and frowned. "Are you okay?" he asked again with a hint of annoyance.

The other man didn't acknowledge him. He was standing in the same place. He hadn't turned his head; it didn't even look like he'd taken a breath. His eyes were lowered and looking out at something indefinable.

"Garrett!" Ty barked loudly.

A few more silent moments passed before Zane looked up at Ty deliberately. His face was now set in the emotionless mask he'd not worn for a couple days, and his eyes were dry. But the light in them was gone, and his gaze was empty.

"What the hell, man?" Ty questioned in annoyance. "Are you okay?" he repeated.

"Have you found what you were looking for?" Zane asked. His voice was brittle, but he didn't look away from Ty.

Ty's brow furrowed in confusion and he cocked his head. He looked around the cemetery, knowing he could spend the entire dreary day there and still not find what he was looking for. But it was no use if Zane was going to go all wonky on him. "Sure," he finally answered. "Let's go."

Zane turned smartly on his heel and started walking.

Ty remained where he was for a moment and watched him in confusion. Finally, he bent and picked up one of the perfect yellow leaves and slid it into his pocket, then followed after his partner slowly.

The long, even strides didn't stop until Zane was through the gate and back out at the street, flagging down a cab. The first one kept going, and so he kept a sharp eye out. He still felt ill. It had come out of nowhere, the specter of memories five years old that he'd thought were just as buried as his wife.

Ty jogged to catch up to him as a second cab stopped at Zane's summons. They climbed in and shook off the water, and Ty gave the driver the name of their hotel. He had hoped to see more of the scenes, but he would rather do it alone than like this.

Five minutes into the ride, Zane finally closed his eyes and relaxed a little. He propped his elbow against the window and rubbed his eyes. God, he hated memories sometimes. They brought back nightmares he didn't want. Frankly, he didn't want the good or the bad, because the good were even worse. He knew Ty wanted to know what was going on, but Zane wasn't sure he could even spit out the words.

"Whenever you're ready, man," Ty prodded irritably.

Zane slanted an equally annoyed glance Ty's way. "Bad memories, okay?" he muttered.

Ty glared at him from his side of the cab for a moment and then looked away with a long sigh. Obviously there was more to it than that, and Ty found himself annoyed that he even gave a damn. He wouldn't ask again, though.

After another long silence, Zane gave a quiet sigh. "Becky died this time of year," Zane said quietly. "Weather's about the same. Fancy graveyard." He shrugged.

"Who is Becky?" Ty asked in exasperation.

Zane kept his eyes focused out the window. "My wife."

Ty stared at him for a long moment, eyes drifting down to the wedding ring Zane still wore but they'd never talked about, then he looked away without commenting. He pressed his lips together tightly as they rode in silence. "I'm sorry," he finally offered.

Nodding slowly, Zane finally said, "Thanks." It was almost inaudible. Ty didn't respond. His immediate reaction was to point out that if Zane had a fucking problem with graveyards he should have said something instead of wasting their time by zoning out in there. He would have been better off leaving Zane at the gate and taking his time. A day ago he would have said it out loud, but now he held his tongue. It was an action he wasn't accustomed to or comfortable with. Forcing himself not to say anything too harsh to the man fueled the resentment Ty felt building.

A few minutes passed. "Need to go back?" Zane asked neutrally.

Ty watched the architecture pass by and sighed inaudibly. "We'll see," he finally answered curtly.

Zane turned off the portion of himself that felt bad that he'd apparently messed with Ty's work. It just didn't compare to the thoughts and dreams and dying lights that swirled through his mind.

He'd need some time to clear those cobwebs away. Then he could get back to work.

The rest of the taxi ride passed in tense silence.

Chapter Seven

Ty was undeniably pissed off, and he spent the rest of the day distracted by it. The more distracted he became with his and Zane's little personal interactions, the angrier he found himself. They had a murderer to find and Ty had the death of a brother to avenge; he didn't need to be absorbed in this little fling they had started up. And he couldn't even shout at Zane to release the frustration anymore. It didn't seem right after what had happened between them. He wasn't used to being angry without an outlet, and it was wearing him down.

They had finally returned to Federal Plaza and given their accounts of what had happened with the exploding computer. They were questioned about the bruises both men displayed, and about why they had left the scene when they knew they would have to be questioned. Ty had been forced to put in a call to Dick Burns in order to get the disgruntled investigators off their backs, and they had been sent on their way.

The rest of the day had been spent at the hotel, combing over files and notes as they searched for a thread.

It was beginning to rain once more, the drops hitting the hotel window lazily when Ty finally put his work down and rested his elbows on the table. He rubbed his hands over his face and groaned plaintively. "Did we eat lunch?" he asked sulkily.

"Nope," Zane answered distractedly. He'd finally managed to sink himself in autopsy reports a couple hours ago, and that subject matter was more than enough to quash any physical urges: hunger, sex, or otherwise.

"Can we eat lunch now?" Ty asked sarcastically.

Zane threw down his pen with a soft sigh. "Sure," he agreed.

Ty leaned back in his chair, watching Zane studiously like he would a lion in the zoo. He was irritated with him, for more reasons than the fact that he had been made to leave his site early. Mostly, Ty was irritated because now when Zane did something, he found himself wondering why.

Pushing the file folders away before scooting back from the table, Zane stretched once he was standing, arms above his head, eyes closed as he rolled his neck. He'd been tense all morning, and sitting hunched over case files all afternoon hadn't helped either.

"Want to call it a day?" Ty asked neutrally.

Zane arched his back and several vertebrae popped. He relaxed in relief before opening his eyes. "I'll be fine after a break. All this shit is swimming around right now," he muttered with a wave of his hand at his head.

Ty merely nodded, watching Zane impatiently.

Zane returned the look impassively. "So. Room service? Going out?" The thought of a cigarette was reassuring, since it didn't look like he'd be having another fuck anytime soon. The fact that Ty was pissed was pretty easy to decipher.

Ty pressed his lips tightly together and cocked his head to the side thoughtfully. "Going out could be risky," he observed in a flat tone. "I haven't spotted a tail yet, but that doesn't mean we don't have one."

Zane nodded absently and walked over to the dresser where he'd tossed the hotel book with the menu in it. He'd thought Ty would want to get out and roam, as restless as the man obviously was. But he'd learned yesterday that there was no telling what Ty would do. Trying to anticipate him was an effort in futility, one that often produced a headache. He paged through the book where it lay on the top of the piece of furniture. Ty's eyes stayed on him as he moved. He seemed to be waiting for something. The silence stretched thin as Zane did his best to ignore it.

"Should I go back to my room tonight?" Ty asked out of the blue. "Or will we be able to work together and fuck each other senseless at the same time?"

Zane jerked his chin around to stare at Ty with wide eyes for a long moment. He opened his mouth to say something and closed it right back before trying again. "I can work with the fucking," he said. Jesus Christ, he sounded like an idiot!

Ty snorted. "Good," he said flatly, the smile dropping again. "As long as we keep it at that, we're fine."

Narrowing his eyes, Zane turned toward Ty, bringing the menu with him. "Keep it at that?" he asked curiously. Yeah, they seemed to have a hell of a lot of chemistry, and there had been a few scarily tender moments, but Zane knew better than to read anything into it.

"Right," Ty answered, either oblivious to the implied question or not caring to elaborate.

Rather than pushing for an answer, Zane held out the menu, but he kept his eyes on Ty, watching him.

"I'll take what I had last night," Ty answered as he looked down at the menu and back up at Zane with a small smirk.

The other man raised an eyebrow, giving Ty a look of wry amusement as he yanked the menu back. "I figured you'd want what you had for breakfast," he tossed out as he walked over to the phone.

Ty chuckled darkly, the sound almost disturbing as he sat in the shadowed corner of the hotel room and rocked back in his chair. He watched Zane, tracking him like a predator tracks its prey as the bigger man moved.

Zane dialed room service and ordered a couple dinners and a dessert—very aware of Ty's eyes following him. Murmuring a curt goodbye, he hung up the phone and sat back down at the table, pushing folders around and taking the opportunity to look at more autopsy photos before the food arrived. He studiously avoided looking at Ty. It was better for his mental health that way.

Ty cocked his head, idly wondering why Zane was so diligently ignoring him now. Finally he shrugged it off and pulled out a thick file from the package a courier had delivered from Washington earlier that day.

Ty had called on a buddy in the main office to search up any unexplained murders in the past ten years, and then had him fax a list. He had picked and chosen from the list of murders, requesting files that could possibly fit their case to try and track the man responsible.

He also had a stack of files on every agent that had worked in the New York office in the past ten years, including one on himself. He would go through them all after he finished with the old files, and he would make a list of the locations every agent had worked before being assigned to New York. All he had to do was find a murder that fit their serial, which was more easily said than done, considering the guy had no MO to speak of, and then match up locations.

"This shit is easier with a computer nerd doing the work," he grumbled around the pencil in his teeth.

Zane glanced up at him and snorted softly, then went back to his notes.

Ty looked up at him, frowning unconsciously, then back to the file he had in his hand. It was an unsolved murder in Baltimore from roughly five years ago. As he read, he began to frown harder and harder. "I know this," he murmured as he flipped through the pages. "Jesus, I remember this," he muttered to himself. "January nineteenth," he continued, not caring if Zane was paying attention to him or not.

The victim had been found on the campus of the University of Maryland's School of Law. He had died—after being dragged through the streets behind what appeared to have been a small, slow-moving vehicle of some sort—of alcohol poisoning. The really interesting thing that Ty had remembered from this case was the identity of the victim. He had been rumored to be Baltimore's infamous Poe Toaster, the man who had, since 1949, visited the grave of the author Edgar Allan Poe and toasted him with cognac. The visits, which had actually been observed by many in the city, had stopped after that year.

"Find anything interesting?" Zane asked as he watched.

Ty answered with a grunt. A piece of paper had joined the pencil in his mouth, the file spread on his knees, and each hand was holding several sheets of paper as he read over what he remembered. He waved at Zane and pointed down.

Zane smiled almost fondly before forcing it back, and he pulled the paper and pencil from between Ty's lips when he stopped at his side. He looked down at the file. "Maryland School of Law, huh?"

"I remember this," Ty said to him. "It has all the earmarks. Unfortunately it's just as random as all the new ones. But there was a token left," he said almost excitedly as he pointed at the notes in the original file. "A quill. We know he was in Baltimore," he declared in a voice that was almost surprised.

"If he was in Baltimore at the university, he could very well have applied to the Bureau straight out of school," Zane murmured. "Or he went into forensics or law enforcement and got familiar with the Bureau just because of proximity."

"We should cross-check all agents who were in Baltimore in '04," Ty suggested.

Zane nodded in agreement. "Sounds like it might be a break."

"Here," Ty grunted as he handed the file over. "Take a gander."

Zane took the file and moved back to his seat as he began to read over it.

"I remember that one happening," Ty told him as he stood up and began to pace. "It was labeled a hate crime kind of thing," he went on. "You see, the victim was this guy called the Poe Toaster. He was actually the grandson of the original Toaster, the man who would sneak into a graveyard every year on Edgar Allan Poe's birthday and toast him with cognac. Sometimes he left notes. Well, in ninety-nine this new guy started it after his father died, and he left more elaborate notes. One year he said that French cognac wasn't good enough for Poe; that was right after 9/11, I think, and the French had refused to join the terrorist hunt. Then in two thousand four he left a note saying the Ravens were going to lose the Super Bowl. It pissed a lot of people off."

"God, anything but NFL rivalries," Zane muttered. "So, alcohol poisoning—that takes a hell of a lot if it's a one-time thing, especially if he wasn't an alcoholic. It'd be more like drowning." He flipped through the pages, looking for the autopsy report.

"He was also dragged through the streets," Ty pointed out. "Left in the snow. But if it didn't matter who the victim was, like they initially thought, then the death itself is even more important."

"Odd combination of methods," Zane murmured, reading the report. "He wasn't an alcoholic. His liver was fine."

Ty watched Zane without responding. There were things about this case that were flitting at his mind, like bats around the mouth of a cave. They were driving him crazy, and he couldn't catch a single one. "Thoughts?" he asked softly.

"Either someone got him to drink a huge amount or he was injected," Zane said with certainty. He read over the report again. "But no tracks found."

"You think he knew his attacker?" Ty questioned softly.

Zane's brow furrowed. "No signs of struggle, except the marks from the ropes used to drag him. No scrapings under fingernails. He was already unconscious when he was dragged." Shaking his head, he let his eyes go out of focus. "I bet he did. I bet he knew him. Even trusted him. A friend or colleague. Someone to celebrate with, to drink more than usual with. Slip him a drug to make him pliable and apt to drink even more."

Ty was nodding in agreement. "It's the epicenter," he murmured. "I'll call Burns, tell him to have someone get on it."

"Tell him about the flagging we want done. Require Baltimore—hometown, school, even family," Zane said distractedly, still looking through the file.

"Uh-huh," Ty responded as he unclipped his phone from his belt.

As Ty talked, Zane got deeper into the file and, squinting, got up to shift stacks of papers for other case files on the desk. Ty relayed what they had uncovered to Burns as soon as he was assured the line was secure. The man seemed dubious about the Baltimore connection at first, but it didn't take long for Ty to convince him, Zane noted. As much of a fuckup as Ty seemed to have been in the Bureau, Burns had always trusted him and treated him almost like a son. Zane couldn't help but wonder why.

Soon, Ty was off the phone and pacing again. Finally he stopped and glared at Zane. "I'm hungry."

"Mm-hmm," Zane answered faintly, three case files laid out in front of him. Ty frowned and watched him.

"You find something?" he asked hopefully.

"No," Zane said, drawing it out since he was still reading. "I didn't. No struggle."

"What?" Ty asked in confusion.

"No struggle. No signs of struggle. Sometimes the victims were tied or wrapped up, but there were no bruises, no claw marks, no abrasions. No sign that they fought before they were murdered," Zane said, frown deepening as he grabbed for another file. "That can't be right."

"How is that possible?" Ty asked softly. "He can't have known all his victims. You think he's using a badge to keep them cooperating?"

"Why couldn't he have known them?" Zane asked calmly as he looked up.

"'Cause it'd be sorta obvious to his other acquaintances that they were slowly dwindling in gruesome ways," Ty snapped. "Unless they're professional contacts," he corrected slowly.

"Or a mix. Professional. Personal. Family. Past friends from school or college," Zane proposed.

"You know how unlikely that is?" Ty asked dubiously, unconsciously taking on the same tone Burns had with him. "Besides, I don't care how well I know someone, they start trying to chop me up I'm going to fight back," he declared.

"It's not probable. But it's possible. New York is a hell of a big city. You could have friends in all kinds of places and they'd never know each other," Zane said, closing the files and stacking them together.

"Oh, fuck you and your logic, Garrett," Ty sulked as he began to pace again.

"Give me geometry any day," Zane muttered. "I hate algebra."

Ty stopped. "We should check the victims for priors," he stated. "If the killer's a Fed, he might be finding his victims through his job."

"We need their workups. Priors, work, church, family, school . . . any one of those could be a connection. Hell, moonlighting. Boyfriend. Knitting circle," the other agent mumbled.

"We should also check witness files," Ty murmured. "They may not have been perps if he was investigating. Could have been witnesses. But no one's going to convince me that a badge could keep someone from fighting for their life."

"Chloroform," Zane said suddenly, pointing to the paper in front of him. "The ME notes traces of chloroform in some of the autopsies."

"That'll do it," Ty conceded with a frown.

"Yeah," Zane agreed, nodding. He jerked a little when there was a knock at the door.

"I got it," Ty muttered as he stood and began to shuffle barefoot to the door. The hairs on the back of his neck suddenly stood on end, and the feeling that something was amiss assaulted him like it sometimes had back when he was in the service. He slowed as he neared the door, evaluating the gut reaction to the knock and licking his lips as he hesitated. Finally, he stepped up to the peephole and peered through, his hand on the gun at the small of his back.

Zane stiffened as he saw Ty reach for his gun, and he picked up his own from the dresser right next to him. He watched carefully, staying just out of a direct line of sight from the door.

But Ty relaxed as he saw the hotel server outside with the food, and he wondered why he was so edgy. He opened the door and greeted the server without further alarm, and after the food had been placed and the server left, Ty looked at Zane and shrugged. "I'm a little tense," he admitted abashedly. It wasn't the first time he had said the words to Zane.

"More than a little." Zane looked at him evenly. "Don't ignore those instincts. Yours are sure to be better than mine."

"Shut up," Ty huffed immediately. He narrowed his eyes as he lifted the lid off his plate and he cut a glance at Zane and smiled. "Why do you think I'm sleeping in here with you?" he asked wryly. "'Cause I get skeered easily."

"Thought it was for my scintillating conversation," Zane said drolly.

"For your scintillating something, anyway," Ty responded distractedly as he sat down and pulled his plate to him.

Zane chuckled and took up his plate, but not until he snatched a fry off Ty's. He had mozzarella sticks instead of fries. He'd decided spur of the moment to pass on the onion rings. Just in case.

"Thief," Ty murmured sulkily.

Zane winked and held out a mozzarella stick to placate him.

Ty glared at it stubbornly and then snatched it out of Zane's hand. "Have you noticed anyone tailing us?" he asked before biting off the tip of the mozzarella stick and yipping as the hot cheese hit his tongue.

"Sure; I just didn't say anything because I'm an idiot," Zane answered flippantly.

"Jesus, you didn't tell me these damn things were nuclear," Ty grunted as he pulled the cheese out of the breaded exterior and tried to no avail to shake it off his finger.

"I figured the fact they were still steaming might be a clue," Zane drawled.

"Shut up," Ty muttered as he shifted in his seat, unconsciously betraying a bit of lingering soreness.

Zane's brow furrowed as he watched Ty move uncomfortably, and he blinked when he realized why. He was really hard-pressed not to grin, but his lips still twitched.

"Stop it," Ty muttered at him as he tried to eat the cooling cheese off his finger.

Zane very carefully schooled his face, though his eyes were still bright and dancing. He got the better of Ty so rarely, he couldn't let it go just yet. "Just let me know if you can't handle hot and spicy," he teased, taking another bite of the hot cheese stick. He was probably pushing his luck, but what the hell.

"Another bad pun, and I'm going to hit you," Ty warned.

Zane couldn't resist. "How do you know I wouldn't like it?"

Ty glared at him, pondering that question with narrowed eyes, reviewing Zane's persistence in that fight. The cell phone at his hip began to ring demandingly, probably saving Zane from another left hook to the chin.

Ty snapped it off his belt and looked down at the readout. He cursed as he flipped the phone open. "It's about fucking time," he groused into the phone as he set his plate down. "Are you Steve Number One or Steve Number Two?" he asked the detective on the line sarcastically.

"Hey," the man on the other end of the call protested. "We were just told about you guys, shithead. Don't start with me."

"We've been cooling our fucking heels for days!" Ty shouted as Zane pushed his plate away and got up to head for the bathroom.

"It's not my fucking fault you government boys need someone to hold your dicks for you," Detective Steve Pierce chastised. "How soon can you get here?"

"Give us thirty," Ty groaned as he pushed his own plate away and glanced toward the bathroom, hearing the water run. "No. Give us an hour," he corrected as he tried to calculate the afternoon traffic. He got up and began pacing as Zane walked back into the room and began pulling his shoes on.

Ty exchanged a few more words with Detective Pierce and then ended the call, flopping back onto his bed with a long, heartfelt groan.

"So. Did they even know we were here?" Zane asked knowingly.

"Said they found out this morning," Ty answered dubiously. "I'm really beginning to feel a little like a salmon here..."

"Swimming upstream? Yeah, I get that feeling too," Zane agreed as he pulled a plain gray dress shirt over his head and tucked it in. He stilled and looked Ty over. "You look exhausted," he said frankly. He hadn't noticed before, but Ty had the look of a man who had been burning both ends of the candle. "Have you been sleeping at all?" he asked worriedly.

"Don't take my insomnia personally," Ty responded wryly. "I don't."

Zane glanced up. "Insomnia." He frowned and went back to his boots. "Sorry," he said curtly. "I've heard it sucks."

"What?" Ty prodded as he saw the reaction.

"What what?" Zane asked, not looking up from his lacing.

"What was the look for?" Ty asked defensively.

Zane pushed away the threatening nerves and clamped down on his emotional reaction, one that came to the surface far too quickly for his liking. "There was no look," he said stubbornly.

"Bullshit," Ty huffed as he sat back up and leaned back on his hands.

Zane finished tying off the shoe and started in on the second, deliberately not looking up at all. He wasn't getting back into all the screeching-violins stuff. He'd finally fucked Ty into a somewhat human condition. No way did he want to ruin that. Zane already felt totally off-kilter—something he'd very much like to blame the other man for—and his handle on himself felt shaky. He hated feeling shaky. It reminded him too much of withdrawal.

Ty picked up a pillow and chucked it at him, hitting him on the top of the head as he bent over. Zane closed his eyes and growled dangerously deep in his throat. Okay, so maybe in human condition was a slight overstatement. He kept on lacing. Next thing, he predicted, Ty would accuse him of clamming up again.

"Fine," Ty sighed with a roll of his eyes as he pushed himself off the bed. "You wanna have an ulcer at forty, be my guest," he grumbled.

"Fuck off," Zane muttered. He'd missed out on the ulcers by some miracle, but he didn't remember his fortieth birthday. He wasn't sure he remembered any of that year, actually. He leaned on his knees and closed his eyes, head bowed. Zane wished he didn't remember the horrific and heart-wrenching dreams that had plagued him after Becky died. And he certainly didn't want to try to explain how he'd wished and wished and pleaded for insomnia, time and time again.

"Oh, Christ, not again, Garrett," Ty muttered in exasperation. "Really?" he asked incredulously. "Do we need to get a shrink in here for you?"

Anger flared, and Zane stood abruptly. "There's no goddamn shrink that can help me at this point, asshole. You want to know what I was thinking? I was thinking that there have been nights I would have taken insomnia for a blessing. Now, stick the fucking orchestra and get dressed so we can get out of here."

"Idiot," Ty hissed derogatorily. "You're so used to running and hiding from your problems you can't get your head out of your ass. You're letting your past run your life, and I'm getting fucking tired of it."

"And I suppose you have all the answers, Dr. Grady? Got that head-shrinking degree in your back pocket all nice and shiny? You have no idea what I've got in my past to deal with," Zane growled.

"And I don't wanna know," Ty stated with no compassion. "Past is the past for a reason."

"And some of us had a good enough one at some point to want to remember it, despite all the nightmares," Zane snapped back. "Until you understand what it means to have your head put in a goddamn blender while you try to hang on to something precious, quit giving me this shit."

Ty gaped at the man, wondering if he even had the right to bring up all the nights of hell he and his Recon boys had gone through over the years. If Zane knew the things he dreamed, he might not be complaining quite so much. Finally, he decided that this stupid argument wasn't worthy of bringing it up, and he waved his hand dismissively.

Zane blinked as Ty just blew him off. "Un-fucking-believable," he muttered, turning to start shoving his things in his pockets. He was working with an emotionally stunted asshole. Come to think of it, it explained so much. Zane had to swallow as much on the residual anger as on the pity he didn't dare let the other man see.

Ty changed quickly into something that wouldn't get him kicked out of the federal building. He stood in front of the bathroom mirror and shook his head angrily, muttering to himself. Zane was starting to piss him off again. Which was good, he supposed. It meant the urge to lick him all over was passing, at least. He took a deep breath and went stalking back out into the main room and grabbed for his leather jacket. Zane stood at the window, arms crossed, staring out at nothing while lost in thought.

"Back to brooding, I see," Ty observed wryly as he patted his chest down, making certain his guns weren't overly obvious before he shrugged into his jacket. "Better than actively whining, I guess."

Zane was silent for a moment longer before grunting and moving to the table to start stacking folders. "Yeah, well, I guess you haven't fucked it out of me yet," he muttered.

"Gonna take more than I could ever do," Ty shot back as he gathered his badge and wallet.

Shaking his head, Zane fell quiet again. He couldn't keep up the argument if he had any intention of conducting himself properly on the job. All it would take would be one good complaint back to Burns about his lack of professionalism. And as much as local cops hated Feds? Zane didn't want to take any chances. He shoved several files into a canvas briefcase and then reached for his gun.

It was going to be a long fucking day.

Chapter Eight

Detective Steve Pierce's gaze slid from his partner back across the table to Zane. "We've been on this case from the beginning. There isn't anyone else who can give you more information, and we got none. Talk to the coroner, maybe. Or that lady profiler of yours, Scott."

"We've spoken to Scott," Ty told him with a curl of his lip. "We don't want to be told what's happened. We want to be told what you think. Here's your big chance to let us know you actually have synapses firing."

The detective leaned back in his chair, eyes flickering from Ty to Zane, sitting across the table from him. He crossed his arms stubbornly and regarded them silently.

Zane's eyes narrowed ever so slightly, and he looked away from Pierce, instead addressing Holleman. "You've been to all the scenes. Surely you have some sort of feeling worked out about all this."

Ty rolled his eyes and looked away, his attention wandering to the wanted posters on the walls. He despised these men. Cops he liked, on a whole. Sometimes, he thought he would have been better as a cop than a Fed. But these two men in particular were complete dicks.

"You wanna hear my feeling?" Holleman responded with hostility. "My feeling is that you people are so concerned with your meetings and paperwork that you're wasting our time with them. We could be out there right now—"

"Yeah, you've been doing a bang-up job so far, Steve," Ty drawled without looking away from the nearest poster.

Zane would have laughed if he weren't already so annoyed. These two assholes had been jerking them around for almost an hour now, making snide remarks about the victims and even more insulting comments about the FBI's operation. "The only reason we're in this meeting is to try to get some help. Like Pierce said, you've been here the whole time. No one else knows more about the case. The sooner you fill us in, the sooner all of us can be out there."

Pierce smiled smugly. "All right, then, I'll give you the rundown. Some of these cases are a serial, sure. But not all of them. How's that for insight?"

"Which ones don't you think fit?" Ty demanded.

"The drug addict, for one. The hooker, for sure. And the other two girls, the roommates. We did some digging; turns out they got around quite a bit," Pierce told them.

The hand Zane had on his thigh below the table clenched into a whitened fist. "Got around, huh?" he asked, voice deceptively quiet. Earlier comments about victim carelessness had been bad enough. This was enough to make Zane's blood boil.

"So what?" Ty asked nonchalantly, not even registering his partner's annoyance. "They got around. So did your momma, but nobody dyed her hair purple and suffocated her."

Pierce's face twisted. "Asshole," he snarled. "They got around a lot more than any self-respecting college girls ought to," he insisted.

"Christ." Ty laughed incredulously. "Have you been to a college campus lately?" he asked.

"We figure they were out hooking casual," Pierce continued, undeterred, "and just got the wrong guy to take home. Fits."

"What makes you think they were hooking?" Ty asked as he leaned forward and cocked his head.

"Client list," Pierce grunted.

"Otherwise known as an address book?" Ty asked wryly.

"Fuck you, Grady," Pierce snarled.

Zane could feel the fury just roiling in his stomach as his teeth ground together. He directed his question to Holleman. "Are you sure you don't want to add something constructive to this conversation, to oh, I don't know, make it worth more than a waste of oxygen?"

"Unlike you two lovebirds, my partner and I tend to agree on these things," Holleman answered calmly.

"So," Ty said loudly as he leaned forward in his seat. "You decided the two co-eds were hooking. That's wonderful. Did you write them off immediately or did you attempt to track their relatively small circle of 'casual clients,' as you call them, and include it in the cross-reference done on all the acquaintances of the victims?" he asked pointedly.

"Waste of time," Pierce insisted. "Those so-called serial tokens—a real slim thread of shit holding these cases together, by the way—the one found with the girls was obviously a rip-off. Little plastic trinket rings. I mean, come on. Probably the guy got his rocks off, did a copycat, and went jonesing for another whore."

"A copycat?" Ty repeated with a predatory smirk. "You mean you released that detail to the public? That he leaves meaningless tokens with his kills?" he drawled knowingly.

Pierce stopped mid-breath. "I didn't say that," he barked.

"Actually, yes, you did," Zane snapped, unable to keep quiet any longer. "Just like you said you blew off common procedure for connecting murder cases."

"Fuck off, Garrett. You got no idea what NYPD procedures require," Pierce snapped.

"Yeah, IQ over forty probably helps," Ty drawled in amusement.

Holleman held out a hand and glared at them. "Shut up, wiseass. The tokens have not been released to the general public, all right?" he told them.

"At least you've done something intelligent," Zane muttered. He knew he was quickly losing hold of his temper.

"Something better than you two assholes, trying to lord it up over here in this ivory tower," Pierce snarled at Ty. "If you and your little paper-pusher here even got out on the street to see a scene, I'd probably have a heart attack and die."

"Promise?" Ty responded calmly. In contrast to the other men, Ty seemed to actually be enjoying the meeting, and that was just making the two detectives angrier. "Look, despite the fact that you're idiots and I'm bored, we're all working at the same thing here. You arrange for us to see some more scenes, we'll consider your theory about a copycat," he bargained. "Even though it's fucking stupid," he added after a brief pause.

Pierce looked between the two men facing him before answering. "You know, Grady? You're more annoying than I remember. You make Garrett here feel like a walk in the fucking park," he said, almost pleasantly. "The Bureau had to dig real deep, I guess. You want to see the scenes? You go through the chief's office and request access like everyone else."

Holleman sighed slightly, shaking his head and closing his eyes. "Look, even if we could personally grant you access, which we can't," he was careful to inform the FBI agents as Pierce grew more and more ornery, "all of the scenes have long been released. There's nothing to see anymore."

His stubborn partner sat back, looking like he was chewing on a lemon.

"There's nothing for you to see," Ty corrected with a pleasant smile.

"You can't tell me you think you've got some special skills or something to let you re-create a goddamn murder scene weeks or months old," Pierce scoffed, his skepticism clear.

"He's got skills you couldn't learn even with a cattle prod up your ass," Zane said, temper boiling.

Ty glanced at Zane but remained silent. He was slightly surprised to hear Zane defending him, and not a little flattered, but he didn't want Zane snapping, not here.

"Oh, how touching," Pierce said with a goading laugh. "I got no reason to like you, Garrett, much less trust you and your skilled partner. You two Feebs come riding in here like Hell's Angels expecting to pick up our cases and magically solve them. Well, I'm calling your bluff. No access to scenes, no goodwill, and no sharing of information. You want to chase off and try to find whoever those girls were fucking, you do it without us."

His blood pressure rocketing, Zane stood up so fast his chair slammed back and hit the floor. "I need some fresh air," he muttered as he stalked past the detectives to the door and walked out, letting it shut loudly behind him.

Holleman watched the man storm out and then turned to Ty with a raised eyebrow. "Never thought I'd see the day when you were the calm part of the equation," he remarked in amusement.

"Yeah, well. I'm the calm one, you're the smart one," Ty sighed as he stood slowly. "Yes, Virginia, there is a Santa."

Pierce sat back with a satisfied chuckle. "What'd you do to get stuck with that fucking suit?" he asked Ty.

Ty walked around the table slowly, hands in his pockets as if he were idly wandering the room. He stopped behind Pierce's chair and bent over him, placing a not-so-friendly hand on his shoulder. The man stiffened nervously, turning his head slightly as if he expected Ty to actually hurt him. "Be seein' y'all later," Ty drawled in a low, friendly voice before he straightened back up and left the room.

Pierce relaxed and gave a small sigh, shaking his head in annoyance.

As soon as Ty had closed the door behind him, Holleman turned in his chair and glared at Pierce. "I know it's fun to poke them, but Christ, man, what the hell?" he asked.

Pierce snorted and waved his partner off. "They needed to be knocked off those damn high horses they always ride in on. But hey, at least we don't have to worry about a serious Fed investigation."

Holleman frowned and shook his head. "I don't know. Grady doesn't seem to give a shit, but Garrett seemed pretty . . . into it."

Pausing, Pierce turned to eye his partner. "Don't let him fool you. I've had the rundown from Serena Scott on that one. Garrett used to be slightly useful, but now he's got a bad record and gets shuffled around. He's probably blowing somebody in DC."

"Or he fucked Serena and ran off so she's pissed," Holleman pointed out in amusement. "Look, whatever. I don't know about you, but I'm more than happy to hand this over to them. Let them chase their tails with this whack-job so we get back to our real jobs."

"But they're our cases in our backyard, and I don't want them out there screwing around," Pierce insisted.

Holleman frowned slightly. "Why not?" he asked curiously.

Pierce's shoulders stiffened, and his face darkened. "'Cause Feebs don't belong on the street. They make us all look bad, that's why. And Garrett's a prick."

"So are you," Holleman laughed fondly. "Come on. I'm hungry."

Pierce muttered under his breath and followed his partner out.

Zane pushed roughly through the reading room door, ramming it back against the wall as he stalked in, immediately pulling out his cigarettes and lighting up. No smoking policy be damned, he thought darkly. After such a piss-poor day, he figured he deserved something for not going totally postal up there.

After the first cigarette, he stopped long enough to light another and kicked a chair for good measure, sending it clattering across the room.

Ty took his time following, visibly irritated enough that people got out of the way as he walked through the halls. He opened the door to the reading room—the only place he really knew to look—and was just in time to watch the little tantrum silently.

"What the hell do you want?" Zane growled as he flicked ashes onto the industrial-grade carpet. He didn't have to be polite to Ty. He didn't even have to be civil.

"What's the problem?" Ty asked calmly, sliding his hands into the pockets of his khaki pants and leaning against the doorway.

Zane turned his back to Ty to stare at the whiteboard. Some of their notes were still written on it from the day the computer exploded. He forcibly calmed himself and buttoned up the anger and frustration. "They're assholes. That's the problem."

"I'll tell them to go play in another sandbox, then," Ty responded wryly.

"They shouldn't even be in the one they've got if they're so blasé and uncaring as to suggest two young women deliberately lured the killer to their house for sex," Zane spit out.

"That's how they're programmed to think," Ty responded in a patient voice.

The unusually placid sound of Ty's voice did the trick. Against Zane's will—because he really wanted to stay angry—the heat drained out of him, replaced by a hollow chill. "I just kept thinking," he said quietly, "about how scared those girls must have been. And here they are sitting and laughing and making light while that bastard is out there, probably picking out his next victim." He gave his head a tiny shake, taking another long drag on the cigarette.

"Wait till he kills a few men in blue. Then they'll be all over it," Ty responded in the same calm, almost uncaring tone.

Zane snorted and shook his head, taking another long drag. "Did they say anything after I left?"

"Nothing about you, no," Ty answered shortly. Looking over his shoulder, Zane raised a brow in question. Ty simply shrugged negligently and half-turned as if he was going to leave. "Food."

Grinding his teeth, Zane dropped the cigarette, ground it under his shoe on the carpet, and followed along, chewing on his annoyance and trying to shove it where the sun didn't shine so he could be Mr. FBI again. He wasn't all too sure he would be successful.

Ty strolled easily down the hall and glanced over his shoulder finally as he felt Zane catch up to him. "They enjoy getting in your craw, y'know," he advised neutrally.

"Yeah," Zane muttered. "I used to be better about shrugging it off. Off my game."

"No shit," Ty responded wryly.

Zane suddenly grinned. "Fuck off."

"Sit on it and spin," Ty shot back as he pushed through a pair of security doors.

"More your style lately," Zane sniped.

Ty stopped short, then he snorted and smiled slightly. "Got me," he snickered good-naturedly.

Zane chuckled, relief washing through him after the stressful day, and pulled out the car keys. "Have to catch up; I'm behind," he said with a shrug. He hit the key fob button as they approached from across the garage.

A few moments later and a few steps closer, the car exploded in front of them.

The bomb set off a chain of reactions that Ty observed in a detached sort of "I think my arm is on fire" manner after they both hit the concrete. Car alarms began to scream, sprinklers overhead kicked on as the flames from the wreck of the car licked at the cement ceiling, alarms blared inside the government building behind them, and bits of flaming plastic and bent metal rained down amidst the smoke. Soon, they heard running footsteps—dress shoes smacking on cement—and shouts from voices Ty didn't recognize as sirens began to wind up in the distance.

Zane shook his head as he sat up. "Fuck. This just got a hell of a lot worse," he muttered as he turned to his side to look at Ty, flat on his back. "You okay?"

All Ty could do to respond was close his eyes and let his head loll to the side. The thick leather of his jacket had saved his arm from a piece of smoldering shrapnel and it smelled like burning cow. He couldn't seem to form words or thoughts.

"Shit. Who decided we were taking turns?" Zane plucked the leather at Ty's arm; it appeared to have survived, though it was scorched. He slid an arm under Ty's back and helped him sit up. "I'm thinking the same disappearing act as the other day is a good idea," he urged. "That was our car."

Ty sat staring at the flaming vehicle as blood began to trickle down his neck. He shivered and lowered his head. "Help me up," he requested hoarsely.

Zane nodded and got to his feet before crouching to help Ty, and he caught sight of the blood. "Ty? You hit your head? Something hit you?"

Ty turned his head obediently for Zane to look and closed his eyes, shivering again. The blood already matted his hair and covered the entire back of his neck.

Zane's lips compressed and he took Ty's arm. "Come on," he said, pulling Ty up and along toward the side stairwell, away from where anyone would appear as they came to investigate. The fact that Ty didn't protest being led anywhere should have caused Zane more worry. The injured man practically kept his eyes closed as they moved. It was obvious his head was swimming, and the blood flowing down his neck was working its way under his collar and down his back.

Getting them inside the stairwell, Zane held Ty up against the wall while looking back through the small window as agents swarmed into the garage, yelling and circling. Frowning, he got Ty's arm over his shoulder and walked him down the steps to the ground floor. He helped Ty sit on the bottom step and touched his cheek, trying to get his attention. "Ty? Stay here. I'm going to get us a car, okay?"

Ty cleared his throat and blinked up at Zane, narrowing his eyes. "I think I might need a doctor, man," he rasped slowly.

"I'll take you to an emergency room, without other agents around. Stay here, okay?" Zane said intently, holding Ty's chin.

"Yeah," Ty muttered, afraid to nod for fear of his head spinning faster.

Zane moved quickly and with a purpose, making no pretense at hiding. The clerk in the key cage was gone, so Zane grabbed the first keys he saw. Once in the motor pool, he hit the unlock button and saw the flashing headlights of a mid-size SUV. Soon, he brought it to a halt at the stairwell and climbed out to get Ty. When he got back into the stairwell, he found Ty on the stairs where he'd left him, unconscious. Tim Henninger crouched next to him with his hand on his shoulder, supporting him. The younger agent was still bandaged from the explosion in the records room, his face and arms cut and stitched in places. His head was lowered, trying to look into Ty's face as he slid his hand into his jacket, apparently reaching for a phone to call for help.

Henninger turned and half-rose when the door opened, tensing, and then relaxed slightly when he saw Zane, who stopped in place, eyes narrowed. "Henninger. We're getting out of here," he said as he knelt in front of Ty and slid his arm under his partner's. The movement seemed to rouse Ty slightly, and his hand clutched in the material of Zane's jacket. "Keep your mouth shut about it."

"What the hell?" Henninger questioned. "Look, he's hurt. Why don't we get the EMTs down here and—"

"Because it's too risky. I'll take him to an emergency room. Now, are you going to help or not?" Zane asked in a flat, no-nonsense tone as he helped Ty to his feet, worried when the other man didn't even look up at him.

"Too risky?" Henninger asked as he followed them through the door. "What the fuck is wrong with you two? Let them take care of him!"

"No," Zane said as he got Ty to the passenger side. "You're going up there and telling them we walked for coffee and were nowhere near that car, you got it?"

Henninger opened the door, hand gripping the side of it until his knuckles turned white. "But why? They're going to know it's your car," he said logically.

"Yeah, and by then, we'll be where no one can get at us," Zane said as he practically lifted Ty into the back seat of the SUV.

"You think someone in the Bureau is trying to kill you?" Henninger asked incredulously, brows nearly up into his hairline.

"It might not be a bad idea for you to hide out for a while after this too," Zane said without answering the question. "You were too close to that computer."

Henninger blanched and repeated himself. "You really think someone from inside's trying to kill you? But that means they'd have to know why you were really sent here."

"And now you see the problem," Zane answered, shutting the door carefully. He turned to the other agent. "But right now, kid, you're the only person I trust besides him," he said with a jerk of his head at Ty, who had slumped in the back seat. "Look, call my cell phone once they pick apart that car and let me know what they find, okay? There's obviously someone on the inside helping, if nothing else."

Henninger's face went hard as he followed Zane around the SUV. "Got it," he murmured in a low voice.

Zane nodded and climbed into the truck. Before closing the door, he stuck out his hand, which Henninger shook. "Take care of yourself. Get Morrison to watch your back."

Henninger nodded. Zane shut the door and drove out of the garage, leaving Henninger behind to cover for them. By the time the SUV hit daylight, Ty was unconscious.

Carrying his bloody partner into the emergency room didn't even raise any eyebrows until Zane was able to flash his badge, and then everyone got busy, fast. Ty had a nice crack on the head; a long, thin gash that had bled badly but didn't even need more than a few stitches, and some minor burns and bad bruising down his arm. Aside from the unpredictable head wound, the worst injury was to his rib cage. Nothing was broken, but he had pulled muscles and suffered deep, painful bruises along the intercostals that would impede his movement for quite some time. Weeks, definitely. Possibly months, the doctor had told Zane.

Zane sat in a chair, leaning over with his elbows on his knees next to the bed where Ty sprawled, hooked up to an IV and all kinds of monitoring equipment. He needed to get them out of here soon. Since he'd used his badge to get in, word would get back to the office sooner rather than later. The admitting doctor had insisted on keeping Ty overnight, to watch the concussion and make certain it didn't turn ugly. They had kept Ty awake most of the night, and it had made him very cranky, very sulky, and very difficult to deal with. Even more so than he usually was. Now he dozed as Zane waited impatiently for the doctor. He checked his watch yet again just as the doctor walked in.

"He's got a little internal damage, swelling in the skull that might bother him a few days, and a nice, big lump on the outside," the doctor offered before Zane could even question him. "He got his bell rung, but he seems to be doing okay, other than the pain. Take him home, put an ice pack on it. Keep an eye on him, keep him up for an hour or two before you give him pain meds, just in case. If he doesn't need the pills, don't give them to him. I'm talking writhing in agony pain," he said sternly. "And keep him in a nice quiet place for a few days until that swelling goes down. A head injury like this can turn bad quickly, though, so like I said, keep an eye on him. If there's pronounced dizziness, blurring of vision, slurring, shakes, confusion, nausea and so on, call an ambulance. That swelling in his head is the worst problem, and it might cause some memory issues. Any questions?" he asked. Zane shook his head silently. "I'll have an orderly in to help him out, then," the doctor said.

Zane stood, shaking his head. "No, just clear the hall, and I'll get us out of here."

The doctor scowled and inclined his head stubbornly. "Either he leaves here in a wheelchair attended by an orderly," he said calmly, "or he doesn't leave at all."

Zane's nostrils flared angrily. "I'll make you a deal," he grated. "I'll push him, and your orderly can follow along behind."

The doctor narrowed his eyes and nodded, removed Ty's IV, and skirted around the curtain to start the paperwork.

Figuring he'd try to make a quick escape, Zane shook Ty's shoulder lightly, bending over close to the other man's ear. "Ty? You want to wake up so we can get out of here?"

Ty turned his head slightly, his temple nudging Zane's chin as he groaned in answer. "Just leave me here with the drugs."

Zane chuckled. He knew they hadn't given Ty anything for the pain because of the concussion, but Ty wouldn't know any different as out of it as he was. "I've got a couple pocketfuls of drugs to keep you happy," Zane crooned to him. "Let's get you up, big boy." He slid his arm under Ty's shoulders and started to slowly lift him to a sitting position.

Ty swatted at him, shivering as his head throbbed. "You sure it's good to move me?" he asked dubiously as he swung his legs off the bed. He wasn't typically too bothered with injuries, but getting conked on the head and losing time bothered him. He couldn't remember a thing from the time he'd walked out of the doors of the Federal building until he woke in the hospital. "Quit touching me," he muttered with a weak swat at Zane's hands. "Isn't there supposed to be a pretty little nurse getting me out of bed? I think you scared the doctors into releasing me," he accused as an orderly wheeled in a wheelchair.

"Sure I did. Because I'm a big, scary guy," Zane said with a note of pride.

"That's not entirely a good thing," Ty grumbled as he stood carefully and shuffled over to the wheelchair. He had seen men try to refuse the wheelchair ride out of the hospital before. Most were macho idiots, and many of them wound up doing a face plant into the floor for their troubles. Ty had never seen the point. Even if he had been the type, though, he knew he couldn't walk a straight line right now anyway.

Zane chuckled as he walked out alongside the chair, his insistence on doing the pushing having dissolved as soon as Ty spoke again, though he kept a sharp eye on their surroundings, just in case. They walked out the entrance where he'd had the hospital valet pull up the SUV in anticipation of loading Ty into it. "It's bed rest and an ice pack for you tonight," he said as the orderly helped Ty into his seat.

"Ice pack," Ty sneered. "A fucking ice pack, that's all I get?" he asked incredulously. "This is a serious head wound," he insisted with a gesture to the back of his head and an insulted look. "It needs at least a sponge bath."

"You barely even got stitches, you big baby," Zane said as he reached over to help with the seat belt once the orderly shut the door.

"Feels like my brains are leaking out my ears," Ty grumbled as he watched Zane's hands. "Do I really have to be buckled in?" he asked with some amusement.

"Yes, you do," Zane said doggedly. He buckled his own belt and drove away from the hospital, eventually bypassing their own hotel and moving into a slightly ritzier block.

"New digs?" Ty asked distantly as he watched the scenery pass by. He winced and turned his head away from the window.

"Sort of. I figure there's a couple real nice, upscale rooms already waiting with our names on them that no one would think to look in," Zane said.

Ty nodded absently. "Good thinking," he mumbled. "No new rooms with our names to give anyone a lead."

Zane nodded, almost disappointed that his forethought hadn't warranted more of a reaction from Ty. "I'll go get our stuff after dark while you rest," he said as he pulled into a parking spot in the hotel's parking garage.

"Shouldn't go alone," Ty reminded, though his voice still had the slightly detached tone to it.

"I'll be careful. Let's go," Zane said after he parked and shut off the engine. "You need to get horizontal."

"Not the best pickup line I've ever heard, but it'll do for now," Ty responded, his voice lighter again, if not still slightly groggy.

Zane made sure he followed along as he went to the front desk at the Tribeca Grand and checked in. The slow, distracted way Ty was moving and looking around at his surroundings as he trailed along behind made him look slightly like Rain Man, and Zane had to fight hard not to laugh at the image. Soon he was leading Ty to the elevator. They zipped up several floors and moved down a richly appointed hallway, where Zane opened the door to an executive suite.

"Nice digs," Ty muttered as he stopped in the entryway of the minimalist guest room and narrowed his eyes. "Bureau went all out on us, huh?" he asked as he looked at the bedroom longingly.

Zane dropped the key cards on the low wooden table in front of a swank white padded couch. "Why don't you go lay down, and I'll get you some ice for that bump. And some codeine, if you want. Doc said you were okay to take painkillers after a few hours."

Ty swallowed as he looked around before finally meeting Zane's eyes. "I'd rather be aware when we go back to get our things."

Zane held his gaze for a long moment, and then nodded slowly. "All right. Go on," he nodded toward the bedroom and grabbed the ice bucket, heading out the door with key card in hand. He made sure the door shut behind him.

As soon as the door clicked, Ty carefully reached his hand up to the back of his head and gingerly prodded at the goose egg there. He winced as pain lanced through his head, and when he brought his hand back to his side it was trembling slightly from the pain. Slowly, he made his way to the bed, and he crawled into it and burrowed under the layers of soft chocolate-colored sheets as he admitted defeat for the day.

It was only a few minutes before Zane returned. He shut, locked, and latched the door before pulling off his jacket, knives, and gun. He filled the heavy plastic bag that came with the bucket half full of ice and carefully crunched the ice on the carpet, not making too much noise. He wrapped it in a towel and walked to the bedroom. Ty was obviously under the sheets and high-thread-count blankets. Setting the ice pack aside, Zane started peeling back layers. A soft groan met his efforts, and finally he uncovered Ty, who hadn't even bothered to take off his jacket.

"Ty," Zane sighed under his breath. The other man looked miserable. "Come on, sit up and get some of your clothes off. You'll be a hell of a lot more comfortable." He helped Ty sit up and started pulling off the ruined jacket first.

Ty huffed and whimpered softly as the jacket was removed, his sore arm and ribs protesting. "Want out of the rest?" Zane asked quietly as he sat back down at Ty's side.

"Fuck," Ty groaned. "Just let me be miserable, okay?" he requested grumpily.

"Okay," Zane said soothingly. "Lie back down and turn on your side—bump up, of course," he said, smiling a little.

"Shut up," Ty huffed even as he obeyed the directive. Zane didn't answer the barb, instead lifting the ice pack and settling it carefully over the swollen area of the back of Ty's skull and holding it there. The hair was still matted with dried blood. Ty hissed in protest and closed his eyes, shivering hard.

Zane rubbed his free hand along Ty's shoulder and side, just behind the bruises; he didn't want Ty jerking around in pain. "Want anything to eat or drink? I'm supposed to keep you awake at least a couple more hours," he said.

"Ugh," Ty answered pitifully. All he wanted to do was sleep.

"I know. Been there. How about you hang onto this ice, and I'll call out for some room service? Got any favorite foods that might keep your attention?" Zane asked as he clasped Ty's shoulder.

"No," Ty murmured as he closed his eyes.

Sighing, Zane got to his feet. He snapped on both lamps and turned on the HD television, pumping up the volume on what looked to be a violent action movie. He tugged on the toes of Ty's boots as he walked by. "No sleeping," he reminded.

"Mmkay," Ty mumbled as he pushed his head under his pillow and promptly began to drift off.

Zane looked down at him and yanked away the pillow and then all the covers. "Ty, I mean it. Do not go to sleep," he said firmly.

"Nap Nazi," Ty accused miserably.

"Yeah, sure, hate me for wanting to make sure you don't go into a coma," Zane said as he nudged Ty's lower back. "Now sit up, and don't forget the ice pack."

"Look, Florence Nightingale, blasting the TV on a guy with a headache is just cruel," Ty pointed out grumpily.

Zane waved him off and walked into the front room to find the menu before returning to the bedroom. Ty sat cross-legged on the bed, but his head was lowered as he held the ice to the back of it, and his eyes were closed. His brow unconsciously furrowed in pain.

Zane sighed quietly and dropped the menu on the nightstand. He grabbed the remote and clicked off the TV, then sat on the edge of the bed slightly behind the other agent. "Here, let me," Zane murmured, lifting his hand to touch Ty's on the ice pack. "Sure you don't want something to take the edge off?" he asked quietly.

"I told you," Ty mumbled, the words barely audible, "if you're going back there, so am I."

Scooting back a little, Zane pulled Ty back against his chest, still holding the ice pack. "It'll wait," he murmured.

Ty shuddered as he leaned back, but he was too hurt and tired to protest being coddled.

"Come on, tough guy, I'm sure you've had worse than this."

"My head hurts, jackass," Ty muttered, his eyes staying closed as he rested back against Zane's chest.

Zane smiled, knowing Ty couldn't see him. "Does it hurt worse than your ass?"

"Shut up," Ty whined, diving into a sulk like a pro. "Jesus, just stop fucking talking."

Zane chortled. "You can't win, heads or tails." He curled one arm around Ty's waist to hold him securely. "Buck up, Marine; you're made of sterner stuff."

"Bite me, Air Force," Ty groaned as he tried to turn onto his side and curl up.

Zane grinned and turned so Ty could lean sideways against him. "Tell me something, Ty. How much of this badass bastard is really you, how much is the Marine, and how much is a show?" he asked.

Ty was silent, the only sound his soft breathing as he lay unmoving. Finally, he breathed in deeply and asked groggily, "Are you taking advantage of a concussion to pump me for information?"

"Damn straight," Zane said immediately.

After a long moment Ty simply gave an admiring, "Nice."

Zane smiled a bit and lifted away the ice pack to look at the head wound. "Learned it from you."

"Not a complete loss, then," Ty murmured.

"Nope," Zane said as he turned over the ice and reapplied it gently. "Not at all. I would never have thought it, but there you go."

"Hmm?" Ty asked drowsily as the ice started him shivering again.

"Ty," Zane said warningly, a little louder. He set down the ice pack, took the other man by the shoulders, and pulled him up into an upright position. He sat beside him as he turned his shoulders and ducked his head to try to catch Ty's eyes. "Don't you go to sleep on me. I mean it. I'll do evil and dastardly things to your body if you do."

Ty opened his eyes wide and blinked the sleep away, giving his head one little shake as he cleared his throat. "You've already done that," he reminded Zane seriously.

"I'm glad you remember," Zane said wryly. "You did recently take a knock to the head."

"Just let me fucking sleep, huh? They kept me awake all fucking night, you sadist," Ty groused sleepily as he closed his eyes.

"Damn it, Ty, don't make me shake you. Jesus. All right. Cold shower time," Zane said, practically dragging Ty with him off the bed and toward the bathroom.

"No!" Ty cried in alarm as he dug his heels in. "Hell, no!" Zane ignored him, pulling him along into the large tiled bathroom. Ty kicked the back of his thigh and tugged at his arm, determined not to get a cold anything.

Shamelessly exploiting Ty's slight weakness, Zane wrapped both arms around him, pulling him against his chest. "Are you awake now?" he asked, trying not to laugh.

"Yes," Ty whimpered pitifully. Zane grasped his chin and tilted it up to look at his eyes, looking at the pupils in the brighter light. Ty just blinked at him miserably, allowing the manhandling without so much as a frown.

"You're looking a little better," Zane said. "So no cold shower. But you do get to sit over here and let me wash the blood off," he said, plucking at the stained shirt.

"Peroxide gets the blood out," Ty offered, not thinking that peroxide would be slightly difficult to come by right then.

"Sure thing," Zane said indulgently. "But warm water will be fine for your neck and back." Zane led him over to the cushioned chair at the stainless-steel counter and got him sitting before going to the sink to soak a washcloth. "Haven't you ever had a concussion before?" he asked.

Ty finally cracked a slightly tired, mischievous smile and answered, "Not that I can remember."

Zane grinned over his shoulder as he wrung out the rag. "Shirt off, please."

Ty groaned, smile faltering as he shrugged out of his bloody shirt with difficulty. He examined it with a distant frown. It was a plain brown shirt with crossed paddles on the front in white. The words read, Schitt Creek Paddling Co. The white of the letters was marred with dried, dark blood stains.

"What?" Zane asked as he walked over and started wiping the crusted blood off Ty's neck.

"I like this shirt," Ty answered softly.

Zane looked down at Ty's hands and just kept wiping. "I'd rather have the shirt be bloody than you."

Ty frowned as he looked at the dried blood and felt Zane's gentle swipes clean the back of his neck. Finally, he looked down, finding a spot of interest on the floor instead, and he asked, "Were you worried?"

Zane pressed his lips together, deciding what to say that would offend Ty the least. "Nah. You're tough. I knew you could handle it." But his voice was soft, no edge or joking to it. Ty's expression was hidden from him, and the only response Zane could see was Ty's head lowering so the cloth could slide more easily against his neck.

Rubbing gently, especially close to the wound, Zane took care of the rest of the blood he could reach. At the last moment, he sighed, leaned over, and pressed his lips to the back of Ty's neck. "There you go," he murmured, unable to explain the unusual gesture.

Ty lowered his head further and shivered again, finally turning his head to brush his cheek against Zane's.

"Are you cold?" Zane asked, frowning a little, but rubbing his cheek lightly against Ty's in return.

"Quit rubbing cold water over me and I won't be," Ty murmured in answer, his head turning just a little bit more until his lips moved against Zane's skin.

The wet cloth was still warm in his hand, but Zane pulled it away from Ty's neck anyway, carefully not moving. He closed his eyes as he held still, letting Ty do as he liked. Ty's entire body trembled as the cool air hit the wet skin on the back of his neck.

Feeling Ty shiver again, Zane went down on one knee beside him. He wasn't sure what to think. Zane knew a concussion could make you really feel off—Lord knows he'd had enough of them himself—but the shivering was new. Maybe Ty was still hurting? He had a lot of injuries to deal with, and being in pain could do odd things to your body. "I feel like I'm not helping a lot here. Warm shower?" he suggested.

"That's a big change from the hard-ass cold-shower threats," Ty muttered.

Zane smiled fondly. "Worked, didn't it?"

Ty groaned and closed his eyes, leaning over until his chin rested on top of Zane's head. He closed his eyes, fully prepared to sleep just like that.

Zane sighed. Ty could be so damn difficult to deal with, mainly because even when he was being stubborn it was almost endearing. "Up you go. You need to stay awake at least another half hour. Lord. How am I going to entertain you for that long?"

"Shadow puppets?" Ty suggested as he stood carefully.

Chuckling, Zane got to his feet, giving Ty some room but staying close by. "How about food? I'll order us some burgers. We missed breakfast."

Ty frowned as he turned his clunking mind to food. "Sounds good," he said in a slightly surprised voice.

Zane smiled. "Good." He walked back to the bedroom, got the menu, and called room service.

Shuffling after him, Ty leaned against the doorframe and closed his eyes as the room began to spin just a little. He concentrated on Zane's voice instead.

Zane hung up the phone and glanced around to see Ty stopped in the doorway. "You okay?" he asked cautiously.

Ty grunted in response and opened his eyes. "I need to sit," he admitted.

"Need a hand?" Zane asked neutrally, not wanting Ty to take offense. Instead, Ty just nodded and held out his arm unsteadily. Zane strode over and took his elbow, then slid his other arm around his waist. "Nice, comfortable armchair over here. You can sit and insult me all you like," Zane said.

Ty merely nodded, either not hearing or not caring. Zane helped him to the chair, then sat down on the edge of the bed nearby and started unlacing his boots, keeping an eye on Ty the whole time. The other agent wore only a thin undershirt now—and there were bloody streaks along the back of it, as well.

Leaning back into the deep and surprisingly comfortable armchair, Ty closed his eyes as soon as he saw that Zane intended to remove some clothing. He might actually be able to fall asleep while Zane was distracted.

Ditching the boots, Zane stood up, took two steps, and knelt down right at Ty's knees, pushing them apart. Ty's eyes snapped open, and he jerked back as he looked down at Zane with wide eyes. "What are you doing?" he asked in a slightly higher voice than usual.

Zane looked up at him innocently as he started in on Ty's cowboy boots. "You want to be comfortable so you can crash after we eat, right?"

"No," Ty insisted almost nervously.

"Don't be silly," Zane dismissed, not touching, not rubbing, not doing a single thing untoward as he worked on pulling off the boots.

Ty closed his eyes and shivered again, leaning back in the chair and slumping as he rested his elbow on the arm of the chair and held his head up. Finally, he opened his eyes and watched Zane blatantly, giving in to the fact that he enjoyed it. Zane's lips turned up as he slid his hands up past Ty's ankles to pull off each sock, tossing them aside. Then he pushed Ty's knees a little further apart and leaned forward.

"Tease," Ty accused softly.

"Do I have your attention now?" Zane drawled.

"You never lost it," Ty responded before thinking better of it.

Zane grinned and set each hand on a knee and slid them slowly up Ty's thighs. "I almost like you better when you're concussed," he said softly.

Ty blinked at him and swallowed hard, unable to respond.

A heavy knock on the door interrupted them. Zane pushed himself up and captured Ty's mouth in a gentle kiss before going to get the food. He left Ty sitting there, confused and slightly dazed as his head and side both throbbed.

Zane got the tray, locked the door behind him, and carried the food into the room. He popped open the Cokes, and while pulling the tops off the food containers, pulled three gel capsules out of his pocket. He split them, put the powder into one of the cans, and threw the capsules into his mouth and swallowed them, chasing them with some Coke from the other can. "Ty, come and eat," he called out as he set Ty's plate with the full Coke can on the sturdy metal and wood table and started unwrapping the cake.

Ty blinked at the doorway and licked his lips again. Finally, he stood carefully, waiting until he was sure that he was steady before unbuttoning and unzipping his jeans and pushing them down to his ankles. He gingerly kicked out of them. "Jackass," he called softly as he padded out into the outer room. As soon as the smell hit him, his mouth began to water, but it also made him slightly nauseous. It was an unusual feeling.

Zane just grinned as he sat down and took a bite of his burger. "Compromise," he said after swallowing. "Eat and then you can sleep."

"Hmph," Ty offered as he sat opposite and licked his lips slowly. Shrugging, Zane squeezed out some ketchup onto his plate to go with his fries and got to eating. Ty followed suit, eating his fries slowly just in case he got sick. He couldn't manage to eat anything but the fries; just the smell of the burger made him shudder. His Coke was disgusting, but then Coke always was. Give him Dr Pepper or give him death.

Zane finished his burger and fries and sat back with the bag of Doritos, taking sips of Coke between bites. "How are you doing?" he asked, looking over at Ty.

"I'm tired," Ty answered, annoyed, as if that should have been obvious from all the begging to nap he'd been doing.

"Fine. You've eaten enough if you want to lie down," Zane said in a long-suffering tone. He dropped his bag of chips on the table and stood up. "Your cake will just have to wait until later."

Ty put his half-eaten fry down and glared across the table at him. "Why?" he asked as another shiver ran through him.

Zane frowned. "You said you were tired. Eat your cake now, if you want. I figured once I finally let up on you, you'd be in that bed in a shot. The doctor said an hour or two, and . . ." he looked at his watch. "It's two ten now. So, bed. Or I could resume where I left off," he said, eyes flaring with heat as he smirked.

Ty glared at him for another moment before pushing out of his seat unsteadily. "I'm going to bed," he mumbled.

Zane hovered close by as Ty walked into the bedroom and sat on the bed, and then he turned off the lights, throwing the room into quiet and shadow.

"You're going to stay, right?" Ty asked softly, peering at Zane through the dim.

Zane sat down next to him on the bed. "Of course I am," he said quietly, smoothing Ty's short hair back from his face.

Ty fought the light-headed heaviness that he was unaccustomed to, and he turned his head slowly to narrow his eyes at Zane. He had Zane pegged as the type who would be out the door to do something dangerous the moment he was asleep, just to prove that he could. But just then, there was nothing Ty could do about it, and he was fucking tired. He rubbed his eyes and turned away, crawling slowly up the bed and sliding under the covers as he laid his head carefully on the pillow.

Zane pulled up the sheet, face turning stony. He knew well and good that Ty would have an absolute shit fit when he figured out what Zane had done. But he'd done what he felt was right. With that kind of knock on the head, Ty absolutely had to rest, and Zane felt that he wouldn't until he absolutely collapsed no matter how much he begged to sleep. Zane couldn't have that—not after today. They both needed to be at the top of their game, because the stakes had just gotten a lot higher. He could trust Ty to stay in bed for at least a few hours now, and he could go and retrieve their things while the man slept.

"Don't you leave," Ty murmured in warning as he fought back the sleep.

Zane sighed, reconsidering. He could wait to go back to the Holiday Inn. Or he could go now, an action that would surely incense his partner beyond any hope of them even being civil to each other again. "Why are you so worried?" he asked spur of the moment. "I can handle myself."

"Because he's on us," Ty slurred in answer. "He's ahead of us."

Zane nodded seriously, though his voice was light. "And here I thought you hated me."

"I do," Ty murmured as his eyes closed involuntarily. Zane stared down at him for a long time before making his decision. He stood up, gave Ty one last glance, and left the bedroom.

Chapter Nine

The low whir of the air conditioner was the only sound in the well-soundproofed room. There were no crying babies or shouting couples to be heard. The lights had all been turned out, and the drapes were closed against the morning sunlight, allowing only the faintest light to appear around the corners of the heavy fabric. Two bodies sprawled on the king-size bed.

Ty groaned softly and rolled over, burying his head under his pillow to drown out the filtered light. He jerked and pulled his head back with a gasp of pain as the pillow hit the throbbing knot on the back of his head. Suddenly hyper-alert, he pushed up onto his elbows and looked around the room in a near panic, trying to remember where he was.

Eyes blinking open as the bed tossed, Zane pushed himself up slightly. "Ty, it's okay," he said sleepily. "We're at the hotel."

"Fuck," Ty groaned as his head whirled unpleasantly. He pushed up onto his hands and knees and closed his eyes, then began crawling clumsily to the edge of the bed.

Zane sat up to watch him move. He hoped the other man didn't fall off the edge of the bed and hit his head again. Zane winced at the thought. But Ty made it off the bed cleanly and staggered into the bathroom, barely making it to the toilet before he was retching violently.

Zane sighed and rubbed his face. He was screwed. With the concussion, Ty might have been sick like that. But in Zane's experience it didn't hit you so suddenly. Unless he was sensitive to drugs. Shit. And Zane had given him a lot. He dragged himself up and pulled on his jeans. This wasn't going to be pretty; he could feel it in his bones.

Ty was on his knees on the expensive tile, head hanging as he panted for breath. As soon as he'd moved quickly after waking so suddenly his stomach had turned, and he'd known he was going to lose last night's miniscule dinner. As he slumped miserably in front of the toilet, he knew that most likely there was more to this than the concussion. Zane had given him something—probably something to get him to sleep so he could go off on his own and do God knew what. His head hanging in the toilet this morning pretty much confirmed that. Ty had never handled any sort of chemicals well. Even too much Tylenol had a tendency to make him queasy.

As soon as he was sure he wouldn't fall over, he pulled himself to his feet and grabbed the sink counter, holding onto it as he splashed his face with water.

In the outer room, Zane's face was grim. They had a lot to do today, including finding out who had tried to kill them. Again. Deciding not to wait, he started getting dressed. He pulled a T-shirt over his head. He wished briefly for a less shitty start to the morning, but he supposed he only had himself to blame. Shrugging into the holster, he dismissed it. He was here to work, not get touchy feely or indulge himself—and he'd already gone over the line with Ty too many times.

"You fuck-shit!" Ty called hoarsely from the bathroom.

Zane snorted. It was about what he had expected to hear. Slightly more creative.

"What did you give me?" Ty demanded angrily.

Zane's lips twitched. "Diphenhydramine hydrochloride," he answered, pulling socks and a long-sleeved button-up out of his duffel.

"Fucking Benadryl? What the hell, man?" Ty asked in a hoarse, incredulous voice. "Were you trying to put me in a coma?" he asked angrily. "How much did you give me?"

"Just three capsules," Zane answered flatly.

For Ty, three capsules was damn near an overdose. Christ, he would be twitching for weeks after this. He closed his eyes and snorted like a bull preparing to charge, trying to calm himself. "Did you get our things?" he asked in a barely controlled voice.

Zane appeared in the doorway, pulling on his holster over his shirt, and then stood there looking at him for a long moment. "No," he said shortly before walking out to the main room.

"Get your ass back here," Ty snarled at him as he left.

Ignoring him, Zane stopped at the low table in front of the couch and started filling his pockets. Wallet, keys, paper with phone numbers, Holiday Inn key card.

Ty turned and followed unsteadily, furious again. Zane had no fucking right to be pissed off. He watched him, waiting for him to turn around again.

Zane knew Ty was behind him. He also knew Ty was angry, but so was he. He wished Ty hadn't got hurt, because Ty's attitude being so reduced bothered him quite a bit. He wished now he'd gone ahead to the hotel. He might as well have had their things if Ty was going to be utterly pissed at him. Zane turned around and looked at him, waiting.

Ty met his eyes, nostrils flaring as he tried to keep calm. He had actually trusted the fucker. Even something as small as being slipped Benadryl in his Coke was a huge deal to someone who was accustomed to having his life on the line every day. It was taking a massive effort not to overreact, and it was making his head hurt.

What hurt the most was that he still had to work with Zane—and try to trust him—even after this shit. He took a slow, deep breath. "Tell me you won't do it again," he requested after a long moment of silence, his voice finally calm again.

Raising a brow slowly, Zane considered. That wasn't what he'd expected. He'd figured Ty would blast him or even take a swing at him. But would Zane dose his partner again? Knowing what he did now about how Ty would react physically, there was only one logical answer. "All right," he said slowly. "I won't do it again."

Ty was silent, waiting for more, for an apology of some sort.

"I'm going downstairs to get us some coffee and breakfast," Zane added. With that he turned and left the room, door snapping shut behind him.

Ty was left standing in the middle of the room, confused by Zane's anger and feeling betrayed by someone he hadn't known he'd completely trusted.

Zane was back in twenty minutes, a white bag of food in one hand and a carafe of coffee in the other. He pulled out the key card and opened the door, making sure it shut firmly behind him. Ty wasn't immediately visible in the suite. A brief survey of all the rooms produced nothing. On closer inspection, however, the Ty-shaped lump under the covers in the bed said that his partner had given up the fight and crawled back under his pillow.

Setting the bag and carafe on the table, Zane felt another flare of anger. Why the hell was Ty doing this? Should he take him back to the hospital? Zane didn't figure a minor concussion would keep a former Recon Marine down, hence the sleep aid. He was starting to think Ty was seriously hurt, in which case drugging him had been a very bad idea. The anger ebbed briefly, but it was immediately replaced with worry, and then another flare of irrational anger.

Pressing his lips together, he walked through to the bedroom and stood at the side of the bed with his hands on his hips. "Ty, are you getting up or not?"

"Go fuck yourself," came the muffled, groggy reply.

"I'm not that flexible," Zane muttered. "You know, I really didn't think a concussion would keep you down. Why else would I try to get you to sleep and sleep well? It's been two times this asshole has gotten close enough to hurt us. You can't be out of commission and vulnerable."

"Good thing I'm not the type to drug myself for sleep, then," Ty's disembodied voice responded icily from under the pillows.

"I didn't drug myself, now did I?" Zane said just as coldly. "Get your ass up or I'm going without you."

"Why the fuck are you pissed off?" Ty asked in an angry, slightly slurred voice as he sat up without first removing the pillow. It flopped melodramatically to the floor, and Ty glared at Zane with narrowed eyes. "Just tell me that. Why are you pissed at me?"

Zane pinched the bridge of his nose. "I'm not angry at you," he said, voice taut with repressed tension. "I'm angry that you got hurt so bad, okay?" He gritted his teeth. What a fucking useless thing to have to say. Here came the pansy-ass comments again.

But Ty was silent, glowering petulantly for a moment before relaxing a little. "Well, stop taking it out on me, all right?" he finally mumbled. "I've got a fucking headache."

Sighing, Zane sat down on the edge of the bed next to him. "I'm sorry," he said quietly. He could say more, but it wouldn't make a bit of difference.

"You're damn right you are," Ty muttered.

"How do you feel?" Zane asked softly. "Really?"

"I don't . . . I don't really remember much from last night and yesterday," Ty admitted, his voice low. "And some further back from that."

"Yeah, I guess you hit your head pretty hard," Zane said. "So you don't remember streaking through the room and dancing on the bed?" he asked solemnly.

"Shut up," Ty shot back with little feeling.

Zane sighed, reaching to push Ty's hair away from his eyes. Ty's eyes closed automatically, and he leaned into the touch unconsciously. "I'll do anything I can to help you feel better," Zane offered softly. "That doesn't include drugs, I promise."

"Ugh," Ty offered as he rubbed at his eyes.

The vibrating of Ty's cell phone on the table beside the bed caused him to jerk and jump, then groan plaintively as he slowly laid his head back down and held it in his hands to keep it from spinning.

Zane rubbed Ty's shoulder soothingly and picked up the phone, snapping it open. "Yeah?" he asked quietly.

"Grady?" the voice on the other end inquired doubtfully.

"No. Who is this?" Zane asked. His voice was low and emotionless. To him, anyone was a suspect now. Anyone but the man practically in his arms.

"Who the fuck is this?" the voice demanded in outrage. "Where the hell is Ty?"

"Not available. You can talk to me," Zane answered, his voice flat.

There was silence on the other end of the line. Finally, the voice asked in a low tone, "Is he hurt? Did he get hurt?"

Zane's brow furrowed, and he looked down at Ty, considering. "He's okay," he said noncommittally, but his voice wasn't as hard.

Ty turned his head and looked up at Zane with narrowed eyes. "Who is it?" he asked as the silence on the other end of the line stretched on once more. Zane held out the phone, and Ty took it with a frown, sitting back up slowly.

"Hello?" he said into the phone as soon as he had it to his ear. He listened for a long minute, the shouting on the other end of the line loud enough that Zane could hear it, and finally Ty smiled tiredly and responded with, "And I love you too, jackass... No, it wasn't our car... No. No, I'm not lying to you. I would never lie to you," he went on wryly, which produced more cussing.

Finally, Ty told the man that he had to go, and he didn't wait for the last curses before he ended the call with a small smile. "Those ex-Recon boys can mother you to death," he told Zane by way of explanation. His face clouded over, though, and he frowned slightly. "Word of the car bomb is out, and so is the fact that we were the targets."

Nodding slowly, Zane processed that more people than the killer would be looking for them, and that Ty had people who worried about him and kept track of him. It made the other man a little more human. "I don't trust our own right now," he said as he tried not to think about Ty. "But we don't have much choice but to work with them. We need the contacts."

"Contacts," Ty muttered in frustration. "Call Henninger. We'll meet him somewhere... the other hotel room," he suggested. "Kill two birds with one trip," he grunted as he crawled out of bed slowly.

"You doing okay?" Zane asked, watching Ty move so carefully.

"I'll live," Ty muttered.

Zane pulled his cell out of his back pocket, flipped it open, and made the call. It took a few rings to pick up.

"Henninger," came the clipped answer.

"It's Garrett," Zane said shortly. "What's the climate?"

"Pretty tame, considering," Henninger answered in a completely different voice, one that was slightly more accommodating. "They're asking about you, but not too diligently. People are wondering how fucking long it takes you two to get a cup of coffee, but other than that they're still too distracted with the scene in the parking deck to give a damn about you," he went on in a low, almost whispered voice. "Where are you?" he asked carefully.

"In a secure location," Zane said vaguely. "We're going to need some assistance, and you're our man. Are you in?"

There was a long silence. Finally, Henninger answered carefully with, "I'll do what I can."

"We're having lunch at the Hard Rock," Zane said, deliberately picking a busy place way across town despite Ty's suggestion. "Try to keep the goons off our backs, all right?"

"What time?" Henninger asked softly, his voice far away, as if he had turned to look behind him as he spoke.

Zane looked at his watch: 10:30. "Noon," he said curtly, and he ended the call.

Ty watched him with one eyebrow raised. "Hard Rock?" he asked with a frown.

Offering the other man a grin, Zane shrugged. "Popular. Busy. Noisy." He tucked the phone back into his pocket and stood to stretch slowly, getting out the kinks.

"How romantic," Ty responded flatly as he rubbed the wet rag he'd retrieved over the back of his head and looked around for his clothing. "He say he'd meet us?"

"He said he'd do what he could," Zane answered. "I think he'll show. Eager, wet behind the ears and all that." He groaned as his arms reached far above him and he rolled his neck. "Christ. How long have I had this job? Calling him a damn puppy. He must be in his late twenties."

"His file said thirty," Ty responded without thinking as he finally located his pants.

Zane looked at Ty in amusement. "You read his file?" His eyes narrowed. "You read my file too, didn't you. At least the unclassified one." It wasn't a question.

Ty looked up at Zane and flushed slightly. "I didn't read yours," he answered in slight embarrassment.

Tipping his head to one side, Zane settled his hands on his hips. "The way you say that makes me think you acquired my file, then. Why not read it?"

Ty pursed his lips and shook his head. "Files don't tell the whole story," he finally murmured. "I guess I was hoping you'd make me read between the lines."

"Did I?" Zane asked, not moving.

Ty was silent and unmoving for a long moment. Finally, he gave an almost imperceptible nod and said, "I certainly never expected you to drug me."

Zane's lips twitched. "You sort of got a hard-knocks pharmacist on your hands, man," he said before walking over to the table for his holster. After a long moment, he added, "Wasn't any malice behind it."

"I know," Ty responded before he could stop himself. "Fucker."

Zane couldn't hold back the snort. He just shook his head and shrugged into the holster. It seemed like they'd be okay. For now, anyway. "Get into your pants, Ty. We don't need to attract that kind of attention."

"Yeah, my ass is so sore there's probably a bull's-eye on it," Ty grumbled as he stepped into his jeans.

"Whiner," Zane said with a quiet chuckle as he turned to look at Ty while he shrugged into his shirt. "You'd think you went skiing and had a terrible time."

"I did," Ty huffed. "Barely remember it."

"You've already proven what a good liar you are; no need to practice," Zane retorted.

"I am not a liar," Ty responded with an affronted grunt.

Zane raised an obviously disbelieving eyebrow. "'No, it wasn't our car, I would never lie to you,'" he repeated back with a smirk.

"Pft," Ty offered as he shrugged into his shirt. "He knew I was lying through my teeth."

"Doesn't change the fact that you were lying. Through your teeth. Gleefully, even," Zane said.

"Shut up," Ty grunted.

Zane crossed his arms. "Aren't you ready yet? You're as bad as a woman, taking forever to get ready to go out," he dug.

Ty stopped what he was doing and looked up, meeting Zane's eyes. "Chalk it up to working off the roofie," he shot back.

There was nothing to say to that. Zane had been there, many a time. He knew he shouldn't have pushed. He sighed, nodded, and headed out to the front room.

Ty just rolled his eyes and sat to pull on his boots. "You know if I was really pissed I would have just hit you, right? Or tried to, anyway," he called wryly, even though he was slightly pissed about it, and would remain so. It had been a stupid fucking thing to do.

"That's actually what I expected," Zane called back as he opened the forgotten bag of breakfast and pulled out yogurt and a couple bagels. Ty would have a conniption when he saw it. Zane grinned.

"Want me to hit you, then? So you won't be disappointed?" Ty offered hopefully as he stood slowly and made his way into the other room.

Zane didn't look up from the table. "If it'll make you feel better," he said as he mixed sugar into his coffee. He was hyper-aware of where Ty was, though.

"Maybe when my head doesn't hurt." Ty shrugged negligently as he peered down at the breakfast. "What the shit is this?"

Zane snickered and added cream to his coffee.

"You fucking pansy," Ty muttered under his breath.

Zane sniggered a little more. "They've got hot food down in the lobby, but since we're going to lunch we don't need to eat this crap."

Ty picked through the slim offerings, grumbling wordlessly. "Let's get the fuck out of here," he finally muttered as he grabbed his battered leather jacket. He stopped and sighed as he examined it. "Need to get a new jacket, I guess," he said almost to himself, his voice wistful and slightly sad.

Stepping close and rubbing a finger along the sleeve, Zane said softly, "Now it's got character."

"It had character before," Ty muttered with a frown as he practically cradled the jacket in his arms. "Now it's got blood on it. And it smells like burnt cow."

"Are you worried about the jacket or worried about yourself?" Zane asked, still sliding his fingers along the leather.

"I smell like burnt cow?" Ty asked innocently in return. Zane shook his head, wryly expectant. "What?" Ty asked as he held the jacket to his chest defensively.

Zane couldn't believe that of all things, he was utterly charmed by this side of Ty. He took Ty's chin between his fingers, leaned closer, and kissed him firmly.

Ty stiffened in surprise, then relaxed slightly and returned the unexpected kiss. It wasn't soft or sweet, but it wasn't out-of-control hot, either. He mumbled softly against Zane's lips, confused by the actions but enjoying them anyway. "That's not nice to do to a man with a concussion," he admonished in a low voice when their mouths parted.

"Why not?" Zane asked, lips quirked, dropping his hands and waiting.

"Because I'm easily confused," Ty answered without thought to the many meanings the words could have.

"I rather doubt that," Zane murmured. They were standing chest to chest, not touching but for the jacket between them.

Ty poked him gently in the stomach, trying to put some distance between them again to dispel the uncomfortable warmth.

"Is that the best you can do? You must be more hurt than I thought," Zane needled.

"I am," Ty responded softly, taking a step back and licking his lips nervously.

Zane slowly nodded. All right, that's how it was going to be. He picked the keys up off the table. "Let's go, then," he said as he pocketed the key cards.

"Are you . . . are you feeling this too?" Ty asked against his better instincts.

There was a hitch in Zane's movement that gave away his reaction to Ty's words, and his hand stayed jammed into his pocket as he shifted his weight and then his eyes returned to Ty. Zane searched the other man for some clue, some sign, as his mild apprehension was overwhelmed by want. Want for something of Ty he couldn't define. Zane didn't say yes . . . but he didn't say no.

"We need to go one way or the other with this," Ty went on earnestly with a little wave of his hand.

The tone of Ty's voice made Zane smile. "One way or the other, huh?"

"You're big on rules, right? We need rules," Ty responded with a sincere frown. "I prefer rules that still allow fucking."

Zane's eyes widened. He cleared his throat and rubbed the back of his neck with one hand. "Rules that still allow fucking," he repeated, voice a bit shaky as he was really trying hard not to grab Ty, throw him on the table, and suck him off until he screamed. "What sort of rules? What do you want?"

"No more surprise kisses," Ty demanded with a wag of his finger.

"Okay," Zane agreed, a bit mystified.

Ty cleared his throat and pursed his lips as if he had thought there would be an argument. The impulsive kisses, while very enjoyable, were blurring the lines for him. He didn't like blurry lines unless he was trying to cross them.

"That's all I can think of," he finished with a frown and a slight blush.

"You don't look too sure about that," Zane pointed out helpfully.

"I reserve the right to add rules," Ty responded with a deeper flush as he crossed his arms protectively over his jacket.

"What about me?" Zane asked, fascinated by Ty's mind at work despite the shuffling it had suffered. The man was obviously struggling with something he didn't want to admit. Zane thought, perhaps, Ty wanted him and didn't want to say so. Perhaps.

"What about you?" Ty asked uncomfortably.

"Do I get to make rules?" Zane asked, moving slightly closer. Something about Ty had changed. He seemed more approachable, more moldable. Definitely more fuckable. Like the hit on the head had knocked some of the abrasive stubbornness out of him.

"Maybe," Ty allowed warily.

Another step forward, so they were practically chest to chest again. "Only maybe?" Zane rumbled.

Ty breathed out heavily through his nose and tilted his head to the side restlessly.

Zane tilted his head to match him. "How about we take turns making rules?" he purred, putting both hands on the leather jacket and pulling it out from between them. This he could do. Sex he could do. Sex with Ty he could definitely do.

Ty just licked his lips and watched the jacket as if it were a lifeline slipping away. Zane laid it aside on the table, reached up, and turned Ty's chin toward him. Hell, sometimes just looking at him made Zane hard, and all good sense went flying out the eighth-story window. What being this close was doing to him . . . Ty was a goddamn narcotic.

"What about not-surprise kisses?" Zane rasped.

Ty swallowed heavily and inclined his head slightly, his chin still in Zane's grasp. "I don't think those have been banned yet," he finally answered hoarsely.

Zane realized that he finally had Ty just as off-kilter as Ty had him. And Ty was a very strong man. Strong of will and strong of opinion.

"Good," Zane replied. "Just wanted that clarified. Now. You want me to not-surprise kiss you or walk away?"

"Neither," Ty answered gruffly, lowering his head stubbornly before reaching up and grabbing the back of Zane's neck to pull him that last inch closer and kiss him.

Joining in the kiss, Zane pulled Ty hard up against his body, wrapping his arms around him. Fuck, why did they always talk so much? This was the way they related best. This was the way they clicked. What were they supposed to do with that?

Ty finally pushed away and held him at arm's length. "Now what?" he panted breathlessly, his breath hitching painfully as his ribs protested the festivities.

Zane shook his head. "Are you feeling this too?" he rasped. This insane, blown-away pleasure, the near impossible-to-assuage hunger, the ache deep inside, contrasted by short moments of tenderness that seemed so out of place. Zane certainly wasn't sure where they came from, but oh, God...

Ty watched him, still trying to slow his breathing and holding him at arm's distance. "No," he lied blithely.

Knowing full well what Ty was saying, Zane let out a pent-up breath before slowly shaking his head. "Me, either," he said, voice more intent than he'd meant it to be. His eyes stayed unswervingly on his partner.

Ty was nodding almost fervently even as Zane spoke. "Good," he breathed quietly. "That's good."

Zane nodded slowly. "Yeah... good."

Roughly an hour later, Zane and Ty sat in a booth at the Hard Rock Cafe, Ty shifting restlessly in a new jacket he had sworn he would never like as they both pretended not to be watching the door.

"I don't know why you're pissy about the jacket," Zane said to him, admiring the black leather as he tapped his unlit cigarette on the table. Damn no-smoking-in-restaurants ordinances. "I should have gotten one. Been a few years since I had a leather jacket."

"It's black," Ty huffed. "And it smells new."

"They had brown," Zane pointed out, eyes studying the busy crowd. "There's no help for it smelling new, unless you want to find some dirt and roll around in it, maybe drive over it a few times with the SUV."

"My other one got run over by a motorcycle once," Ty responded hopefully, leaning forward on his elbows. "And the brown ones was all too small."

Zane smiled, noticing the way Ty's accent was stronger and his grammar was worse when he was irritated. The more he got to know him, the more obvious it was becoming that a lot of Ty Grady was a façade—or layers of several masks. Zane wasn't sure if he would ever see the real man, and it made him slightly sad. He thought maybe he would really like the real man.

"You could have waited," he pointed out. "Lord knows there're enough stores in this town." He sat back, stretching his legs out to the side of the table almost into the aisle. "Maybe I'll go get one yet."

"Yeah, that'll be fun, being twins," Ty muttered under his breath. Finally, he growled and shrugged out of the squeaky new leather and tossed it across the table at Zane. "Fucking take it," he muttered.

Catching the jacket just before it hit him in the face, Zane grinned and shook it out, looking over it gleefully. Without even blinking away from the jacket, he murmured, "Henninger's here," before saying louder, "Thanks, Grady, it's not even my birthday."

"You can go fuck yourself," Ty muttered, loud enough for Henninger to hear as he approached the table.

"Well, it's . . . good to see you're still the same sweet pair," Henninger murmured as he nodded at them and glanced around idly before sliding into the booth beside Zane.

"What can I say, it's still the honeymoon phase," Zane answered dryly, picking up his iced tea.

"My condolences," Henninger responded flatly, nodding at Zane. "What the hell is going on?" he asked as Ty growled wordlessly.

"You tell us," Zane retorted, still sitting back, relaxed. "I imagine the shit's still hitting the fan at the office."

"And it's dripping off the walls," Henninger nodded in answer. "Is there a . . . particular reason, by any chance, that you two haven't come back in yet?" he asked carefully. "Are you okay?" he asked Ty with a small frown.

Zane glanced at Ty, who was doing a good job of looking bored and disinterested. That or his head was still pounding and he really wasn't paying attention. It was hard for Zane to tell. "He's got a little headache. He's fine," he answered for the other man. "And we're rather fond of our skins," he continued. "The office seems to be a hotbed of opportunity for assassinations right now," Zane said. "Can you get the information we need?"

"You think someone in the Bureau is trying to kill you," Henninger murmured almost under his breath, repeating his words from the day before but sounding slightly more convinced. The noise of the busy restaurant covered their conversation perfectly. "How did he find out why you were here?" he asked, apparently wanting them to know that he agreed with their assumptions. "And why risk confirming what, up to now, has just been a suspicion?"

Zane just raised his brow, and they sat back quietly as a server appeared to take Henninger's drink order and drop off Ty and Zane's appetizer. Snapping out of his supposed daze, Ty reached forward and snagged a chicken finger, crunching on it as he watched Henninger thoughtfully. The kid seemed to be having a hard time coming to terms with the fact that the serial really was an FBI man.

"It ain't just us he's trying to off," Ty said to the younger man. "There was an attempt on you as well, in case you forgot," he reminded softly. "This boy knows what we're doing before we do it. He knows how to get in and get out without getting on tape. He's a step ahead of us all the way."

"Look, we're not going back in there, and we're not reporting in again until we get some hard evidence to take to someone high up," Zane said. "You can get us the information we need from inside—and you've proven you can keep your mouth shut." He reached out and took up a loaded potato skin. "We'll take care of the rest," he murmured, meeting Ty's eyes.

Ty merely sat and stared, and Henninger looked between them with a frown. "I don't like this," he finally muttered. He shifted uncomfortably and looked away. He had several healing cuts on his face and a laceration that had been stitched up on his neck.

Ty watched him with a small frown. It had taken a lot of guts for the kid to come out here and meet them, knowing they were AWOL.

And he appeared to be legit, which Ty found almost surprising. No tail that Ty had seen. Risking his neck to try and help them just days after getting metal and plastic shrapnel to the face, the kid was earning Ty's grudging respect.

"Okay," Henninger finally said softly as he looked back at Zane and then at Ty.

Zane smiled crookedly. "Good. Here's what we need."

Standing outside the SUV smoking, Zane waited as Ty finished talking with Henninger before they went their opposite ways. The kid had balls, that was for sure. He still seemed so damn naïve, though. Shaking his head, he leaned back against the door, tapping ashes to float to the ground.

"That shit'll kill you, y'know," Ty murmured as he walked up to stand beside the SUV.

Zane gave him an amused look as he pulled the cigarette from between his lips. "This was the least destructive of my vices. Quit as many as I did and see if you don't need one to keep the others in line." He thought about that for a minute. "I suppose I could have kept whoring instead."

"That'll kill you too," Ty responded simply.

Taking another drag, Zane tipped his head. "Maybe I'll think about it when I don't need the stress relief," he allowed. He blew the smoke up into the air away from Ty and chuckled darkly. "They were all good for that."

"Why not troll the bars?" Ty asked curiously, unable to help himself. "You're a good-looking guy. Did you just get a kick out of paying for it?"

Zane smiled. "Did I catch a compliment in there?" he asked, flicking ashes to the side as he looked at his feet. He took another pull off the half-gone cigarette before answering. "Breaking the rules is addictive too."

Ty inclined his head slightly and peered at Zane through the dark lenses of his brown aviators. "How in the hell did you make it past the psych exams?" he asked finally in exasperation.

Breathing in deeply and blowing the smoke out and away, Zane looked resigned. "You're not the only one good at lying through your teeth."

Ty was silent for a long moment before he leaned closer and lowered his sunglasses enough to meet Zane's eyes. "If you turn out to be the killer, I'm going to be all kinds of pissed off, got it?" he warned.

Zane threw back his head and laughed. "I got plans for a lot more fucking before any mercy killing, man," he said, taking a last drag of the cigarette before dropping it and grinding it under his boot.

Ty snorted in response and looked up and down the sidewalk slowly before reaching for the door handle and opening the passenger-side door. "Let's get the fuck out of here," he muttered. "I got a headache."

Keys jingling in hand, Zane climbed into the SUV along with Ty.

"Henninger said he'd put in the paperwork for the car so they won't tag us for it," Ty said as they both got settled. "He also said I never actually called him about those damn personnel files. I could have sworn I did."

"I think we got distracted by food, then the NYPD called and off we went," Zane answered regretfully. "Did he say he'd get on it?"

"He said he'd need the original files. They're in the old room," Ty answered.

"Holiday Inn?" Zane asked.

Ty nodded. "I want my other jacket," he grumbled in answer.

Zane looked down at his dandy new black jacket and smirked. "Off we go, then." He went quiet for a long minute as the radio played. "Whiner."

"Shut up," Ty muttered, trying not to watch the traffic passing so it wouldn't make him sick. He took his sunglasses off and rubbed his eyes. "I should not have eaten," he murmured after a moment, and he leaned his head against his hand and covered his eyes with his fingers.

Glancing over at the other man, worry showed on Zane's face. "We can go back to the Tribeca for a while," he offered. "I don't particularly want to see you puking your guts up."

It spoke to just how lousy he was feeling that Ty didn't argue. He just swallowed heavily and nodded in agreement. Zane turned at the next right and twenty minutes later they pulled up at the doors. "Go ahead. I'll go park the truck," Zane said.

"No," Ty answered with a shake of his head as he looked up at the hotel. "We need to stick to each other as much as we can."

Without saying another word, Zane put the SUV back in motion and drove down into the parking garage. When he stopped the truck, one glance at the other man worried him more. "Ty, you don't look so good."

"I don't feel so good, neither," Ty muttered. A violent shiver ran through him, and he looked over at Zane with a frown. He had lost his color, and he was feeling slightly light-headed.

Zane's eyes widened. "Is this left over from before? Are you that sensitive to drugs?"

"I think it's the concussion thing," Ty murmured as he unbuckled his seat belt and opened the door with a slight lurch. "I been fighting it all morning," he muttered. "And no more drugs!" he called as he got out of the car and pushed the door shut.

Sliding his way out of the seat belt and getting out of the truck, Zane met Ty at the back bumper, reaching forward to catch the other man when he staggered. "Christ," Zane hissed below his breath. He slid an arm under Ty's and helped him walk.

"Told you I should've stayed in the fucking hospital," Ty grumbled as he held to Zane tightly. "Jesus. At least I didn't do this in front of the kid," he muttered as he tried and failed to walk a straight line. "Maybe I need to go back," he said doubtfully.

"It wasn't safe at the hospital," Zane answered. He tightened his arm around Ty when they stopped at the elevator and he reached out to hit the button. "Anyone can walk into those rooms. You're better off here. But this time you're taking some Tylenol to help with the swelling and fever," he chastised. Zane could feel the heat radiating off his partner.

"Fever," Ty huffed dubiously, closing his eyes and staving off another wave of nausea. "I've never had a concussion before," he added in a distant voice.

"Never?" Zane said in disbelief as he helped Ty into the elevator. "You were Recon in the Marines and undercover for the FBI, and you've never had a concussion? How the hell did you manage that?"

"I ducked," Ty answered in a childishly honest voice.

"You ducked," Zane muttered. "Smart-ass." He shifted Ty closer against him as he made sure he had the other man on his feet when the door opened. "Think you can make it under your own power to the main elevator?" he asked, looking out into the corridor.

"Uh-huh," Ty answered with a nod that made him wince. He swallowed heavily and straightened up, closing his eyes and trying to use sheer willpower to force his head to stop spinning. "Maybe," he amended.

Zane looked over him doubtfully, but led the way out of the elevator, hovering right next to Ty as they strolled slowly down the hall to the main bank of elevators. Luckily, being the middle of the afternoon, people were sparse. He hit the Up button.

Ty didn't know what was worse, keeping his eyes open and seeing the room spin or closing them and feeling it. He placed his palm against the wall and leaned heavily against it, going whiter as he tried to plow through it. "Which hotel was this?" he asked Zane as he finally closed his eyes again.

Zane's eyes flashed to Ty, seeing him pale. "The Tribeca Grand," he murmured, moving closer to slide his arm around Ty's lower back.

"So I can crash?" Ty ventured hopefully, leaning into Zane again as the elevator doors opened.

"Yeah, you can," Zane agreed, not letting go of him as they stepped into the elevator. Five minutes later they were in the room, and Zane helped Ty to the bed. "Here we are again," he said with a sigh. "Can you sit up long enough for me to get the Tylenol?"

"Yeah," Ty answered with a deep blush of embarrassment.

Zane crouched in front of him and cupped his cheek. "Hey. It's not you, okay? It's the crack on the head. Nothing to be ashamed of, feeling like shit. Believe me, I've been there."

Ty merely nodded, barely meeting Zane's eyes.

Zane lifted Ty's chin. "Stubborn jarhead," he muttered, a smidgen of fondness in his voice. Then he stood up and walked to the bathroom.

Ty lowered his head and licked his lips slowly, sighing in relief as the dizziness began to ebb. He hated not having control over his body. He hated being hurt at all, but head injuries had always been one of his greater fears. He'd seen what they could do to even the strongest of men days, even months after the initial injury.

Walking back with two pills and a glass of water, Zane crouched down again. "Real Tylenol, see? Only two," he joked quietly, offering them palm up. "Bottoms up, then bottom down. You need to sleep."

"Ugh," Ty commented quietly as he took the pills and downed them. "Just a few minutes," he insisted stubbornly.

"What for?" Zane asked.

"We've gone AWOL," Ty said with difficulty, using the wrong terminology and not even realizing it. "Gotta get something done."

Zane frowned. "What is it? Something I can do?"

"No, just . . . something. Anything," Ty clarified.

Shaking his head, Zane settled a hand on Ty's arm. "What you need to do is sleep," he insisted. "Then we can do something. But we can't if you can't even walk."

"Point," Ty allowed as he let himself slowly curl on his side.

Zane nodded and tugged off Ty's boots before pushing his legs up onto the bed and pulling up the sheet. "Yell if you need me," he murmured, sliding his hand through Ty's hair gently. Ty grunted in answer, already drifting off.

Getting to his feet, Zane rubbed his face with one hand and sighed, looking around aimlessly. If he left the room, Ty would smack the shit out of him when he woke up. Zane was certain of that. So with a sigh he pulled off the leather jacket and walked out to the front of the suite to wait.

Hours later, Ty awoke with a gasp, reaching for a knife he hadn't slept with in almost seven years.

Zane glanced up from where he sat at a small table in the corner of the bedroom, writing notes on a hotel notepad. "Ty?" he said quietly.

Ty looked over at him, wild-eyed and tense for a brief moment before he seemed to calm himself. His breathing was still labored, though, and he was still taut as a bowstring.

Cautiously, Zane laid down the pen and kept both hands above the table, moving as little as possible. The man looked really spooked.

And a spooked Force Recon Marine with a head injury was not someone to fool around with. "How are you feeling?" he asked.

Ty watched Zane for a long time before lowering his eyes, as if looking for the answer to the question. He glanced at the window with its heavy drapes drawn, and he looked down at the toes of his socks briefly before licking his lips and nodding. "Okay," he answered cautiously.

"Need some more Tylenol? Something to drink?" Zane asked, watching closely. He thought that the other man did look better. Not pale, not sweating, steadiness back in his eyes. Sort of. But no sign of any recognition on Ty's part sent a cold slice of worry through him.

"No," Ty answered in the same cautious tone. He reached out slowly and patted his left calf, not finding what he was looking for and frowning as he looked around the bed for whatever was missing.

"What are you looking for?" Zane asked, brow furrowing.

Ty glanced back up at Zane as if he wasn't sure he was real. "My knife," he answered dubiously. He licked his lips and watched Zane for another second before clearing his throat and muttering, "I didn't have my knife, did I?"

Zane pressed his lips together. "No," he said, shaking his head.

Ty looked slightly stricken as he stared at Zane. He watched him warily, then finally nodded in acceptance.

"You know who I am?" Zane asked evenly.

Ty nodded again, rolling his shoulders to try to ease some of the tension invested in them.

"How about some water?" Zane asked, scooting his chair back from the table.

"Okay," Ty answered cautiously, still scowling at Zane and watching him warily.

"You know who you are, right?" Zane ventured, stopping at the foot of the bed.

"Yes," Ty muttered grumpily. "Jackass," he added to let Zane know he really did remember him.

Zane grinned and leaned over. "Hmmm. I'd kiss you to welcome you back from la-la land, but it's against the rules."

Ty blinked at him, eyes widening slowly at the highly unusual pronouncement. "Rules?" he asked in a suddenly hoarse voice.

Biting his lip, Zane shook his head. "Well," he muttered, "despite what you think, I never was one for rules." He reached forward to hold Ty's chin and kissed him firmly, a little bit of relief easing the tension in Zane's body.

Ty tensed and returned the kiss as if he was merely too surprised not to do so, but then he relaxed slowly and leaned forward into it. "I hope to hell I can remember where that came from," he murmured with a small smile.

Zane hummed against Ty's lips lowly. "Good," he said, voice a little rough. Just one kiss and he was aroused. Zane closed his eyes for a moment, taking a steadying breath and pushing himself away from the bed.

"That . . . that's pretty damn nice," Ty said softly as Zane moved away from him. Zane paused, looking back at Ty with darkened eyes before he sank to sit facing him on the bed, waiting to see what he would do. Was this the real Ty? The one who stayed hidden under layers of Marine training and forced sarcasm? Or was it just the conk on the head?

Ty watched him quietly, eyes unusually calm and thankfully clear once more. "I remember wanting you pretty bad," he finally admitted.

Zane stayed quiet for several heartbeats. "Wanting . . . then?" he asked quietly.

Ty just shook his head and gave a small, embarrassed half-smile. "Just . . . in general."

A smile slowly pulled at Zane's mouth. "The feeling's mutual."

Ty licked his lips and grinned slowly. "I'm going to deny saying that when my head stops hurting," he told Zane gruffly.

"I wouldn't expect any less. Can't have you threatening my pansy-ass status in this relationship," Zane quipped.

Ty raised an eyebrow and jerked his chin to the side at the word. "Relationship?" he asked with a small laugh. He remembered screwing around with the man. He didn't remember any "relationship," so to speak.

Zane rolled his eyes despite the jump in his pulse at Ty's reaction. "Don't read into it. We are partners, after all." He shifted his weight to stand back up. Ty's hand shot out with surprising speed and grabbed him. Zane stopped in place, turning dark, questioning eyes on Ty.

Ty inclined his head in a beckoning gesture and gave Zane's hand a slight tug.

Sliding over onto his thigh, Zane shifted closer, interested, but also somewhat suspicious. Ty was a devious little fucker. Zane could hope for a kiss . . . but he figured it was about sixty-forty Ty would shove him to the floor. All in jest, of course.

"Are we doing the right thing?" Ty asked breathlessly as he looked up at Zane.

Zane looked down at the hand that still grasped his wrist, then up at Ty, the desire written all over him. "I don't know," he admitted in a rasp, facing the quandary of the two of them together head-on. "But it sure as hell feels right."

Ty just shook his head and licked his lips, attention rapt on Zane's eyes. "I don't mean us. I mean the case. Should we even still be here?" he asked in a rough voice.

Cheeks reddening, Zane blinked rapidly at him. "The case. I don't know anymore," he said quietly.

A moment passed in silence, not even the sound of their breathing breaking the moment. Finally, Ty tugged Zane closer and kissed him passionately.

"Goddamn, Ty," Zane rasped once they separated to breathe.

"I think maybe a shower is in order," Ty muttered with one final kiss. He felt himself searching for any reason not to go through with what he had started. It felt too much like spinning out of control for him to be comfortable. He kissed Zane again impulsively and then pushed him away to crawl off the bed and start for the bathroom carefully. He felt like he might fall over if he moved too quickly.

Rolling to his side, Zane watched Ty walk away. "Yeah," he whispered. Christ, what a view. He squeezed his eyes shut for a few seconds. What would he do when Ty went back to being . . . Ty? As much as he found this Ty endearing and sexy as hell, it was disconcerting to have him be so totally different from the man Zane had come to know, sex and all. It was like meeting a new partner all over again, one that was easy to work with and actually friendly and affectionate, and Zane just didn't know what to think of it. Even worse, he could feel the dangerous allure of it, threatening to drag him under with wanting it.

Ty clanked around in the bathroom for a few moments before the shower started, and soon he was out again, a towel around his shoulders and running it through his short hair carefully as he watched Zane and moved closer. His entire right side was covered with nasty purpling bruises, and he walked with a slight hitch to his step. "What day is it?" he finally asked with a wince.

"Friday," Zane murmured. He was on his back again, arm thrown over his eyes.

Ty frowned but said nothing in response, instead walking closer to the bed and flopping the towel down on Zane's thighs. "You okay?" he asked.

Zane lifted his arm. His brow was furrowed as he looked at Ty. "Yeah?" What was Ty asking about? His state of mind? Zane moved his hand to grasp the towel as he looked up at Ty, who was towering over him. God, he was incredible-looking like this—even all beaten up—flushed and soft after a hot shower.

"You sure?" Ty asked. "I feel like I'm becoming more a hindrance than a help," he admitted.

"Not to me," Zane answered evenly.

Ty nodded and lowered his head, retrieving his towel from Zane's grasp without another word.

Zane sat up and peered up at his partner. "How fuzzy are you, still? Do we need to lay low until your brain pulls itself out of the frying pan?" he asked worriedly.

Ty lowered his head and looked at Zane from under lowered brows. "Things are fuzzy," he admitted after a moment of honest self-examination. "I remember most of the important things. Mentally I'm okay. Physically, not so much. I think if we were in a fight tonight I'd be a liability," he added with a wince as he bowed his head again.

"Then we'll stay in and take it easy. I do want to make a few phone calls and go pick up our stuff, get those personnel files to Henninger. Right now, that's our only lead. Other than that, we're sadly lacking in choices to pursue on the case. I hate to say it . . . it's going to take another killing—and some lucky evidence—to give us a break."

"Maybe if we weren't ducking and covering every other day, we'd have made more progress," Ty muttered sulkily as he sat down on the edge of the bed. "Where are the files again?"

"At the other room," Zane answered evenly, trying not to show how worrying it was that Ty was having trouble remembering. "I'll run out and pick them up, get us some food other than room service and some snacks, and head back this way," he continued nonchalantly.

Ty looked up at him, something like hurt resentment in his eyes. "What about Henninger? Can you call him to go with you?" he finally asked resignedly.

Zane turned his chin and looked at him evenly. "I'd rather have you there. But yeah, I can call him."

Ty merely looked up at him blankly, his façade from the first several days slowly returning. Zane's lips twitched ruefully. There was "his"Ty. It was something like protective armor. If Ty was feeling threatened, he turned into that man. Zane stood and walked out to the front room to call Henninger. At least this Ty he knew how to handle. The other, softer man threw him totally. But oddly, Zane's chest hurt. It was something he had said that made that newer man disappear again.

"I'll go with you if you trust me to," came a soft call from the bedroom.

Torn, Zane held the cell in one hand. The past day and a half, Ty had threatened him with bodily harm if he went back to the Holiday Inn without him—something Zane had first thought was disdain for his abilities, but later discovered was concern. Now, Ty was acting like Zane was the one who was sitting in judgment over his abilities. Sliding the phone into his pocket, Zane walked back to the bedroom door.

"You know I'm not all here," Ty said to him flatly as he sat on the edge of the bed with his hands clasped between his knees.

"Even not all here, you're better than I am," Zane said conversationally. "It's up to you to believe me or not." Ty was Recon. A goddamn Marine. A top undercover agent. Survival was ingrained in his instincts and reflexes, things that just didn't come naturally to Zane.

Ty jerked his head slightly and looked up at Zane appraisingly. "Give me a minute to get dressed, then," he finally muttered.

Zane nodded and walked to the dressing table where he'd set out their guns and started adjusting his holster. Ty dressed slowly, quietly dreading another attack of dizziness or nausea. Finally, he looked over his shoulder as he buttoned his shirt and muttered, "I don't like feeling useless."

"I know," Zane replied, not turning around from where he was checking over the guns. Ty turned and watched the movements of Zane's shoulders as he checked that the guns were loaded and working properly. He moved closer, bare feet on the carpet letting him move almost soundlessly. He stopped just out of arm's reach and slid his hands into his pockets.

"Is there anything else I'm not remembering, Zane?" he asked softly, the words slow and pointed.

Zane looked up, though he didn't turn, hands still moving knowledgeably on the weapon. "Such as?"

"I couldn't say," Ty answered in quiet confusion. He could feel that Zane expected something of him, and he knew whatever it was, he wasn't delivering.

The falter in Ty's voice made Zane's shoulders stiffen. He turned around. "Ty," he sighed. "I'm just worried, all right? This isn't . . . exactly . . . you. It's not bad, it's not wrong, just not the same, and it worries me. It worries me what you'll think about it after. What you'll think about me. Okay?" He held out Ty's gun, butt toward the other man.

Ty looked down at the weapon and then back up at Zane in confusion. "What I'll think about you?" he echoed, sounding slightly lost.

Zane's smile was self-deprecating. "I'm fairly sure that, fucking aside, you're not at all fond of me. Remember the pansy-ass comments?" He offered the gun again. "You meant them wholeheartedly. And not undeservedly, I guess." He shrugged and looked at Ty evenly, and his voice was slightly flatter. "Don't think too hard about it. Give it another day or so, and you'll be okay. Then all this can be as unfond of a memory as you want."

Ty frowned harder as he took the gun. "Fine," he said softly, checking automatically to see if the gun was loaded.

Why it hurt when Ty turned away, Zane didn't know. And he refused to think about it.

On the way to the Holiday Inn, the call came over the radio. Another murder. The dispatcher gave the address, the name of the hotel, and the room number, and Ty inhaled sharply.

"I know that number," he said softly. "Why do I know that number?" he asked Zane in frustration. His head was pounding, but Zane didn't need to know about that. Or about the black around his peripheral vision.

Zane glanced over at him worriedly as he drove. "Go there," Ty requested. "Go to the scene."

Zane nodded and punched in the address on the GPS, then turned on the siren as they made their way through traffic toward the hotel. The front entrance was already busy with city cops and FBI forensics. An ambulance idled in the tow-away zone.

Ty was opening the door and getting out of the car before Zane even had it in park, and Zane cursed creatively and followed him hastily. Ty walked out into the middle of the road, and Zane spared a thought that it was a damn good thing the street was cordoned off, or Ty would have just wandered into traffic unheeded. The fact that his partner was definitely not all there came crashing down on him so quickly that it hurt.

"Jesus, Garrett," Ty gasped out in horror as he stared up at the façade of the hotel building. "It's her," he said breathlessly.

"It's who?" Zane asked in confusion.

"I've been here. That room number," Ty answered as his breathing began to accelerate even more. "It was hers."

"Whose?" Zane asked in frustration.

"The little stewardess," Ty whispered. "From the flight."

"The girl you fucked the other night?" Zane asked in dread as he looked back at the ordered chaos of the police vehicles.

"I'll be all over that room," Ty told him quietly. "She was leaving that night. If it's her, I was the last person with her."

"Fuck," Zane hissed as he ran his hand through his hair.

"Yeah," Ty murmured as his mind reeled. "I think it's time we report in," he whispered, "before I get framed for this fucking murder."

Zane swore, pulled out his cell, and started dialing.

Four hours into the night, they were standing outside the room, talking quietly with Special Agents Sears and Ross as members of the forensics team and others worked busily.

They had been given a chance to look at the scene before anything was touched.

Isabelle St. Claire's body had been hung up in the window against a clean white hotel sheet. She was naked and bloody, covered with various colors of water-based paint, and framed by the painted wooden casing of the window like a portrait.

Ty had stared at the scene motionlessly, going dangerously pale as he looked up at the obscene parody of a framed portrait on the wall. Zane had finally taken his elbow and pulled him away, unable to watch the effect the scene had on him.

"So you knew the victim?" Sears asked Ty as they stood out in the hallway.

Ty nodded, but then shook his head. "She was an acquaintance," he said hollowly, unable to take his eyes off the doorway.

"Meaning you fucked her, then left," Ross supplied.

Zane cleared his throat, but Ty merely nodded again in answer, not taking exception to the harsh words.

Zane hovered closer. "He was gone for less than two hours that night," he supplied in a hard voice. "He wasn't covered in paint or blood when he got back. I think I would have noticed that, at least. We've been with each other pretty much twenty-four/seven since," he told them.

Ty turned to stare at Zane briefly, but added nothing.

Ross and Sears looked between themselves, silently communicating before Ross turned his attention back to the agents. "All right. We've got your numbers in case there's anything that comes up. Get out of here," he muttered.

Ty didn't move; his feet were rooted to the floor in front of the yellow police tape that now cordoned off the room. "How'd she die?" he asked in a hoarse voice. "Was she still alive when he put her up there?" he asked as the elevator dinged down the hall.

He waited as their two fellow agents looked at each other again. Sears answered, finally. "There's a lot of blood. It looks like maybe she was," she murmured regretfully.

Ty closed his eyes and turned his head to the side, fighting back the urge to be sick. Zane had to fight hard not to touch him or comfort him in any way, and finally he placed a gentle hand on his shoulder.

There was a sickening thud as the coroner lowered the body and sheet to a piece of plastic on the floor.

Sears closed her eyes and looked away. "Sometimes, I hate my job," she muttered, turning to look at her partner, who was watching dispassionately.

Another hand on his other shoulder caused Ty to open his eyes again, and he turned to see that Henninger had joined them. Ty didn't even think to ask why or how.

"What are you doing here?" Zane asked, frowning a little. He looked over the younger man's shoulder to see Morrison several feet away, getting paperwork from one of the city cops who had been called in to secure the scene.

"I figured you might be here when I heard the call," Henninger answered quietly. "Are you sticking around?"

Zane looked at Ty. The man was obviously shell-shocked. "No. We're leaving. Come on," he murmured as he took Ty's arm, pulling him along behind to the stairwell at the opposite end of the hall. Henninger followed them, glancing over his shoulder to see Morrison absorbed in discussion with his back to them.

"Stop," Ty muttered as they got to the fire door. He shook his head and looked at both men, then turned to look back at the activity behind them. "If we disappear again, it'll make us suspects," he reminded hazily.

Lips pressing hard, Zane bit down on his urge to protest. Although Ross and Sears had cleared them—for now—that didn't guarantee it would stay that way. "Shit," he swore under his breath. "Fuck it. I don't want to be where that bastard knows where we are." He turned and waved Henninger back to the activity, then took Ty's elbow and put his hand on the heavy stairwell door.

Henninger nodded and headed back down the hall to the crime scene and his partner, glancing over his shoulder worriedly at them.

"I've got a bad feeling about this," Zane muttered as he opened the stairwell door and gestured Ty inside.

Ty didn't reply as he entered the stairwell and stood staring down the steps unseeingly.

Zane started down the stairs, then stopped and turned when he realized Ty wasn't following.

Ty's hands hung limp at his sides and he cocked his head slightly. "He knew I'd been here," Ty murmured. "He followed me. He knew he could hurt us through her. He knew we'd take different rooms than the ones we were given and he found us. He knew we'd stay on it even after being hurt and he planned for it in case we weren't killed," he rambled slowly. "He's profiled us," he whispered with a bit of shock in his voice.

"Yeah," Zane agreed. "So we're not going to get anywhere." He paused a long moment. "Unless we break profile."

Ty shook his head and frowned. "We need to take this to Burns," he said softly, as if they might be overheard. "'Cause right now my number-one suspect would be me."

Zane's eyes narrowed. "Was your last assignment here in New York?" he asked.

Ty pressed his lips together tightly, prepared to offer the usual that's classified. But there was really no point in that. "Yes," he answered finally.

Jaw setting, Zane stared at Ty for a long minute. "You're not the killer," he finally said evenly. "There will be evidence to track and clear you. Just like there's evidence to track and trap him. We just have to find it."

Ty returned the look with one that was unreadable. Finally, he nodded and looked down at his booted feet.

"Ty," Zane said, trying to get his attention. "I can't do this without you."

"You know they'll take us off this case, right?" Ty responded softly. "We're both probably looking at probation until I'm cleared."

"You said it before. Burns put us on this case for a reason; both of us are already fuckups who should have been fired or buried. He'll keep us on it," Zane asserted as he studied the other man. "How much is still missing from your head?"

"Why?" Ty asked defensively.

"We can use it to our advantage. If you're off your usual style, that may throw him," Zane pointed out seriously. "Of course, you might wake up after a thirty-minute nap and be back to your usual irascible self."

Ty stared at him for a minute and then his lips twitched in a half-smile. "Irascible?" he echoed weakly. Rubbing his hands over his eyes with a sudden sigh of frustration, he shrugged. "It's like swimming through cotton, trying to remember the past couple weeks," he answered. "I remember some of the smallest details. But other things, bigger things, I can't recall at all."

Taking the few steps up so he could reach him, Zane pulled Ty's hands away from his eyes. "Don't push it—that's what the doctors told me. Trying consciously to remember will just give you a bad headache."

Ty looked down at him, nonplussed. "I already have a headache," he admitted.

Zane smiled sadly and looked over Ty carefully, still holding both of Ty's wrists in his hands. "You look . . . unwell," he murmured with a frown.

"I can't think," Ty murmured in response, fidgeting as much as a man could when he was perched on top of a staircase with both hands being held by someone else.

Zane sobered and watched his agitated movements, slowly releasing his hands so he could pace if he wanted to. "Ty. You've got to calm down. There's only so much we can do right now; that doesn't mean we won't be able to do more later."

"I can't," Ty finally told him with an uncharacteristic show of emotion. He sat down hard on the top step and bent over, placing his hands on each side of his head and squeezing his eyes shut as if he were trying to block out everything. He began to rock back and forth slowly as he spoke. "I can't concentrate on anything, not when all I can think about is you. And now with this fucking headache," he ground out in frustration, not finishing his thoughts as he closed his eyes once more and held his head in his hands. "I feel sick," he finally added pitifully.

Zane's breath was caught in his chest. This wasn't what he'd expected at all. Ty was obviously having more difficulty with the concussion than he had been outwardly letting on, and the slip of admitting that he couldn't concentrate on anything but Zane made his body warm uncomfortably. It was hard to decipher what Ty really meant through the babbling.

"What do you suggest?" Zane asked softly, trying to stay as detached as possible, at least for a little longer.

Ty pressed his lips tightly together and breathed out slowly through his nose. "I think I need to request medical leave," he answered finally, his voice hoarse and full of pain. It was obvious that he had never before been forced to admit he was not physically capable of something.

The mask broke, and Zane looked stunned. "Ty...I..." He didn't know what to say. His hands curled into fists.

"This can't be done alone; we've already established that," Ty breathed. "And I can't think," he ground out in frustration. "If I request it before they can suspend us, the suspension won't go in your file," he added.

Zane nodded slowly, feeling helpless. Powerless. Again. He lifted both hands and rubbed at his eyes.

Ty sat there and bowed his head with a sinking feeling. "We both know I'm no good to you," he said finally. "Hell, I'm light-headed right now."

Dropping his hands, Zane pulled open his eyes to look at Ty. "Lie back before you fall over," he said quietly, tone soft, even worried. "Please."

Ty tilted his head up, and his expression softened as he looked up at Zane. "You won't miss me," he murmured to him softly. He knew it was the right decision, to pull himself off the case. It didn't mean he had to like it.

Zane reached down to run his fingers through Ty's hair, but just as the tips of his fingers touched, the loud clank of the stairwell door being pushed open startled them both and interrupted the tender gesture.

Ty lowered his head again as an agent stepped into the stairwell, and then he looked up to meet Zane's eyes again. They looked at each other intently for several heartbeats before Ty climbed to his feet unsteadily and turned to face the man.

"I need a doctor," he said hoarsely to the agent.

"And I want you both to know this will in no way negatively impact your records. Grady, you've been cleared of any involvement in the murder, not that we really expected trouble there," Assistant Director Burns said as he looked at the two men. He received no answers, much the same as the last ten minutes he'd been talking. "Garrett, you've been put back on active duty for immediate assignment," he continued.

The two agents in the room with him were about as different as night and day from the last time he had seen them. Ty sat quietly, slightly distant and reserved. He'd been kept at a hospital in New York under observation for nearly a week, diagnosed with a severe concussion and PTSD. When they released him, he'd been flown directly back to DC and driven to this very meeting. Burns noticed that he still wore the little hospital bracelet on his wrist.

Meanwhile, Zane had been taken straight to Washington to be debriefed over and over as the internal investigation continued. His attitude had understandably been for shit the whole time. Getting him to cooperate with anything had been a fight, but Burns didn't really blame the man.

Now, Ty was scheduled for medical review over at Walter Reed in two hours, and looking at him as he sat in his office, Burns wasn't sure he would pass muster. He had never seen Ty Grady look so defeated. And Burns had his doubts about Zane's willingness to go back to work at all. Zane stood at the window, staring out with his arms crossed, face schooled blank. Burns suppressed a frown. The Zane Garrett of old seemed to have made a reappearance: dark jeans, T-shirt, black leather jacket, two days without shaving, at the least. Burns could smell the cigarette smoke coming off him from ten feet away. It was only because he'd seen Zane's medical review the day before that Burns knew the man hadn't gone back to any more of his old habits.

It was almost like the two had switched places. He shook his head. This had not been his aim when he had paired them up. He should have known Ty could corrupt anyone.

"Do you two have any questions?" Burns asked. Ty shook his head, and Zane merely stared out the window without responding. Burns sighed. "You're both being reassigned," he continued. "I've not shared the whereabouts with anyone but you individually. If you tell each other, that's none of my business." And Burns would leave it at that. He looked between them one more time. Neither man spoke. "Well. I have a meeting downstairs. Take care." And with that he departed, leaving them alone in the room when the door clicked shut behind him.

Ty sat staring at the floor listlessly, unable to look up at Zane as he sat with his knee bouncing. Zane didn't move from the window, and silent minutes passed. It wasn't tense. It was just empty.

"You wanna know where I'm going?" Ty finally asked, doubt clear in his voice.

Zane didn't turn from the plate-glass window. "Medical leave. They'll poke and prod and pick your brain apart at Walter Reed and a few specialty places for a while, then send you off to another city; Norfolk maybe, Atlanta. Possibly back to Baltimore. To live quietly for a predetermined amount of time and see a doctor three times a week," he said in a monotone. He knew the drill; he knew it too well.

"Guess that's a no, huh?" Ty affirmed flatly. He cleared his throat and stood, taking his cues from Zane and not asking where the other man was being sent. "Well. Probably for the best, right?" he muttered as he shrugged into his coat carefully. His ribs were still tender even after the weeks that had passed. "Good luck, Garrett," he offered with a small sigh, not allowing himself to think about why he regretted this ending.

"Get better, Grady. The Bureau needs you," Zane said, not moving. He tried to decide why this hurt so much. They'd known each other barely a week. Granted, they'd screwed each other like crazy. But why did this feel so wrong?

Ty watched him for a moment, a sinking feeling in his chest as he realized that Zane didn't even intend to fucking turn around and say goodbye. He moved silently toward the door, worn boots soundless on the industrial carpet.

"Ty—"

Ty stopped with his hand on the doorknob, turning to look back at Zane.

He had turned around to look at him, and some of the cold was out of his demeanor, revealing a hint of unusual vulnerability. "You said I wouldn't miss you." He drew in a long breath, and his voice was even quieter when he spoke again. "You were wrong."

Ty was silent, unmoving as he met Zane's eyes across the room. "I was wrong about a lot of things," he said finally, his voice soft and wistful. He turned the knob and quickly slid out of the room.

Turning back to the window, Zane leaned his forehead against the glass and closed his eyes.

Chapter Ten

The motorcycle sped down the well-lit freeway, far above the speed limit, the hunched figure aboard shrouded in black leather and a full-face helmet. The bike swerved through traffic, darting around cars and trucks without a hint of hesitation before exiting and rolling to a slower speed at the bottom of the ramp.

The bike sped up again as it entered an older, run-down, darker part of town, where the city rotted from the inside out. The rider guided it down a maze of streets before stopping in front of a small warehouse. With the hit of a button, a large bay door opened, and the rider steered the bike inside before the door closed behind him.

Once the bike stopped, the rider stood up and swung his leg over, leaving the keys in it as he walked over to a scarred table. He pulled off his helmet and set it there before looking around.

Zane had been in Miami almost four months, working the inner city, trailing down some major drug deals with quite a bit of success. A lot of it was sheer cussedness and bravado; his Bureau contact had already warned him to be more careful three times. But safety didn't matter to him, as long as he got the job done.

He tossed his gloves next to the helmet and unzipped his jacket as he walked further into the warehouse toward a loft. He climbed the steps, tossing the black leather over the railing, revealing a skin-tight, sweaty T-shirt, covered by a double shoulder holster, and sheaths holding wickedly sharp knives with well-worn handles at his wrists.

After disarming but shoving one gun in the back of his waistband, he went to a cabinet and looked tiredly over several bottles—many empty—and pulled out a half-empty one of rotgut tequila. He screwed off the top before he shook a cigarette out of a crumpled pack. He collapsed on the lumpy couch, lit up, and took a long pull of the harsh liquor, leaning his head back to stare at the ceiling and lose himself in his vices. It would be a lonely, silent, hot night.

Ty sat on the balcony of his row house in Baltimore, smoking a Montecristo No. 4 Reserva and blowing smoke rings into the starless sky. The cigar was a limited production (only one hundred thousand had been made down in Cuba), and they were packaged in sleek black boxes of twenty cigars, each box labeled with a gold number between one and five thousand. In the back of Ty's closet, he had five boxes in a safe, numbered twelve to sixteen.

It was good to have resourceful friends stationed at Gitmo.

"Ty?" a woman's voice called from inside the bedroom. "If you don't come back to bed, I'm leaving."

Ty lowered his head and tapped the tip of his finger on his beer bottle.

"I mean it, Ty. I'm going home."

Another smoke ring drifted its way toward the clouded moon, and somewhere in the city a horn honked angrily.

"You shithead!" the woman called. "I fucking knew this was a mistake," she mumbled to herself as the rustling of sheets and clothing drifted out to Ty's ears. A few moments later the front door slammed shut.

Ty sighed heavily and inhaled the cool air with its hint of fragrant cigar smoke. He sat with his bare feet propped on the railing, nothing but a worn pair of sweatpants protecting him from the chill, and he watched the sun rise silently.

It had been almost four months since his medical leave had been granted. He had been evaluated—both for his injuries and for what had been deemed severe exhaustion and shock—observed, treated, treated again, observed some more, and finally given three weeks of vacation to "get his head back on straight." He had another thirteen days of nothing to do but barmaids. He might actually go crazy before then.

Zane pulled off his jacket and threw it to the floor, stamping up the steps to the loft and making for the bathroom. He flipped on the light and turned toward the mirror to look at the angry, bloody gash across the meat of his upper arm.

He muttered in harsh Spanish. Fuckers. Taking potshots at him like that when he'd delivered what they wanted and more. He'd taken more satisfaction than usual beating the shit out of a couple of them before he called in the cavalry to arrest the whole lot of them.

He hissed angrily as he poured peroxide liberally over the gunshot wound, covered it messily with antibiotic cream, ignoring that it was still gaping and bleeding, and wrapped it up. He walked toward the kitchen, still muttering angrily as he slid a cigarette between his lips.

Walking by the answering machine, he turned up his nose at the blinking red light and lit up. The only person who called him here was the Bureau contact, and he definitely didn't want to talk to her. Cursing under his breath, he hit the button and pulled out his guns, checking them as he disarmed.

"Special Agent Garrett, this is Assistant Director Richard Burns." Zane's head shot around so he could stare at the machine. "Don't you dare ignore me. Call me. It doesn't matter what time." He left an unfamiliar return number and hung up.

Hitting the erase button, Zane frowned and tapped the ashes from his cigarette. It was odd to hear English not made rapid-fire by an accent. "What's he want?" he murmured to himself, the Spanish flowing easily. He tapped his fingers on the phone for a long moment before picking up and dialing the number he had easily memorized.

Two minutes later, he was connected to Burns, presumably at home, since it was the middle of the night.

"Special Agent Garrett. Thank you for returning my call so promptly," Burns said by way of greeting, no hint of censure or sleep in his voice.

Zane walked with the handset over to the couch and pulled out a bottle of painkillers. "What do you want, Burns?" Zane muttered in his well-practiced accented English, setting his cigarette in an overfull ashtray. He poured a handful of pills into his hand and popped three into his mouth, sitting on the edge of the couch and holding his arm out to look at it.

"Ever the conversationalist. Nice accent, by the way. Have you been following the Tri-State murders?"

Zane's jaw set. "No," he said shortly.

"Good. Get to DC. I want you here by three thirty tomorrow."

"DC?" Zane objected. "I'm in the middle of all kinds of shit here, Burns. I can't just drop it!"

"You will turn over all information and material to Special Agent Black, who is waiting quite patiently right outside your door. Be here, and don't be late."

Burns hung up, leaving Zane staring at the handset. After a long moment, he hurled it at the wall, foreign expletives flowing off his tongue as it shattered.

Ty didn't sleep at night. He never had, even as a child. While the military had forced him to change that, the subsequent years of working undercover mostly at night had hardwired his body once more to sleep during the day and prowl restlessly during the late hours when he had nothing else to keep him busy. And so, when his phone rang at roughly two in the afternoon, it sent Ty straight up and into a full-out panic before he was able to track down the vibrating cell phone and growl at it.

"What?" he answered in a huff, rubbing sleepy eyes and shaking his head to wake himself fully.

"Special Agent Grady," a familiar voice greeted warmly.

"Dick?" Ty responded in shock. "I didn't do it," he said immediately. "Whatever it was, I didn't do it. I'm on vacation," he insisted defensively.

There was a chuckle in response. "I know you're on vacation, Ty. That's why I'm calling. How do you feel?"

"Uhh..."

"I need you to cut it short," Burns told him solemnly. "Have you been following the Tri-State murders?"

"No," Ty answered immediately.

"Good. Get in here. One hour."

"What?"

"And don't come in smelling like beer and cheap cigars!" Burns chastised before hanging up.

Zane let the bike coast as he pulled up at the gate to the Bureau parking lot. He showed his badge and was waved through, although he got a couple of odd looks. He hadn't bothered to dress up, just bringing the basics in the saddlebags on his bike. And the leather, of course, since he was riding. His favorite jacket had that gash in the arm from last night, but he wouldn't give it up. He parked the bike in the garage and pulled his leg over, boot hitting the pavement with a clunk. He pulled off the helmet and ran a hand through his overgrown hair. He left the helmet on the bike and stalked toward the building.

The receptionist blinked at him as he entered the Assistant Director's office. "They're... waiting for you," she stuttered at him.

Zane offered her a rakish grin before reaching for the knob to open the door.

"And I can assure you the cigars are not cheap," a voice was saying conversationally on the other side of the door. "The beer is," the man added, "but never the cigars."

"I don't need to know about those cigars," Burns responded in a tired voice.

Zane stopped just inside, having caught words in a voice he knew he'd never forget. Instead of focusing on Burns, who looked up at him, Zane focused on the back of the man who sat across from the Assistant Director.

"Garrett. Nice of you to join us. Over half an hour late," Burns greeted, but he didn't sound too perturbed.

Ty stiffened in the chair and went still. Slowly, he turned his head to look back at Zane, and the stunned reaction was too instantaneous to conceal.

Zane swallowed hard, looking over Ty's face. He looked... good. Really good. Finally, he found the nerve to speak. "Hello, Grady." The words came out still tinged by an accent.

"Garrett," Ty greeted in shock as he stood uncertainly. He turned to Burns and asked, "What is this?"

Zane tore his eyes away from Ty and looked to Burns.

"Despite how your last collaboration ended, we need you two in New York again," Burns answered. His smile faded. "The killer went quiet, without showing so much as a shadow, for about three months after you two were removed from the case. As if he... missed you," he told them with an odd uncertainty. "Until two weeks ago. Since then there has been one more murder, and two days ago, the two agents we had on the case were seriously injured in a gas line explosion."

"You're putting us back on the Tri-State case?" Ty blurted in shock. "Together?"

The Assistant Director nodded. "In a way," he answered vaguely. "You two are the only ones left who've worked the case at all and are around to tell about it. The others might not make it." He sighed. "And I know it's important to you both. For many reasons," he added quietly with a glance at Ty.

Zane took a few steps toward Burns's desk. "Are we gonna be handcuffed like last time?"

"Handcuffed?" Burns asked in confusion. "What you two do on your own time is none of the Bureau's concern," he added with a wink at Ty, who rolled his eyes and sat back down slowly.

"Very funny," Zane said flatly. He'd just ridden over fifteen hours on a motorcycle to get there and he wasn't amused. No matter how much he jumped inside at the chance to see Ty again, Zane knew they'd be walking right back into an uncontrolled fire that could too easily torch them both—but it was the best news he had heard in months. "We had a tail up our asses and too many people looking over our shoulders. It didn't stop that bastard from tracking us down somewhere else." Zane's words were clipped and run together, blending his accents. He glanced to Ty, trying to get some feel for him after four months apart.

Ty sat silently, head slightly bowed and body completely still as he watched Burns from under lowered brows. There was no nervous bouncing of his knee or jittery twitching like there had always been before when he was forced to sit still. He was also clean-shaven, and his hair was still closely cropped. The only remnant of his previous wardrobe was the slightly wrinkled white dress shirt he wore beneath his suit coat, untucked and unbuttoned at the collar. He stared at Burns emotionlessly, none of the usual fire in his eyes or features.

"You'll be sent in unofficially with no other Bureau resources aside from what I have here for you," Burns answered seriously as he waved a manila envelope. "The two of you have unique experience, you understand."

Zane was still watching the other agent, seeing the stamp of medical overload and a bureaucratic smackdown all over him. He'd lived it himself, and it was a fucking mess to deal with. He'd wondered, more than once, if he'd have broken the self-enforced conditioning if he hadn't met Ty. How in the hell was Ty supposed to break free of it?

"Grady?" Zane asked abruptly. "Are you in?"

"This is not really a request, gentlemen," Burns said gently.

Zane barked back something rough in Spanish before catching himself. "Kiss my ass, Burns. After what we went through last time, I think we have some say," Zane growled.

The Assistant Director narrowed his eyes, but didn't disagree.

Ty's eyes moved from Burns to Zane, and he merely nodded in answer.

Zane studied him for a long moment, trying not to get lost in the details. "All right. We're in. Give me the stuff; I want out of here. We shouldn't have come in to the office to start with, if we're supposed to be under the radar. Word will get around."

Burns slid an envelope across the desk. "Approval for this directive comes from the Director himself. Having a killer on the inside like this is a terrible failure on the part of the system. It has to be corrected." He looked between them. "I won't be able to repeat this. You have carte blanche. Those credit cards do not have limits. There are alternate identifications in that envelope, if need be. Just take this bastard out."

"You don't want him in jail?" Zane asked sharply.

The Assistant Director turned and walked to the window. "Good luck, gentlemen."

Ty stood and watched Burns for a moment, then turned to meet Zane's eyes. He licked his lips uncertainly, unable to think of anything to say. He just nodded his head at the door and gave Burns one last glance.

Zane picked up the envelope and led the way out, not another word for the Assistant Director. He assumed Ty would follow, but he still stopped in the outer room to wait and get another good look at the man he'd thought about far too much the past four months. Ty did follow, ignoring the batting eyelashes of the secretary who had previously looked at him with such disdain.

Instead, he came to stand beside Zane, not looking him in the eye. "You're looking good," he commented softly.

Zane raised a sardonic eyebrow, not that Ty would see it. He looked like a hell-bent-for-leather biker, with the clothes, the three-day whiskers, and his messy hair. It was an image he'd cultivated for a while now, and one he was pretty much comfortable in. But Ty...

"You're looking different," Zane answered, voice low. "Good. But different."

"Shut up," Ty muttered as he began moving slowly to the elevator.

"Glad to hear that wry sense of humor is still in there," Zane murmured to him.

Ty looked over at him as they walked, a small, slightly sad smile gracing his features. They were both quiet on the elevator as it took them down to the parking deck level.

When the elevator doors opened, Zane asked, "You got a ride?"

"I took a cab," Ty admitted. "Wasn't quite sober when I got the call."

A grin pulled at Zane's lips as he unzipped his jacket, slid the envelope inside, and zipped it back up. "You can ride with me then," he said casually as they left the elevator and stepped out into the parking deck.

"Why do I get the feeling that's a bad thing?" Ty asked warily as he followed.

Zane's answer was a low, smug chuckle, and a minute later they stood next to his cobalt blue Honda Valkyrie. Zane held the helmet out to Ty, a dare in his eyes.

"No," Ty answered immediately. "Hell, no," he added.

"C'mon, baby, don't you want to feel this much power purring between your thighs?" Zane drawled.

"No," Ty answered earnestly with a shake of his head as he patted the seat of the motorcycle apologetically.

Zane pouted. "I suppose I can just meet you somewhere," he offered, lips twitching. He mounted the bike and turned the key and the motor came to life; a growling, rolling, beautiful purr—just like Zane had said.

"Home," Ty answered immediately. "I'm going home to get my shit."

Glancing back to Ty, Zane sat with his legs splayed as he pulled on his gloves. "And where is home?" he asked. "You actually want me there rather than going ahead to get us some rooms somewhere?"

Ty sighed heavily and looked Zane over as he sat on the bike. "Yeah," he murmured almost dejectedly. "I want you there," he said pointedly.

Zane smiled slowly under Ty's frank appraisal. Maybe they were still on the same wavelength. "Tell me where," he requested. "Unless you want to change your mind . . ." he tilted his head to the seat behind him.

"My dignity and common sense won't allow it," Ty answered as he nodded to the entrance of the garage. "Follow," he said succinctly as he turned and began heading for the daylight.

Chuckling, Zane waited a moment and then coasted the bike behind him. A harrowing ride through DC traffic later and they were in Baltimore, bumping over cobblestone streets as they made their way through the warren of the old city toward Ty's home. Zane parked in the walkway that led to the row house as Ty paid the hefty cab fare.

Ty stood back and watched the car drive off, then turned slowly to look back at Zane. He cocked his head and narrowed his eyes as Ty walked closer. "I know that jacket," he murmured as he stopped right in front of Zane, hands in his pockets.

The leather was broken in and beaten up, well-lived in with a few scuffs here and there, a couple rips, and one gash across his upper arm. Abused, but loved.

"Do you, now?" Zane asked innocently.

"I would have taken better care of it," Ty responded haughtily as he reached up to finger the gash in the arm that didn't look near as worn as the other rips and tears. "This new?" he asked seriously.

Zane looked at his arm. "Last night. Didn't move out of the way fast enough. Even I can't dodge two bullets at once."

Ty tutted and shook his head sadly. "Not the man I thought you were, then." He sighed sorrowfully as he tugged at the slice in the leather and peered in at Zane's arm. Zane shook his head and obligingly held his arm out. The white bandage was still there, extending out from under the red T-shirt he wore under the black leather. What he didn't know was that a few splotches of dark blood colored the gauze. He hadn't checked it since he had stopped for breakfast about ten hours ago.

"You're bleeding," Ty told him matter-of-factly as he tilted his head toward the front door. "Come on. I'll pour some rubbing alcohol in it and make me feel better," he offered with a grin.

"You want your eardrums broken too? You'll finally get to hear me scream," Zane muttered, closing his palm over his arm protectively and looking petulant.

"Bonus," Ty crooned as he took Zane's good arm and led him forcefully to the door. Zane grumbled under his breath but didn't resist as Ty pulled him along. "You look like you've been somewhere rough," Ty observed as he unlocked the door. "They put you undercover?"

"Yeah," Zane said, just looking at the other man, soaking in his features. He'd thought about him so much the past four months, he still couldn't quite believe he was here looking at him. "Inner Miami."

"Explains the accent. It was a waste of your time," Ty muttered as he pushed the door open and gestured for Zane to go in. "Only thing that'll fix Miami is a fucking nuke."

"True," Zane agreed with a shrug. "Kept me busy and out of Burns's nonexistent hair, I figure." He walked into the house and paused a few steps inside the front room. The rooms were immaculate, completely at odds with the façade Ty showed to the world. The furnishings were comfortable and well-kept—not to mention actually matching—and not a single item seemed to be out of place. Framed pictures lined the walls of the little living room, each frame identical to the next. They were all black-and-white prints, and told the story of Ty's life and career, showing him smiling and laughing with a variety of heavily armed, uniformed individuals in various exotic and not-so-exotic locations. There were several others that Zane felt certain were of Ty's family.

Ty watched Zane from behind, letting him observe.

Zane's lips pressed together hard. "You sure you got the right house?" he finally asked. Christ. This was nothing like what he would expect from the man he thought Ty was. The dichotomy of the man he had known had run deeper than he had ever suspected.

Ty frowned at him. "I'm a neat guy," he pointed out softly.

Zane slanted him a grin. "I'll have to check the hospital corners on the bed, Jarhead." He unzipped the jacket and slid it from his shoulders, pinching the bandage.

"You can bounce a quarter off my bed," Ty boasted as he led the way into the kitchen. He dug under the sink and brought out an antique metal First Aid cabinet. The red cross on the front was faded and scratched, and the metal was dented and scarred. When he opened the door, the contents were all modern, though, and he pulled out some gauze, a tin of Rawleigh's medicated salve, and some medical tape.

Zane tossed his jacket over the bar and pushed up his sleeve as he plopped himself onto a stool. He jerked the bandage off in one go with a grimace and poked at the oozing gouge. It was a good three inches long across his upper arm, and had taken out quite a chunk of flesh. He supposed now that a few stitches might not have been a bad idea.

Ty glanced over at it and immediately groaned softly. "What the hell?" he muttered. "I'm not stitching you up in my kitchen," he insisted. "That needs a doctor."

"Just bandage it up," Zane said stubbornly. "Another scar won't matter."

Ty frowned doubtfully, but he cut the tape into strips and stuck them to the side of the counter, then opened the tin and slathered a good deal of the salve inside the wound without waiting to see if Zane would allow him to touch it. He worked quickly and finally pulled the wound together, placed a thin piece of gauze over it, taped the damaged skin as closed as he could, and wound it all up without a word. Zane sat there unmoving, gritting his teeth. It hurt. A lot.

"Glass of water?" he requested after Ty was done.

Ty simply nodded and went to a cabinet near the refrigerator to retrieve a glass. He filled it from a bottle that sat on the counter and handed it wordlessly to Zane. Reaching over to the jacket, Zane dug into the pocket and pulled out a battered bottle of Tylenol, got a couple pills, and swallowed them down.

"Tough guy, huh?" Ty asked sarcastically. "I bet you got all kinds of action with that routine in Miami," he muttered as he watched with a frown.

Zane lowered the glass and looked at Ty appraisingly as he tucked the bottle away. "Depends on what kind of action you're talking about," he said, being deliberately vague. Ty could be talking about fighting action. Possibly. If Ty were true to form . . . that wouldn't be it.

Ty just raised one eyebrow and shrugged. "If you got called papi more than once, then I want blood tests before I touch you again," he said as he turned to the sink behind him and began washing his hands.

Chuckling, Zane pushed off his stool and reached out to snag Ty around the waist and start pulling. "Not even once. Didn't pay anybody, either."

Ty huffed a laugh and let himself be pulled closer, swatting the faucet off before he was out of reach and pulling away only enough to make it seem like an effort. "Bucking the trend, then," he drawled. "How proud you must be."

"Mmm." Zane reached out with his other arm to drag Ty closer, facing him, then slid his lips along the curve of Ty's neck. "I got some ass," he admitted before scraping his teeth on Ty's skin for a moment. Then he added, "No men."

Ty lowered his chin until his cheek brushed against Zane's, and he frowned and nodded. "Good," he replied softly.

Closing his eyes, Zane inhaled Ty's scent slowly and let himself fall under the sound of his voice. It aroused him like nothing else. "The ass? Or the no men?" he rasped, moving slightly to rub their cheeks together.

"I don't care," Ty breathed in answer as he turned his head and pressed his lips to Zane's in an open-mouthed, hungry kiss.

Zane's hand closed around the back of Ty's neck as the other man beat him to the kiss, one he joined with just as much desire. Christ, he'd missed this, missed Ty. He'd never expected it, and he'd lied to himself about how much it had hurt to be without him, unable to understand how he'd grown so attached to this man in the space of seven hectic, awful days. His other hand tightened around Ty's waist, hauling him up against his body.

Ty flailed briefly, trying not to grab the upper arm he had just bandaged, and he groaned softly into the kiss. He had tried not to think about their brief stint in New York together. Parts of it he still didn't remember, and that just made it worse as he tried to force the memories out. Now, though, it all seemed to come rushing back and he let it, wrapping his arms around Zane and pulling him closer until there was no room left between them.

Ty's soft sounds made Zane's gut cramp with more than just passion; it was powerful enough for him to shudder. Emotion he'd packed away in a tiny little box somewhere inside broke free, and everything he'd tried to deny bubbled up. Once the kiss finally broke, he dropped his head to Ty's shoulder, turning his face into Ty's neck, and he clutched him tightly, unwilling to let go. Not just yet. Not until the lonely ache that had been building the past four months faded.

Ty gave a little whuff of surprise when Zane clung to him, but he slowly slid his arms around him and hugged him, resting his chin against Zane's cheek. "You okay?" he asked in a whisper.

Zane slowly nodded, waiting a few heartbeats before admitting, "I am now," in a matching whisper. There was so much he wanted to say but didn't dare.

Ty closed his eyes as the answer sent a shiver through him. He had been afraid of this. Terrified of this. He had known Zane had meant something more to him than just a weeklong partnership or a few wild fucks. He had known, given the chance, that Zane could mean quite a lot to him. Now, it seemed that Zane returned at least a portion of that feeling. Maybe more. And Ty didn't know how to handle it. He didn't even know if he wanted it.

He swallowed heavily and slid his hand up Zane's back into his hair, cradling his head as he ran his fingers through the short, messy curls.

"You need a haircut," he murmured finally, unable to say what he really wanted.

Zane shrugged slightly, not willing to move unless Ty pushed him away. He was trying to memorize the feel of the other man's body against his.

"And a shower," Ty continued in a soft voice. He turned his head and pressed his nose and mouth against Zane's cheek gently. "And some sleep, I bet."

Zane knew he was exhausted, but he was so used to it he hardly felt it anymore. He'd been numb until he saw Ty again. Or maybe he'd lost his mind. "All of the above?" he answered. "And food?"

"Yeah," Ty laughed as he smiled against Zane's skin. "What do you want to eat?"

"Anything but Cuban," Zane said immediately before grinning and gnawing a little on Ty's shoulder.

Ty laughed again, louder this time as another shiver ran through him. "I don't have any Cuban in me, but I doubt I'll taste great," he warned as he pulled away. "How about pizza?" he suggested. "I'll go get it while you shower."

"I suppose," Zane said reluctantly, meaning Ty leaving rather than the food choice.

"You don't sulk as well as I do," Ty informed him dispassionately as he moved away.

"I just need practice," Zane objected, leaning forward to snag Ty's arm before he got too far away. "How about a counter offer?"

"Depends on which counter you're talking about," Ty answered warily as he looked from Zane's hand up to his eyes.

Zane tugged gently. "How about you shower with me, and then we'll both go get pizza?" It was overt, Zane knew. An outright play for attention.

But now that he had Ty this close, he didn't want to let him out of reach. He could feel the heat spiraling between them and all he wanted to do was stoke the flames.

Ty raised an eyebrow and stepped closer with the tug. "You want me to shower with you?" he asked in amusement. "Need help reaching your back, do you?" he asked with a smirk.

"And other places," Zane said, looking Ty up and down significantly.

"I can go next door and ask the lady neighbor for her loofah," Ty teased gently. "Bubble bath, maybe?"

"Whatever gets you in there with me," Zane responded earnestly.

"Subtle, Garrett," Ty laughed softly. "Man, you really did shed the fake layer, didn't you?" he observed.

Zane shrugged. "Somebody reminded me it was best to be myself," he said seriously, tugging on Ty's arm again. "He seemed rather fond of me that way."

"Must have been a genius you were dealing with," Ty said cheekily as he remained a few steps away.

"Yeah, I have to admit, he was pretty smart, though I teased him otherwise," Zane said, curling his arms back around Ty and relaxing as he moved closer. "I regretted that, later. The teasing, I mean."

Ty frowned and leaned back so he could look into Zane's eyes without going cross-eyed. "One of the advantages of teasing a man with a cracked head is that he doesn't remember it after," he offered.

Zane's face went still. "How much do you remember?" he asked quietly, eyes filled with silent questions.

Ty licked his lips nervously and shrugged. He hated when people asked him that. He hated admitting when he couldn't recall something. "Enough that I know kissing me wasn't a really weird thing for you to do," he answered vaguely.

Rather than being surprised or confused, Zane looked disappointed. So, Ty remembered they'd had a good time. Sort of. But that was all, apparently. Zane nodded and offered a small, forced smile. At least he had that. It would do while he figured out how to make the longing for that fire between them to stop.

Ty watched his reaction carefully, confused by it. "What am I missing?" he asked in frustration. He had worked for weeks to regain the memories he had lost. He knew he was still missing quite a few, some that he would never get back, but until right then he hadn't come across any holes that had seemed important, either to him or to someone else.

Zane swallowed hard as he slid his hand to take Ty's and laced their fingers together. "Are you feeling this too?" he asked, echoing what they'd asked each other months ago, only to have it pushed aside. But not forgotten.

Ty watched their fingers intertwine, fighting back the fluttering in his stomach when Zane spoke. He jerked his head up sharply and met Zane's eyes. That one he did remember, although he had regretted that conversation for months, blushing furiously whenever he thought of it even when he was alone. He shook his head and swallowed. "No," he answered hoarsely, echoing the answer he had given before.

Slowly, Zane raised his other hand to cup Ty's reddening cheek. "Me, either," he breathed before leaning forward to kiss Ty gently.

Ty groaned plaintively to break the kiss, and he took a step back to put some distance between them. "Jesus Christ, Zane," he muttered in exasperation. "I was horrible to you. Why are you even here?"

Zane clamped down on the emotion swirling inside him, forcing himself to be as reasonable as he could. Some insane declaration would get them nowhere but upset and blustering. "I missed you," he admitted hoarsely. "All the damn time."

Instead of asking why in the hell Zane had missed someone who'd been so shitty to him for the majority of their time together, Ty decided to accept it as a gift and shook his head, moving closer again. "I missed you too," he admitted.

A small smile pulled at Zane's lips as Ty stepped back into his reach. "Missed a pansy-ass poster boy?" he teased as he pulled Ty to him.

"I had a head injury," Ty answered defensively, mumbling against Zane's cheek.

"You called me that before the head injury," Zane needled.

"Exactly," Ty affirmed with a small smile against Zane's skin.

Ty's lips against him made Zane happier than he could remember being in some time. Four months' time, if he was honest, which he really tried to avoid.

Ty turned his head, breathing in Zane's scent. "Why don't you go back to the shower idea," he suggested softly, pulling away gently again.

Zane kept hold of Ty's hand even as the other man backed away. He felt both relieved and scared, and it was a toss-up as to which was stronger. "Your shower idea? Or my shower idea?"

Ty snorted softly and looked back down at their joined hands. "Which do you prefer?" he asked with a small smile.

"My idea," Zane admitted, tilting his head to one side as he raised their combined fists. "But that won't get me food anytime soon."

Ty grinned mischievously, acknowledging the obvious joke he could make and passing it over. "Tell you what," he murmured as he tugged at their hands and brought Zane closer. "You go shower, and I'll order pizza and change the sheets on the bed," he offered.

The purr started low in Zane's chest and built as he stepped right up against Ty for one more enveloping kiss. "Deal," he murmured.

Ty grinned against his lips and gently extricated himself. "What do you want on your pizza?" he asked as he moved away before Zane could snag him again.

"Anything but onions and fish," Zane said as he reached for the jacket. "I'm gonna duck outside for a smoke first, okay?"

"Those things'll kill you," Ty admonished as he headed for the phone. Zane had the cigarette between his lips already as he headed for the back porch.

"I think the bullets will get me first," he said wryly as he stepped out and pulled the door shut behind him.

Ty stared after him for a moment, unsettled. He wasn't sure what it was about the situation that left him feeling odd. He sighed heavily and dialed the nearest pizza joint, placing the order and giving his phone number for delivery. Then he headed up the narrow stairs to the bedroom at the front of the little row house and began yanking the sheets off the bed. They smelled like the girl from the bar and expensive cigars and possibly Mike's Hard Lemonade. Ty was a little hazy on the details. Regardless, Zane didn't really need to catch a whiff of any of those things.

Taking his time with the smoke, Zane stared off into the city that sprawled out down the hill from the roofs of the brownstones. He spent a few long minutes picking apart his own feelings—why he felt simultaneously steadier and shakier than he had in months. Steadier, because he was with Ty. It had to be. But just the implications shook him. He had no idea how he had become so dependent on the other man without even seeing it happening. How did he do something about it? More importantly... did he want to do something about it?

Christ. He shook his head. Zane didn't even know what "it" was. But he knew he was afraid it would disappear. He didn't want to watch Ty walk away again. He finished the cigarette, stubbed it out on the concrete, and dropped it into the planter that looked like it had been used for that purpose before. Zane briefly wondered who had been smoking out here if Ty was so against cigarettes, and he drew in a deep breath. He knew Ty's habits. It didn't bear thinking. Shower first. Then he'd see what other emotions reared their heads. Hopefully they'd be ones he understood.

He found Ty upstairs, searching for the spare set of sheets and muttering to himself as he rummaged through the top shelf of the closet.

Zane stopped in the doorway. "Towels in here?" he asked, taking in the length of Ty's body and pushing back the desire that revived inside.

Ty glanced over his shoulder and shook his head. "Bathroom," he answered. "I was just looking for clean sheets."

Zane nodded and glanced into the closet briefly. He was surprised to see an old, beat-up motorcycle helmet sitting on the top shelf. He didn't say anything about it or even show that he saw it, but he looked at Ty curiously as he wandered away. The bathroom was easy to find. He stripped down, then frowned at the fresh bandage.

"Well, damn," he muttered. He scrunched his nose. Might as well take it off. It would just get wet and sticky and gooey and that was just gross. He pulled the tape as fast as he could, pleasantly surprised when it didn't take off too much skin. He turned on the water, poked at the side of the gouge again, and watched a thin stream of red trickle from the deepest cut of it.

"You know, I think that's gonna hurt even more if I get it wet," he muttered to himself. He grabbed a washcloth from the counter and climbed into the shower, holding the cloth over his upper arm.

"Need help?" Ty's voice asked softly from the doorway.

Zane turned his chin to look through the clear shower curtain. Ty was a little wavy, but recognizable. "I forgot about the bandage," Zane said. "I took it off so it wouldn't get . . . gloppy."

"Gloppy," Ty echoed with a nod, as if that made perfect sense. "Need help?" he repeated.

"Yes."

Ty gave that a small smile and moved into the bathroom, pulling his buttoned shirt over his head and tossing it to the floor. He then slid out of his suit pants and briefs and left them on the ground as well before he stepped into the shower and gently pressed a hand to the rag over Zane's arm.

Once Ty held the cloth, Zane turned his back to the water and leaned his head into the spray, wetting down, running one hand through it to soak his hair. He let the hot water pour over his face, groaning quietly as it sluiced down over his shoulders and body. Without warning, Ty stepped into him and pushed him hard against the shower wall, kissing him hungrily as the water cascaded over them both.

Zane's groan didn't abate as it came out over Ty's lips. He wrapped his good arm around Ty and gave as good as he got; the sizzle popped inside him, just like every time before. He'd craved it. He'd tried the oblivion of alcohol and the high of drugs, but he'd not been able to find anything to match this. Ty's touch was unique and irreplaceable. The idea stunned him, and he wavered a little, catching himself against the wall with one hand.

Ty murmured to him soothingly and pressed himself hard against Zane's body with a growl. Zane lowered his chin to rub his cheek against Ty's temple, flattening himself against the wall—practically out of the water—to keep Ty as close as possible. He shifted his hips, sliding his more-than- interested cock against Ty's wet thigh. Ty murmured quietly and bit down on Zane's lip, rocking his hips into Zane as his hands traveled down his wet body to slide around and grab his ass possessively. Gasping, Zane shifted into the rhythm of Ty's hips so they ground against each other. A hoarse moan from his throat echoed around them before being drowned out by the falling water.

Ty pulled away with a gasping pant suddenly, and he put his hand on Zane's chest and stepped back carefully in the shower stall. "You finish your shower," he rasped breathlessly. "Then we'll do this right," he promised.

Reaching up to hold the cloth to his arm, Zane lifted glazed eyes to look at Ty as he dragged in breaths. He was flushed all over, both from the hot water and the attention.

Ty was obviously just as turned on as he was, chest heaving as he tried to regain his composure, and body on full alert as the water pounded down on him. "We may even eat first," he added with a crooked smirk.

"Get out of the shower before I turn you around and fuck you right here," Zane warned in a growl.

"Pushy," Ty observed as he turned and stepped out of the shower, standing there for a moment to calm himself before he grabbed a thin robe and shrugged into it.

Zane closed his eyes and turned to the side, pressing his heated cheek to the cool tile while the water started to soak into the rag he held over his arm. What was it about Ty that made him lose control? Inhaling sharply as his arm twinged painfully, he merely dropped the rag and turned around to grab the soap and clean up.

By the time he was done, Ty had retrieved the pizza from an unimpressed delivery boy who was apparently used to people answering the door while soaking wet and still in a robe, and he'd set a couple sodas out on the kitchen counter.

As soon as he got out of the shower, Zane shook his jeans out and frowned at them. They were a mess. He just dropped them and wrapped the big towel around his waist. Wasn't like he'd need clothes for that long. He thumped down the steps to join Ty in the kitchen and groaned happily. "Pizza. Food of the gods."

Ty just gave him a crooked smile and pushed the pizza box in front of him. It didn't take long for them both to eat. Despite being hungry, they both wanted something else.

Finally, Zane got up from the stool, towel dipping precariously low on his hips, and took his empty drink can to the trash. Ty watched him as he finished his drink. Waiting.

One hunger fed, the greater one was almost overwhelming. Zane turned and walked back to Ty, took the can out of his hand and set it on the bar, and grabbed his chin. "I want you on that bed, under me, now."

Ty's body reacted instantly to the words. He licked his lips in anticipation and stood, pressing their bodies together. "Missed me, huh?" he wagered with a small smirk.

"Fuck," Zane murmured, pulling Ty closer. "You're worse than heroin."

Ty stopped short and cocked his head at Zane. "Not sure that's a compliment," he muttered.

Zane tipped his head to the side and sighed, not able to meet Ty's eyes. "I crave heroin."

"Ah, Christ," Ty groaned as he moved again and pushed away from Zane. He walked slowly to the sink counter, rubbing the back of his neck and grumbling to himself. "You know, you keep turning into a worse and worse idea."

Zane sighed and shifted to sit on the nearest stool again. He leaned his elbows against the counter. "You're right," he said, scrubbing at his face with one hand. "And another addiction is just the thing I need, let me tell you." Never mind that he feared this addiction was already rooted deep inside him.

Ty stood with his back to Zane, his hands flat on the sink top as he stared at the reflection of the overhead lights in the stainless steel. Being called an addiction was not sitting well with him, especially from an addict, and he began to worry about how Zane was seeing this arrangement. Ty lowered his head and frowned down at the drain. A lot of things occurred to him to ask of Zane at that point. The only thing Ty knew he could ask without making a damn fool of himself, though, was, "Are you using?"

Zane closed his eyes. Only you, was the best answer, the answer he wanted to give. But it wasn't the correct answer, and he had no right to lie. "Nothing hard core," he finally admitted. It had been a self-destructive couple of months, when he first got to Miami. He wondered if Ty would care.

Ty straightened and turned to stare at Zane. "You back on the bottle?" he asked neutrally.

Nothing other than a flat-out negative while steadily meeting Ty's eyes would convince him otherwise, and Zane couldn't do it. He shrugged a little. "Yeah."

Ty looked away and shook his head, walking to the steps wordlessly and heading to the second floor. Zane sighed as he sat in the kitchen before slowly getting up to follow. Ty retrieved the pair of sweatpants he had been wearing before he was called in to Burns's office, tossed his robe aside, and he was stepping into them when Zane topped the stairs.

"Well, then," he said as soon as he heard Zane enter the room. "You won't mind if I have a drink," he said curtly as he brushed past Zane and headed downstairs for the kitchen again.

Zane sighed. That answered that question. "By all means," he said, going to the bathroom to put his briefs and dirty jeans back on and taking another look at the rip in his arm. He sniffed at it and ventured back down the narrow stairs to face Ty, who had retrieved a bottle from the refrigerator and was standing at the kitchen counter, drinking it as he played the bottle top over his fingers like it was a poker chip.

Zane sat on the stool across from him, sliding a hand through his wet hair. "Now what?" he asked. It was a question that had many meanings.

"Want a drink?" Ty offered sarcastically.

Narrowing his eyes, Zane shook his head sharply. "Only when I'm in for the night," he muttered.

"Well, that makes it better," Ty responded in the same sarcastic tone. "We all know the chicos in Miami sleep like babies."

Zane's face went hard. "Why are you giving me shit over this if you don't care?"

"Do I sound like a man who doesn't care?" Ty asked, trying to keep the hostility out of his voice.

That brought Zane up short, and his sharp reply died in his throat. Ty sounded . . . upset? He certainly looked angry. After four months apart, he was angry because Zane had started drinking and popping again. He didn't know what to say without going back into that dangerous emotional territory. "So you want me to leave off it again?" he asked, voice even.

Ty closed his eyes and snorted in exasperation as he lowered his head. Rubbing his eyes and wincing, he shook his head and said, "That is sort of the idea of the whole being-on-the-wagon thing."

"And I obviously have so much respect for the whole being-on-the-wagon thing," Zane retorted, sliding off the stool and heading back upstairs to get his shirt. This wasn't going to go well, and he saw no reason to stick around for more abuse. He'd made his decision at the time, and at the time it had made sense. The sound of Ty's bottle crashing against the nearest wall followed his exit.

Zane stopped midway up the stairs and turned to look down at Ty as the man stood in the middle of the kitchen. "What the fuck is your problem?"

"You don't even care, do you?" Ty asked heatedly as the wall dripped and fizzed with Hard Lemonade. "You didn't give a damn if you were killed down there."

Zane leaned his shoulder against the wall, tipping his head back to glare at the ceiling. What did you say to a question like that? The truth? "Why should I give a damn? I got the job done, and no one I worked with was hurt."

Ty glared at him for a moment before lowering his head once more and placing his hands flat on the countertop to calm himself. "All right, then," he finally said in a soft voice.

Anger flared again in Zane, and he wasn't of any mind to repress it. "So now you're going to sit in judgment over four months of my life with no explanation? Fuck you, Grady." He stalked up the steps and into the bathroom. For a long moment there he'd almost been convinced Ty did care.

"You told me," Ty called after him angrily, coming up the steps behind him, "how long it had been since someone gave a damn about you! You make it fucking impossible to do it!" he shouted as he rounded on the bathroom door.

Zane froze, hands on the sink as he looked at the hurt that surfaced in his eyes and crossed his face despite his effort to swallow it down. After a tense silence he felt Ty standing nearby, and he said hoarsely, "Add four more months to the tally."

"You going for a record?" Ty asked heatedly. "Because I don't give a flying fuck about the people you were working with in fucking Florida."

"What are you saying, Ty? 'Cause I've changed my mind about four times about what I think you're saying," Zane snapped back before turning on him. "I didn't give a shit about anybody for five years, and then when I did, I didn't do a damn thing about it slipping away."

"I'm saying," Ty answered in a slow, stubborn tone, "that I would be hurt if something happened to you."

Zane's anger wilted, and he just looked at Ty while he stood there and ached inside. "I don't want to hurt you."

Ty had nothing to say to that. He sighed heavily and shook his head. "Is this going to interfere with what we have to do?" he asked resignedly after a long moment of tense silence.

"I'll stop with the drinking," Zane finally promised after a long pause, turning to pick his shirt up off the floor.

"And your other... addictions?" Ty asked slowly.

Zane tilted his head, trying to stretch some of the tension out of his neck before looking back to Ty. "I'll get it under control," he murmured, settling his dark eyes on Ty's body appraisingly.

Ty shivered slightly in the cool air of his bedroom, and he looked away toward the window and the small balcony. "You staying here tonight?" he finally asked in a beaten voice.

Looking up at himself in the mirror, Zane knew what his reply had to be, as much as he didn't want it to be. "No. I'll go on ahead and find somewhere for us to work," he said quietly. It would not be a good idea for him to stay so close to Ty. It was far, far too tempting, and he knew he'd never be able to resist.

Ty sighed and rolled his head back and forth. "How 'bout this, then?" he said in exasperation. "I would like for you to stay," he told Zane slowly.

Zane sighed and turned to walk over to Ty, sliding his arms around his waist and leaning to press their foreheads together abruptly. Ty had asked; Zane would go for broke. "So," he murmured. "Is this one addiction I can indulge?"

Ty's eyes closed as soon as they made contact, and he turned his head to the side and sighed softly as he slid his arms around Zane. "At least it's not one that'll kill you," he answered flatly.

Zane's mouth tipped up at the corners. He wasn't too sure he'd say that. "I'll stay," he murmured.

Ty just nodded in response, not moving from the tentative embrace. He rested his chin on Zane's shoulder and exhaled slowly. Zane squeezed his arms tentatively. "Never a dull moment," he muttered. They'd been flash and bang from the first moment they'd met.

"Yeah, well, if you weren't such a dick..." Ty murmured with a small smile.

Zane snickered. "Works out well since you're an asshole."

"We're gonna have to talk about these puns." Ty groaned as he pulled away and shuffled slowly for the bed. Neither man was thinking of sex any longer. It was obvious from the slump of Ty's shoulders that he had exhausted what energy he had left on being pissed off.

"Mm-hmm," Zane answered, following along. Some sleep wouldn't go unappreciated, depending on if he slept at all without several whiskey shots first.

"Next bad pun you make I'm kicking you in the shin. I don't care where we are," Ty threatened as he turned and raised his chin.

"Ah ah ah, you forget, pain is not an incentive for me to quit," Zane prodded, crossing his arms.

Ty responded with a swift kick to Zane's shin. Zane laughed and caught Ty around the waist, hefting him practically off his feet and swinging him around. Ty flailed gracelessly. A man of his size and demeanor was not accustomed to being tossed around like a rag doll, and it showed. Zane's size advantage was finally paying off.

He snickered and let Ty get his feet under him. "You love it," he teased.

"Jesus," Ty snapped as he held to Zane for a moment longer to make sure he really was on the ground again. Zane kept his arms wrapped around him, and he leaned forward to nuzzle the side of Ty's neck. "Well, that's . . . sort of embarrassing," Ty muttered almost to himself.

Zane grinned and pressed his face close so the other man couldn't see it and get cranky again. Ty simply let himself be cuddled with a resigned sigh. Unable to hold back a yawn, Zane mumbled against Ty's skin, unwilling to move just yet.

"Bed, huh?" Ty murmured as he finally wrapped his arms around Zane and patted him on the head.

Zane nodded, feeling drowsy for the first time in a long while without the help of copious amounts of alcohol.

"Take off those nasty jeans before you get your ass in my clean sheets," Ty warned. Zane disrobed obediently as Ty watched him, leaving only his briefs to sleep in, then Ty stepped back and nodded for him to get into bed. "Fucking later," he promised with a tired smile.

Zane grunted at him and crawled over the foot of the bed and slid down to lay on his belly with a soft sigh, not even bothering to reach for a pillow. Ty stood watching him for a moment, then walked over to the door and flipped off the light before crawling in after him.

"You'll be here?" Zane asked sleepily, shifting one hand to just barely touch Ty's arm.

"If I'm not, look on the balcony," Ty answered softly as he rolled onto his side and slid his hand over Zane's back.

The other man hummed softly and dropped quickly off to sleep. With his eyes closed, the shadows and thinness of his face became more pronounced. Ty sighed softly as he looked over him.

There was an obvious familiarity to this situation. Except before, their roles had been reversed, and Ty hadn't yet been forced to resort to substances to keep his sanity. He reached up and ran his fingertips down the side of Zane's face with a frown. There wasn't much to be done for him, either, nothing that Zane wouldn't resent.

Chapter Eleven

Zane managed to sleep a couple hours before the dreams and the shakes woke him with a startled gasp. He sat up quickly, reaching for the gun that wasn't there, looking around in confusion. The man in bed beside him groaned in response to the bouncing of the mattress and flopped onto his side. Seeing that, Zane remembered where he was and why, and his heart started to calm. He looked down at Ty, though he couldn't see much in the dark. He glanced to the clock and sighed. Two damn hours. He was wide-awake now with little chance of more sleep.

He scooted up to lean against the headboard and stare off into the dark, trying to order his thoughts. A day ago, he would have hit a bottle. Now . . . he pulled one knee up to his chest and sighed.

"It's harder to go back to sleep when you're sitting up, numb-nuts," Ty muttered sleepily without moving or opening his eyes.

A smile pulled at Zane's lips. "I didn't realize that, thanks," he murmured, reaching out to smooth a hand through Ty's hair. It was comforting to have him there, though Zane wouldn't have admitted it aloud. Although, he figured, he'd already said it in a way, hadn't he?

Ty swatted at him grumpily and muttered again, tossing an arm over Zane's lap as he sat there beside him. He rested his face against Zane's hip and sighed sleepily. Settling his hand in Ty's hair again, Zane petted him gently as he let his head loll back. No more drink; it would be hard to get to sleep at night, hard to gear down. He'd probably be a worse mess in the morning, and Ty sure wasn't going to tolerate him popping pills to wake up and stay up. He winced. He should get that other tin out of his jacket before Ty had reason to find it.

"Go to sleep," Ty muttered against his hip. "And stop thinking about drinking."

Zane thumped his shoulder. "Bastard," he cursed quietly before allowing himself to slump. He stilled and calmed, looking at the dark shadow of the man curled up against him. It didn't seem like they'd spent enough time together all those months ago to have developed this sort of comfort, but it was there nonetheless.

"C'mon," Ty muttered as he lifted his head and scooted back, patting the bed next to him.

"Ty," Zane said tiredly. It wouldn't work. As soon as he went back to sleep he'd wake right back up. Too much time spent on a hair trigger. But he didn't want to keep Ty awake, so he slid down and turned to his side, facing him, and laid his head down.

"Roll over," Ty ordered in a hoarse, sleepy voice as he slid his arm under Zane's head. He gave his shoulder a push for good measure.

Frowning, Zane let him push him to his back. Ty manhandled him until he was on his side again, facing away, and Ty snuggled against him. He wrapped his arm over Zane protectively and nuzzled his nose into Zane's hair with a sigh.

"Sleep," he whispered soothingly, knowing if Zane didn't, then he wouldn't either. It was impossible for him to rest with a tense body next to him.

Zane laid there for a long moment, surprised, but he started to relax more as Ty held him close. It was . . . indescribable. He could feel sleep encroaching again, and Zane hoped he might rest for a change.

He twitched slightly as he started to fall asleep; the warmth of Ty's body and the sound of his breathing eased Zane enough that he dozed off, feeling safer in Ty's arms than he had in a long time.

The next time one of the two men awoke, it was Ty, waking without moving. The morning light was seeping through the windows and he groaned softly. Zane still lay on his side, just where Ty had maneuvered him, deeply asleep with Ty wrapped around him. He hadn't even moved, much less woken up again. Ty extracted himself carefully and padded into the bathroom, making as little sound as possible. When he returned, Zane still hadn't moved.

Ty slid back into the warm bed and up next to him. He slowly kissed his neck, nuzzling into the warm skin. Zane shifted slightly and his breath caught as he started to wake, recognizing the touch as out of the ordinary.

"Morning," Ty murmured softly as he felt Zane stir. Zane hummed quietly, almost questioningly. "Wake up," Ty whispered.

Starting to move a bit, Zane drew in a deeper breath and turned his face up toward Ty, eyes still closed. "Time to wake up already?" he asked, voice soft and heavy with sleep.

"You've got an hour or so before we have to get out of bed," Ty answered as he continued to nuzzle against Zane's skin.

Zane made a few appreciative sounds and shifted closer to Ty. "Don't wanna wake up . . . this is nice," he mumbled.

"Want to sleep a little longer?" Ty asked in a softer voice.

"Mmm. Only if you stay," Zane murmured faintly, about to drop back off into a doze.

"If I stay, I might do unseemly things to you," Ty warned in a low voice as his hand moved slowly down Zane's side.

The corner of Zane's mouth turned up. "Mmmm. As long as I'm not dreaming it," he murmured, smoothing his hand down over the mattress in front of himself.

Ty scooted closer, pulling Zane back by his hip as he lifted himself up more. "This is becoming distracting," he informed Zane softly, lips moving against Zane's ear.

Zane laughed hoarsely and finally opened his eyes. "This?" he asked, covering Ty's hand with his own, just to touch. Ty's fingers dug into Zane's hip slowly, and he flexed his hips against him.

"Waking up like this every morning would have its perks," Ty murmured without thinking as he kissed at Zane's neck.

Biting his lip, Zane tried to ignore how much that thought pleased him—but he couldn't ignore the curl of desire. "Yeah," he agreed.

Ty pushed up further and pulled Zane to lie flat on his back, kissing him languidly as his hand roamed up and down warm skin. Zane slid his arm over Ty's waist as he let him control the kiss. God, he could get used to this. He wanted to get used to this.

Groaning softly, Ty straddled one of Zane's legs, pushing his knee between them and forcing them apart.

"Yeah," Zane encouraged, sliding his hands down Ty's back and gripping his ass, pulling their groins closer together. Ty growled and kissed him harder, insinuating himself between Zane's legs and sliding his hands under his shoulder blades to hold him still. Body relaxed and malleable from sleep, Zane moved as Ty moved, his mouth giving as Ty took, Zane's body quickening as he tried to rock against him.

Ty gasped softly into Zane's mouth and reached up to tangle one hand in his hair, sliding their groins together for the friction. The phone on the bedside table began to ring and vibrate demandingly, and Ty practically snarled at it before stealing another kiss. Zane's hands tightened on Ty. He wanted so much to say Forget the phone, you're supposed to be fucking me, but he let the kiss end instead of lengthening it.

Ty stretched and reached for the phone, groaning as his hips pushed into Zane even harder, and he snatched the phone up and flipped it open. "What?" he barked in answer as he settled back down over Zane's body. The voice on the other end was loud enough to almost be distinguished, and it was obviously female. Ty bent his head to nip at Zane's neck as he listened.

A hum rumbled in Zane's chest as he settled his hands on Ty's hips, giving him the angle to pull the other man against him as he slowly rutted against his body.

Ty reached again for the bedside table, letting the voice on the phone ramble on as he grabbed the drawer pull and yanked at it. He fumbled in the drawer, finally extracting a tube of lubricant and then a torn box of condoms. He kissed Zane again, bringing the phone close enough to Zane's ear that he could hear a brief but heartfelt curse. Zane smiled against Ty's lips. Obviously it wasn't critical enough to stop Ty from fucking him, so he couldn't care less that the person on the other end of the line was pissed off. To help out, Zane lifted his hips and snagged his briefs with one hand, pushing them down to his thighs.

"Yeah," Ty whispered to him as he reached down to help, pushing the briefs further down and kissing him again. The phone fell from his hand and slid down the pillow, and he reached for the lubricant as he pushed Zane's legs further apart with his knee. Zane kicked the briefs to the side and spread his legs more to make room for Ty. His cock was already erect and standing. It hadn't taken long, not with Ty touching him. It never did. As he sucked in a breath, he turned his head and could hear the feminine voice still talking.

"Ty?" the little voice questioned angrily. "Ty! Are you even listening to me?" it shouted.

Ty reached for the phone and put it to his ear again as he reached between Zane's legs with the other. "Listening," he grunted unconvincingly before moving the phone away from his mouth and kissing Zane again as he slid a finger inside him.

Biting his lip against a soft cry, Zane arched into Ty's hand, squeezing his eyes closed and gripping the sheets. Fuck, he wanted this so badly, and the fact that Ty was doing it despite the phone call just made him crazier. Zane lifted one hand to curl around himself, lightly running his thumb over the head of his aching cock.

Ty could barely form complex thoughts, much less deal with the woman on the other end of the phone. He wanted Zane and just Zane, and he wanted him right that minute. He slid another finger into him slowly, practically vibrating with the desire to go faster.

"You owe me an apology!" the woman's voice shouted from the cell phone, and Ty dropped the phone again to grip Zane's hair and pull his head back roughly so he could bite at his neck. "Ty!" the woman shouted.

Zane gasped for a breath, tipping his head back and clenching his hand into Ty's sides as he felt teeth scrape against his skin. Zane tightened his hold on his own cock, pleasure already lapping through him. It would only get better. The annoyed voice was a tiny buzz he couldn't be troubled to notice. All his attention was on Ty's hands. And Ty's hands were going ever further, his fingers twisting wickedly inside Zane as he dragged his teeth down Zane's neck.

Another screaming demand from the woman on the phone caused Ty to pull up short and grab the phone. "Stacey, I'll call you back," he grated into the phone before hanging up and tossing it over his shoulder to land precariously on the edge of the bed at their feet. He bent to kiss Zane again, letting himself moan loudly with the contact.

Zane couldn't stand it anymore. "Ty . . . please," he whimpered.

As if to accentuate his point, the phone began to ring and vibrate at the end of the bed. Ty ignored it, instead focusing all his attention on Zane and preparing him for a nice, rough fuck. He kissed him hungrily as the phone hopped around angrily on the tangled bed covers, and he reached for the condom wrapper and ripped it open after pulling his fingers out and sliding the palm of his hand up the length of Zane's cock teasingly.

Zane choked down a cry as he felt Ty's hand on him, and he couldn't stop his hips from snapping up into Ty's hand. "Fuck," he breathed. "Fuck, Ty..."

"Not yet," Ty rasped as he rolled the condom on and reached to tug at the back of Zane's thigh. The phone finally stopped ringing, and Ty kissed Zane again messily. Seconds later, Ty was pushing slowly into Zane's body as the landline began to ring.

Zane growled. "Who the fuck is she?" he demanded, keeping his hands on Ty, smoothing them over hard muscles. "Never mind," he gasped as Ty moved inside him. "She just wants what I've got." And he purposefully tilted his hips and rocked up to sink Ty deeper inside him.

Ty groaned, the sound close to a whimper as he pressed his lips to Zane's jaw and pushed harder.

Ty's voice on the answering machine could be heard from the kitchen, warning not to leave a message because he never returned them anyway, and then a loud beep sounded as Ty pushed up onto his hands and flexed his hips. "Don't listen," he told Zane in a tight voice as he began to rock into him.

"Fuck," Zane breathed. "You think I can pay attention to anything but you?" He struggled to focus on Ty moving inside him; he'd been missing this for four months and now that he had it? He wasn't going to miss it anymore. "Come on, fuck me," he growled, fingers digging into Ty's shoulders.

Ty obliged with a little growl, one hand going back to Zane's hair to hold him in place as he began to truly thrust into him. The bed rocked with their movements, the headboard groaning in time, and in the distance an angry female voice shouted into an answering machine. But Zane's ears were filled with the sound of his own heartbeat and Ty's panting gasps. He cried out Ty's name as he started to rock against him, intensifying the effect of the thrusts. He snaked his hand back between them to pump his cock, and the shock waves multiplied.

"Fuck, yes," Ty hissed as he buried his face in Zane's neck and used the muscles of his back and legs to thrust.

The motions made Zane arch his body, the slow, almost languid rocking driving him even more insane than any amount of frenzied pounding could have done. Under it all, he could hear the girl's voice, but he couldn't think about that right then. This felt too damn incredible to focus on anything else.

A low groan built in Zane's chest as he pulled at his cock, Ty's slow, rhythmic movement building the fire higher but not providing quite enough spark. "Ty... for God's sake... have I got to beg?" Zane asked helplessly, pulling his knees up to try to get Ty to move faster, thrust harder.

Ty didn't answer him, instead speeding the rhythm of his thrusts with a grunt of effort.

Zane gasped out encouragement, throwing his head back as he felt the orgasm clenching inside him. He tightened his fist on himself. "Not long..." he ground out.

"Come on, Garrett," Ty coaxed in a low, rumbling voice. "Come all over me," he whispered against Zane's skin.

Zane's body started to tighten up, and his hand moved faster on himself. "Ty..." he hissed. And with another few thrusts, he jerked in place and yelled as he came, the hot liquid smearing between them with each pulse as he cried out each time, nearly delirious with pleasure.

Ty closed his eyes and groaned, thrusting harder and grunting with each push of his hips. "One day," he ground out with difficulty, "I'm just going to sit in a corner and watch you jerk off," he promised as his belly rubbed against Zane's slick knuckles. Just the thought was enough to send him over the edge, and he tried to slow his movements to stave off the orgasm. But the friction from the slow rocking was still too much, and he came with a shout that was loud enough to drown out the final beep of the answering machine.

Zane's gut jerked again in reaction to Ty's words. Fuck, Zane would love that, to feel Ty's eyes on him. He moaned Ty's name long and low. Ty rocked through the torturous friction and finally collapsed with a small gasp, panting. The cell phone on the end of the bed began to vibrate and sing, dancing itself to the edge of the bed and then falling to the floor with a clatter.

Ty pushed up shakily and kissed Zane breathlessly, pulling out of him carefully and groaning as he did so. Zane clutched at him mindlessly, trying to pull him close again, but Ty rolled onto his side instead, pulling Zane with him. He kissed Zane one more time, almost gently, and then flopped onto his back. The phone ceased its singing somewhere on the floor at the end of the bed, and Ty sighed loudly and closed his eyes in relief.

"I was with her night before last," he admitted in a low, breathless voice.

Sighing softly, Zane shifted to lie against Ty's side, settling his cheek on his upper arm. He thought idly about how much more cut Ty seemed to be now. He didn't look different, but he felt harder somehow. Perhaps Zane had just been too caught up before to notice the changes. He could imagine that Ty had had very little to occupy himself with other than physical endeavors, though. He remembered well what it was like on medical leave, under orders not to do anything mentally "strenuous." The only thing left to someone as active as Ty was physical.

"Hope it was better than what I did that night," Zane murmured absently, his mind turning to the gunshot wound that now throbbed angrily.

Ty turned his head slightly and rested his chin against Zane's head as he wrapped his arm around him carefully. He didn't say anything, knowing that everything coming to mind would either really piss Zane off or be a lie.

Zane lay just breathing for a while, and finally he smiled. "Sit in a corner and watch me jerk off?" he drawled. "My, my."

Ty blushed slightly, though in the early morning light it wasn't entirely noticeable. "Sounds fun," he explained shortly.

"Mmm. I agree," Zane murmured as he turned his lips to Ty's skin and stretched out against him. He sighed, the sound muffled against Ty's shoulder. "What is it about you that makes me want to chuck everything and just fuck you again?" he asked seriously.

Ty blinked in surprise and turned his head slightly. "Must be the Old Spice," he joked weakly.

Zane snorted and shook his head, though he did turn his head to inhale the scent of Ty's sweaty skin.

"I don't know, then," Ty murmured more seriously with a tilt to his chin.

Zane went quiet for a long moment, but there wasn't anything he felt like he could say without sounding like an absolute fool. The nerves were creeping back, and he could feel the shakes threatening. He rolled to his back, lifting both hands to rub at his face before having to curl them into fists because they were shaking visibly. Damn damn damn. He'd hoped he'd have a little longer before the cravings hit. And he couldn't drink when it was time to get to work. "We need to get going," he murmured faintly. He winced as it came out sounding totally weak.

Ty lay still for a moment, nonplussed by the sudden change in subject. "Yeah," he finally agreed with a grunt as he rolled and swung his feet over the edge of the bed. He hefted himself up and shuffled to the bathroom to clean up.

Zane watched Ty walk away with a swirling of confusing emotions. Fuck, he needed a hit. Flipping his legs out of the bed, Zane headed downstairs, first to the little bathroom under the steps, then to his jacket. He had to get rid of the damn pills or he'd be popping them like crazy—and that would make it so much harder to control himself around Ty. Not to mention royally pissing Ty off.

Ty heard the rustle of the sheets as Zane slipped out, and he stood in front of the bathroom mirror with the damp cloth and waited a few moments before giving into the suspicion and following silently. He took his time getting into his briefs and jeans, hoping he wouldn't find Zane doing what he thought he was doing. The fact that he was already jonesing was pretty obvious, and Ty knew enough addicts to know that Zane's stash would be close.

Zane rifled through the jacket and found the tin he carried the pills in. He didn't open it, just tapped the tin nervously on the leather sleeve, again trying to make himself get rid of them. He was still there when Ty came up behind him and leaned quietly against the kitchen counter. Zane was so wrapped up in his internal struggle that he didn't hear Ty, and the tin kept tapping nervously, speeding up, slowing down, speeding up.

Ty watched him silently, frown deepening as Zane continued to visibly struggle with himself.

Zane's hand shook as it curled around the tin, and he closed his eyes. He could give it up. He could. It wasn't his body that wanted the drug. It was his head. He took a deep breath, opened his eyes, and turned, freezing in place when he saw Ty there. Ty met his eyes emotionlessly and then slowly looked down at the tin in his hands.

"Mints?" he asked flatly.

"No."

Ty's jaw clenched and then relaxed again. "Bit early for those, hmm?"

Zane debated explaining—for about two seconds. Instead, he reached out and grabbed Ty's hand. He set the tin in his palm, curled his fingers over it, and then brushed past him, heading upstairs to the bathroom. Ty watched him go, then looked back down at the tin and pursed his lips. With a sigh, he slid it into his back pocket and headed back up to the bedroom to start getting packed.

Zane turned on the cold water in the shower and sank down to sit on the edge of the bathtub, cursing himself. It should be easier than this. He'd quit before, and it had been much more hard-core shit. These poppers were no big deal.

He climbed into the shower. So why did he feel like he had so much more to lose? The craving for the drugs echoed through his head, the urge to find a drink curled in his gut, and the wish for a cigarette set his fingers to twitching. God, he'd fucked himself up. At the time he hadn't cared anymore. He'd figured he wouldn't last long enough for it to be a problem. Body shaking, he leaned against the wall, fighting for control.

Not much more was said between the two of them until they were at the airport waiting for the commercial flight Ty had hastily booked. They sat in the lounge area of the airport bar and watched CNN, Ty rapping his fingers on the table impatiently.

Zane had been shaky and distracted all morning, nervous and tense as he waited for the other shoe to drop. He was just as twitchy from coming off the drugs as wondering what Ty might do about it. He knew there was nothing he could do to change Ty's opinion about them, and that was what still bothered him; that he'd damaged Ty's opinion of him. For Ty's part, he hadn't even alluded to the pills Zane had handed over.

Finally, after half an hour of delay and being too restless to keep quiet any longer, Ty looked from the television mounted in the corner of the bar to Zane and tilted his head. "Got any preferences as to where we stay in the city?" he asked flatly.

Zane blinked, pulled out of his thoughts. He glanced to Ty and shrugged. "Somewhere... unpredictable. Queens, maybe," he mused. "Or Chinatown."

Ty nodded and sipped at his orange juice. "Good idea," he responded, unable to think of anything further to say to the man.

When Ty went quiet again, Zane fell back into thought, trying to focus on his memories about the case, pushing aside his worries. He wasn't having much success, though, especially with the seeming party in the bar across the room. He winced when a raucous group clanged bottles together. God, he didn't want to be here. He wanted to be back at Ty's apartment, curled up and warm like early this morning.

Ty sat and watched without emotion. He sighed and looked down at his watch, knee bouncing restlessly. "You can still step away from this case," he said to Zane softly.

Zane raised his eyes to meet Ty's. "The case isn't the problem. I'm the problem," he murmured, shifting to set his elbows on his knees.

"You're my problem," Ty reminded.

"Your problem?" Zane asked, frowning a little.

"If you can't get your shit together, then you're my problem," Ty clarified. "We established before this isn't a job that can be done alone."

Zane's face went still and he sat up, averting his eyes toward the windows. "I'll have it together," he said gruffly. It wouldn't be pretty inside, but he'd deal with that when he came to it.

"What are you so afraid of?" Ty asked suddenly.

Dark eyes going bleak, Zane didn't know if he could explain the answer to himself, much less to Ty. "I..." He pressed his lips together and tried humor. "Afraid of embarrassing myself?"

"I don't buy that," Ty replied after a moment of thought. He cocked his head and looked Zane over carefully. "What is it? Dying? Being alone? Dying alone?" he ventured sarcastically. "At least those are legitimate things to be afraid of," he added before Zane could answer.

"I'm not afraid of dying," Zane murmured. It was the complete opposite, actually. He was afraid that it would be someone else doing the dying. Wasn't that just all sticky and sentimental, he thought darkly, sending his mood even further down.

"Come on, Garrett," Ty murmured as he leaned closer. "If we can fuck each other senseless, we can be honest with each other."

Zane's eyes shifted sideways to meet Ty's and they shifted away just as quickly. When he spoke, it was a bare whisper. "You remember when I said I didn't give a shit about anybody for five years? And how that had changed?"

"Yeah?" Ty answered questioningly. At the time, he had thought Zane had been referring to the wife he'd lost, but now in this new context he had a sinking feeling that he had been wrong.

A sad smile twisted Zane's lips. "Becky was killed five years ago," he mentioned, seemingly offhand.

"That was your wife," Ty said carefully, getting a little more confused.

"Yes. I never thought I'd care about anyone after her," Zane answered quietly. "We'd been married almost ten years. It was like half of me was suddenly gone. I can't explain it any other way."

Ty nodded slowly, sliding his plastic bottle top on the table restlessly. "Go on," he invited.

Christ. Zane felt like an idiot. "I didn't care about anybody, even myself. And when I did . . ." Zane's jaw clenched, and he kept his eyes focused on the window. Anything but on the man sitting across from him. "I let him walk away."

Without even really realizing it, Ty had produced the tin of pills in his hand as Zane spoke. He tapped the hollow tin almost angrily. "So, this is you," he said with a rap, "pining over someone you let get away."

Zane glanced over at the table in surprise, seeing the small tin. He looked up at Ty in shock and realized that Ty either hadn't caught the meaning of his words or simply didn't apply them to himself. Although he felt relieved, he also felt worse than before. He stared at the tin. "You shouldn't have brought those here." Avoid the question.

Avoid the question. Forget about the question, Ty. You don't want to know the answer.

Ty merely looked at him blankly. "Figured if you kept this up, I might need them," he finally snapped.

"Goddamn it," Zane hissed, hand flashing out to scoop up the tin. "It's you, you asshole," he said.

"What's me?" Ty demanded defensively. "Give those back," he added with a hiss and a motion of his hand.

Zane leaned over and grabbed the front of Ty's shirt, yanking him forward. "You are the one who walked away," he growled before shaking him slightly and pushing him back into the chair.

Ty's chair rocked precariously before righting itself again, but Ty never seemed to notice as he stared at Zane with shocked hazel eyes. "What?" he asked stupidly, his voice hoarse and slightly higher than normal.

"Fuck," Zane muttered, getting to his feet and pocketing the tin. "I need a drink." He stalked off toward the bar. What a fucked-up situation.

"Garrett," Ty barked after him.

Zane stopped dead in his tracks just four steps away, his body jerking itself to a halt in response to Ty's commanding voice. He slowly straightened his shoulders and turned his chin to indicate he was listening.

"You don't need a drink," Ty said to him in slow, measured words.

Inhaling sharply, Zane held his breath for a long moment as he closed his eyes and dropped his head. His hands slowly rose to burrow into the pockets of the leather jacket, and he just stood there. So, what now? Go forward? Go back? He wished again for the oblivion of too much alcohol—but Ty's words echoed through him, and he stayed in place.

"Let me have those pills," Ty requested after a moment of tense silence.

Zane turned automatically, walked back, and held out the tin, looking everywhere but at Ty. Ty took it, eyes on Zane and piercing through him. He slipped the tin into a pocket inside his canvas jacket and then shifted in his chair. With a long sigh he closed his eyes and rubbed the bridge of his nose.

"So, you're saying . . . what?" he murmured finally with a wave of his hand. "You're in love with me?"

"No," Zane was quick to insist. "I'm saying that I figured out I cared about what happened to you and then let you walk away," he answered stubbornly. He had no idea about loving Ty. The whole concept scared the absolute shit out of him, and he simply refused to even consider the possibility. He could care about his partner, though, right? No harm in that.

"Okay," Ty responded slowly, nodding his head. "So now you're either trying to push me away or you're trying to self-destruct," he ventured. "Maybe both," he shrugged as he continued to stare at Zane, waiting for eye contact. "What I don't get is why."

Zane gritted his teeth, then his shoulders and demeanor sagged, and he just looked exhausted. He looked up, and his eyes were filled with resignation. "Can't exactly pull you closer, can I?" he asked quietly.

There was a long, tense moment of silence as Ty met Zane's eyes emotionlessly. "Maybe not in public," he answered finally.

Zane stared at him, silent, and he shook his head minutely. Was Ty joking at his expense? He sounded inexplicably solemn.

"Seriously," Ty warned, lowering his head slightly and looking up at Zane with narrowed eyes and a barely perceptible twitch of his lips. "Don't grope me in public."

Zane blinked and flinched a little, totally surprised. This wasn't at all what he'd expected in the way of reply from the man sitting in front of him. "Okay?" he replied, brow furrowed. He still wasn't sure that Ty wasn't yanking his chain. Christ. All Zane wanted was to be able to fuck Ty and make sure the man didn't get killed. Wasn't that simple enough?

"Okay," Ty repeated with a nod. He looked around the airport lounge and then back up at Zane towering over him. "You're drawing some attention," he informed his partner casually.

Still not sure what had just happened, Zane shook his head, turned in place, and headed for the men's room. No liquor, no uppers, and a crack-job partner who Zane couldn't keep his hands off of. Well, fine. They were just getting used to each other again, right? The insanely satisfying and addictive sex was just a bonus. Anything else he felt was shoved away as far as he could push it.

Left alone, Ty rolled his eyes and sagged his shoulders as Zane walked away. It was far more difficult to deal with Zane when he didn't have the heart to be an asshole to him.

Zane got to the bathroom and splashed his face with cool water, looking up at his face and the dark circles under his eyes. One night of sleep did not make up for months of deprivation. He realized how shitty he looked; why hadn't he noticed before? He almost looked like death warmed over. No wonder Ty was worried. Zane splashed more water on his face. He had to get this shit out of his head or he was going to go insane over it.

As he stood over the sink, the loudspeakers in the ceiling crackled to life and announced that the flight he and Ty were awaiting was now boarding. After one last breath, Zane grabbed some paper towels, dried his face and hands, and left the bathroom to rejoin Ty.

As soon as they got into their seats, Ty turned to Zane with a small frown. "When Burns called you for this, did he ask you if you'd been following the case?" he asked abruptly.

"Yeah," Zane answered as he pulled out the seat belt and messed with it. "Why?"

"What did you tell him?" Ty asked.

Zane raised a brow as he glanced over at his partner. "I told him no."

"Did you tell him the truth?" Ty pressed.

Zane frowned. "Yes. I'd been buried in the barrio for almost fourteen weeks. I hadn't heard or read anything that wasn't in Spanish in at least that long." He moved in the seat, trying to stretch out his long legs.

Ty nodded. That was the answer he'd expected. "I lied," he admitted.

"Why?"

"I'm not sure," Ty answered with a shrug. "It was the first thing that came out. He asked if I'd been following, and I said no before I even thought about it."

"And after you said it?" Zane prodded.

"Didn't look back," Ty answered immediately. He produced a thin leather binder and handed it over to Zane.

"What's this?" Zane asked in surprise as he took the portfolio and looked at it warily.

"It's all the clippings I kept about the case when I was in the hospital and after," Ty answered as he crossed his arms over his chest defensively and shifted in his seat.

Zane looked up in surprise. "You kept up with it the whole time? Why would you do that? With all the mess in your head you were trying to straighten out?" He clearly remembered the look on Ty's face when they'd seen that girl hanging in the window.

"I don't like being outsmarted," Ty answered in a soft, determined voice. "And I don't like feeling guilty," he admitted.

Zane raised his head and looked at him seriously. He'd taken for granted that a man like Ty would be able to shrug off the past easily. His behavior and his attitude all implied that he lived in the here and now, but Zane knew him well enough now to see that he took everything to heart, especially his failures. And Zane knew Ty considered that woman's death his fault. The killer never would have set his sights on her if Ty hadn't led him to her. Suddenly, whatever Ty had collected in that binder seemed very important to Zane. It would tell him about more than just the case. It would tell him about Ty, about the man he thought he could care deeply for.

"I highlighted some bits. Underlined and . . . scribbled. I was cooped up," Ty muttered defensively.

Zane tipped his head, eyes warming, and he smiled slightly. "Okay," he said quietly, trying not to laugh. He schooled his features and looked back down at the portfolio solemnly. "Anything I should know before looking?" he asked, sliding his hand over the leather.

Ty pursed his lips and then nodded his head. "The last murders were . . ." He seemed to hesitate, unsure of how to continue. Zane frowned worriedly. "They found them in the morgue," Ty told him hoarsely.

"The morgue?" Zane asked with a sudden drop in the pit of his stomach.

"The ME and her assistant," Ty answered as he lowered his head.

Zane's head snapped up. "Karen? What the hell?" he asked.

Ty didn't look up, merely kept his head bowed as if it was somehow his fault. Zane looked back down at the binder with dread, then opened it and turned it to look over the first page. The articles weren't in any sort of order. They were merely put in as Ty had found them.

The first page, however, was about the woman. It detailed her discovery with all the gory relish of the popular press, and Ty knew it word for word. He looked away from the photograph included of Isabelle St. Claire in her airline uniform. "The way she was found," he said in a hoarse voice, "made me start thinking the way the bodies were found was even more important than we thought it was."

Zane glanced up at him before going back to the article. "Go on," he invited.

"It's not really the victims he's after," Ty conjectured. "It's the situations," he went on with a point at the next page. "His vics have to fit the situation he's after, but other than that he doesn't care who they are. He went after the ME and her assistant next."

Zane glanced up at him with a wince.

Ty nodded grimly. "But it wasn't in the same manner as the agents he killed, or like us or the other people he was trying to merely get rid of. It wasn't like they stumbled across him as he was doing something. It was methodical. I think they were planned victims, killed in the morgue for some reason," he said with emphasis.

Flipping through the pages, Zane stopped on that article, seeing the picture of the dark-haired woman they'd worked with. He shook his head. Ty must have done this just in the last few days, right before he got the call from Burns. He was still keeping up, somehow. Zane's chest hurt with the thought. "Goddamn," he murmured. "They were locked in the autopsy lab. But why? You're right; there's something off about it. Always before, there's some sort of odd positioning. They were just there."

"Right. In the morgue. I started looking back at the other ones. The first with the meth guy found in his bed. The second with the hooker found in the graveyard, which happens to be one of the most elite burial grounds in the city," he added with a point of his finger at the binder. "Then the two girls with the dyed hair who were switched in each other's beds. I don't think it mattered how they were killed or who they were. Just how they were found."

"What about the guy with the bird flu? Or the twins that looked like a mutual execution? What was off about them?" Zane asked.

Ty sighed heavily and shook his head, looking out the window as the plane began to taxi down the runway. "That's the problem with my theory," he admitted. "The twins were the ones that were killed across state lines. They were the reason the FBI was brought in at all. That is the importance of their location. But aside from that? There wasn't anything special about where or how they were found, just what they were killed with."

"The one man with a rare disease and the others with their own twin?"

"Uh-huh. Nothing else stands out."

"Other than they were different from all the others," Zane said.

Ty muttered as he looked out the window diligently. "There's an answer there, but I'm just not seeing the big picture," he added in frustration.

Zane kept paging through the binder quietly, reviewing the older cases and then reading up on what had happened since.

A shiver ran through Ty and he closed his eyes and bowed his head again. "I hate knowing this fucker is smarter than I am," he muttered.

Zane's head snapped up. "He's not smarter than you," he said firmly. "He just has inside information."

Ty sneered at that bit of logic and snorted. "You saying he's the kid in class with the teacher's copy of the textbook?" he asked wryly as his knee began to bounce restlessly.

"That's exactly what I'm saying. It's easy to beat the other kids' test scores when you have the answer key," Zane pointed out.

Ty closed his eyes and rubbed them. "Still doesn't mean the other kids have to like it," he muttered as the engines roared and the plane lifted off.

Once they arrived in New York, a brief discussion established that they would contact Tim Henninger at the Bureau. It was fairly safe and probably the most expedient way of going about things. He'd risked his neck to help them before, and despite Ty's inherent lack of respect for the kid, they both trusted him in their own ways.

When they called him, he sounded almost happy to hear from them. Ty could practically hear him vibrating over the phone as he asked where they wanted to meet.

When Henninger arrived at the diner, Zane was eating as Ty drank a glass of juice. They sat on the same side of the table, Zane somewhat sprawled in the booth, Ty sitting up straight and slightly stiff. Henninger blinked at them, noticing the outward changes; Zane's scruff set off by Ty's more polished, professional look. For the first time, it was easy to see the former Marine in the FBI agent.

"Guys, it's great to see you," Henninger said quietly as he slid into the booth across the table from them, looking at them in mild confusion. He leaned closer, looking at them both oddly. "But why are you back?" he asked with a frown.

Ty gave Zane a glance and then looked back at Henninger seriously. "They wanted someone who could fly under the Bureau radar, as it were. And the . . . the general feeling was that the killer . . . missed us," he answered hesitantly.

Henninger's dark eyes lit up with amusement, and he smiled and nodded as he laughed softly. The smile gave him an entirely different look, one that Ty probably would have found appealing in other circumstances. "It would appear that he did," Henninger said with some amusement as the waitress sauntered over to take his order. "So, you're here to draw him out?" he went on after he ordered. "If you're under the radar, how do you plan to make yourself known to him?"

Ty just frowned. That wasn't exactly why they were here, but it made a certain kind of sense when put that way. If the killer had gone silent because they had abandoned the case, then it stood to reason that their mere presence would kick him back into doing something stupid. That also meant that their mere presence might cost someone else their life.

Zane pushed a bite of waffle around on the plate in front of him. "That's not exactly the plan," he murmured half to himself.

"But you hope to catch the killer's attention?" Henninger asked as he watched Zane's fork distractedly.

"We don't want his attention," Zane answered carefully. "We want him. Tell us about the cases. We've both been out of the loop."

"Have you?" Henninger responded with wide eyes, looking back and forth at them. "So you don't know anything about the last two murders?" he asked, his brow creasing.

Ty shook his head in answer, lips pressed tightly together.

"They didn't even tell you about the other agents?" Henninger asked them in disbelief.

Zane shook his head. "Just the basics," he said tightly.

Henninger looked between them, clearly surprised. Ty stared back at him, not appearing at all fazed.

"The murders when he resurfaced, medical examiner Karen Bryce and her assistant, Mina Holmes," Henninger told them regretfully. "They found the two of them in the morgue, locked inside. Looked like a nasty, bloody fight. Karen's throat was cut, and Mina had been strangled."

Zane cursed quietly and looked away, fighting back the desire to throw something.

Henninger frowned. "How do they expect us to make progress on finding this guy if we keep starting over? I mean, you got pulled right in the middle of things. You hadn't been killed yet; you were ahead of the curve," he pointed out wryly. His eyes shifted back and forth between the two, still puzzling over the changes in them.

"That knock on my head was a bit worse than we thought at first," Ty answered shortly. "I wasn't making much sense there at the end."

Henninger watched him silently for a moment, frowning and pursing his lips. Finally, he seemed to accept that and sat back.

Zane pushed his plate away, unable to eat any more after the news about Karen. "The Bureau has pretty much accepted that he's one of us now, right? Has anyone done anything about security in the offices?"

"Aside from more locked doors in the building and lengthier pass codes? Not really," Henninger answered with a shake of his head. "They don't want to spook him."

"Jesus fucking Christ," Zane spit out under his breath, sitting back with a thump and crossing his arms.

Henninger boggled at them. "What'd you two do? Switch brains?"

Ty sat silently and glared at the kid, remembering why he might have disliked him. Zane's glare matched Ty's, and Henninger shrank back a little. "Sorry," he muttered.

"This is what's going to happen," Zane bit off after a little more glaring. "You're going to get us all the case files—the originals, not copies—and the personnel files we were working before. I want the manifest lists from evidence, including everyone who's touched every single piece, and everyone who's filed a single piece of paper in this case."

"And you have clearance from on high this time," Ty added. "No sneaking required."

Henninger blinked, looked vaguely worried, and opened his mouth to utter a very obvious word, but caught it just in time. "I don't want to know, do I?"

Ty just shrugged and looked back down at his untouched food.

"Just get it. Then call us when it's together, and we'll meet again to pick it up. You've got my number." Zane scooted out of the booth and stood up, pulling a wad of cash out of his pocket and tossing a twenty on the table.

Henninger watched him rise with a slightly stricken look and then looked back at Ty, who was still sitting and staring at him blankly. "I kind of liked him better when he was you," Henninger grumbled to him.

Ty gave him a weak, sympathetic smile and slid out of the booth. Zane rolled his eyes and nudged Ty to get moving. Ty nudged him back, hard, and snarled at him as they left the restaurant. Henninger turned in his seat and watched them go, frowning at them thoughtfully.

Zane pulled out a cigarette and lit up as soon as they were outside. "I still don't like him," he said as they started walking.

"What do you mean, still?" Ty asked.

"He's a puppy dog. Didn't we have this conversation?" Zane said around his cigarette. He stopped at the curb to wait for the light to change.

"I didn't think you had a problem with him?" Ty questioned.

"At first I didn't, but I think that's because I was so wrapped up in being annoyed with you," Zane admitted. "But damn, he's eager. I was never that shiny."

Ty gave Zane a sidelong glance and shrugged. "Guess that depends on who you ask," he said.

Zane looked at Ty with narrowed eyes. "You met a caricature. You know that."

"Yeah, but it's still fun to watch you get all puffy over it," Ty laughed softly, a glimmer of the man Zane had first met shining through in his eyes.

Chuckling as they crossed the street, Zane smiled and winked at Ty. "You just like to poke and poke and get me riled up," he said with a purposeful double meaning.

"Damn right," Ty said with a grin, and then he stopped suddenly and kicked Zane in the shin.

"Ow!" Zane cried, though he was laughing slightly in surprise as Ty turned back around and began walking.

"I'm gonna start wearing steel-toed boots," Ty said over his shoulder. Zane snorted as they walked. He stopped without warning as he glanced across the street. "Oooh—detour."

"What?" Ty asked in confusion as he turned and then followed Zane's line of sight worriedly.

"Come on!" Zane ordered. He actually sounded happy all of a sudden. He pulled Ty along to the corner and then crossed to the other side of the street and walked partway back up to stop in front of the classy storefront window of a privately owned bookstore.

"What?" Ty asked again as he looked up at the hand-carved sign.

"I've heard about this place," Zane said, looking up at the sign. "It's all mysteries, suspense, thrillers . . ." He nearly bounced in place.

"Do you not get enough of that shit in your real life?" Ty asked with a roll of his eyes. "Come on," he ordered as he turned away. "I don't do books."

"Well, I do. Get an espresso or something," Zane said, pulling open the door and going inside.

"I don't do espressos," Ty called after him stubbornly. As he stood outside the doors, his shoulders slumped, and soon he obediently followed Zane into the store.

Zane was already browsing on a table marked Old Favorites when Ty stepped through the door. Quiet jazz played in the background, and a slim, white-haired man with spectacles sat behind the counter reading. A full coffee and espresso bar was set up to the side, steaming gently.

Ty forced himself not to groan. He hated these fucking places. Give him McDonald's black coffee and a copy of Guns and Ammo to read on the john and he was set. He didn't even like coffee.

"I see you're a man of action rather than one of reflection," the old man said out of the blue, his twinkling eyes looking over the glasses.

Ty was slightly surprised to be addressed, but he recovered quickly enough to respond with, "I'm prone to paper cuts."

The man chuckled and closed his book, using a tasseled bookmark. "Your friend is happy to be here."

"He's happy to be anywhere," Ty grumbled with an unfavorable glance at Zane.

"Perhaps he'll be better company the rest of the day. Coffee?"

Ty shook his head and glanced at Zane again with a frown. "You can keep him," he told the man in a grumble as he checked his watch.

Lifting his teacup, the man took a sip and looked over at Zane speculatively. "It changes one's appearance so, don't you think?"

Ty looked up at the old man in confusion and then glanced over at Zane again. The agent was practically beaming, another Jekyll-and-Hyde turnabout in five minutes flat. Ty watched him for a long moment, blinking in surprise at the twist in his chest. Finally, he gave the old man another look and cleared his throat.

"Help yourself to a seat," the old man offered.

Ty sighed and moved closer cautiously to take the chair. He realized that he wasn't used to people addressing him at all, especially strangers. Most everyone shied away from him because of his threatening, grumpy air. Was it slipping or was the old dude just crazy?

The man settled back in his seat, picking up his book again. "Perhaps he'll take pity on you soon," he said, opening the pages and going back to his reading, looking through the spectacles that sat low on his nose.

"I doubt that very much," Ty muttered as he turned his attention to Zane and crossed his arms over his chest.

Within a minute, Zane felt Ty's eyes on him, and he looked over his shoulder to favor Ty with a smile. Then he nodded and looked at the books he held. He chose three and put a couple back, then walked over to the counter. "Not even going to look, huh?"

Ty suspected that Zane wouldn't be enjoying this quite as much if he knew Ty didn't mind watching him. So he maintained his slightly sulky air and shook his head.

Zane glanced to the old man who was reading and apparently paying them no attention. "Okay, I'm happy. We can go after I pay for these." It hadn't even been ten minutes.

Ty looked him over and then sighed softly, allowing a small smile to show through. "We've got more time," he murmured in a low voice.

Zane tried not to grin like a fool. He adored bookstores, and it was a welcome distraction from his worries and brooding. "Thanks," he said softly with an indefinable look in his eyes. Then he turned to disappear in the stacks that led further into the store.

As soon as he was gone, Ty rolled his eyes heavenward and slouched in his chair in defeat. That look in Zane's eyes would get him anything.

The old man didn't make a sound or look up from his book. But he was smiling.

"Shut up," Ty muttered to him. He glanced over at him again, reading the gold lettering on the book the man read: The Complete Works of Edgar Allan Poe.

Ty frowned at the leather-bound volume as something buried deep in his memory began to click. Anyone who lived in Baltimore for any period of time had read at least one Poe story. The only ones Ty could remember were the one about the heart in the floorboards, the guy being bricked up in a wine cellar, and the name of the last one he had read, "The Murders in the Rue Morgue."

"Can I see that?" he asked suddenly, sitting up and pointing at the old book.

The man looked up at him, a small smile curling at his lips. "Of course," he said graciously, putting his bookmark in place carefully before he closed it and handed it to Ty.

Ty flipped to the index, where he found a list of the stories included in the volume. "Have you read all these before?" he asked without looking up.

"Many times," the man answered.

"Two people locked in a morgue," Ty murmured.

"That's one, yes," the man answered, mistakenly thinking that Ty was still speaking to him.

"Is there one with a blonde woman and a brunette, maybe switching places?" Ty tried as he looked up at the man. "Or one about a painting? A girl getting her teeth all pulled out?"

The old man nodded with a confused look at Ty and then at the book. Ty stood up quickly, thrusting the book back into the old man's hands. "Garrett!" he called out excitedly.

Zane appeared around one of the long bookshelves, moving toward him quickly and obviously alarmed. "What?" he demanded worriedly.

"I think you just broke this fucking case," Ty said to him with a grin. "Go find a copy of that book," he ordered as he pointed at the hardback the old man held gingerly in his hands.

CHAPTER TWELVE

Zane watched the activity from between the blinds of a small storefront across the street from the crime scene. He'd been watching for twenty minutes, not moving at all. Ty stood beside him, a little further away from the window because he was restless and couldn't quite stand still.

They watched as the local police set up a perimeter to keep out curious bystanders, cordoned off possible witnesses, and spread plainclothes agents through the gathering crowd to spot possible suspects. They watched Detectives Pierce and Holleman stand and scratch their heads in bewilderment, and they watched Ross and Sears arrive with Henninger and Morrison in tow and scratch their heads too. They watched the medical examiner arrive—the new one—followed by two techs and a body bag.

"Looks pretty chaotic. I think we can get in and out and never be seen," Ty murmured to Zane. "The ME is new; he won't know us. And you know he's got it pretty cleared out in there now as he examines the body."

Zane nodded slowly, still watching. He pulled out his phone, hit a few buttons, and waited. Down on the street, Henninger dug out his phone.

"We're going in with the ME. Keep the rest out," Zane said shortly. After a long moment in which the other agent answered, he snapped the phone shut, a grim look on his face. "Let's go," he said quietly. "Around the block and through the back. Entrance through the back."

Ty nodded and followed silently. They'd been leaving the bookstore with their newly purchased collection of Poe stories when they'd received the call, and he was almost eager to see if this newest murder would fit into their theory.

They headed outside and around the block, well away from the gathered law enforcement, and came in through the back alley where the ambulance was parked. There were just a couple cops to stand guard. A quick flash of their badges and some officious government snarls at the overworked men, and they were in.

Zane shoved his hands in his pockets and walked carefully on the narrow runner of plastic laid over the slick and sticky floor. Each room was bloody. They found the new ME in the living room.

The man looked over his shoulder at them. "You're the team from the Bureau?"

Ty glanced at Zane and then back at the ME. "What can you tell us?" he asked without answering the question.

"Occupant of the house is a seventy-one-year-old male. We don't know if he's the victim yet, but he's nowhere to be found. No way to tell time of death just yet except for the congealing of the blood. I'd say anywhere from three to five hours," the examiner told them. He stood up from where he crouched, carefully keeping his hands away from his own body. His gloves were stained almost to the wrists. "We're still finding pieces around the house. I figure most of the victim is here."

"How was the scene discovered?" Zane asked stoically.

The ME glanced between them. "The victim's heart was delivered to Federal Plaza with this address on a return address label."

"The heart?" Ty echoed flatly.

The ME nodded and merely looked at him as Zane rubbed his hand over his eyes, flinching painfully. Ty glanced around and pursed his lips. The blood that was visible was beginning to dry and grow darker. There were indeed pieces, just as the man had said. It was like a scene from some camp slasher movie. But Ty wasn't registering the absolute horror of the scene he was calmly perusing. Instead, he found himself trying to fit it into the profile he had made of the killer all those months ago.

"Anything else remarkable?" Zane forced himself to ask. He wanted—needed—to get out of there. Very soon. It was messing with his head.

"The murder weapon," the ME answered with a nod. He had one of the crime scene techs lead them over to a dresser that was decked out with a white cloth and tapers in silver candlesticks. On a tarnished silver platter in the center of the cloth was a gore-caked hacksaw.

Zane took one good look, nodded sharply and turned away, clenching his trembling hands into tight fists. It wasn't the blood and carnage that bothered him so much; it was the idea that someone did this to another living person, that it was so obviously planned.

Ty didn't notice his partner's reactions. Instead, he stared at the placement of the murder weapon curiously, intrigued by it.

"They found it like this?" he asked with a wave at the platter.

The tech nodded. "We're the only ones who've been in this room, sir."

Ty turned and looked over the room, glancing at Zane and then back at the bloody floor again. "Anything else?" he asked the crime scene guy.

"The only thing we've found that's odd is a hole cut in the floorboards. We're pretty sure the murder weapon was used to do it," the tech answered.

"Where's the hole?" Zane demanded.

"Bedroom. Here, I'll show you," the man answered as he pointed to a nearby doorway. "But it's not a hole. The killer covered it again," he added hastily as he led them into a front room of the house. "We haven't lifted the cover yet. We just finished taking photos."

Ty frowned down at the crudely cut square in the floor. "This dude's nuttier than squirrel shit," he muttered.

The tech glanced at him and bit his lip to keep from smiling.

Zane carefully knelt down, staring at the cracks in the wood. "Gloves," he asked, holding up one hand.

The tech blinked down at him, then glanced at Ty.

"Don't you think maybe you should let the crime scene dudes do this, Hoss?" Ty asked Zane pointedly.

"Give me some fucking gloves," Zane growled.

The tech pulled some out of his pocket and handed them over without questioning. After pulling them on, Zane started slowly tracing the cracks in the floorboards with his fingers. Ty watched wordlessly, recognizing Zane's gears turning but too annoyed with him to care.

All Ty knew was that their perp was getting frustrated with the lack of progress the Feds had been making, and he was now putting on a show. It felt almost like he was excited. The scene had a sense of manic glee to it, something none of the other scenes had carried with them. Ty looked over his shoulder, back in the direction of the room with the platter and the murder weapon, flanked by silver candlesticks.

It felt like a party. Like a welcome home party, complete with bloody confetti. But that wasn't possible, and Ty frowned as he began to wonder about his own mental stability. The killer had no way of knowing they were back on the case yet. If their theory was correct, he had nothing to be celebrating.

Kneeling on the floor, Zane pulled at the cutout of the hardwood floor with his fingers, but it was too tight to lift. He reached into his jacket sleeve and pulled out one of his knives, sliding it into the gap between the boards and applying pressure carefully.

The board lifted easily. He pulled it away and set it aside, then reached for the next one.

"What are you doing?" Ty asked in alarm as Zane began destroying the crime scene.

Zane looked grimly down into the hole as he lifted a second floorboard. "Take a look," he said to Ty as he sat back.

Ty and the tech both bent over the hole and peered down into it. Inside was a simple piece of white construction paper. Drawn on it in blood was a stylized heart.

"Weird," the tech observed flatly.

Ty turned his head to look at the man, then down at Zane. "Probably our token. What'd you expect to find?" he asked curiously.

Zane shrugged distractedly. "I don't know. Had hardwood floors growing up, used to hide things under them," he explained in a troubled voice. He stood up, peeling the gloves off and handing them to the tech. "Thanks," he said quietly before turning on his heel and leaving the room.

Ty stood and watched Zane retreat with a frown, then looked back down at the note left under the floorboards. He sighed and looked back up. Even in here, far removed from what appeared to be the main crime scene, there was blood and gore.

"Takes a real madman to do this to another human being," the ME said to him softly from the doorway where he'd been watching.

Ty gave the ME a glance and shook his head, taking stock of the fact that he himself was trying to figure out how the perp had done it physically, rather than mentally or morally. He stood and walked slowly to the door, standing beside the man.

"Scarier still," he murmured to the medical examiner as he looked through the house to the back porch where Zane stood. "I don't think he's crazy at all," he said softly as he left the room carefully, making certain he stayed on the plastic on his way out.

Zane stood outside, a cigarette already lit. He didn't move when Ty came out onto the porch. The dark circles under Zane's eyes were pronounced, and he looked exhausted and ill. His eyes were still blank, as if he was thinking about something so hard that he was almost zoning out over it.

Ty reached over and took the cigarette from between his lips, putting it out against the thick denim of his jeans. He then put the butt in his shirt pocket and looked away toward the back alley. Zane had to be out of it to be smoking at a fucking crime scene. He didn't know what evidence the smoke might destroy.

"Better get going before anyone else tries to come in," Ty said to him in annoyance. "Henninger can't hold them off for long."

They ducked around the ambulance just as they heard Gary Ross's deep voice, and Zane led the way back out of the alley and down the street, away from the scene. They stopped moving six blocks away, and Zane pulled out another cigarette, getting that deep-in-thought look in his eyes again.

Ty gently reached out and plucked the cigarette from his fingers. "Tell me what you're thinking," he requested calmly.

Zane's eyes followed the unlit cigarette in confusion, and he blinked owlishly when he looked up at Ty. "What?" he asked, reaching to take the cigarette back.

Ty pulled it further away, holding it out of reach as he looked at Zane pointedly.

Zane's brows drew together, and he took a few seconds to review the last minute. "Oh... I was thinking about the floorboards," he said, looking at Ty's hand and then back up at his eyes.

"What about them?" Ty prodded.

"The Tell-Tale Heart," Zane answered with a nod. "You were right. He's re-enacting Poe stories. Where that gets us, I don't know. It's a relief to finally see the pattern though." He wrinkled his nose, gave up on the cigarette, and pulled the crumpled pack out of his pocket to get another.

Ty sighed and handed the cigarette back. "Okay," he said. "So we get that book out, make a list of the murders, and send it to Henninger," he suggested. "But you're right, it gets us nowhere closer to him. That scene was... different," he added in a tired voice, mind still working over the new form of his profile.

Zane took the cigarette and tapped it on the pack, but now he was focusing more on Ty's reaction to giving it back. He didn't want Zane to smoke. That must be it. He remembered Ty's wry voice: "Those things will kill you." He slid the cigarette back into the pack and stuffed it into his pocket.

"How so?" he asked belatedly.

Ty merely shrugged and looked down, frowning. "Come on," he said softly as he stepped to the side and began moving again, "I need to write some shit down."

Zane rubbed a hand over his face, and they headed back to where they'd parked. It took a while to get back to the seedy motel they'd picked out, and they were both quiet the whole way. Once in the room, Zane shucked the jacket, the weapons, and his boots, and immediately laid facedown on the bed. Maybe if he dozed, something would come to him.

Ty didn't follow Zane's lead. Instead, he paced at the end of the other bed, pen in hand, drumming it against his thigh as he moved. He was thinking about the welcome party, about his inability to be horrified by the gore. His frown deepened the more he paced.

"Why are you pacing?" Zane muttered after several minutes. "Can't you sit to think?"

"No," Ty snapped in answer. "Leave me the fuck alone."

Zane sat up, obviously peeved. Growling quietly, he stalked over to his jacket and pulled out the cigarettes and lighter before turning to the door. Ty watched him go, glowering at the cigarettes in his hand. Zane yanked the door open, shoved the latch over to block it open, and stepped out onto the concrete walkway as he lifted an unlit smoke to his lips.

"Why would he set up the scene like that?" Ty called after him before the door could close.

Startling slightly, Zane almost dropped the lighter. He pushed the door back open partway. "The scene?" he asked, cigarette between his lips as he spoke.

"He set up the murder weapon like an offering," Ty answered, voicing what had been bothering him. "Like a... gift."

"On a silver platter, yeah. I wasn't amused," Zane said, blowing the smoke away from the door. "I bet he was."

Ty blinked at him and his lips parted slightly as if he was surprised at what Zane had said. He looked down to the thin carpet and blinked again, mouth working silently for several moments. "We haven't been amused," he mumbled.

Zane watched Ty, confused. "What's going on in that head of yours?" he asked mildly, the snap and frustration gone for the moment.

"I think I completely missed the profile," Ty answered dazedly.

Zane blinked in surprise. He stuck the unlit cigarette behind his ear and reentered the room, shutting the door behind him and turning the bolt. "Tell me," he prompted.

"We've been assuming he was playing games, flaunting how good he was and waiting for someone worth playing the game against," Ty answered quickly as he began pacing again. "Burns said there was an overall feeling that the killer was depressed after we left, despondent and silent. We assumed—because we're FBI and ego is a requirement—that it was because he thought we were good enough to play the game. But why would he think that?" he posed as he stopped and looked at Zane. "We were here for a grand total of, what, seven days? We made no progress, no more than any of the others, and the only thing we succeeded in doing was almost getting killed. He's not trying to play. He's trying to please."

"Trying to please? You mean to keep us busy? To give him our attention? And then when he lost it, he was unhappy?" Zane asked.

Ty shook his head. "You read crime novels and watch detective movies, right?" he said eagerly. "The stereotype in almost every one is a bored cop; he wants something exciting to sink his teeth into, wants action, wants . . . a big case to work on," he rambled almost excitedly. "Right? For all his intelligence and talent, this perp has bought into that image. He admires law enforcement officers," he went on, beginning to form a new profile as he spoke. "His dad or father figure might even have been a security guard or some sort of pseudo-policeman type. That's why he became a Fed, if he is one. He admired them. He wants to please the people he admires, give them something worth their time." He closed his eyes and lifted his chin, raising his face to the ceiling.

Zane bit back a smile. He glanced to the stack of crime and suspense novels he'd bought. "Okay, I can see that. So, he's hoping to give us a good game. So if we figure it out, what's to stop him from changing the game?"

"He has to change it. He'll be well-schooled in forensics and profiling. He'll think he's hiding by switching his MO, but he's still got that pattern. He may have picked it because it offered so many different methods. Or it may have more special meaning to him. He killed the Poe Toaster in Baltimore, we can be sure of that, either as a jumping-off point or practice. He had to have picked him because of who he was. Poe is the playbook he's sticking to in order to stay safe. He's not killing for the pleasure of the kill, not like normal serials. What he enjoys—his real ritual—is the after-effects," Ty explained as the profile unfolded before him like a road map over his mental steering wheel. "What he craves is the attention of the authorities afterward. Not the press, not the public. Just the cops and Feds. He doesn't just return to the scene of the crime; he lives it. He soaks the mayhem in afterward, either by being physically present or thriving on the official reports. That's why he's sending stuff in the mail; he's helping the people he admires try to solve him."

"So, it might not be someone at the Bureau, but maybe a cop from the city who's got access," Zane realized. "Someone who works both sides of the case, although in a minor role. Like the Steves are attached to this case." He tossed the cigarette pack on the table and sat back down on the bed. "I wish we had that damn list of all personnel who've touched anything to do with this mess."

"The new profile screams cop with an inferiority complex," Ty agreed. "But with the access he has, I'm still saying FBI. It also makes me think that something we did, the two of us, told him that we were enjoying what he was doing," he went on more tentatively. "We may have expressed admiration for his skill somehow or shown interest in how or why he did something that none of the other agents had noticed. Whatever it was we did, he thought he'd finally found someone who was enjoying the fruits of his labor."

Zane's face was blank and then he blanched. "So he's been doing this ... specifically to amuse us? You and me?"

"Not at first," Ty answered with a shake of his head. "And not even now. To assume that would be to assume he knows we're back. The two of us, specifically. I think he heard somehow that the Bureau was sending in a new crew. That, back there? That was his welcome party."

Zane closed his eyes, feeling slightly ill at the thought. That had been perhaps the most gruesome scene he had ever witnessed, and he'd seen a lot, but Ty seemed to be thinking of it as merely another stepping stone to finding their killer.

He opened his eyes again and looked—really looked—at Ty, studying him, catching on to the slightly detached air he had about him. He'd had it ever since they'd been reunited. Even back at his home in Baltimore. He remembered Ty's reaction to the woman being found in his hotel room all those months ago, and experience with psychology told Zane what was going on. Ty was still in shock. He'd gone through the treatment like a good little soldier, but he hadn't really processed any of the therapy. He had basically severed any links to deeper emotions to avoid anything hurting too much.

Ty snorted and continued to pace, oblivious to Zane's study of him. "We should call Henninger," he finally murmured. "Tell him to change the profile."

"It'll be several hours till he's off the scene and able to talk," Zane reminded. He felt for Ty. Not just aching because Ty was so removed, but in other ways as well. It scared him, and his chest tightened as he watched his partner pace.

"Call him anyway, this shit is important," Ty grunted in annoyance as he patted himself down for his own phone.

"All right. Call Henninger, then what?" Zane asked. "We need somewhere bigger than this to spread out the files he's supposed to bring us and give them a good study. We should probably change hotels anyway, just in case."

Ty was very still, letting the last words sink in. "You think he knows we're back?" he asked neutrally.

Zane swallowed, thinking back to what they'd talked about minutes before. "Yeah."

"Us, specifically?" Ty asked quietly.

Meeting Ty's eyes, Zane wondered if the curling anxiety showed in his own. "Yeah."

"Me too," Ty responded in the same quiet, calm voice.

"Won't be long until he—"

"He needs us," Ty interrupted confidently. "He needs us to make him feel as if he's doing well. He won't try to hurt us again. I'm sure of it," he lied.

The lie didn't go unnoticed, but Zane had no plan to comment. He looked up at Ty sadly, wanting to say something, anything other than the soft words crowding in his throat. He swallowed on them again. He didn't know how much more "speaking" they could do. Finally, a sentiment broke free in a rasp. "I won't lose you. Not now."

"I don't plan to get any more lost than I am," Ty answered roughly. He turned quickly, pacing away from the bed as he flipped open his phone.

Zane squeezed his eyes shut and cursed silently. Curling his hands into fists, he got off the bed, put on his jacket, and retrieved his lighter, sliding the cigarette from behind his ear as he walked toward the door again.

Ty watched him go from under lowered brows, waiting for Henninger to pick up. When the younger agent answered, Ty quickly told him about the change in profile and the pattern they had discovered.

"Poe?" Henninger asked in a low voice, obviously trying not to be overheard. "You're sure?"

"The latest murder pretty much clinches it," Ty answered. "We got one of those damn anthologies; we're going to go through it and see what we find. Did you get a chance to gather those personnel files for me?"

"Not yet," Henninger answered hesitantly. "I'll have them by the morning," he promised quickly. "You wanted anyone who worked or lived in Baltimore between 2000 and 2002, correct?"

"That's right," Ty answered with an unconscious nod. "Now, go get the word out about the pattern, get Bureau analysts all over this shit. We have to get ahead of him."

"Right. But how do I go to them with this?" Henninger asked worriedly. "What do I tell them?"

"Make up something. Take the credit," Ty instructed.

"What?" Henninger asked in a slightly stunned voice.

"Tell them you figured it out with this latest murder; it's pretty damn obvious when you think about it," Ty suggested. "Tell them about the murder in Baltimore and how you made the connection from there. If they ask," he was careful to instruct. "They probably won't, so don't offer any information you don't have to. They'll probably just be glad to have something to go on. If you get in too deep, just tell them you got a tip from a buddy in the Bureau who didn't want to be named. Give them my name and number in Baltimore if they demand it."

He waited until Henninger got a notepad and gave him the number in case he needed it.

"Anything else?" Henninger asked with a heavy sigh.

"Just be careful. We suspect he may know we're back, and if he does, he may connect you with us," Ty warned worriedly. He didn't like the thought of being responsible for any more innocent lives. He still saw Isabelle St. Claire's face when he slept.

"No worries, sir," Henninger murmured.

Ty ended the call and sighed unhappily. Despite what should have been considered two major breaks in the case, he didn't feel as if they'd made any progress.

Zane stepped back into the room, smelling of smoke and looking troubled. "Time to move?" he asked Ty.

Ty nodded wordlessly, and they began gathering their small number of things and carrying them out to the rental car. The feeling that the killer was on their trail, rather than the other way around, sat heavily on both of them. They didn't say another word to each other as Zane got behind the wheel and began driving with no particular destination in mind.

Finally, Ty glanced over at him and watched him for a long moment. "We could just cut and run," he suggested softly, watching Zane closely.

Forcibly keeping his eyes on the road, Zane pressed his lips together hard, and his hands curled tightly around the steering wheel. "It's a nice dream," he finally answered, his voice as unsteady as the rest of him. "But I'd never be able to sleep. And neither would you," he said softly.

Ty couldn't help but smile. "Yeah," he responded as he looked back out the window.

They were silent for several more minutes as they sat in midday traffic.

"Okay so, change of venue," Zane said suddenly in a slightly louder voice than he'd intended, hoping to dispel the funk that had settled over them. "How about a jazzy place in Greenwich? Good restaurants. Great bars."

"You talking hotels?" Ty asked dubiously.

"More bungalow-type setups. Rent by the week. Artsy places," Zane explained. "It's different."

"Do I look like an artsy type to you?" Ty asked, bristling on principle.

It didn't even faze Zane. "You look like sex on legs to me. You'll blend in, no problem."

"I swear to God, if you try to put me in leather pants or some shit like that I'll kill you," Ty warned with a point of his finger at Zane.

"I was thinking along the lines of no pants, baby," Zane said with a smirk. "In our room, anyway."

That gave Ty pause and he pursed his lips to consider. "Yeah, okay," he finally agreed with a smirk.

Zane found an eclectic neighborhood with bohemian shops, art galleries, and people all over the place. They lucked out and found a furnished studio apartment for rent rather than a hotel, and the landlord was happy to rent to them for an unspecified amount of time as long as it came with the hefty down payment they offered, no questions asked. Hundreds of people drifted in and out of Greenwich each year. These two men were nothing special.

The three-room apartment that was half of the third floor of an old brownstone was decorated in warm colors and comfortable fabrics. There were no electronics, except for a phone, but there was wireless internet coming from somewhere, probably the small café across the street.

Zane dropped his bag and box on the round table in the front room. He turned to see Ty surveying the room warily, and it made him smile. "Coming in?"

"I don't know," Ty frowned. "Does it smell like hemp and incense?"

"Just the bed," Zane said straight-faced.

"Too bad," Ty replied seriously. "That was the only part I was looking forward to."

Zane's lips twitched. "Still have the couch," he said, trying to get Ty into the room.

Ty took a step into the room and stopped stubbornly. "I feel my manhood seeping out of me," he muttered.

Zane dropped his jacket on a wingback chair after pulling the bottle of Mountain Dew out of it. The apartment was cute and quaint; somewhere no one would ever look for two FBI agents. He pulled his gun out of the holster and set it on the table as Ty ventured further into the rooms.

When Zane turned his attention back to his partner, Ty had his back to him, his jacket was off, and his holster sat snug against his pressed blue dress shirt. He was rubbing the back of his neck and looking down at the bed in front of him, his free hand on his hip. Looking at the shined dress shoes and the expensive, tailored suit he wore, from this angle he may as well have been a different person from the one Zane had worked with before.

Zane wondered what had happened to Ty's crazy T-shirts. They had fit his style and his hard-ass image. He'd probably packed them away, Zane figured, packed them away with all his old habits and thoughts as the physical and mental therapy had taken over.

Zane missed those T-shirts.

Watching him, Zane considered pulling Ty into his arms in hopes the man might relax a little. But the vibe Ty was putting out clearly said that touching of any sort was not the way to relax him. Stretching, Zane sighed and dug into his duffel, looking for a clean T-shirt. Unfortunately all of his were plain ones.

He went to the bed and pulled the covers back, smoothing his hand over the sheets before heading to the bathroom. It had been a long day, and he was more than ready to rest.

Ty followed him and leaned against the doorframe that led into the bathroom as Zane went over to the antique oval mirror above the sink. Zane washed up as Ty moved closer to him, and he stiffened in surprise when Ty wrapped his arms around him from behind.

"It's good to have you here," Ty told him impulsively.

Zane shifted back, closer to Ty's body, sliding his arm back and around Ty's waist to press flush against him. Ty held him silently, settling his chin on Zane's shoulder after several breaths. Zane turned his cheek into Ty's and closed his eyes, and Ty waited tensely for some sort of response, flushing at the words he had uttered.

"I wouldn't have agreed to come here, if it hadn't been you," Zane murmured finally. "Don't you know that?"

Ty jerked a little in surprise, but he didn't release him. "Why?" he asked in a whisper.

Zane closed his eyes and kept their cheeks pressed together. "I trust you."

A flush of guilt swept through Ty with the words. He couldn't say the same about why he had agreed to take this case. He would have come alone. It was revenge for him, pure and simple. Unfinished business. He turned his head more and pressed his nose against Zane's cheek. "Then you're a fucking idiot," he said gruffly.

Zane chuckled. "Yeah, but you already knew that." Ty was silent. Zane pulled away gently and moved past him, figuring no other comment on Ty's part meant the talking thing was done. He went out into the main room and reached for his duffel to dig out his shower kit.

Ty let him move away, a heavy feeling in his chest and an unsettled feeling everywhere else. He couldn't seem to feel anything but guilt unless Zane was near him. Why was that? Why did he need Zane in order to feel?

"We do better when we're fucking," Ty muttered to him as he followed him back out into the room.

Zane snorted quietly. "News flash," he said as he sat on the edge of the bed and began unlacing his boots.

CHAPTER THIRTEEN

Zane thumped into the room and dropped the bag of snacks and drinks he'd just picked up at the quick mart down the block. He hadn't been able to sleep, and he was glad that some places were open at four in the morning. He tossed his jacket to the side and headed to the table to unload his gear. He glanced over at Ty, who curled on his side on the bed, apparently sleeping. As Zane watched him in the light from the street that filtered through the window, Ty growled in his sleep and rolled, tangling in the sheets as he did so.

Smiling slightly, Zane stopped to look down at him. Ty never seemed to sleep easy, except when Zane was in bed holding him. He wondered what Ty dreamed about. Usually Ty woke as soon as Zane moved. The fact that he was still asleep meant he'd either already been awake and discerned he wasn't needed, he was very tired, or he was sick. Thoughtful, Zane took care of his gun and wallet, setting them carefully aside.

Ty muttered in his sleep and tossed his head fitfully. Frowning, Zane walked over and crouched down beside the bed, looking over Ty's face as it twisted slightly. Zane wanted to wake him just to interrupt the bad dreams, but he wasn't going to reach out and touch until the other man knew he was there, just in case. Ty had all kinds of ingrained military training that his body instinctively followed, and Zane didn't relish getting attacked by a Recon Marine having flashbacks.

"Ty," he murmured, prompting the other man to wake up a little as he shielded himself with the side of the bed.

"Hmm?" Ty responded as he tossed his head again and rolled back toward Zane.

"You're tossing around so much, you can't be resting," Zane said quietly.

Ty's eyes fluttered open and he looked at Zane without seeming to recognize him. He stared for a moment and then closed them again. He sighed and shifted slightly in the bed, then opened his eyes again. They were clear when he met Zane's eyes. "Shut up," he muttered sleepily.

Zane chuckled. "You'll be crankier than you were when you went to bed."

"I'm not cranky," Ty insisted drowsily as he closed his eyes again and rolled onto his back. He stretched with relish, yawning and curling his toes contentedly. "I was dreaming," he muttered.

"Mm-hmm," Zane agreed, shifting to sit on the edge of the bed and lay his hand lightly on Ty's abs. "Dreaming of?"

"The desert," Ty answered in a mumble. He shifted again, arching up into Zane's hand like a dog getting his belly rubbed.

Zane started rubbing agreeably, watching Ty move. "Desert, huh?"

Ty inhaled deeply and then sighed, opening his eyes again to stare at the ceiling. "Makes my trigger finger itch."

"Sand does itch," Zane replied blithely. "One of the reasons I chose Miami over western New Mexico."

Ty turned his head slightly and looked up at Zane in confusion. Zane raised a brow. "What?"

"What?" Ty asked in a lost voice.

Zane shook his head. "You're definitely not awake. One of the reasons I refused the assignment in New Mexico is because I hate eating sand. And I don't like rattlesnakes."

Ty blinked at him rapidly and then looked around the room before pushing himself into a sitting position. "What assignment in New Mexico?" he asked as he rubbed his eyes.

Peering at him in amusement, Zane decided to explain even though Ty was still out of it. "The one I was offered before they stuck me in Miami. Bilingual agents are scarce lately," he said.

"Oh, yeah," Ty responded flatly with a little nod as he moved. "That's very important," he assured Zane gruffly as he flopped back onto his side and buried his head under his pillow.

Zane chuckled and pulled away the pillow. "Cranky?" he teased.

Ty groaned softly and then huffed in irritation. "Can't a man sleep in peace around here?"

"Apparently not when he dreams of the desert," Zane drawled. He leaned to press his lips to Ty's temple. "Sleep, then," he murmured.

"I always dream of the desert," Ty muttered sulkily as he pressed his face against the mattress, refusing to be roused.

Zane's lips drifted to the corner of Ty's eye. "Why?" he murmured.

Ty twitched and turned to elbow Zane in the ribs. "That's where I lived," he grumbled.

Zane smoothed his hand over Ty's arm in a soothing motion and turned his face to lay his cheek against Ty's for a moment.

Ty sighed again and relaxed under the pressure of Zane's body. "You're very high-maintenance," he mumbled against the pillow.

Grinning, Zane curled his arm over Ty's back and rubbed slowly over his hip. "Yeah, so I've been told."

"Shut up," Ty ordered.

Zane coasted his hand over Ty's cheek and rolled away. "Sleep, oh cranky one."

Ty groaned and rolled back onto his back. "Well fuck, Garrett, I'm awake now," he muttered disconsolately.

"Sorry," Zane murmured, letting his arm fall between them and looking down at Ty.

Ty looked up at him in irritation for a moment before letting the façade fall away and smiling slightly. "You're a damn sight better to wake up to than what I usually do," he admitted.

Zane smiled crookedly. "And what's that?"

"You don't really want to know, do you?" Ty asked dubiously.

"I already know about the woman who was screeching on the phone," Zane pointed out.

Ty cleared his throat and looked away, staring up at the ceiling with a frown. "Usually," he finally said with a scowl, "I don't wake up to anything. So, I guess you'll have to do."

"Is there a compliment hidden in there somewhere?" Zane asked mildly.

"Beggars can't be choosers," Ty muttered with a small smirk.

Zane whapped Ty's hip. "I don't beg," he asserted.

Ty jerked and laughed softly, turning slightly away in case Zane decided to smack him again. "I beg to differ," he snickered.

Zane smacked him again, a little harder this time. "I can't think of an instance. Not a legitimate one, anyway."

"What's an illegitimate reason to beg?" Ty asked as he continued laughing softly.

Zane's hand stilled, as did his face. His eyes shifted across the room blankly. "They exist," he said vaguely.

Ty narrowed his eyes up at his companion and then rolled them as he looked away. "Moody," he accused as he sat back up again and stretched.

"Moody?" Zane's face scrunched. "I was sort of thinking about the last time I begged for my life and couldn't really have cared less. Just figured if I told you, I'd get the violins treatment again."

"You were right. And that's not an illegitimate reason, moron," Ty told him as he swung his feet over the edge of the bed.

"I was referring to the 'couldn't really have cared less' part, actually," Zane said, closing his eyes and letting his head lean back against the wall.

Ty sat with his back to Zane, looking at the opposite wall with his head cocked thoughtfully. "Fuck," he commented with a slight shake of his head.

Zane opened his eyes and looked at Ty's back. "Maybe later," he said as he picked up the file folder again. "Told you I was fucked up while we were apart."

"Why not just let them kill you?" Ty asked. "Why beg at all?"

"Gut reflex, I guess," Zane said quietly. "Didn't really think about it, except that there was something I'd miss. Was scared too. Being shot in the head doesn't appeal too much."

"It'd be quicker than a lot of other ways," Ty pointed out as he turned around slightly and met Zane's eyes. "I was always afraid of dying slow," he said thoughtfully.

Zane's mouth quirked. "I played that game too." He curled his hand into a fist as his fingers started twitching.

"What game?" Ty asked in confusion.

"Figuring out what will kill you slow and easy," Zane said, opening his fist and rubbing his palm against his thigh. "Pain wasn't a consideration."

Ty stared at him for a long moment. "Why'd you want to go slow?" he finally asked.

Zane's mouth quirked. "So I could enjoy it."

Ty raised one expressive eyebrow. He licked his lips and looked away. "My daddy used to mind the mines when I was little," he said suddenly. "I used to dream that I was stuck down there. I wouldn't mind freezing to death," he claimed abruptly. "Going numb and then going to sleep. But I think I'd want it quick. I got too much to look back on and regret to want time to ponder it all." He glanced back at Zane. "Just another thing we don't have in common."

"Regrets? Maybe. Sometimes I think I deserve all the shit I went through. Did it to myself," Zane said. He met Ty's eyes. "I would think you wouldn't agree. You don't seem the type to self-flagellate."

"Let's pretend I don't know what you're talking about," Ty responded with a ghost of a smile. His regrets were one thing he did not plan on going over with Zane anytime soon. Or ever.

Zane nodded slowly. "All right," he murmured. It was obviously a topic to avoid. "So you're saying you think I don't have regrets?"

"No. Just commenting on the fact that you'd rather have time to linger over them at the end," Ty corrected. "This is a morbid conversation. What the hell is wrong with you?" he asked in a huff as he rubbed his hands through his hair.

"Me?" Zane asked in disbelief. "I didn't say I wanted to linger over anything. Just that if I have to die, I want to enjoy it." He shrugged slightly. "You don't have enough focus to ponder much of anything hopped on heroin. That's the allure." His hand twitched again.

Ty sighed and looked away again with a shake of his head. "How long ago was it?" he asked tiredly.

"How long ago was what?"

"The heroin?" Ty asked curtly as he glanced back over his shoulder.

"Four and a half, maybe five weeks, I guess," Zane answered.

"So I'm to assume it wasn't a constant thing?" Ty asked tightly. "Since you're not screaming in pain from the withdrawal, I mean?"

Zane stared at him for a long moment. "No, it wasn't constant. It was all I had to cut the pain when I got shot." His hand went to his abdomen, where Ty knew there was a fresh, barely healing scar. "I know what I can handle."

Ty examined him for a long time, and then turned his head to face the wall again. He sighed softly. "Okay," he finally acknowledged quietly. It just wasn't worth the fight it could turn into to continue the conversation, and Ty was getting tired of talking about it.

"Did you ever use?" Zane asked, curious.

"Never," Ty answered immediately.

"But you drink," Zane murmured, looking down at his hands, wondering if there was any way he could explain so Ty could have some idea of what it was like to be addicted. "Ever drink too much and still want more?"

"Every time I drink too much I swear it off for a week," Ty muttered.

"But I pick the bottle up the next weekend. The next day. Maybe even that night," Zane said softly. "Just until I get my fill. Feels good, not hurting anybody. Once I've had enough, I'll stop. I won't drink too much this time."

Ty turned his head slightly, but didn't quite look back at Zane. "I understand what an addiction is," he said in a low, hard voice. "Not everyone is that weak."

Zane's body went totally still. "Everyone is that weak. Even guys who fuck a different woman every night just to forget somebody else."

Ty's shoulders tensed slightly as he looked back at the wall. "Touché," he said abruptly.

Zane raised a brow, staring at the other man. "Touché? That's it? Five months ago you'd have clocked me for that."

"What do you want from me, Garrett?" Ty asked in frustration. He turned his head slightly but still didn't turn to meet Zane's eyes.

Sitting up, Zane reached for him. "Look at me, Ty," he said firmly.

Ty glanced over his shoulder, his jaw clenching angrily.

"What were you going to say first? Before your newly installed conscience caught your brain and had you say something else?" Zane asked, fingers tightening.

Ty looked down at Zane's fingers as they dug into his arm, then back up to look sideways at Zane. "Some creative version of 'fuck you,' I'm sure," he answered tightly.

"Then why didn't you say it? Christ knows you've called me about every name in the book. Why not now?" Zane prodded. If Ty didn't let some of that anger out somehow he was going to implode. Zane had seen it happen. Zane had had it happen.

"Because," Ty answered stubbornly.

"'Because'?" Zane parroted, refusing to back off. "Think I can't take it?"

"Are you trying to start a fight?" Ty asked as he shook his arm away from Zane's grasp.

"Apparently. And you're determined to sit there all buttoned up and not hurt my feelings," Zane said, catching Ty's arm again, this time the forearm. "Let it go. There's no one here to act for."

"How many harsh words will it take to send you into a bottle?" Ty asked as he yanked his forearm away and smacked at Zane's hand. "Not too damn many, I'm guessing."

"How many times am I gonna have to rip down these walls you keep putting up before you fucking pop and go ballistic at precisely the wrong time?" Zane snapped, fingers grasping and tightening despite the smack. "How long can you keep it all inside? 'Cause believe me, you've got no chance of doing it forever."

Ty reached for Zane's hand suddenly, squeezing his wrist to free his other hand. As soon as Zane's fingers let go, Ty reached out and backhanded him.

If Zane had been a smaller man, he might have fallen sideways under the blow. As it was, his chin snapped to the side from the strength of it, and when he looked back at Ty, he had to lick a trickle of blood off his split lip. When he spoke, his voice was strong and even with the surety of hard-won personal experience. "If you can't learn to let go of the anger and frustration somehow, it will eat you up inside," he advised. "And I don't mean hiding in the bottom of a bottle or between some stranger's thighs."

Ty closed his eyes and looked away, visibly trying to calm himself. "I'm sorry," he finally murmured. He turned slightly and reached back to Zane, sliding his hand against the side of his face as he wiped the blood away from Zane's lip with his thumb regretfully.

Zane pressed his cheek into Ty's hand, looking over him with softer eyes, and his mouth quirked. "Well, I deserved it," he said. "I don't want you to go through what I did."

Ty wasn't quite sure what to say in response, and it showed clearly on his face. Instead of saying anything, he turned his head and let his hand slide away from Zane's face. He picked up Zane's hand and turned it over with a sad shake of his head. "You're quite susceptible to that move," he chastised softly as his thumb slid gently over the pressure point he'd utilized.

Grimacing, Zane rolled his wrist. "Yeah. I've worn the sheaths so long that I'm not used to having my wrists vulnerable. It's hard to change a habit like that."

Ty hummed thoughtfully and set his hands back into his own lap. "Where'd the knives come from?" he asked abruptly.

"Jack Tanner," Zane answered.

Ty raised an eyebrow and tilted his head so he could see Zane better. "You worked with Jack at the Academy?" he asked in obvious surprise. Jack Tanner was an ex-SEAL, employed by the Bureau to teach agents going through the Academy the basics of not getting killed in hand-to-hand combat. By the time Ty had gone through, Tanner was old enough and grouchy enough that he didn't teach classes anymore; he merely picked protégés to run the lessons and supervised them.

Zane smiled slightly and nodded. "I needed the help," he said. "Remember me telling you about having to repeat? Yeah. Jack's the reason I didn't wash out the second time through."

"I didn't know he did one-on-one lessons," Ty remarked with a small smirk.

"Only for special cases," Zane said. "That, and Becky was a really good cook."

Ty nodded and looked away uncomfortably. "Jack was always a sucker for a good ribeye," he muttered.

Zane tipped his head. "Another story there?" he asked.

"There's always another story somewhere," Ty answered vaguely.

"Like why you want it to end quick," Zane said, deciding he'd pushed enough. He already knew more about Ty's past than Ty knew about his. He supposed he was lucky in that respect. Sighing, he rubbed his eyes. "Going numb and then going to sleep," he agreed finally. "I guess that appeals to a lot of people in our line of work.

We're more likely to be beaten up, shot, knifed, blown up, hit by a car, tortured..."

Ty merely nodded distantly, his head slightly turned as he stared out the window.

"Why'd you take this job?" Zane asked curiously. "After they ran you out of Recon? Why not tell the government to take a flying leap and buy a coal mine?"

Ty scratched his chin and cocked his head. "'Cause I was afraid of the coal mines," he answered curtly.

"I knew you were a smart man," Zane said.

"Doesn't take a smart man to be afraid of the coal mines," Ty responded seriously.

"What does it take? For you to be afraid?"

Ty turned his head quickly and frowned at Zane. "You don't think I'm afraid?" he asked.

"If you aren't, then you're way beyond fixing," Zane claimed. "I want to know what makes you afraid. I've seen it, a few times, in your eyes. On your face. But I couldn't figure out why. Not really."

Ty shrugged and looked away before Zane could see anything else in his eyes. "I don't know," he answered defensively. "Normal things, I guess."

"Ty," Zane said quietly, seeing the evasion for what it was.

"What?" Ty huffed.

Zane sighed and shook his head, but he had to laugh just a tiny bit. "I don't think I have ever met someone as stubborn as you."

"Shut up," Ty said uncomfortably.

"It's not an insult. Hell." Zane sighed and leaned back against the headboard. He watched Ty for a long minute. The man looked antsy and unable to settle. On edge. "Ty, chill."

"You woke me up," Ty said accusingly. "Why do you want to know? What does it matter what I'm afraid of?" he asked, obviously unable to let the conversation go.

Zane blinked in surprise. "It matters to me," he said quietly. "I want to know. So I..." His voice trailed off and he swallowed. "So I can protect you."

Ty sniffed. "Protect me from being afraid?"

"Protect you when you're afraid," Zane corrected.

Ty muttered quietly to himself and shook his head. "Okay," he finally ground out. "You want to know what I'm afraid of?" he asked as he turned his head slightly and looked back at Zane. "I'm afraid of small spaces," he said as he raised his hand and began counting off with his fingers. "I'm afraid of small, dark spaces. I'm afraid of small, dark spaces with bugs and/or rodents in them. And I'm afraid of falling when my ass isn't attached to a parachute. Satisfied?" he asked sarcastically.

Zane refused to be baited. "Thanks," he said simply, just watching Ty, wondering what was making him so cranky. He'd tried picking a fight; he'd tried reasoning with him. But Ty was still tense, unwilling or unable to just let the frustration go and shout at him. "Do I still make you that uncomfortable?" he asked, sounding forlorn. "After all we've done?"

Ty closed his eyes and raised his chin slightly, sighing quietly. "A little," he admitted. "I'm not used to answering questions, okay?" he explained defensively. "I just . . . It's just weird for me."

Zane nodded from where he leaned against the headboard, and a bit of his own tension seeped away. "Come here," he requested, reaching out an arm.

Ty glanced over at him to see if he was making light. When he didn't see any signs of joking, he narrowed his eyes slightly. "Fuck off, Priss," he offered with a small smile.

Zane's eyes sparkled and he laid his hand over his propped-up knee. "Who are you callin' Priss, Mr. Suited Up and Shiny?" he taunted.

"If this is going to resort to name-calling, I've already got you beat, Spanky," Ty warned with a smirk.

"How do you figure that, Jarhead?" Zane replied.

"'Cause I rock," Ty explained in an even voice. "And you don't," he continued as he pointed at Zane, pinky finger held out to the side daintily as if he were drinking tea.

Smirking, Zane sat up, grabbed Ty, and dragged him down onto the bed and under his bigger body. "I'd poke you, but you'd beat the shit out of me."

Ty flailed briefly before he was pinned, and he blinked up at Zane suspiciously as he flexed his fingers under Zane's grip. "Power trip," he accused softly.

Zane waggled his eyebrows. "I gave you a chance to come peacefully."

"You're easily distracted, aren't you?" Ty deadpanned.

"Not really," Zane said smoothly, dragging one hand down Ty's chest. "I'm still focused on you."

Ty shivered as Zane's fingers raised goose bumps all over his body. "And that is the crux of our problem," he reminded softly.

"Problem?" Zane echoed, his hand continuing its descent.

"All kinds of problems," Ty affirmed. He reached up with the hand Zane had left free and smacked the bigger man gently on the side of the head. "Focus," he chastised.

Zane screwed up his face before looking down at Ty seriously. "You're not a problem. Not to me."

"Sure I am," Ty argued. "We know the bare minimum about each other, and correct me if I'm wrong, that's just the way we want it. We know we want to take each other to bed, but we don't have much else to go on. To me, that spells all kinds of problems," he pointed out gently. "I didn't say I was complaining," he added.

"Grady . . ." Zane groaned and rolled to his side, then curled one arm around his partner's waist. "I'm not trying to pick a fight here, but what do you propose we do about it? Neither one of us is all that good at talking. In fact, I'd say we suck spectacularly at talking."

"How about you stop asking so many questions," Ty suggested. "And I'll start giving a damn when you look like you need a hug," he added cheekily.

"You already give a damn," Zane chanced.

Ty merely smiled, his lips twitching as if he was trying not to. Zane grinned and stole a kiss.

"Shut up," Ty muttered before jabbing Zane in the ribs gently and rolling out of his grasp.

Restraining the urge to yank Ty back into his arms, Zane instead let go and just lay there watching him. Ty sat up and swung his legs over the edge of the bed, then cocked his head and stared at the far wall thoughtfully.

"What are you afraid of?" he asked after nearly a minute of silence.

That silence extended as Zane struggled with what to say. "Not being there," he finally murmured.

Ty turned his head slightly to look back over his shoulder. "Not being where?" he asked in confusion.

Zane looked haunted. "I wasn't there when Becky was killed. I wasn't there when my first partner went stupid and drove home drunk. And I lost them both."

"Yeah?" Ty responded unsympathetically. "I was there when my partner was shot and killed," he said quietly. "I even took the bullet just like he did," he said as he pointed to the spot low on his abdomen where a scar told the story of a through and through. "Still didn't do him a damn bit of good. Just 'cause you're there, doesn't mean it's any less tragic."

Zane closed his eyes and shrugged a little. "If I'd been there, I might have been able to do something. But I wasn't, and I lost them."

"And if you'd been there," Ty said softly, "I would have lost you."

Zane slowly opened his eyes to look at Ty's back as his breath caught. "I'm not letting you walk away again," he said to him thickly without thinking about it first.

Ty gave a lopsided shrug and then nodded, not turning to look back at Zane. "It's debatable, who walked away," he said softly.

Zane drew in a deep breath, held it, and let it out slowly. "We . . . couldn't have done this then. We didn't know . . ."

Ty nodded thoughtfully as he finally turned to look Zane over, but the look on his face clearly said that he might disagree.

"How?" Zane asked, tilting his head to one side.

"How what, Chief?" Ty asked softly.

"How would it have worked?"

Ty pursed his lips and shrugged again. "Same way it is now, I guess," he answered, displaying the sort of nonchalance with which the Ty of old had always handled emotional situations. "Except without the drinking and drugs and copious amounts of anonymous sex, I'd imagine," he added with a cock of his head.

Zane's lips twitched. "Anonymous sex? I thought you knew all those women."

"Well, I did after a few minutes," Ty pointed out with a hint of a blush.

A smile broke free. "You did better than I did, then," the other man muttered, though he wasn't at all self-conscious about it.

"I don't wanna know," Ty said immediately, closing his eyes and shaking his head.

Zane chuckled and swiped playfully at Ty's arm. "Come here," he said again. "We can sleep until Henninger calls."

"You sleep, I'll wake you up during the middle of a dream," Ty promised crankily.

"You were having a bad dream!" Zane insisted.

"You know what I ain't afraid of?" Ty asked. "Bad dreams!" He swatted at Zane's grasping hand and then began crawling toward him slowly. "Dreams mean I'm sleeping, and sleeping means I ain't lying awake trying to get to sleep. Understand?" he asked as he got right in Zane's face and brushed his nose against Zane's.

"I understand," Zane repeated dutifully, rubbing the tip of his nose against Ty's before lifting just enough to press a soft kiss against his lips. "First night I slept without passing out drunk in four months was that night at your place," he said, his voice barely audible.

Ty closed his eyes and sighed quietly, deflating a little just before he clambered to the side and flopped down beside Zane.

Zane knew Ty didn't want to hear it. But he'd said it to him anyway; the closest he could come to communicating how much he felt he needed his partner. He shifted and lay along Ty's side, letting his eyes close while he just focused on feeling him close.

Ty's arm snaked around him, pulling him closer. "After this case is over," he said quietly as he stared up at the ceiling and idly twirled a lock of Zane's hair, "promise me you'll get help."

Zane inhaled and exhaled slowly. "I promise," he whispered.

Ty merely nodded his head almost indiscernibly and continued to play with Zane's hair. "So, what exactly was the point of waking me up and picking a fight?" he asked finally.

"Hmmm?" Zane grunted. He knew full well what Ty was asking about. For now, Zane was just pleased to have the cranky, gruff Ty back. He could relate to him. This Ty didn't scare him and make him feel incredible, baffling emotions he'd tried to shut away.

Ty rolled his eyes and shook his head again. "Asshole," he accused almost fondly. He was unable to stay quiet for long. "I mean," he said pointedly, "I know why I poke you. But where's the fun in poking me? Why start arguments just for the sake of fighting?" he demanded.

Zane opened his eyes. He considered teasing, but thought it might be bordering on cruel at this point. "You're more yourself now than you've been since I saw you again," he said seriously.

Ty blinked up at the ceiling. "What the hell?" he finally asked.

Raising an eyebrow, Zane raised his head and rested his chin on Ty's chest as he looked up at him. He didn't answer, though.

Ty narrowed his eyes again and sighed heavily. "You're trying to drive me crazy, aren't you?" he finally asked.

"Depends, I guess," Zane said. "If it helps you shake off that damn conditioning, I'll do whatever I have to."

Ty cocked his head and frowned. "Conditioning," he muttered.

"'Proper behavior'?" Zane said, sounding like he was parroting from a doctor. "All those things the shrink told you were the right things to do when you actually felt emotions?"

Ty's eyes narrowed even further and he growled softly in the back of his throat.

Zane considered carefully what to say. "There's a piece of you missing. Or that you've buried. One that I think we're going to need for this case."

Ty was silent as he pushed Zane off him and sat up, leaning against the headboard and staring at his partner expectantly.

"Don't you think so?" Zane asked evenly, watching Ty intently.

"So you're trying to egg me on," Ty responded without answering. "Make me cranky and somehow use me to solve an unsolvable case. What the hell are you, Zane, a Little Rascal?"

Zane's eyes flashed with a little temper before calming, and he sat up to look over at the other man. "It's your passion that's missing, Ty. You want to solve the case. You desperately want to catch a break on it. But that drive you had . . . I just don't see it. I mean, for Christ's sake, you figured out the pattern the guy follows! That drove you insane when we were here before, but now you don't even seem to give a damn!"

Ty leaned forward and his nostrils flared angrily. "Maybe there's a lot of shit you miss with your head so far up your ass," he snarled.

Zane just smiled, watching Ty with something that looked like pleasure mixed with hunger and a tinge of amusement.

Ty stopped short when he saw the reaction, sitting back against the headboard suspiciously. "Don't look at me like that," he muttered.

"Why not?" Zane asked.

"Because," Ty huffed as he rolled off the bed and began to pace restlessly.

Zane shook his head slowly, still watching him. "Come back here," he tried, though he didn't move from his sitting position on the end of the bed. Ty shot him a dirty look and stopped pacing. He crossed his arms defiantly and pursed his lips to see what Zane would do. But the other man just waited for a moment, then patted his thigh and raised an eyebrow.

Ty snorted and looked at him incredulously. "Go fuck yourself," he advised.

"I'd rather fuck you," Zane drawled. Ty merely snorted stubbornly and turned to continue his pacing. Zane grinned and sprawled back on the bed. "Well, whenever," he added, tipping his head back against the headboard to look at the ceiling.

"So is the fucking a part of your little plan too?" Ty asked suddenly.

Zane brought his chin down and focused on Ty. "I want to fuck you, regardless," he said. "You have any idea how far you've gotten under my skin?"

Again, the hairs on Ty's arms rose and his chest tightened slightly. He shook his head wordlessly and scowled.

"Goddamn it, Ty. I get a hard-on just looking at you," Zane snapped. "Don't tell me you haven't noticed."

Ty took an involuntary step back and blinked at Zane stupidly. "I didn't," he insisted and shook his head as he finally looked away.

Zane cocked his head. "Does that bother you?" he asked, voice revealing his surprise.

"No," Ty answered defensively. "I just didn't . . . realize . . ."

"Didn't realize what?" Zane asked softly, sitting up to lean his elbows on his knees.

Ty was slowly regaining his balance, and as he did so he smiled slowly. "That you were so easy," he answered with a smirk.

Zane chuckled and leaned back again. "Blame the hookers."

Ty grew serious once more and took a step closer. "Is it the same?" he asked softly.

The smile on Zane's face dimmed. "Not even remotely close to you."

Ty stopped as Zane spoke and then took another step closer. "Do you have any idea," he said in a low voice, "how far you've gotten under my skin?"

Zane stilled completely. "No," he said honestly, voice low.

Ty moved closer and stood at the side of bed in front of Zane. "You should," he murmured as he reached out and ran his fingers through Zane's hair.

Zane's dark eyes focused on him. "How? You don't believe the same of me."

"I don't?" Ty asked softly.

Gaze going soft, Zane reached up to touch Ty's hand, though he didn't interfere with its movement. "I don't know," he whispered.

Ty sighed softly and bent over, dropping his hands to lean on Zane's thighs. He slid them up to rest against Zane's hips and he knelt there, looking up at him. "The girl who called that morning at my place," he said suddenly. "She was so upset because I fucked her, then spent the rest of the night on the balcony with a beer and a really fucking rare cigar. Thinking about you."

Zane could feel his heart pounding in the quiet. He wondered if Ty could hear it. He moved his hands to rest on Ty's forearms. "Thinking about what?" he asked quietly. "Where I was?"

"And who and what you were doing," Ty answered with a slow nod. "What we had done, what we should have done . . ."

"I should have . . ." Zane stopped and shook his head. "I thought about you," he admitted.

"You should have what?" Ty pressed softly.

Zane sighed and closed his eyes. "I should have stayed," he breathed. "I just didn't know how."

Ty watched him closely, frowning. "You couldn't have stayed," he finally responded.

"I know," Zane answered. "Doesn't mean I didn't think about it."

Ty remained on his knees, frowning at Zane without anything to say. He pulled Zane's hand toward him and kissed the inside of his wrist impulsively. Zane's pulse was racing, and Ty could feel it jumping under his lips. "Why are you nervous?" he whispered in confusion.

Taking a deep breath, Zane let out his greatest fear. "What if something happens to you?" It was out of left field, for sure. But it was eating at him from the inside.

Ty raised his head slightly, looking at Zane seriously as he released him. He slowly eased himself up to sit cross-legged beside the bed and rested his elbows on his knees. This all went back to Zane's wife, he realized. It was a pretty common reaction when someone lost a person they loved: to close off and try to refuse to care or let anyone close. The bitch of it was that there was no way to guard against losing again and again.

"I can't promise that nothing will," he finally answered with a shrug.

Zane nodded. "I know," he said in a pained voice. "But I still want you."

"So what's the problem?" Ty asked gently.

Zane raised one shoulder in a confused shrug. "You said it: we get along best when we're fucking. How do we make that work?"

"Not everything needs to be planned, Zane," Ty answered with a tinge of frustration. "Not everything needs a why or how."

"So we just see how it goes?" Zane asked. Ty answered with a nod and smiled. Zane smiled slightly in return, the vise that had been around his chest finally eased. "I'll try."

Ty reached out and patted his knee almost delicately and then hefted himself off the floor.

Zane's hands almost itched with the need to touch Ty again, but he curled them into fists and cursed his nerves. See how it goes. Well, it wasn't going anywhere right this moment. He clambered off the bed and walked over to his jacket, poking through the pockets for his cigarettes. Ty was watching him silently, a crooked smirk curling his lips.

Zane turned around. When he saw Ty watching, he didn't move; he just stood there with his cigarettes in one hand and lighter in the other.

"Those things'll kill you," Ty advised in amusement.

Looking at Ty ruefully, Zane shook his head and flipped him off as he walked to the door. "Leave me at least one of my vices?" he requested.

Ty sighed and watched him as he reached the door. "The pills are in my bag," he offered quietly.

Stopping at the door, Zane looked back over his shoulder at Ty. Yeah, he wanted the damn pills. Just a single thought and he was dying for them, for the artificial high and confidence he got from them. Having them around was like a burr stuck in his shirt, scraping his skin raw. He turned around. "Give them over, please," he requested quietly.

Ty waited for a moment and then walked over to the bag to rummage through and find the tin. He held it up and rattled it, then tossed it to Zane without a word. Zane caught the tin deftly and looked down at it for a long moment. Then he moved, walking past Ty and into the bathroom, where he worked to pry the tin open. Ty lowered his head, listening intently and hoping to hear the flush of the toilet instead of the running of the water to fill a glass.

Zane stared down at the little pink pills. How big a deal was this? They didn't hurt anyone but him . . . and Ty. Zane turned his chin toward the door. Because Ty didn't want him doing the drugs. Caught in that thought, he turned the tin over and watched the pills fall into the toilet and sink to the bottom to land on white porcelain. Stone-cold sober, he flushed them down and tossed the tin into the garbage can with a clink.

When Zane turned around, he saw Ty standing there. He took two steps and captured Ty's mouth with his own, his hands closing gently about his face.

Ty returned the kiss with feeling, sliding his hands around Zane's hips and pulling him closer. "Good boy," he murmured between kisses.

Chapter Fourteen

Henninger called promptly at nine that morning, just a few hours after Zane flushed his pills. The young agent told Ty he'd arranged to have one of the earlier crime scenes opened for them, because he knew how much Ty liked to go and stare, and they had to meet him as soon as possible before anyone got wind of it. He also had the personnel files for them, and there were some interesting things in there.

"Like what?" Ty asked curiously.

"Like the number of people involved with this case that were in Baltimore in 2004," Henninger answered wryly. "You and me included, Special Agent Grady," he added.

"Ah, fuck," Ty muttered into the phone. "Bring them anyway, kiddo," he requested as he gestured for Zane to hurry and get his shit together. "We'll see you in thirty."

"Yes, sir," Henninger answered before ending the call.

As soon as the call was over, Zane and Ty scrambled, got down to their rental car in record time, and set off to drive across town to meet the other man.

Ty found himself pondering the way Tim Henninger had come through for them as he drove in the seventy-mile-an-hour traffic. He had seriously underestimated the kid. He would have to buy him dinner or something in apology.

In the passenger seat, Zane paged through a notepad of his own scribbling that he'd grabbed on the way out the door. "I'm still unhappy about the evidence missing," he said.

"What?" Ty asked flatly.

"Different things from each case," Zane said. "No pattern I can see. ME supplementary notes from one. Skin scrapings from another. Time notations from a third."

Ty looked over at him and frowned. "And?"

"Large assumption: If he's making a different mistake each time and managing to clean up after himself, we might be able to create additional profile information," Zane said. "Areas he's weak in. That's assuming it's all not just human error."

"Could be," Ty drawled. "It'll be like trying to see a puzzle that's all been painted over."

"You can still match the edges," Zane said distractedly as he started making notations on a yellow legal pad in his lap.

"Is there anything missing from the murders that occurred after the computer exploded?" Ty asked.

Zane flipped through his notes, frowning. "No. Why?"

"I still think he removed that shit as bait," Ty claimed.

"I'm not convinced," Zane muttered.

The loose papers scattered across his lap as their car was thumped hard from behind.

Ty was thrown forward with the impact, but he kept the car straight as his head jerked. He glanced into the rearview mirror and frowned at the yellow cab behind them. The windshield had been illegally tinted until you could barely see through it, and the call numbers had been removed. "Uh-oh," he muttered.

Turning around in the seat, Zane tried to look as the cab hit them again, harder this time. "What the hell?" he hissed. Before they could react, the cab swerved slightly to ram the back passenger quarter panel of their car, pushing them toward the concrete median wall.

Ty tensed, his mind going blank and relying on training and instinct rather than common sense as he handled the nearly out-of-control vehicle. He watched the cab out of the corner of his eye in order to anticipate the next attack, and he kept his attention on the concrete barrier and his hands on the wheel.

Zane pulled his gun out, looking back at the looming vehicle as it hit them again, this time actually revving the engine and pushing them. The collision was hard enough to jostle them both, and Zane had to grab the door handle. Other cars in the two lanes to their left honked and swerved wildly, skidding to keep from hitting them or the wall.

"Fucker," Ty growled. This was the fuck who'd been killing. This was the fuck who'd tried to kill them. He was sure of it. "Hold on," he said to Zane with a dangerous glint in his eyes, and he slammed on the brakes, sending the rear end of their vehicle crashing into the front of the cab in retaliation.

Biting off a curse, Zane braced himself against the dashboard just in time with his free hand as they jerked back and forth. Ty hit the gas once more and sped up, leaving the cab lagging behind.

"Goddamn it, I can't see him," Zane ground out, trying to get a look through the tinted windshield as the cab advanced again, pulling partway up the passenger side to knock them closer to the barrier. "The sides are blacked out too."

"He wouldn't risk being seen," Ty said through gritted teeth as he veered the rental car into the cab with a crunch of metal and the burning stench of rubber. Whoever the man was, though, he was good with a speeding car. Instead of veering out of control, he turned the cab to meet the push, crashing the two cars together so hard that sparks flew and smoke began to churn out of the cab's ruined grill.

"I can't take a shot, even to take out the tires. He'll kill somebody besides us," Zane said sharply as the driver gunned the cab's engine to pull up beside them on the passenger side. The driver swerved over to smash the cars together again, hitting the passenger side, pushing them within a few feet of the wall as Ty tried desperately to keep them from going out of control. Zane could see the cab gaining on his side of the car for another attempt. "He's coming..."

"Shut up," Ty ground out as the side of their car squealed against the concrete. The cab smashed into their side again and the metal of the passenger door screeched and crumpled alarmingly. Ty glanced over at it, taking his eyes off the road for a second to see Zane leaning and struggling to pull his arm away from the door. If the cab smashed them again, one of them was getting hurt, and Ty could easily see who it was going to be. He glanced in the rearview mirror again, seeing that the traffic they had passed was slowing and giving the two dueling cars a wide berth. "Hold on," he breathed as his peripheral vision caught the cab swerving for another impact.

He slammed on the brakes to avoid the coming collision. The back wheels smoked as they locked, and the vehicle fishtailed dangerously as the Ford struggled to go from eighty to stop in no time flat. Despite the seat belt, Zane was thrown forward and his free hand landed on the dashboard to catch himself, his gun thumping to the console between the seats. The cab veered into their lane, finding nothing to slam into since they were no longer beside him, then it accelerated in a burst of black smoke as the Ford finally fishtailed out of control and hit the wall with its back left panel. The front tire blew, then the back, and the rental car left the ground, spinning gracefully into the air and then crashing back down onto its side.

Zane gasped aloud as the seat belt caught him painfully across the chest and snapped him against the door when the car upended. The Ford smashed against the blacktop on the passenger side and slid, only to slow and slam against a hapless motorist before crashing back onto all four wheels.

The crumpled car finally drifted to a weaving, smoking stop just inches from the concrete as the cab disappeared out of sight ahead of them. Ty sat with his hands clutching the wheel, knuckles white and breathing hard as sirens began to sound somewhere in the distance.

Beside him, Zane leaned against the crunched passenger door, his entire right side a mass of swamping pain. Glancing over to the driver's side, Zane didn't see any blood on Ty as the man sat staring out the windshield. Zane glanced up around them to see if help was close, only to see the cab about fifty yards away—facing them—and he could see the tires spinning as the driver held down the brake and revved the engine. All traffic on their side of the highway had come to a stop; the lanes littered with wrecked cars and stunned motorists.

Zane's voice was strained and stunned as he spoke. "Ty. Ty, we gotta get out. Get out of your seat belt." He tried to pull away from the passenger-side door and excruciating pain tore through his entire body in burning waves, taking his breath away.

Ty sat staring at the menacingly crushed front grill of the cab in the distance, unmoving as Zane gave the ruined door several weak sideways kicks, trying to free himself. Calmly, as if in a daze, Ty reached up and began plucking away what shards remained of the moonroof's glass.

Zane swallowed hard as his vision began to fade and blur. He was going into shock. "I can't get out that way," he told Ty, gritting his teeth.

Ty looked at him, still in a calm, detached sort of haze. "You're stuck," he murmured as he reached across Zane's chest and prodded the metal where the other man's arm was captured. He glanced up at the cab, then reached across Zane's lap to the seat handle that would lay the seat back. It didn't budge, and Ty turned his head slightly, his nose brushing against Zane's cheek. He glanced again to see the cab begin its run, heading toward them on a sure collision course. It would gain speed quickly, and then the impact would come. The heavy steel construction of the old car would tear the battered Ford to pieces.

Ty clambered to stand on the middle console, rising up out of the moonroof as he drew his gun. He waited a half-second and then opened fire. The yellow paint on the hood of the cab began to dent and explode as the bullets hit, and the safety glass shattered, but didn't break. The illegal tinting inside the windshield kept it from falling apart as it was riddled with bullet holes. Ty couldn't see the driver or tell if he was hitting him. He lowered his aim and began trying for the tires, but his gun clicked empty and he shouted a frustrated curse.

He reached for his backup as the cab barreled toward them, but he couldn't reach it in the small confines. He contorted with difficulty and snagged Zane's gun from where it had landed on the dash during the roll and straightened back up, aiming for the lower part of the car.

"Damn it, Ty, get out of the car!" Zane yelled, his voice breaking as the pain began to overwhelm his emotional control. His eyes flickered between the oncoming car and his lover, and he pushed against Ty's legs with his free hand.

One of the front tires blew out as Ty emptied the clip again, ignoring Zane's demands, but the cab continued to limp toward them at an alarming speed. It was almost on them. If the crash didn't kill them, the man inside the cab would.

Ty fired the last round, then reared back and chucked the empty gun at the cab in utter frustration before he ducked back into the car. He shook his head wordlessly, awkwardly kneeling on the console as he tried to free Zane's arm from between the torn metal of the door and the crumpled frame. He knew that even if he got Zane free now, it was too late. But it wasn't in him to give up.

"Shit, Ty, you can't take my damn arm off! Please... baby." Zane's voice cracked with agony as he pleaded between uneven gasping breaths. "Get out of the car," he ordered weakly.

Ty responded with a small, chaste kiss. As he heard the roaring of the battered cab's engine coming closer, he curled protectively around Zane, hoping to shield him from the brunt of the crash. He tried not to tense, but his physical discipline was no match for simple human instinct. As the cab barreled toward them, he hunched his shoulders and prepared for the impact.

"I'm sorry," he breathed as he closed his eyes tight and waited.

"Ty..." Zane choked out as he curled his free arm around Ty's back, holding him tight and turning his face into his neck. Christ. Forget about not being there. This. This was Zane's worst nightmare.

The sound of the sirens was closer now, and through his closed eyelids Ty could see the changing light and dark that told him the flashing lights were on top of them. There was a sound of squealing tires and the smell of burning rubber. He raised his head and opened his eyes, knowing the impact should have come already. He turned and looked out the cracked window at the yellow blur of the cab as the driver turned at the last minute, spinning out right beside their wrecked Ford on the highway. He turned out of the spin, gunned the engine, and headed off in the other direction. Several squad cars gave chase, flying by the wreck of their vehicle in a blaze of light and sound.

The driver knew he couldn't finish them off and still get away. He had chosen to fight another day, and he'd left Ty and Zane alive to do it.

When Ty shifted, Zane opened his eyes to blurrily see the cab retreating and police cars stopping around them. He started to shake. Shock. He was going into shock. His arm was already numb, and the pain was still shooting up into his shoulder and down his back. His side was screaming and he couldn't feel his leg. "When we get out of this car I am kicking your ass," he rasped.

Ty didn't respond. He was already climbing through the roof and holding up his badge and his empty gun, handle first, calling out the code for an officer down.

Zane sat in the back of the ambulance with a blanket over his shoulders and lap as the EMT worked him over. He stayed put, cowed by a tiny woman who barked at him when he'd tried to leave without medical treatment. All he'd allowed was an IV of clear fluids, and he'd checked the bags. What she was doing hurt like hell (he'd also insisted on no painkillers after a very few words with her about the past addiction record) so he was focusing hard on what was going on away from the ambulance.

Ty stood talking with some of the cops. Luckily, they'd not given him any trouble, none that Zane saw anyway. The EMT found another broken rib and Zane hissed, jerking away instinctively.

"Doing okay, Special Agent Garrett?" the EMT asked.

"Still here," he answered hoarsely after pulling away the oxygen mask. His eyes were still glassy and glazed with pain.

"Feeling light-headed again?" she asked, pausing in her examination.

"Just get it over with, huh?" he said weakly, leaning his head sideways against the wall.

"I told you already, I can't do anything more for you here. You're going to have to go to the hospital and—"

"Just do whatever you have to do," Zane interrupted. "I have to be able to use that arm." It would be his right arm. He swallowed hard. "Set it and do whatever."

The EMT stared at him silently. When she spoke, her voice was thin. "You know how much you're going to hurt?"

Zane turned his chin so he could look at his mangled arm and then at her. "Yeah, I know. Just do it."

Frowning deeply, she got to her feet and climbed into the ambulance with practiced ease. Zane just closed his eyes. He was going to pass out; he knew it. When he opened his eyes again, he found that Ty had finally managed to break away from the cops who'd been asking him questions and was making his way hastily toward the ambulance.

He glared his way past a man who tried to stop him, and he came up to Zane with a twisting sensation in his gut. He could take pain himself, but he couldn't take watching other people go through it. Especially not people he cared for.

"Why haven't they drugged you yet?" he asked Zane in outrage.

Zane pulled the mask away to answer, but the EMT beat him to it. "He declined pain treatment," she said, voice clearly disapproving.

"Well, fuck that, give it to him anyway," Ty demanded with an impressive scowl.

"No," Zane said sharply. "You pump me full of something strong enough to help, and I'll be out of commission for two days and then suffering another week of cravings."

"A local won't cause drug cravings, moron!" Ty shouted angrily. Zane merely shook his head stubbornly.

The EMT looked between them, scowling heavily. "Special Agent Garrett, please reconsider," she asked, voice soft. "The pain from the broken bones is just going to grow worse; you're already well in shock. And your partner is right. I can give you a local for your arm and it has nothing to do with—"

Zane looked up at Ty and shook his head, cutting her off. "Go make arrangements for a car," he rasped to his partner. "You didn't listen before. Listen now. Go and come back."

"Fuck you," Ty huffed. "Give him the drugs," he told the EMT.

"I can't give him the drugs if he doesn't consent," the woman said helplessly.

The corner of Zane's mouth turned up triumphantly, although his eyes drilled into Ty. But he was still shaking slightly.

"He's severely injured," Ty argued calmly, looking at the woman intently. "He's not mentally capable of making the decision," he said pointedly.

Her eyes narrowed and she looked from him to Zane and back.

"What? The hell I'm not," Zane said hoarsely. "What are you trying to do to me?" he demanded of Ty.

"I'm trying to keep you out of the fucking hospital," Ty snarled. "Give him the shot," he told the woman. "You know if he goes catatonic from the pain you'll just have to do it then, and take him to the hospital, and shoot me because I'll have to kill someone."

"Ty, goddamn it, we have things we have to do. I can't be stoned out of my mind for an hour, much less a day—"

"A local wouldn't do that!" Ty interrupted in frustration.

"What if that son of a bitch comes back after . . . What the hell?" Zane stood up in a rush and his head snapped around as the EMT stepped back, pulling an empty syringe from the IV feed line.

Ty pointed at her and gave a triumphant little "Ha!"

"Now, Special Agent Garrett, you're exhibiting strong symptoms of shock," she said soothingly, laying her hand over the IV shunt in his arm, making sure he didn't yank it out. Her eyes shifted from Zane's badly broken arm again over to Ty. "You need to sit down right now. I've given you a sedative and something to help with the pain."

Zane took two steps right up into Ty's face. "You can't do this to a partner and expect there to be any lev . . . level of tr—trus . . ." His knees started to give out as he blinked slowly.

Ty took him by his good arm and eased him toward the stretcher he had refused to use before. "We'll talk about trust later, Special Agent Garrett," he cooed as he forced Zane down.

Wobbling as he sat back down, Zane's eyes glazed. "Ty," he said pleadingly as he sagged against the stretcher, lying out flat as Ty and the paramedic moved his nearly limp body. "Don't."

Ty held him down until he was certain Zane wouldn't thrash around when released. "I'm sorry," he murmured as his hands slipped away once Zane's eyes closed. He looked up at the EMT and sighed dejectedly. "Thank you."

The woman smiled, but looked nonplussed. "I can't believe he's not out cold. We should take him to the hospital."

"Can't do the hospital," Ty told her softly. "Not safe there."

She nodded as if she understood, then looked between them thoughtfully. "So he's your partner?" she asked carefully.

Ty nodded as he looked back down at Zane, not even catching that there was more than one meaning to the question. "We're working a case," he answered distractedly as he pulled out his badge and showed it to her. The action was completely habitual. "Been a bad one," he murmured quietly.

The EMT glanced at the badge. "So he's your partner at work," she clarified.

Ty looked over at her and blinked stupidly. "What?" he asked in confusion.

The woman smiled a little. "I asked if he's your partner at work. You're looking a little wobbly yourself. Why don't you sit down, Special Agent..."

"Grady," Ty supplied as he frowned. "Yes, he's my partner at work," he echoed, still confused by her interest. "I don't need to sit down," he added stubbornly.

"Okay," she said. "I just thought you might want to stick around. He should be out for about thirty minutes. He's still going to hurt when he wakes up, though. He told me about why he didn't want the drugs." She gave him an even look. "Who are you to him to countermand his decision?"

"I'm his partner," Ty answered defensively, beginning to bristle a little under the scrutiny. "You knew as well as I did that he wouldn't be able to take it. Common sense trumps alcoholism every day of the week, Sunshine. He'll thank us later."

"But you know it's more than alcoholism, right?" she asked as she instructed another EMT to set Zane's arm and wrap it up while he was out. "That's why you're so protective," she continued as she took Ty's arm and pulled him gently away, "of your partner."

Ty was getting annoyed and beginning to suspect that she could tell he hadn't exactly made it out of the car without injuries either. He could feel the urge to bark at the woman and he stamped it down, just hoping to get away without being doctored. "What's your point, Princess?" he asked.

The woman's eyes flashed. "Honestly? I'm trying to decide if you care enough about him to take care of him after this. He's going to be a mess for a couple days, at least. Broken bones all over, the sedative and his reactions to it. Seemed to me you were worried enough that he might be more than just a partner. Maybe a friend?" She stood and straightened, not bothered at all that she was more than a foot shorter than Ty. "Now. Tell me what I want to hear, or I'm shipping him off to Lenox Hill. And unbutton your shirt; I see bruising," she demanded as she pointed at his neck.

"What do you want to hear?" Ty asked as he pulled the top of his shirt together to hide the bruising from his seat belt, his frustrated voice going slightly higher than it normally did.

"Grady?" a soft voice called from amidst the crowd of police, firemen, and EMTs. Ty turned distractedly to see Henninger making his way precariously through the crowd.

"Hold on," he said to the man with a dismissive wave of his hand, looking back at the woman.

"Are you going to take care of him?" she asked bluntly. "Or do I need to find someone else?"

"How about a fucking doctor? That's what he needs, right?" Ty asked in exasperation.

"What the hell happened?" Henninger asked as he jogged up to them. "Jesus. Is he dead?" he asked as he looked down at Zane.

The woman shook her head, face hardening. "Go take care of your business, Special Agent Grady." She turned away and joined the other paramedic in tending to Zane's more severe wounds. They worked on the arm, one holding a preformed brace as the other wrapped his now-set arm into it.

Ty fought back the urge to reach out and throttle the infuriating woman. He looked down at Zane and his features softened unconsciously as he watched them lift him carefully to wrap his ribs tightly. "How long is he going to hurt?" he asked as Henninger stepped closer and peered down at Zane as well.

Zane was jostled as the stretcher was moved around, wheeling him toward the back of the waiting ambulance. The agent didn't even protest as they moved him, just sluggishly stared into nothing when he should have been unconscious. "He's going to hurt for a while. A week, at least. Two is more likely. I wouldn't be surprised if it's three or four. He's dislocated his shoulder, broken two bones in his forearm, cracked four ribs, had his brain rattled around in his skull, and his hip is badly bruised," she said grimly. "Looks like his knee may be out too. He's a mess. I don't know how he expects to operate without painkillers."

"So he's out of commission," Ty muttered with a defeated look at Zane as they moved him.

She shrugged in answer.

"But how . . ." Henninger started, but glares from both Ty and the EMT shut him up.

Ty was torn. He'd already stepped over the line by forcing the anesthesia on Zane, though why the EMT hadn't just done a local he couldn't guess. She obviously knew more about it all than he did.

Should he call Burns and let him know Zane was out of service? He certainly wouldn't be much good to the case now. Perhaps Ty should have Burns send someone new in. Or he could keep going on his own until Zane recovered, although he knew he couldn't do this alone. He wasn't as smart as the killer. He didn't know what to do, and the indecisiveness was as annoying to him as it was uncharacteristic.

"Garrett can't work like that. You're going to have to call in and have him taken off the case," Henninger advised as he watched Ty think it over.

"A case is the last thing Special Agent Garrett should be worrying about," the EMT offered.

"Hmm?" Ty asked them both distractedly. "How did you get here, anyway?" he asked the young agent with sudden annoyance.

"I was waiting to meet you, heard about this mess over the radio, and got a bad feeling about it since you were late. When you got later, I decided to drive up here just in case and I saw you standing by the wreck," Henninger answered defensively. He glanced to the EMT uncertainly, and she rolled her eyes and walked the few steps to climb up into the truck with her patient. "Look, Grady," Henninger continued. "Catching this serial is more important than keeping Zane Garrett on the job."

Ty was shocked that he almost found himself agreeing with the sentiment. He blinked at the man and then looked over at Zane, who was obviously struggling with the effects of the drugs. "You ever been asked the question 'Who would you choose to save? A hundred strangers or one family member?'" he asked softly.

Henninger drew back in surprise and a hint of concern. "No," he said cautiously. "But I'd answer a hundred strangers. That's our job."

"That is the noble answer, isn't it?" Ty murmured as he looked back at Zane.

"We have a responsibility. If that's noble, then . . ." Henninger shrugged, frowning as he noticed Ty's attention wavering. "You know it's the right thing to do," he insisted.

"What do you care, anyway?" Ty asked him in slightly desperate whisper.

"I care about catching the guy who's going around cutting people into such small chunks you could make Hamburger Helper with them!" Henninger retorted. "I'd care about that more than I'd care about one man who I can barely stand to work with."

Ty was still aware enough of his surroundings not to argue that point. "Do you have your car?" he asked Henninger hoarsely without answering.

Henninger blinked at the sudden change in topic. "Yeah," he answered warily.

"Can he ride?" Ty called out to the EMT inside the vehicle.

"If you can make him sign this release, he's all yours," the woman yelled back.

Ty cringed and looked back at Henninger. "Go get your car," he told the kid softly. "We're getting him the hell out of here," he muttered as he headed for the ambulance.

Before Ty could get there, Zane stepped down out of the truck, holding tightly to the grab bar as the paramedic held the clipboard and the signed release form up behind him for Ty to see. Zane's glazed eyes were blazing with anger, and he was trembling from the pain and the drugs. "You goddamn piece of shit," he said thickly, obviously trying to throw off the effects of the sedative.

"I know," Ty agreed unapologetically as he reached out to support Zane. How the man was walking, he didn't know.

Zane was wobbly and weak, and he hated that he felt like he was moving through water and seeing through a haze. A red haze, but still a haze. He had to lean heavily on Ty when the other man slipped under his good arm. He thought about cussing some more, but all that came out was a hiss of pain, and his knees tried to give out on him. "Bitch gave me a shot, goddamn it," he muttered mostly to himself. "I am so fucked."

"I know," Ty repeated as he tried to support him without hurting him or himself. "You're gonna be just fine," he promised. "Henninger's got cigarettes for you," he said as if in consolation as he nodded at the kid.

Henninger watched them with wide, confused eyes before nodding quickly and fishing for his keys. "In the car," he told Zane agreeably.

Zane grimaced. "Why does everything hurt when just one side got banged up? And why did it have to be my gun arm?" he half-whined as Ty got him walking, albeit unsteadily, to follow Henninger, who took off ahead to get his car and move it closer.

"I used all your ammo anyway," Ty grumbled. "And then threw your gun at a car. Have fun filling out that paperwork."

Zane managed to clear through the haze enough to look at Ty as they struggled through the crowd. "Are you hurt?" he asked.

"If I say yes, will it make you not mad at me?" Ty asked almost teasingly, his voice slightly strained under the bigger man's weight.

"No," Zane bit out. He went quiet as they walked several steps. "I asked you to get out of the car."

"Must not have heard you," Ty murmured in response.

"I begged you," Zane said weakly, but his hand tightened on Ty's arm. "Bastard."

"I know," Ty repeated softly, looking around at the various pods of people being tended to and interviewed as they made their way practically unnoticed through them, following Henninger toward the concrete barrier. Henninger pulled up nearly in front of them as they broke free of the perimeter of the wreck site on the other side of the closed-off highway, and Ty groaned as he looked at the two-foot-high concrete median wall.

Henninger hopped out and stood on the other side indecisively, unsure of how to help.

Zane focused on the wall and sighed. "Shit. It's never easy, is it?" Taking a deep breath, he blinked hard and lifted his weight off Ty to stand up straight. By force of will he walked the two steps to the barrier and stepped over it. Both Ty and Henninger had their hands out around him, hovering protectively and looking like parents watching their firstborn take a step. Zane couldn't help but chuckle at the two of them as he took the three more steps to the car and sagged against it. "Okay, I'm done," he whispered as the pain from his whole right side echoed through him.

Ty hopped the barrier behind him as Henninger opened the back door for him. "Where to?" Henninger asked worriedly as Ty helped Zane into the back.

"I don't care," Ty answered in a low growl. "Somewhere safe."

Zane sagged back against the seat and closed his eyes, holding his arm close against his chest protectively. His jacket sleeve hung loose over the sling, sliced in several long pieces.

Nodding, the young agent pulled into traffic and got them moving. "You're going to need help, Grady. Should I call Sears and Ross?"

"No," Ty grunted in answer. "You're gonna help me," he said in a low, even voice.

"Me?" Henninger bleated, looking into the mirror again. "I don't have field experience. Sears and Ross would be a lot more help since Garrett can't—" Ty was glaring at him in the rearview mirror, and he trailed off and cleared his throat. "All I'm saying is we need backup," he continued quietly. "You don't think your presence in New York is going to be all over the Bureau now that this shit has gone down?"

Ty rubbed his eyes and looked out the window, then back at Zane once more. He had laid his head against Ty's shoulder and wasn't moving at all, and Ty thought he might have passed out. "Call 'em," he grunted softly.

Henninger nodded. "What are you going to do with Garrett?"

"I don't fucking know!" Ty answered in frustration as he fought with the decisions. "Any suggestions?"

Henninger looked at him hesitantly. "Could take him to my place," he offered.

Ty frowned at him, nodding. Zane trusted Henninger, and for the most part, so did Ty. They could leave Zane at his place with a guard detail and then they would go after the fucker. There was a hot trail to follow, and part of Ty resented the fact that he was in this car with his injured partner rather than on that trail right now.

"It's secure," Henninger assured him. "Key card to get in, that kind of thing."

"Take us there," Ty ordered as he pulled his mind off the man who had gone slack against him and back on the man who had once again almost killed them both.

A thirty-minute drive through thick traffic later, Henninger parked the car in the garage under his building and turned to look at them. "How are we getting him upstairs?"

"How far is it?" Ty inquired as he took stock of his own injuries. He had failed to mention the possible cracked rib or sprained wrist to the EMT, and his chest was killing him where the seat belt had cut into him. But he could carry Zane if he had to.

"About forty feet to the elevator, then another fifty to the apartment," Henninger said, looking unsure. "Could be more."

Ty groaned and shook his head. He wouldn't make it that far, and there was no way he'd risk dropping Zane and causing further injury. "Garrett," he murmured in Zane's ear. "Wake up, man. We need you to walk."

Zane stirred. "I'm awake," he mumbled. "We there?"

"Yes," Ty answered with a flood of relief. He hadn't relished the idea of dragging Zane's heavy frame through the building. "Come on," he murmured with a pat to Zane's head, fighting back the urge to make a gesture more intimate in front of Henninger.

The bigger man groaned and sat up. "I feel like I got hit by a truck, and it's all your fault," he accused weakly.

"I know, it's all my fault," Ty murmured agreeably as he slid out the back of the car and pulled Zane carefully with him. "Technically, you should be feeling really good," he corrected.

"Too much pain negates the effects of happy juice," Zane croaked as Ty got him out of the car. "Too much abuse negates the body's reaction," he added, all too familiar with the medical reasoning. He leaned on the door. "Where to?" he asked tiredly. His face was gray, and his shoulders hunched as he cradled his arm and babied his ribs.

"Elevator," Henninger said. "Come on. When we get upstairs, I'll call Ross and Sears, fill them in."

"What for?" Zane asked, voice sharpening in surprise.

"Backup," Ty answered in almost a whisper as he slid under Zane's good arm and urged him to walk before he fell over.

"What for?" Zane repeated as they made their way to the elevator. He wasn't leaning on Ty as much, but he was still dizzy and wobbly.

"They're going to babysit you," Henninger offered.

Zane stopped dead in his tracks. "What!?" he barked.

Ty winced and tightened his hold. "Thank you, Henninger," he snapped in annoyance. "Garrett, come on before you fall over."

"This conversation is not over," Zane growled as he got to walking again.

Henninger got to the elevator first and hit the Up button. "Come on, Garrett, be realistic. You can't go out in the field in this condition. You're dead weight now," he observed clinically.

Ty winced again at the delivery of the logic, but he knew it was true. "I'm sorry," he whispered to Zane. "It's this or the hospital, either way with a guard detail. You ain't going back in the field," he declared with finality.

Zane didn't answer as they got into the elevator, and he didn't say anything the rest of the way to the apartment. His face was strained and white as they went inside.

Henninger pointed them toward the bedroom. "This is a restored building from the turn of the century, so the doorways are wide; that ought to help," he said. "I love the architecture."

Ty nodded disinterestedly.

"The parking garage was the best perk," Henninger rambled on. "Not many buildings like this have them. And they even kept the original tunnels below the building intact for storage units. Nobody uses them, though. They used to be—"

"Fascinating," Ty grunted as he guided Zane toward the bedroom. The bed was made neatly, with an almost military precision that even a Marine could appreciate. The room, like the rest of the apartment, was uncluttered, almost Spartan in its simplicity. Somehow, it didn't fit the image he had of Henninger. "Garrett?" he breathed as he helped him to the bed.

Lowering himself to the edge of the bed, Zane looked up slowly, not at Ty, but at the other agent. Henninger took a step back. "Uh. I'll go call the others and get them over here," he said before disappearing.

Left alone with Zane, Ty was silent, waiting for either the blowup or—what he feared worse—complete silence. And that was what he got as Zane dropped his chin and stared at the floor. He raised his hand to rub his eyes. He looked like he was ready to fall over. Ty swallowed heavily and put a hand to Zane's forehead. "Why don't you lay back?" he said softly, his tone resigned.

Zane reached up to take Ty's wrist in a firm grip and pull his hand away, but he didn't let go. Ty was still, holding his breath as he waited. Slowly, Zane looked up at him. His dark eyes watered with pain and emotion. "We can still cut and run," he whispered.

Ty's chest tightened, and his insides seemed to lurch with the words. He nodded as he let his fingers curl over, trying to touch the hand that still gripped his wrist. "We will. But I need revenge first," he said softly.

Zane's brow furrowed as he loosened his fingers. "What for?" he asked quietly.

"You," Ty answered simply.

Zane exhaled painfully, and he tugged gently at Ty's hand, trying to get him to lean over. Ty moved with the tug and licked his lips nervously. Zane merely looked him in the eye as he got closer. "You come back, you understand?" he rasped intently. "If I have to come after you there will be absolute hell to pay."

Ty closed his eyes and butted his head against Zane's forehead. "What could go wrong, hmm?" he asked softly, a small smile playing at his lips. "I've got the kid with me, we don't know where we're going, who we're after, or what we'll do when we find him . . . It's foolproof."

Zane's fingers gripped Ty's chin, and he moved to kiss Ty desperately, palm sliding down to cup the nape of Ty's neck as their lips moved against one another. Ty breathed out heavily into the kiss, almost losing his resolve not to do exactly what Zane had suggested: cut and run. Leave this all behind and just get the two of them to safety. He slid his hand across Zane's cheek and kissed him as if it were the last time.

All the pain and fear and upset and desire balled up in Zane's gut, and his breath stopped as he gripped his lover's shoulder. "Come back to me."

"I will," Ty assured him softly. From the outer room they heard the obvious crackle of a radio and Henninger's muffled response. Ty pulled away and looked down into Zane's eyes. He slipped him his backup sidearm. "Anyone comes too close, you blast 'em," he murmured. "Badge or not," he added pointedly, his voice so low it was a whisper.

Letting out a shaky breath, Zane took the gun in his left hand, then slid it with a wince into his sling. "Yeah," he agreed, eyes trained on Ty.

Ty stood up and slid a plastic prescription bottle out of his back pocket, setting it by Zane's side.

The other agent blinked at it. "What's this?" he asked suspiciously.

"Pills I took from the EMT," Ty murmured. "Should get you through."

Zane looked at the bottle and then at Ty. He nodded slowly.

Ty began backing away from the bed slowly. "See you soon," he whispered before turning and exiting the room quickly.

Zane drew a breath to speak, but Ty was gone, and Zane didn't have the strength or ability to chase after him. He slowly lay down on his good side, head resting on a thin pillow. The words he'd wanted to say were stuck in his throat, and he squeezed his eyes shut tight, tiny drops sparkling in his eyelashes.

In the front room, Henninger turned as Ty reentered. "Got him settled?"

"Settled as he's gonna be, anyway," Ty mumbled as he rubbed a spot of tension at the back of his neck.

"I just got a call from a friend in the NYPD," Henninger told him excitedly. "They located the cab that was used."

Ty perked up and stared at him expectantly. The buzzer beside the door rang, and Henninger started toward the intercom to answer it.

"Well?" Ty demanded impatiently. "Where'd they find it?"

"Not two blocks from here," Henninger answered with a grin as he pushed the button that would let Sears and Ross in.

Adrenaline began to pump through Ty's body as the prospect of catching the man became more plausible. If they had the cab, then they could follow the trail. And Ty could track anything and anyone, whether it was in backwoods, desert, or the streets of New York City, he was confident of that fact. They had him.

It was only a minute or so before Sears and Ross stepped through the door, but waiting for them to arrive was torturous. As they waited,

Ty and Henninger stood at the large windows that lined the far side of the apartment, and Henninger explained to him what was around the neighborhood as they formed a plan of action.

"Grady, I can't say it's good to see you again," Special Agent Sears greeted, brushing her blonde hair over her shoulder. "How is he?" she asked with real concern.

"He's hurt bad," Ty answered grimly.

Ross stood at her side, looking annoyed. "We tried calling you," he said to Henninger.

"This building's got shitty reception," Henninger muttered uncomfortably as he looked at his phone that had never rung.

Ty nodded at them both, suddenly very aware of the splatters of blood from the crash that spotted his rumpled clothing and the fact that he looked like he'd been tumbled on high spin for an hour. It seemed to him that it spoke of his failures so far, that he hadn't even been able to protect his partner, much less catch the killer he'd been set on.

"Thank you for coming," he said to them both quietly, not a trace of apology or embarrassment in his tone. There was impatience, however, and he was practically vibrating in his shoes.

Sears looked over him, but didn't comment. "We can stay a couple hours before they start asking us where the hell we've disappeared to," she said apologetically. "So you better get going unless we make this official."

"I left our notes on the case in there with Garrett," Ty told her gruffly. The unspoken reason—in case neither of them lived long enough to share what they'd found—wasn't lost on anyone. "And there's a stack of personnel files here that has the name of our killer in it somewhere," he added as he pointed to the files Henninger had put on the coffee table.

Henninger nodded and glanced between them uncomfortably. "You want to change your shirt, Grady?" he asked finally, eyes drifting over the small amount of blood.

Ty glanced at him and then quietly shook his head. "There'll be more on it when we're done," he said in a low, soft voice.

Ross and Sears glanced at each other. "Don't hesitate to call in backup," Sears reminded disapprovingly.

Henninger nodded, turned to grab a small bag, and led the way out the door and to the elevator.

Neither man spoke as they headed out of the apartment. They rode down in the elevator in silence, Henninger glancing at Ty every few seconds as if wishing to say something. Finally, as the elevator came to a jolting stop at the parking deck floor, he cleared his throat and said, "Before we start this, I just want you to know, Special Agent Grady, it's been a real pleasure working with you. Both of you."

Ty glanced at him as the doors whooshed quietly open. "Likewise," he said softly to the kid.

He stepped out of the elevator as Henninger gave him an almost shy smile. He looked out into the dark parking deck and stepped forward, but his progress was halted as a hand suddenly covered the lower part of his face. He struggled as he breathed in the sickly sweet scent that covered the handkerchief, but he had already inhaled too much of the chloroform, and he sank helplessly to his knees, not able to reach his gun or even strike out at his attacker.

The last sound he heard was a shout and struggle that seemed to be miles away and a distant thunk as his limp body hit the concrete floor.

Chapter Fifteen

Zane laid on Henninger's bed for a while, dozing, until he started hurting too much to rest. Dragging his eyes open, he spent a long minute looking at the bottle of pills Ty had left him. There was nothing more tempting than a bottle of painkillers when you had a legitimate reason to take them, but he didn't pick them up. Instead, he lurched out of the bed and walked out to the main room to find Ross pacing and Sears sitting and watching her partner calmly.

"Hey," he rasped.

They both looked at him as if they hadn't expected to see him at all. "You shouldn't be up," Sears admonished as she stood and made her way over to him. "What do you need?"

"A stiff drink," Zane muttered, moving to sit in an armchair.

"I would be more comfortable if you returned to the bed," Sears said to him soothingly, looking over at her partner pointedly.

"Let him sit there if he wants," Ross replied with a wave of his hand.

"Can I have a drink? Please?" Zane asked pitifully. "I don't care what. Tap water, anything."

Sears sighed, accepting the fact that Zane wasn't planning on listening, and she headed to Henninger's kitchen as her heels rapped on the wooden floors and echoed to the open ceilings. She began rummaging in the refrigerator as Ross came closer to Zane.

"So, the Bureau sent you in under the radar," he said to Zane with obvious disdain. "Because they thought we couldn't handle it on our own?"

Zane rolled his head around carefully. "Because six Bureau personnel had already been killed or injured," he corrected. "You didn't happen to work in Baltimore in 2004, did you?"

Ross snorted unhappily but shook his head in answer as he moved away again, pacing restlessly in much the same manner Ty always did. Zane watched him with a frown until Sears came out with a glass of sparkling liquid. "This was all I could find besides water," she said. "It's pomegranate juice. Figured some sugar might do you good."

"Thanks," Zane murmured, taking the glass and a long drink. "So, you two get to babysit me."

"We're on the shelf right now, anyway," Sears answered loudly before Ross could respond. "If we weren't here," she went on more gently as she sat on the coffee table opposite Zane and crossed her legs daintily, "we would be drowning in paperwork."

Zane glanced between the two with a growing smile. Ross grimaced and started pacing again. "Gotta love paperwork," he commented, eyes actually brightening a little. "Lately, I wish I'd had more of it and less death and destruction."

Sears reached out and put a hand on his knee gently. "Are you sure you don't want to be in the hospital?" she asked quietly. "It's all over the wire, what happened. We could set up a guard there. You've got to be in a lot of pain."

"Christ, Marian, leave the man alone," Ross huffed. "And stop batting your eyelashes at him," he added grumpily.

"I am doing no such thing," Sears responded calmly as she maintained eye contact with Zane. "Did they give you painkillers?" she asked.

Zane looked at her steadily and lied through his teeth without giving anything away. "Yeah, I took some already. And I'm fine. Just worn out."

Sears narrowed her eyes but then nodded as she accepted what he said for truth. She seemed out of ideas, and she looked up at her partner for help. Ross, who was still pacing behind Zane restlessly, just shrugged and gestured at him in agitation.

"You should be resting," Sears insisted as she sat and observed Zane. She wasn't just watching him. She was observing. It reminded Zane of the way Ty watched people sometimes. Everything seemed to remind him of Ty lately. Ross came around to flop gracelessly into a nearby chair.

Aware of Sears's interest, Zane let his injured shoulder sag a little and the exhaustion show. No need for them to know exactly how bad of shape he was in . . . just in case. He wasn't all that sure about Ross. "You trust Henninger enough to hop to and come running when he calls like that?" he asked. "I barely know the kid."

"Henninger's a better agent than he's given credit for," Sears answered neutrally. "If he says he needs help, then he needs help."

"You barely know the kid and yet he's your inside contact?" Ross asked dubiously.

"He's who we got tagged with by the New York office when we got here," Zane allowed. "When we came back, we used him 'cause he'd helped us before. We needed someone who could get us information fast and dirty."

"No wonder he's been so jumpy lately." Ross laughed softly.

"Poor kid," Sears added with a fond smile.

"What? He getting flack at the office?" Zane asked.

"Every time there was a loud noise somewhere, he would hit the ceiling," Sears told him with a smirk she tried to hide. "Apparently, he had a guilty conscience."

Zane frowned a little. "He seemed okay when he was talking with us," he murmured. "Huh." He shifted and slumped in the chair a little. "So. What's the story on you two?" he drawled, looking between them.

Both agents looked back at him with suddenly unreadable expressions. Finally, Sears smiled slowly. "I'll show you mine if you show me yours," she answered.

Zane immediately broke out in wheezing laughter. "You're joking, right?"

"Come on," Sears wheedled with a grin. "I'll spill on my partner if you tell me about yours."

Zane snorted and peered at Sears as Ross protested noisily. "Watch out," he told the woman with a smile. "I've seen how Grady behaves around a woman. He's an utter bastard." He sighed and some of the amusement died away. "As for me," he said quietly, dropped his eyes, and looked at his ring thoughtfully, "I can't see another woman without thinking of my wife."

The teasing dropped away, and Sears smiled softly. "I'm sorry," she murmured in the tone of voice that said she knew Zane's wife had died rather than left him.

"You girls finished getting your nails done?" Ross asked with a huff.

"Fuck off, Ross," Zane bit out, aggravation showing.

"Boys, boys," Sears murmured as she stood and rolled her eyes.

Ross snapped his mouth closed and gave Zane an infuriating smirk. "You look a little restless, Garrett," he observed with false sympathy. "Henninger told us about your Poe theory when we demanded to know why he needed us here. Why don't you explain that one to us if you need something to do?"

Rolling his eyes, Zane glanced over at the wall of bookshelves nearby. "See if you can find a copy of Poe over there," he requested. "We'll see what we can find."

The sound of scraping and the musty smell of something old and wet were the first things to batter Ty's senses. He groaned involuntarily and his head lolled, his chin resting on his chest as if he were upright rather than prostrate.

Slowly, with more effort than he liked, he forced one eye open. His eyelid was too heavy, though, and he soon closed it and raised his head to let it rest back against the cold, rough surface behind him. He was upright, he realized, but he didn't understand how he was capable of standing, or even sitting up. He was soon aware of labored breathing that wasn't his own coming from somewhere close, and then more scraping sounds came with it. There was an odd, wet sound, followed by a few thuds that echoed hollowly, and more scraping.

"Grady? Special Agent Grady, are you okay?" The unfamiliar voice echoed in the darkness, bouncing around in the damp and distorting in a surreal manner.

Ty wasn't even sure he had really heard it. "Okay?" he echoed with difficulty. His tongue felt swollen and dry, and his throat was scratchy and painful as he spoke. His head pounded as if his ears had been filled with concrete. He blearily recognized the aftereffects of chloroform, and a cold fear began to twist in his chest.

"Yes, you're okay. I thought you might talk to me while I work. Make the time pass faster."

Ty raised his head slightly, forcing his dry eyes open again and blinking in the weak, flickering light of a candle that was sitting on the floor next to him. It was dark otherwise, utterly so. Not a bit of natural light flowed around him, and the cold and damp gave him the distinct feeling of being in his grandmother's root cellar.

"Work," he repeated as if testing the word. He swallowed painfully and then cleared his throat. The odd scraping noise stopped for a moment.

"Well, yes. You get to hang there and rest while I'm working. Doesn't seem very fair, does it? But I'm pretty sure you wouldn't cooperate otherwise. Which is why you're tied up."

Ty let his head rest against the cold surface behind him again. It was rough, like brick or hewn rock. He had thought his limbs were just too heavy to move, but he tugged at the restraints on his arms with the sinking realization that he was restrained. A sound like a chain clanking met his ears, and he frowned in confusion. He was chained to a wall? Seriously? He realized, after hearing the man's words, that there was a rope of some sort wound under his arms and around his chest, holding him upright even as he slumped, and there were shackles around his ankles as well, keeping him pinned to the wall.

He squinted back out into the flickering darkness. The man seemed to be working by candlelight as well. Ty glanced down at the candle sitting in a pool of melted wax at his feet. Staring at it, he remembered tidbits from his childhood that had never really surfaced in his adult life. The old miners in his hometown in West Virginia had always told stories about the candles they carried with them underground, as well as flashlights. When the light died, you had to hustle your ass out of there because the oxygen was either going or gone and you were next. It was cheaper than a canary.

"We're underground," he stated stupidly.

"Very good!" the distorted voice said sarcastically. "You must be shaking it off quicker than I expected. Luckily, I planned for that."

Ty frowned harder and turned his head to the side, groaning as the motion caused his head to swim. "Did you kill the kid?" he asked the man with a tinge of anguish he was ashamed to let creep into his voice.

The man responded with a short laugh. "You'll find he's just fine," he answered drolly, then paused as if in thought. "Actually, no, you won't. But someone else will. Perhaps your partner."

Ty closed his eyes at the lance of pain that went through him at that thought. Zane. His mind was foggy, and he tried desperately to rally. "Garrett's not gonna be amused by this," he told the man, trying in vain to squeeze his hands through the antique shackles. They were far too tight, though, and the rough metal cut at him as he tugged. "You picked the wrong one to play with."

"I don't think so," the man answered, his voice bouncing off the subterranean walls. "You're much more dangerous than your partner, you see. He's an addict and an alcoholic, and you were the only thing keeping him from fucking himself into the ground. You and I both know it." The voice sounded oddly pleased.

Ty felt himself go cold as he listened. The man knew them well, almost as if he had been with them through their personal struggles. And Ty knew this man had no intention of leaving Zane alive, either. Ty had just been picked off first because Zane was hurt.

"Did you see my welcome back present?" the voice asked abruptly. The question made him sound almost hopeful, like he was trying to please.

Ty was silent, listening to the odd scraping sound as a violent shiver went through him. "I did," he finally answered softly, sensing that talking about Zane would get him nowhere. "I especially liked the confetti."

Another soft laugh greeted his words. "That took a lot of planning. I wanted you to know how much I appreciate people who paid attention." There was a thoughtful pause while the scraping "work" continued. "Shame. If you hadn't found my file so quickly, you would have been able to keep going."

"Your file?" Ty asked hoarsely.

The man hummed in response. "I'm in that little stack you have; Baltimore '04," he answered regretfully. "I understand you're the one who caught on to Poe, as well. Bravo, Ty, I must say. I expected Zane to get it first, him being the brains of your operation and all."

Ty frowned. If he knew about both the files and the fact that Ty, and not Henninger, had been the one to figure out Poe, then he had to have taps. Probably all over the Bureau.

"You're still trying to solve it, aren't you, Grady?" the distorted voice asked in amusement. "You were enjoying yourself, weren't you? Maybe not your partner, but you were loving this case," he said with confidence. "Where did you stash Special Agent Garrett, by the way?" he asked slyly, as if he might have already known the answer. "I do hope he's safe."

Ty swallowed heavily and licked his dry lips. As their conversation continued, the man still sounded completely sane. That was possibly more frightening than even his situation. It would have been easier to deal with him if he had been delusional or something.

"He's safer than you are," Ty murmured, cursing his earlier stupidity. If he'd been thinking clearly he would have told the man Zane was dead or severely injured from the wreck. Now, he had practically sealed Zane's death sentence as well.

The scraping stopped, and the voice that responded was one of pure sympathy. "He's hurt, isn't he? He's hurt, and you left him behind to go work on the case, didn't you, Grady?" He tutted in disapproval. "You just couldn't let it go, that need for revenge. Oh, don't be surprised. I knew about you and Sanchez. He found the Baltimore connection too. He even put a call into his old Recon buddy Ty Grady down in Maryland to ask him about it, but you never answered your phone, did you, Ty? You've been wondering what that call was about since you got here, haven't you? You weren't there for Sanchez, and you won't be there for Garrett."

Ty closed his eyes and lowered his head, pain lancing through his chest at the killer's accusations.

"Ah. You did leave him, didn't you? Embarrassed, are you? That's no way to treat a partner. You should be ashamed of yourself. What will he think when you don't come back? He'll think you abandoned him; left him because he was worthless."

Ty licked his lips and opened his mouth to speak, but no words came. He swallowed with difficulty and then tried again, managing a hoarse, "I'm sure he'll be relieved to be rid of me."

"Hmmm. I'm not sure I believe you, Grady. Who else will he work with? Who else would work with him? He's a loose cannon." There was a soft chuckle. "But then, so are you. At least you're firing real ammunition. He'll be even easier to take care of without you around."

Again, Ty was silent, and the odd sounds started up again. It was a slow, squishing sound, like a shoe stuck in the mud, and then a long scrape followed by several shorter ones. Ty couldn't quite identify it, but as he listened, he accepted with a sinking sensation that he was going to die.

Sears brought Zane another glass of juice while he sat and flipped through the pages of the leather Poe anthology Ross had found. Ross sat with a pen and paper, making notes as Zane searched for similarities between the cases and the stories he read.

"'The Murders in the Rue Morgue,'" he said softly.

"The ME," Sears provided with a wince.

"Right. In the story, one woman's head is practically cut off. The other was stuffed into the chimney." Frowning, Zane shook his head.

"The location is what's important there, right?" Ross asked as he made a note.

Zane nodded and moved onto the next. "'Ligeia,'" he announced. "First thing, the wife in the story dies," he said woodenly. He grimaced and kept reading. "The man in the story remarries, but he's convinced that his new wife is the old one, reincarnated or something, and he slowly poisons the second wife, who then dies as well. The second wife was described as raven-haired. The first wife was blonde," he stated in clipped tones.

"The dye job roommates," Ross said with a nod without looking up from his paper. "That wasn't location; it was body positioning."

"And the wife thing explains the plastic wedding rings," Zane supplied tiredly. "Hooked together to symbolize they were really one person, no doubt."

"Jesus," Sears murmured with a shake of her head. She was thumbing through the files that sat nearby, making notes. Henninger had pulled only the files of anyone who had lived in or around the Baltimore area in 2001, which included large areas like Washington, DC. The stack was huge.

An odd feeling of dread settled into Zane as he looked at the files. It was like searching for one particular needle in a fucking needle factory. How would they know which file was relevant? Even Ty's file was in that stack, and Zane's fingers itched to search for it. Instead, he paged through the book and found another story, one he'd read over and over while in school. "'The Tell-Tale Heart,'" he announced.

Both agents looked up from their notes. Zane didn't need to explain that one.

"You've been a fine conversationalist, but it's almost time for me to leave." The distorted voice was more muffled, and the light had grown very dim.

It took a while, but Ty had finally decided that he knew what the sound was. In hindsight, it bothered him that it took him so long to figure it out. He had spent one summer when he was thirteen years old helping his father build a small outbuilding on their property. It had been nothing but cinderblock and beam, but they had still needed mortar and a trowel. He had grown to love the sound of laying the mortar that summer. He was trying to come to terms with the fact that that sound would be one of the last ones he heard.

The fucker was bricking him in. He recognized "The Cask of Amontillado" now that his head had cleared and he knew what was happening. This had been the only Poe story Ty had read and actually enjoyed. Ironic that it would be what killed him.

He turned his head in the darkness. He could see the outline of the man at the top of the wall he was building. When he spoke, his voice echoed off the cavernous walls of the catacomb and came back too distorted to even decipher an accent, much less if it was familiar.

Again, Ty felt the cold dread creep over him. It was his worst nightmare, one he had never actually dreamed; knowing his lover was in danger and he couldn't do a damn thing about it. His wrists and ankles were bloody from his silent struggles with the shackles. He was shivering from the damp and cold. But he hadn't yet given up. He couldn't, not while knowing that the killer's next stop would be Zane.

"He'll kill you," he told the man who was in the process of murdering him. "He'll make it hurt."

"I'll be disappointed if he doesn't try," the man answered sincerely. "Well, three bricks left, Special Agent Grady. Time to say goodbye, if you like."

Ty was silent as the man made some rustling sounds, as if he were crumpling a trash bag. Soon, a handful of white plastic was stuffed through the hole left in the brick wall. It was a plastic suit that had obviously been protecting the man's clothing from the mud and mortar. It fluttered to the ground and the candle flickered threateningly. As soon as it landed, the plastic caught the flame and flared, bathing the little room in a burst of light. It illuminated the tiny space, making the water dripping down the old brick walls shimmer.

Ty could see the heavy drilled brackets that bound him to the bricks with thick chains, and the solid wall of brick a couple feet in front of him that closed in the tiny alcove. He knew instantly that no one would find him here. Not in time.

He glanced up at the face in the hole in the brick wall and swallowed past his shock as he finally saw the man's face.

"Congratulations," he managed to utter to the face looking down at him.

"Why, thank you, Ty. That's very kind of you. By the way, don't worry about the kid. He needs to be alive enough to pass on the news about you disappearing. But I'm afraid I can't make the same promise about your partner."

Three bricks left.

Ty fought back the panic that bubbled up. Even the glimpse of the man's face didn't make a dent in the cold curtain of fear that had fallen. What good did it do to finally know who they had been hunting if he was going to die here?

Two bricks.

The candle flickered as the wall was nearly finished. A soft gust of cool, damp air flushed through the small hole remaining. Then there was a thump, a wet plop, a long scrape, and a quiet slide of sticky mortar.

The last brick.

Ty swallowed as the outside world was shut out. He looked down at the candle, the flame unwavering but weak. When it ran out, so would he.

"We have five more victims to explain," Ross told Zane as he scribbled quickly.

"'Berenice,'" Zane answered as his entire right side burned with throbbing, incessant pain. "The woman whose teeth were all yanked and she was wrapped up in a shroud and dumped at the cemetery. Then we have 'The Oval Portrait,' the woman who was painted with her own blood and stuck up on a canvas."

"God, it's so easy to see now," Sears groaned.

"A few more and we have them all. All except the agents who got too close." Zane was shaking as he continued to turn through the book.

"Jesus, it was right there all this time," Ross whispered.

"You told the Assistant Director about this, right?" Sears asked suddenly.

"Henninger was supposed to relay it," Zane answered with a sigh.

"Better make sure," Ross mumbled as he pulled out his cell phone and started punching buttons while Sears took his notepad from him.

Zane turned to the front of the book to look at the index as Ross swore at the phone and moved to the window.

"Let's see," he murmured as he scanned over the names of the stories he remembered reading years ago. "'The Fall of the House of Usher,'" he announced to Sears as she wrote quickly. "The character is suffering from extreme hypersensitivity. That's got to be the first guy, the meth overdose."

Sears nodded without looking up from her writing.

Zane paged through some more with his good hand. "There's one. 'William Wilson,'" he said. "A man kills his double. That explains the twins." He continued to scan and passed on story after story. "There's a classic," he murmured to himself. "'The Raven,'" he mused. He made to turn the page to go to the next page of the index.

"Wait," Sears said as she reached out and took Zane's hand. "Bird flu," she whispered.

Ross paused in his pacing, still messing with his phone, and he looked over at them sardonically. "Well, that's sort of clever," he commented before tossing his phone onto the couch and pulling Sears's off the strap of her purse.

Zane's face was grim. "That's all of them. There's got to be twenty more stories in here that he can play with."

"Now what? So we've figured out the pattern, but it doesn't get us closer to him," Sears protested in disgust.

"It helps us understand how he thinks," Zane pointed out.

"Until your profiling buddy comes back, that doesn't do us much good," Ross pointed out as he paced and waited for the call to go through.

"We still know next to nothing about him," Sears pointed out. "Even if we did, we can't leave you alone here to go do anything about it."

"Yes, you most certainly fucking can," Zane insisted. "I don't need a babysitter, and Grady and Henninger are going to need backup. Call for someone."

"We can't call anyone from here. Something in the building's blocking cell service," Ross informed them in frustration as he waved the useless cell phone.

"Use Henninger's phone," Sears suggested logically. Except Henninger didn't have a landline.

"I'm going down to the garage and then up to the front of the building, okay? I'll be back," Ross declared, and he was out the door.

Zane nodded and pushed himself out of the chair to grab one of the personnel files. "Christ. There's got to be some way to find this asshole," he muttered.

Special Agent Gary Ross hadn't gone far into the darkened parking deck when he stumbled over something on the ground as he jogged with his phone held out in front of him, and he almost went sprawling. He righted himself and turned to look, cursing creatively when he realized that it was a man on the ground. He knelt beside him and felt his pulse.

"Fuck," he hissed, recognizing Henninger's dark, curly hair, now matted down with blood. "Tim?" he murmured as the man groaned.

"Why the hell don't you have a fucking phone?" he asked in annoyance as he began to gather the man off the ground. He glanced toward the exit signs attached to the ceilings of the parking deck, knowing that just a few more steps would give him a signal, but he needed to get Henninger inside and safe before he could go call for help.

"Phone?" Henninger mumbled weakly as he stirred.

"Come on," Ross grunted, hefting Henninger up and dragging him back toward the elevators.

Sears was pacing and Zane would have been as well had he been able to walk, waiting for Ross to return.

"How do we find him?" Zane muttered from where he leaned awkwardly to one side, trying to keep the pressure off his broken ribs. "We need another murder, another city he lived in. Some dots to connect."

"He's got to slip up sometime, especially since we know what to look for now," Sears assured. "The net's closing on him."

"Which only makes him more dangerous," Zane gritted out through the pain.

A thump on the door interrupted them. Zane glanced to Sears, who pulled her gun out from under her jacket and nodded toward the door. She carefully walked to the side of the door until she was right up against it before looking through the peephole. "Shit!" she yelled, throwing the door open.

Ross was panting as Henninger tried and failed to stand. They staggered through the door together. Ross dumped the man on the couch with a gasp, and Sears kicked the door closed as she rushed to help them.

"What happened?" she demanded as she knelt next to Henninger on the couch, trying to check the head wound.

"We got jumped," Henninger croaked in answer as he winced away from her touch. It looked as if someone had hit him in the side of the head with something nice and blunt. There was enough blood that it had caked down the side of his face, and it would probably hurt like hell, but he was in no mortal danger. "I saw him take Grady down with a cloth or something and then the lights went out. There must have been two of them."

"Cloth?" Zane breathed. He squeezed his eyes shut tightly. "Chloroform," he groaned. They had been right about that aspect, anyway. "Henninger," he said thickly. "We need to call the Bureau."

"What?" Henninger asked dazedly.

"He's so out of it, he won't have a clue what you're talking about," Ross muttered, walking over to the window to peer out as if someone might be out there now, looking guilty. Sears sniffed and went to the kitchen for ice.

"Focus, Henninger," Zane tried desperately, not even able to think about Ty being at the hands of this monster.

"Okay," Henninger mumbled as he sat up and held his head, squinting at them all. He seemed to be having difficulty comprehending the urgency of a phone. Their need was even more urgent now; they needed every unit in the city on the lookout for Ty and his captor.

"We need to call out. How the hell do you get any of your messages?" Ross asked him testily as he jabbed at his phone again.

Henninger swallowed and rubbed at his ribs gingerly as he looked up at the other agent. "I turn off the signal blocker on the window," he answered flatly.

Ross turned to him, confusion flitting over his features, and Sears stepped back into the room to look at them oddly. Henninger shrugged apologetically to them both before pulling a silenced gun from under his jacket. With two quick, quiet pops, the gun sent both agents to the hardwood floor. He stood quickly and turned to Zane, who'd only had time to scramble out of the chair and get a few steps away.

"You son of a bitch," Zane whispered through a sudden stupor. Henninger gave a lopsided shrug and a small smile, the gun trained on Zane unerringly.

Zane remained motionless, hand lowered out to his side, injured right arm useless in its sling. "Where's Ty?" he rasped.

"Dying," Henninger answered bluntly, his head cocking to the side with the word.

It took everything Zane had to hold it together as agony ripped through him. "Why?"

Henninger laughed softly, amusement written all over his slightly bloody face. "You know, Grady had the good sense not to ask me such a stupid question."

Zane let out a shaky breath. Dying meant not dead yet. He held onto that thought tightly. "He's a smart man."

"He was, indeed," Henninger drawled. "And so are you. If you two were a little less smart, we'd not have two dead agents on our hands," he told Zane with a nod of his head at the two bodies on the floor. "Had you found my file amongst the stack, yet?" he asked.

"We got too close," Zane realized aloud. "Just like Reilly and Sanchez. You killed them in their hotel room. You were meeting with them, weren't you? About the case. They trusted you," he ground out. "We trusted you."

"Look at me." Henninger laughed. "Everyone trusts me, Garrett. Even strangers." He grinned impishly.

Zane shook his head slowly, hefting his hurt arm up against him with a wince. "Why all the murders? You're too sane for this."

"Stop moving, Garrett," Henninger ordered seriously. "You know, every time someone's asked me that I gave them the answer they wanted. It's such a trite question, really, but it's the only thing a dying person can think of, apparently. But you," he went on as he began stepping a little closer, "you, I can't read well enough to give you an answer. I'm not sure what it is you want to hear."

"How nice for you," Zane snarled, pushing aside desperation for anger. "Put down the goddamn gun."

"You're not really in a position to be giving orders, Special Agent Garrett," Henninger murmured. "Any more questions before I kill you? I'm rather short on time, you see, having all these unexpected dead bodies lying around," he said in amusement.

"What do you need from me to give me the answer?" Zane tried, wincing and gasping in pain as he bumped back against the door with his injured arm. He could feel the gun Ty had given him resting heavily in his sling, though he'd have to use his left hand to shoot.

Henninger tilted his head and narrowed his eyes, intrigued by the challenge. "Why did you come back?" he asked finally, the amusement and enjoyment clear in his voice. "Why did you come back with that asshole for a partner and the very real probability that you would die? Grady, he came back for revenge. But you? Why didn't you just stay away? Stay away and drink and drug yourself to a quiet death?"

Zane jerked backward in apparent surprise, slamming his useless arm against the door. He yelped and grabbed for his elbow, his good hand sliding under the sling to support it. He made a conscious decision to let the pain show clearly on his face. He was going to need his strength for other things . . . he hoped.

Weighing his options as Henninger watched in lurid amusement, Zane tried to decide what to say to get the most reaction. Enough reaction. He drew a breath. "I love him."

At that, Henninger stopped short in surprise. Then he began to chuckle. "Love him?" he echoed with a gleeful laugh. "Oh, that is rich! No wonder he looked so crushed when I told him it was his fault you were going to die."

The chilling edge of Henninger's words cut through him, and Zane drew another breath. "I love him," he repeated, voice stronger.

Henninger laughed harder in the face of Zane's conviction. Within a heartbeat's time, Zane snapped his left arm out away from him, sending the slim stiletto from its sheath hurtling toward the killer with enough speed that Henninger couldn't dodge it. The knife buried deep into his upper chest, close to the shoulder of his gun arm.

Crying out in anger and surprise, Henninger jerked to one side as the knife hit, his gun firing uselessly off to the side, giving Zane just enough time to pull out his own gun and fire. The shot hit him in the gut—the perfect wound since Zane wanted to interrogate him as he died a slow, painful death. Henninger staggered back, looking down at the burgeoning stain of blood in shock. Slowly his knees gave out, and he began to sink to the floor.

Arm shaking, Zane kept the gun trained on him as he stalked over and kicked the weapon out of Henninger's hand, sending it sliding to wedge under the couch. He crouched down in front of him, took hold of the hilt of the knife sticking from Henninger's shoulder, and twisted it hard.

Henninger cried out in shock and pain and struck out, hitting Zane's injured hip with as much force as a fatally wounded man could muster. Zane gritted his teeth as his entire leg exploded into fire, but he kept twisting. "Where is he?" he ground out. "Tell me where he is, and I'll call you an ambulance."

The blood drained from Henninger's face as the pain took him over. "You're so smart," he slurred as he struggled weakly. "Figure it out," he rasped.

"Talk or you can bleed out here."

Henninger merely laughed at him hoarsely. Growling, Zane drew back his fist and hit Henninger in the gut, close to the gunshot wound.

The edges of Henninger's vision darkened as he gurgled and gasped, but when the pain receded he managed another laugh. "He said you'd kill me," he murmured as blood began to dribble out of the corner of his mouth. "He said you'd make it hurt," he told Zane tauntingly.

Anger and terror building equally, Zane stood up and yanked the knife out of Henninger's shoulder, ignoring the agonized cry of pain. He lifted the gun and pushed it to the killer's forehead, staring down at the man who knelt before him. "He's right. Where is he?"

Henninger closed his eyes and shook his head. He knew he would be handed the death penalty if they found Grady alive. He also knew, deep down, that Garrett was going to kill him even if he did tell him where Grady was. Garrett was just that kind of guy. Grady had too much honor to do it, but Garrett would pull the trigger in a heartbeat. He probably should have taken him out first, now that he thought of it.

It was too late now, considering there was also the surprising factor of the fact that he had been gut shot and was going to die a slow, painful death if Garrett didn't do it fast. He preferred fast. It wouldn't be difficult to get Garrett angry and make him lose his temper, and then . . . sweet oblivion.

Henninger's lips twitched in a slow, amused smile. "You've thought about what happens when I die, haven't you?" he asked in a weak, pained voice. He would win either way, even in death. "No one will believe you. You'll become Suspect Number One without Grady to back you up," he said with a quiet confidence. "How will you live with knowing that it wasn't love that made you so desperate to find him?" he asked as he opened his black eyes. "How will you remain sober?" he asked with a disdainful sneer. "Knowing it's only self-preservation that's making you so desperate?"

Zane's face went very still as his emotions settled into solid certainty, momentarily blocking out the pain. He used the gun barrel to nudge Henninger's chin up so he could see his eyes, and he put the gun back to the other man's forehead. Then he smiled coldly.

Henninger's eyes flickered open, filled with a sudden doubt that quickly faded back into the depths. Out of them all, Garrett had turned out to be the biggest problem for him; like a chameleon who couldn't decide on his color. He had been predictable at first, but then had begun to change to the point that Henninger couldn't decide what to do with him. Even now, Henninger wasn't sure what to do with him. As Garrett looked down at him, Henninger could feel, for the first time, the possibility of defeat creeping in on him.

Zane stood and drew a steady breath to speak. "Luckily, you don't have to worry about that," he said softly, and then he pulled the trigger.

Henninger's body jerked and thumped to the floor. Gathering himself, Zane went over to the window to search for the signal blocker. Finally, he found it and yanked the cord out of it, then grabbed the phone out of Ross's limp hand and hit buttons with his thumb as he swayed dangerously. He sank to his knees as his entire right side throbbed and burned viciously. The call was answered immediately. Zane gave the codes for officers down and perpetrator down, and then the location to the best of his knowledge before tossing the phone onto the coffee table, still open so it could be traced.

Painfully, he pushed himself to his knees and crawled to check Ross for a pulse. Grimacing when he found none, Zane shifted awkwardly and moved to Sears. She was gone too. He hung his head, an agonized whimper escaping. He looked back at the murderer's body. No need to check a pulse there. The feeling of grim satisfaction gave him the strength to grab for the book he'd left in the armchair. The answer was in there, somewhere. He felt sure Henninger had thought of Ty as another victim, not just someone in the way. Sitting there sprawled on the floor, he started paging through it again, shaking as he prayed it would give him some clue.

"Fuck all," he hissed toward the body. "God, please . . . Ty . . ." he whispered as he kept turning, story after story, anguish encroaching as no inspiration hit until he couldn't hold it off anymore. It gripped him hard, and he curled in on himself, hot tears slipping loose and dotting the pages. He could hardly think through the pain and loss of blood.

Defeated, he looked up at Henninger's body. Blood was matted in his hair. Ty's blood? More stained his hands, along with traces of what looked like grit and dust from where he had lain on the concrete of the parking deck.

He must have taken Ty down with chloroform—because Zane knew Ty would have hurt him badly if he had tried some other method—hidden him away, then hit himself in the head just hard enough to make blood flow. All he had to do was lay on the ground pretending to be unconscious until someone found him.

The tears gave way to an ill resignation as Zane's eyes continued down the killer's body, looking for some hint. Henninger had been on his knees and fallen backward, his heels pushing to one side as he had died.

It took a long moment for Zane to register what he was seeing. The bottoms of Henninger's dress shoes were covered in gritty, gray mud. It was ground into the treads and covered the insteps. Zane pulled himself closer, almost out of energy. Reaching out slowly, Zane drew shaking fingers down the sole, and they came away covered with thick, damp mud. He stared at the dead body. They were in the city, and it had been dry all week. Where would he find fresh mud?

"They even kept the original tunnels below the building intact..."

"Jesus," Zane hissed, grabbing for the book, ignoring the gritty muck coming off his hand onto the pages. He found what he was looking for: "The Cask of Amontillado."

"Jesus!" Lurching to his feet, Zane collapsed again with a harsh cry, catching himself on the couch's arm with his good hand. He was too weak, and he hurt so badly he could barely tolerate it. He focused on the one thing he could. Ty. Ty would be going crazy, stuck somewhere small and in the dark, like in the story.

He needed something to pump him up until he could get to Ty. Stumbling into the bedroom, he made it to the nightstand and swiped up the bottle Ty had given him. Pulling the top off, he saw the caplets marked OC inside and shook them all out onto the bed. Ten pills. Without a thought to the dosage, he scooped up a handful, tossed them in his mouth, and started chewing. The dry, sharp chemical taste filled his senses when he swallowed, and he pushed himself out to the front room again and found his gun and the bloody knife. He grabbed

Sears's gun for good measure and drew a deep breath as he felt the first wave of drug-induced energy. He wove dangerously as he headed to the door, the drugs already taking effect since he'd bypassed the time release by chewing them up. By the time he got to the elevator, the high was rushing through him.

"I'm coming, Ty," he murmured to the closing elevator doors. "I'm coming."

Ty struggled and called out for help until his voice was hoarse and his abused wrists were dripping blood down his arms. The chains held fast, though, and nothing but the flicker of the candle noticed his distress.

Soon he found himself hyperventilating, and he forced himself to breathe slowly in a desperate attempt to calm. He would surely die if he didn't remain calm. He closed his eyes, but realized immediately that the darkness felt heavier without the light of the candle. He opened them and stared longingly at the bricks. They were so close in the small space, but still unreachable.

Tim Henninger—and Ty was still trying to get his mind around how horribly he had misjudged the kid—had left everything incriminating inside Ty's tomb with him. His plastic protective gear, his tools, the bucket of drying mortar, and probably the cruelest of all, the keys to Ty's shackles, just out of reach on the ground.

Ty looked back at the candle with a growing sense of calm. He was going to die here. In the dark. He swallowed past the tightening of his throat and watched the candle. The flame had weakened alarmingly, and now its circle of light didn't even reach Ty's feet. As Ty watched it, the flame went blue, stuttering in the growing darkness.

Ty took in a deep breath of the stale, damp air.

His head shot up at the sound of a voice echoing faintly on the other side of the wall. Was he hallucinating? He could have sworn that he'd heard a shout somewhere in the distance. He stared at the brick wall in front of him, shaking convulsively with cold and encroaching shock. At his feet, the tiny flame spit and flared violently, then sputtered one last time and died.

He tried to call out for help, but his voice was gone.

The desire to simply close his eyes and let sleep take him over was almost overwhelming. Ty cocked his head as he heard the sound again. "Zane," he whispered to the hallucination, the sound barely a word as his head spun and he gasped for the nearly nonexistent air.

Zane emerged into the darkened basement, lit only by a couple of bare, hanging light bulbs. He was shaking again, this time with manic energy instead of pain and exhaustion. The drugs had taken hold quickly and adrenaline and chemicals shot through his body at warp speed. He walked past the large furnace, looking around quickly, gun in his hand. He had no idea if Henninger had an accomplice or not. He came upon a long, ill-lit hallway that had doorways covered by chain-link fence on each side. Storage units.

"Ty!" Zane yelled, his voice echoing through the large space as he moved down the hallway. The echo was the only thing that answered his calls. Finally, he spotted a darker hole in the wall at the end of the hallway, one that wasn't lit at all. Tunnels, Henninger had said.

Zane couldn't see into the rough-hewn passageway, and he quickly started patting his jacket pockets and found his lighter. Thank God he'd talked Ty out of making him stop smoking. Annoyed with the restraining sling, he pulled his arm out of it and dropped it, then held up the flaming lighter and looked down at the dirt. It was gray, just like Henninger's shoes.

"Ty!" he yelled again, heading into the catacombs, bypassing the insets filled merely with old crates and construction debris.

Walking in long strides, hurt arm raised to shelter the flame, Zane almost kept going before he noticed that he had passed a space of wall where an inset should have been. Backtracking, his heart plummeted as he saw a square of clearly new brick in the wall.

"Ty... Ty!" he yelled, running to the inset and touching the wall. The mortar was wet. He pulled out his knife and started prying at a brick with one hand and pushed it in. He heard it thump to the ground inside the little alcove, accompanied by the rattle of plastic. Then he dislodged another, and another.

From inside there was a clank of chains and a soft groan.

Zane frantically started pulling at the bricks, easily ignoring how they scraped and cut into his hands. The bricks reluctantly pulled loose; the mortar was closer to setting than not. When he had a rough opening, Zane leaned over with the lighter.

"Ty?" he rasped, pulse pounding with adrenaline.

Ty was strapped to the wall of the tiny alcove, his hands stretched out to the sides and above his head, blood running down them and clotting at his wrists. His feet were spread shoulder-width apart, shackled to the wall so that he couldn't even kick out, and a rope around his chest kept him from sagging forward. Everywhere the restraints touched him, there was blood. His head was bowed, his chin resting on his chest, and his fingers hung limply from his shackled hands. He didn't move, but a small groan told Zane that he was still alive. Barely.

Glancing around inside the alcove, Zane saw the plastic and the bucket of mortar. He cursed under his breath before seeing the candle and a rusted set of iron keys. "That son of a bitch," he breathed. Leaning over the bricks, he reached to light the candle so he could pocket the lighter and start digging at the bricks again. The drugs filtering through his system built up his manic concern, and he worked feverishly, heedless of the pain or his ever-increasing heart rate and light-headedness. Once the hole was big enough that he could get a leg in and duck under, he did so, which put him right up against his partner. There wasn't much room. There wouldn't have been much air, either, and just standing there made him claustrophobic.

"Ty?" he whispered, gently cupping his chin and raising it, praying he wasn't too far gone. Ty's head was heavy in his hand. But another groan came from his cracked, dry lips and he stirred.

Breaths harsh, Zane carefully lowered Ty's chin before moving to grasp for the keys he had seen lying on the ground. Fussing and cursing the locks, he started with Ty's feet, then moved to unlock the shackles on one bloody and cut-up wrist.

He'd struggled, Zane noted with a lurch of his stomach. Oh, Lord, he'd struggled. Zane's heart hurt with the mere idea of how hard Ty must have fought to cut into his wrists and chest like he had. When Ty's body sagged, Zane draped the free arm over his shoulder and fought to unlock the last shackle. The other man collapsed against him. Trying to pull him free, though, Zane couldn't get him away from the wall. He fingered the rope, and with a growl pulled out one of his knives and cut through it. Glancing to the uneven hole, he gathered Ty against him and turned them both toward it.

"Zane," Ty breathed pitifully, the tortured sound barely audible.

The sound of his name almost tore Zane's heart out. "I'm here, baby. I'm getting you out of here," he promised.

Ty seemed to be coming around, gasping at the stale air as if it were the sweetest thing he had ever tasted. "Are you real?" he asked Zane as he tightened his weak grip. His words were hardly recognizable.

Zane's laugh was tinged with a little desperation. "Yeah. I'm as real as it gets," he answered, stopping at the bricks. He drew several fast breaths, gritted his teeth, and lifted Ty totally from the ground. He moved very slowly and cautiously to step over the broken wall, setting his feet amongst the tumbled bricks, where he stumbled.

Ty's feet hit the uneven ground as Zane set him down, and he sank to his hands and knees. "Henninger," he gasped as his head swam. "It's Henninger," he said urgently, his voice still hoarse and abused from the harsh chloroform and the desperate shouting for help.

Collapsing to his knees beside him, both of Zane's hands hit the ground in an attempt to catch himself. The jarring didn't hurt, and neither had the lifting. Instead, he felt hot, dizzy, and light-headed. His pulse raced dangerously, and his gut burned with nausea. He was buzzing all over. He knew what was happening.

"Dead. He's dead," Zane bit out viciously as he tried to remember when he'd last eaten anything solid and how many of what kind of pills he'd taken. There had been a whole handful, but his memory seemed bright and fuzzy.

Ty blinked at the man, both of them on their hands and knees and looking as if they'd just lost the fight rather than won it. He swallowed and nodded, unable to think of anything to say as confused relief washed through him.

Zane curled his hand around Ty's, looking up with glazed eyes. "I've got to get you out of here," he said roughly as another strong swell of adrenaline and haze swamped him. He just barely quelled the impulse to laugh hysterically. "Running out of time."

"What's wrong with you?" Ty asked. His head was clearing and he was beginning to actually function once more. "Did he hurt you?"

Zane managed to shake his head and climb awkwardly to his feet, helping Ty up as well, and they leaned heavily on each other as they started moving toward the dim light. Zane was sweating now, and his arms and hands were clammy and trembling even where he held Ty tightly. "After I took him out, I could hardly move. I took the pills you left me so I could find you."

"All of them?" Ty asked in horror.

Zane actually laughed: a high, thin noise totally unlike him.

"You've overdosed," Ty murmured. "Fuck," he groaned as he tried to gather his strength and take more of Zane's weight. He stumbled with the attempt.

Managing a weak chuckle, Zane tried to hold on, but his entire body was shaking uncontrollably. "I've had worse." Not really, though . . . "Had to get here. Had to find you." He lurched to the side as dizziness hit him, and both men fell to their knees, neither one strong enough to fully support the other. "You were in the dark."

They stayed there wallowing for too many moments before Ty pushed himself up and grabbed Zane's uninjured arm to pull him to his feet weakly. "Come on," he murmured. "I thought I'd never see daylight again; I can't die in here with you now."

Zane laughed again. "Daylight. I've already got stars in my eyes," he drew out as he stumbled along beside Ty. He swallowed hard as they emerged into the basement. "Ty . . ." he gasped weakly.

"Don't," Ty growled almost angrily, his knees weak and his hands numb from being without blood for too long. "Don't you dare."

Jerking away, Zane turned and fell to his knees to retch violently, too far into the drugs to be embarrassed or concerned. All he could do was try to breathe. Behind him, Ty sagged to his knees again, unable to remain standing. He bowed his head and shivered. After a moment he forced himself up again and pulled Zane to his feet with difficulty.

"I need you, Ty, more than anything," Zane admitted hoarsely as the elevator came into sight.

Ty closed his eyes, leaning against Zane and rallying with the unexpected words. He took more of the other man's weight on himself and practically dragged his gasping partner toward the doors of the service elevator. By the time he managed to get them inside and rising toward what he prayed would be help, Zane was no longer breathing.

Chapter Sixteen

Ty walked slowly down the sterile hallway of the hospital, watching his feet carefully so as not to think too hard about why he was here. After traversing what he knew had to be the longest hallway in history, he found the room and stepped into the doorway, unconsciously biting his lip as he looked at the still figure on the bed.

He swallowed heavily and made his way slowly into the room, stopping at the bedside and looking down. Zane looked awful. His skin—what of it wasn't mottled with ugly bruises—was an unhealthy gray color under the soft light of the hospital room. Ty fought back the urge to feel sorry for himself as he sat down beside the bed and looked at the myriad of tubes and IVs that attached to Zane's hands and arms.

Hopped up, Zane hadn't realized that he'd torn his hands all to hell on the bricks, and the further abuse to his broken arm had meant surgery to fix it. The bandages around his palms and fingers glared white against his dark tan.

He'd been in the hospital for a week and still looked this bad. Like death warmed over. And the cliché fit. The overdose had done a real number on him. By the time the EMTs had gotten to them, Zane had been in full cardiac arrest.

But he was alive, and that was all that Ty cared about. He sat silently, merely watching Zane as he slept. After a while, his vision unfocused and he was simply staring at the hospital blanket that covered Zane's still body as he sat by his side.

"Hey."

Ty winced at the soft word.

He hadn't had a chance to see Zane since they had taken him out of that service elevator. During the past week, no one would let him see his partner until he himself was officially discharged, and he had only just been released himself. They had merely told him that Zane was alive, and left it at that. During the time he'd been confined to his hospital bed, Ty'd had a lot of time to think about what he wanted to say to Zane. Ever aware of the prying ears and eyes around them, though, he bit back the more tender words he might have said. They didn't feel right on his tongue, anyway.

"Hey," he echoed hollowly.

Zane's dark eyes were sunken, but they were open, mostly clear and focused. "How're you?" he whispered.

"Horrible," Ty managed to answer with a weak smile. "They tell me I'm not allowed to kick your ass yet."

One brow slowly edged up in question. "Kiss my ass, did you say?" Zane's eyes twinkled and the corners of his mouth turned up slightly.

Ty glanced over his shoulder quickly and then stood to press a kiss to Zane's lips. "I thought we'd lost you," he muttered accusingly.

Zane brightened a little after the kiss. "I'm too stubborn to die when I have a reason to live," he murmured, watching Ty reverently.

"You damn well better be," Ty murmured as he sat back down, wringing his hands together as if he wanted to do something else with them. "'Cause I'm gonna beat the living shit out of you later."

"Promises, promises," Zane said quietly. "I owe you a hell of a beating too." He paused for a moment as they just stared at each other. "Wanna call it even?"

Ty made a show of thinking over the offer and then smiled slightly. The smile fell slowly, and he looked over Zane seriously. "You are getting out of here, right?" he asked softly.

"Yeah. You are waiting for me, right?" Zane asked.

Ty's lips compressed into a thin line and he looked away, flushing guiltily. Zane tilted his head to the side, and his smile turned slightly sad. After everything they'd been through, even after what he'd just said, it appeared that the military mindset was far too ingrained for Ty to be comfortable admitting what he felt for his lover now that the dire situation had passed. Zane wondered if he even felt anything at all.

"Either way." Zane sighed tiredly, letting his eyes close. "Let me know."

"They're not gonna let me stick around," Ty said softly as he lowered his head.

Zane stilled for a long moment, then opened his eyes to see Ty at the bedside, head bowed. "'They' being the Bureau," he said, not questioning.

Ty looked back up at him with open desperation, as if he were begging Zane to tell him what to do.

Pure joy swelled quietly inside Zane. "You don't want to go," he realized, lifting his hand with difficulty to brush Ty's cheek.

"Not right now," Ty whispered in something close to outrage. "What, you thought I'd just leave your sorry ass after all this?" he asked incredulously.

Zane shook his head slowly, smile reappearing. "Sorry. Little slow. I'll blame the drugs they gave me to counteract the drugs," he murmured. He didn't have to be scared. All of a sudden it was easy to accept that. "You care about my sorry ass," he added quietly, turning eyes that spoke volumes on Ty.

Ty was silent, his knuckles turning white as he clasped his hands together. "I do," he finally agreed. "And stop forgetting it," he chided gently.

Rather than replying right away, Zane turned his head fully to the side so he could rest and watch Ty at the same time. He studied the bed hair and the thinner face, dark with stubble. He realized Ty must have come straight here from being released. But to Zane, he was gorgeous. "Okay," he agreed, then licked his lips. "So they're sending you off somewhere?" he asked, back to the "they."

"Lecture circuit," Ty answered bitterly. "Again." He looked away and then lowered his head, blushing deeply. "They can't put me on a case until . . . they're sure I won't freak out in the dark." He sighed and closed his eyes, unable to look back up. "They had to leave me a nightlight," he admitted sheepishly.

"C'mon and look at me, Ty," Zane murmured.

Ty didn't respond, other than to open his eyes. He stared at the thin blanket over Zane's body for what seemed an eternity before slowly raising his eyes to meet Zane's.

"You're a brave man," Zane rasped. "I hope that the next time I'm with you and it's dark, you'll let me hold you," Zane said.

"You're gonna have to," Ty responded in a broken laugh, "'cause all the current evidence points to the fact that I'll cry like a little girl."

"That's okay," Zane murmured without humor, raising his left arm so he could stroke Ty's cheek gently with shaking fingers. "Still want you."

Ty glanced over his shoulder nervously and then back at Zane guiltily.

Zane smiled. His eyes flickered to the empty doorway and back. "Don't worry," he said softly. "There's no one watching."

A pained look came over Ty's face before he looked away again.

Zane nodded, relaxing some against the pillows. "I understand," he said gently. He didn't have the years of habit to break. He lowered his arm and rested it on the bed again. "When do you leave?"

"Now," Ty murmured, unable to look up.

Zane's breath caught for a long moment until he forced himself to exhale. There wasn't anything else to say, then. And nothing else to be done. One more time, he'd have to watch Ty walk away, and he couldn't do anything more about it than last time. "Quick kiss before you go?" he requested, knowing it would be hard if Ty was truly as on edge as he was acting.

Ty closed his eyes and shivered. "I do want you," he whispered. "I want you to find me, as soon as you're free," he murmured as he looked up.

Zane nodded and watched the battle warring in Ty's expressive hazel eyes. It hurt more than he would ever have expected. "Take care of yourself," he said, exhaustion breaking past his bold front.

Ty reached impulsively and smoothed Zane's hair back from his forehead. He stood, bending over him to press a kiss to his forehead. "We can still cut and run," he whispered against the warm skin.

Swallowing hard, Zane shivered as hope shot through him. Hope for something other than the occasional flyby as they passed each other by while working. He had to try to ignore the twang he felt at the thought of leaving his hard-earned and well-loved job behind.

"Just say the word," he said thickly.

Ty closed his eyes, his fingers tightening in Zane's hair. He was proposing they both give up a job they loved, give up everything either of them knew. "We can open up a flower shop and sell black market orchids from the back," he offered with a slight hitch in his voice.

Zane smiled at the flash of humor, though he knew it was Ty's defense mechanism. "Just say the word," he repeated quietly, though he knew Ty never would, and he wondered what he himself would do if it ever came to that. "Go on. Go, while I'm too drugged to stop you."

"Even if I quit now, I couldn't stay here," Ty responded almost defensively, as if trying to convince himself to go. "I couldn't stay with you."

Calm in the face of Ty's struggle, Zane nodded. "You're right," he said evenly.

Ty moved quickly and pressed a kiss to Zane's lips. "Be careful, Zane," he breathed, then stood and swiftly walked away from the hospital bed, not looking back as he disappeared through the door.

※

The motorcycle sped along Interstate 35 under the bright sunlight, skillfully handled by the rider in brown leather and a full-face helmet. The bike moved steadily through the thin traffic. The rider reached out and thumbed a button when the headphone in his helmet beeped for a phone call.

"Garrett," he shouted over the roar of the engine.

"Special Agent Garrett."

Zane blinked and looked from side to side as he gunned the bike to speed up. "What do you want, Burns? I'm on vacation."

"Yes, I know. Five months of Miami earns you three weeks of vacation. How are you, Zane?"

Even more surprised to be called by name, Zane tilted his head. "I'm good," he answered cautiously.

"Where are you, pray tell?"

"Home," Zane answered slowly.

"How is Texas? Sunny?" Burns asked politely.

"No, we're in the middle of a blizzard," Zane deadpanned.

"Well, your wit is still as sharp as a broken toothpick," Burns said with a sigh. "Vacation is over in four days. I want you here in DC on the fifth."

Zane pressed his lips together as he guided the bike off the interstate onto a lesser highway. "You're the boss," he finally said.

"You're not going back to Miami," Burns said placatingly.

"Miami's a cesspool," Zane muttered, unconsciously repeating a sentiment said to him what seemed like years ago.

"Be here in five days. The Bureau will pay for transport, if you like. Get your head wrapped around the idea of a few easy assignments and a new partner while you're at it," Burns instructed.

Zane's gut clenched painfully. "I've told you. I don't want a new partner. What happened to my old partner?"

Burns usually blithely ignored him when he asked about Ty, but now he cleared his throat and said, "That's classified. See you in five days, Special Agent Garrett." And the Assistant Director hung up.

Zane had to force himself to pay attention to traffic as his stomach roiled. He didn't want another partner. He only wanted Ty.

God. Ty. Almost six months had passed, and not a word. Not a message. Nothing but blind hope to keep him going. Work made it easier to forget. But after the second time being injured in Miami this past tour, Zane snapped out of the dangerous, depressive funk and figured out he had better listen to Ty's request for him to be careful or he'd cut his chances of seeing him again to nil. He put in the vacation and transfer requests, and for the first time in five years, went home to Texas.

The last three weeks had been full of memories: old and new, good and bad. Ty was always there, on the edge of his periphery, and Zane felt like a part of himself was missing. What were the chances Burns would put him back together with Ty? Zane figured on absolutely none, and that was optimistic. If Zane had been put back in deep cover, then Ty had to have been as well. That was the other man's specialty, after all, and the "That's classified" answer pretty much confirmed it. But he couldn't help hoping. At least Burns might be willing to tell him how to contact Ty when they spoke in five days.

The bike sped out of the city and into the flats, giving its rider time to think.

Ty sat at the end of the bar, watching the Orioles get the shit kicked out of them again and drinking a Sam Adams fresh out of the tap. He knew the bartender by name. He knew the waitress by name. He knew the drunk dude throwing darts at the public health poster in the corner by name. He had spent a great deal of time in this bar.

"Want another basket, sweetie?" Cindy asked him as she leaned against the bar next to him, a tray of dirty glasses and empty beer bottles resting on her hip.

Ty glanced at her and shook his head, offering a weak smile. He slid the empty basket of chips toward her, and she smiled at him as she took it and went on her way. Ty looked back at the television, watching but not seeing. The Orioles were just painful this season. Finally, he drained his beer, setting the empty glass down with a clunk and slapping down a fifty with it.

He waved goodbye to all the people who thought they knew him and stepped out into the warm night air. He sighed and turned away from the corner where the cabs frequented, walking instead toward his row house near Fell's Point. It was a long walk, but Ty didn't mind it. The walk helped quell the part of him that prayed one of the cars racing along the narrow roads would just hit him as he shuffled across the street. Life was no fun anymore. The job was no fun anymore. The bad guys kept getting away, and shooting them wasn't worth the paperwork. He couldn't even watch baseball without feeling the need to slit his wrists.

Fucking stupid Orioles.

He had tracked Zane right back to Miami, to an undercover job where Ty couldn't possibly contact him. They couldn't have sent him back down there unless he had accepted the assignment, and Ty was left with nothing but to wonder why Zane would do that.

The cell phone in his back pocket began to vibrate as he walked slowly behind a couple out enjoying the night. Ty growled under his breath and then reached back for it, flipping it open and answering with a negligent, "What?"

"Stop walking," the voice said on the other end of the call, "and wait for your ride to pick you up."

Ty stopped dead in his tracks and swallowed heavily, resisting the urge to look around. "You're having me followed?" he asked incredulously.

"Only when you're thinking about going AWOL," Assistant Director Burns answered with a smile in his voice.

Ty was simmering as a black Yukon Denali pulled up beside the line of parked cars next to the sidewalk and waited for him patiently. "And when is that?" he demanded in a growl.

"Midnight to 4 a.m.," Burns returned knowingly. "How're the broken fingers?"

"Broken," Ty grunted in answer. "Why am I being tailed?"

"You have a new assignment."

"But—"

"Señor de la Vega had a nasty plane accident down in the Caribbean," Burns informed him quietly. "Seems the mechanic working on his plane had some broken fingers no one knew about, didn't get all the nuts and bolts tight enough. Get in the damn car and let it take you home. I want you in DC by noon."

"You and your new assignments can go fuck yourselves, Dick," Ty grumbled. "My fingers hurt. And the important one won't stand up by itself."

"So hold them all up and call it a flock," Burns advised in mild amusement.

Ty snorted. "Flock of birds. That's funny," he muttered disconsolately to himself as he stared at the government vehicle stubbornly.

"Ty," Burns sighed, his voice taking on the tone of the mentor he had once been. "Don't toss everything you love out the window, hmm? You've tied up your loose ends, and you get to torture your new partner tomorrow. Noon. I'll see you then," he said before ending the call.

Ty looked down at the phone as if it had offended him somehow, then up at the agent patiently waiting for him by the open back door of the Yukon. Ty's jaw tightened as he looked up and down the sidewalk. Finally, he sighed and trudged over to the waiting vehicle, sliding into the back wordlessly.

Zane ignored Burns's offer of transport, instead spending a couple more days with his parents before getting on the bike and heading east. He really didn't care what time he got to DC on the fifth day. Burns hadn't specified, after all. He stopped both nights along the way and tried a lot not to think about what was waiting for him. A new partner.

It was a few minutes after noon when he pulled into the Bureau lot and showed his identification. Once he parked, he got a hit of déjà vu. He'd arrived like this last time. Same bike, same leather, different jacket. His mother had insisted he cut his hair, though, so it was trimmed and neat once more. He had a few more scars. He'd not told anyone about those. No one to tell, really, and they'd mostly healed up.

Wrinkling his nose, Zane dropped the helmet on the seat and clomped his way into the building, grumbling to himself.

With all his contacts, he'd managed to find out only that Ty had been released from Walter Reed on the day Zane had last seen him, but then he hit a dead end. How it was possible for Ty to just walk out of the hospital and disappear, he didn't know; agents not on assignment were usually pretty easy to find through the Bureau. He hadn't gone on the lecture circuit like he'd said he was, that was for certain. The only thing Zane could come up with was that Ty was working something off the books—not even undercover, but serious black-ops stuff—and that meant he wouldn't be found at all. It had been frustrating as all hell as Zane searched for him. And now here he was, faced with a partner he didn't want, in a job that was swiftly becoming more like work and less like something he enjoyed.

"Good to see you doing well, Special Agent Grady," the secretary offered insincerely as Ty entered the outer office.

"Good to see the stick still firmly lodged, Princess," Ty responded as he walked right by her and waved for her to tell Burns that he was there. She puffed up angrily and jabbed at the intercom to announce him.

Ty entered the Assistant Director's office and stopped short. Over the past five or six hours, he had allowed himself to hope that his new partner would really be his old one. That Burns had finally pulled Zane out of that hell in Miami and brought him back to the Special Crimes unit. But now, he saw with a sinking sensation that his new partner was already here, sitting in one of the chairs opposite Burns with a leather portfolio in his lap, taking notes.

Holy Jesus, he was taking notes.

The young man looked up and over his shoulder to study Ty as Burns started talking. "Special Agent Grady, thank you for joining us. This is David Reese."

The blond man stood, clutching the folder to his chest. Bright green eyes shone through wire-rimmed glasses. "Special Agent Grady," Reese said. "It's great to meet you."

Ty remained planted where he was, staring at the kid. He looked to Burns with sheer outrage glinting in his eyes. "What the shit is this?" he asked.

Reese blinked and looked back at Burns, who was smiling. "David is a junior at Georgetown. He's interning with me this summer. Say hello, Ty," the Assistant Director ordered pleasantly.

Ty stared at him, slightly nonplussed as he looked back at the kid. "Shit," he finally muttered apologetically as he stepped closer and took his hand in greeting. "I thought you were my new partner," he said with a laugh.

"Jesus," Reese muttered as he shook Ty's hand. "I feel for your new partner, man. He'll be crapping his pants."

Burns snorted.

"Yeah well, he also won't look twelve, so he'll be fine," Ty huffed in return.

Reese smiled slightly, but he didn't appear amused by the crack about his age.

"David, Special Agent Grady here is one of the more unconventional agents you may encounter here at the Bureau. Do not include him in your summaries," Burns cautioned with a smirk as he leaned back in his chair.

Reese nodded and smiled wryly. "I should hope not, sir," he answered. "I don't know how you'd keep new recruits."

"We'd feed them to the military," Ty grumbled as he went over and flopped down into the empty chair. "So where is this asshole, anyway?" he asked with frown. "You can't tell me I'm the one on time."

"Actually, you are, although he's not far behind. Security said he came through a few minutes ago," Burns said. Then he looked to Reese. "You see, David, one of the more arduous jobs we have here is figuring out how to gather agents who work effectively together. Special Agent Grady here presents a particularly difficult challenge, as I'm sure you can imagine." The young man glanced to Ty, obviously agreeing with the sentiment.

Burns cocked his head when he heard the outer door open and footsteps clomp in. The office door opened and Reese turned curiously to look. Ty was almost afraid to do the same, but curiosity got the better of him.

Zane Garrett stood totally still just inside the doorway, his eyes already settled intently on Ty.

"Special Agent Garrett, how lovely of you to join us," Burns drawled. "This is David Reese, my newest intern. I believe you already know Special Agent Grady."

After a short pause, Zane nodded slightly.

Ty found himself struggling for something to say as he blinked stupidly at Zane. The lack of reaction was disconcerting. Ty had tried every trick in his book, trying to find a way to get in touch with Zane after the medical leave had ended. But an undercover operation trumped even fake family emergencies, and Ty hadn't been able to get anywhere before his own assignments commenced. He found himself wondering, not for the first time, whether Zane took an assignment he knew would keep him under on purpose, just to keep away from him after the haze of the drugs had cleared.

"Well, David, it's time for your next appointment," Burns said pointedly, ushering the student out the door past Zane. The Assistant

Director shut the door behind him and turned to look at the two men. The office was quiet.

Ty finally swallowed down his shock and looked from Burns to Zane uncertainly. "Hey," he offered.

Zane glanced to Burns as well, and back to Ty. "Hi," he said quietly, taking in Ty's features.

And there seemed to be nothing more to say. Ty finally looked down, unwilling to meet Zane's unreadable eyes.

"Well," Burns said as he moved back to the chair behind his desk. "Garrett, if you choose to move from Arlington closer to your new assignment, the Bureau will pay for temporary accommodations until you can get yourself settled in DC or surrounds. Paperwork's in the mail," he told them as he waved his hand through the air in dismissal, though there was the slightest twist of a smile on his lips.

Zane blinked, surprise and hope emerging in his eyes. "You're... partnering us again?"

"As long as you don't blow anything up again or kill anyone else, yes," Burns answered with some amusement as Ty glanced back up at Zane in surprise. "You'll be working the DC area for now. No undercover work, no big cases until you're both... mentally stable," he said with a wry smirk.

"Does that mean this is a permanent assignment?" Ty asked, his voice low and slightly hoarse.

Burns merely laughed and leaned back in his chair again.

Zane had to tear his eyes away from Ty. "No objection," he said softly.

"Good!" Burns responded with a smile. "Now get the hell out of my office," he said as the smile dropped back into his customary scowl. "And take a fucking shower," he ordered. "Both of you."

Zane took an awkward step backward, watching Ty again, and reached behind himself to grasp the doorknob. He pulled open the door and waited. Burns's lips twitched as he watched, and he shook his head ever so slightly.

Ty looked back at the Assistant Director uncertainly and then nodded obediently, glancing at Zane as he passed by him out the door. Zane watched him the whole way and then followed, pulling the door shut as they left. He was completely oblivious to the secretary staring at them.

Ty slowed to a stop and turned to meet Zane's eyes. He glanced at the secretary and then back at Zane, turning again to keep moving without ever saying anything. After a moment's pause, Zane blinked and strode after him, out into the hall, catching up at the elevator.

Ty had his head down, waiting for the doors to open. "How have you been?" he asked quietly without looking up.

Zane cast over the five months of hell in Miami. "Shitty," he answered in the same soft tone. "You?"

Ty looked up slightly but didn't answer. The doors whooshed open, and he stepped inside the elevator car. Zane didn't hesitate to follow. He punched the button for the parking garage, and the doors slid shut. "I tried to get in touch with you," Ty finally murmured without looking at Zane. "They said you were unreachable. You went back to Miami," he said bitterly, his voice almost accusing.

"I didn't have much of a choice. It was that or New Mexico," Zane said. He didn't try to apologize. "I . . . I didn't know you were looking for me. We were buried." He leaned back against the wall. "I called in a couple times. They wouldn't tell me anything about you," he growled.

Ty glanced at Zane sideways, really looking at him for the first time. "You've been shot again, haven't you?" he asked in resignation.

Zane didn't try to lie. He just let his eyes drop. Ty nodded and looked away, the swirling in his stomach nearly unbearable.

"Did you get your head on straight?" Zane asked. The elevator stopped and the doors opened.

Ty stood there, looking out into the parking deck with a sort of distance to his expression that was fairly common lately. "No," he answered softly.

Zane swallowed, hurting. He reached out and blocked the door open and waved Ty through.

Ty walked past him with his head down again, hands in his pockets as he headed for his car. Suddenly, he stopped and looked up, inhaling deeply. "You did have a choice," he murmured.

Zane halted in place. He'd considered the other option. Once. Fleetingly. "No," he said clearly. "I didn't want to give up on seeing you again."

Ty's eyes wandered along the cement ceiling of the parking structure, his back still turned as he considered Zane's answer. "But it wasn't worth it to leave," he finally murmured, as if talking to himself.

Swallowing on the pain, Zane closed his eyes for a long moment. When he spoke, it was a rasp. "We can still cut and run." His shoulders tightened. "But now we don't have to."

Ty stood there for another moment before turning slowly to look back at Zane. He looked at the leather and the fresh scars, letting his eyes carry over them pointedly. "You didn't listen to a damn thing I told you," he said softly. "Did you?"

Zane flinched, and true regret was clear on his face. "No," he said miserably. "Not for a while. I wasn't . . ." He huffed. "I wasn't . . . there," he said weakly, waving at his head.

"You shouldn't have to be there to be careful," Ty growled in response. "It's common fucking sense, Garrett!" he shouted suddenly, his voice echoing through the structure.

Nervously licking his upper lip, Zane winced and straightened his shoulders. "What do you want me to say, Ty?" he asked. "It won't change it."

"I want you to say you're sorry," Ty demanded stubbornly. "And I want you to tell me how pissed you are at me for leaving when I did!"

"I was so angry I saw red for weeks," Zane admitted. "Even though I knew there wasn't a goddamn thing you could do about it," he went on, voice getting louder as he allowed the emotion to break through. "I was furious with the Bureau for chucking me back into hell, and I was pissed with myself for letting them. For a while, the best thing I could come up with was hoping an injury would land me back in the fucking hospital," he growled, incensed, his eyes flashing. "I would have done anything. Anything to get back to you. I can't say I'm sorry for that."

Ty exhaled slowly, calming. "Better," he said softly with a nod.

Shaking, Zane took a couple steps toward Ty, set a hand on his chest, and pushed him hard against the concrete pillar behind him. "That's all you have to say?" he demanded, the fury still clear.

Ty moved suddenly, shoving Zane away before grabbing his face with both hands and kissing him forcefully, right there in the parking garage. Zane reeled back a couple steps as Ty's weight hit him. He got his balance and grabbed both of Ty's upper arms, taking those steps forward again and pinning Ty against the wall. It was a gloriously violent kiss that he poured all his anguish and anger into.

Ty gripped him mindlessly, not even concerned about the possibility of the security cameras catching them as they took out the past five months of frustration on each other. Finally, he shoved at Zane roughly, gasping for breath. When pushed, Zane turned and stalked a few steps away. He stood there, trying to get his breath, and he wiped his mouth with the back of his hand.

"I'm not sorry," he muttered as he dragged a hand through his short hair.

Ty rested his head back against the concrete wall and closed his eyes. "I am," he whispered.

Zane's emotions played openly across his face. He wasn't even trying to hide them. He was hurt, he was confused, and he was scared. "What for?" he asked, voice aching. He couldn't bring himself to move again, to rejoin Ty four strides away.

"Leaving," Ty answered as he opened his eyes again.

The frustration and anger faded as Zane took a good long look at him. He looked like hell. He was tan enough that it spoke of time in some exotic location, but the arduous past five months fairly clung to him. His eyes were flat and tired, his face was scruffy, and even though he'd slept, he still looked haggard. Three of the fingers on his right hand were badly broken and bandaged. The smoke of the expensive cigars he smoked was strong enough for Zane to smell without trying.

Zane considered barking at him for not taking care of himself, but it just wasn't in him. After so long apart, he didn't want to hurt anymore. Slowly his feet moved, taking him closer to Ty until he stood less than an arm's length away. Zane couldn't stifle the sigh, and he resisted the urge to reach out and touch. "I thought you were supposed to get better on convalescent leave," he murmured.

"Maybe I had some unfinished business to tend to first," Ty responded wryly, his voice low and hoarse.

"Christ," Zane muttered. "We're both such a fucking mess."

"I worried about you," Ty admitted.

Zane sighed and lowered his head, looking up at Ty from under lowered brows. The proximity alone was easing his pain as much as anything. "I couldn't stop thinking about you."

"Why the hell didn't you come home?" Ty asked, letting the anguish leak through.

"The same reason you walked away," Zane whispered.

"'Cause you didn't know anything about black market orchids?" Ty asked weakly.

Zane's laugh was choked, but it was still a laugh. "Allergies?" he offered, trying to dip his head to meet Ty's gaze.

Ty lifted his chin and made eye contact. "I still drink," he blurted. "And I still smoke illegal Cubans. And I still take barmaids home and fuck them when I start thinking about you too much."

The slight humor left Zane's eyes, replaced with a carefully guarded look. He hadn't touched a drop. He hadn't touched a pill. He hadn't touched a cigarette, because that was what Ty had wanted. And he couldn't bring himself to touch anyone else. It was the only way he had to stay connected to Ty, to convince himself that Ty might still want him when they finally met again. "Is that supposed to scare me away?" he finally asked.

"Needed you to know," Ty answered quietly.

Zane nodded slowly. "And what do you need to know?"

"You still want me around?" Ty asked after a moment of consideration.

"Yeah," Zane said softly, not yet touching like he wanted to. "Do you still want me?"

"Yeah," Ty breathed, the word barely audible.

Zane let out a pent-up breath and looked away. "Let's get out of here," he suggested as he reached for Ty. The sound of one of the elevator doors whooshing shut made Ty jump imperceptibly. Zane jerked his hand back, then he nodded and looked around them; he'd forgotten they were in the goddamn parking garage. "You're going to have to check out a car or get a cab," he said apologetically. "I'm on the bike."

"I drove my truck," Ty murmured. "I didn't figure my new partner would want to drag me home," he said with a slightly sly smile.

"Damn it. I wanted to get you on the Valkyrie," Zane muttered.

"Not a chance in hell," Ty answered instantly. "I got those things out of my system a decade ago."

Zane rolled his eyes and stepped back. "Shit, Grady. I gave up drinking, drugs, and smoking for you. I am not giving up my motorcycle."

Ty grinned slowly, a hint of the former mischief entering his eyes. Zane crossed his arms stubbornly, sulking.

"Well, that's unbecoming," Ty murmured as he reached out and took Zane's elbow. "Ride with me," he suggested with a smirk that faded into a smile. "We can catch up on the ride home."

"Fine." Zane gave a put-upon sigh and started to walk alongside him. "But we're coming back for the Valkyrie."

"Whatever you say, Hoss," Ty muttered agreeably.

Zane's smile was big and silly. "So. Baltimore, huh? Think I can find any action there?" he asked as Ty led him to an old green and tan Ford Bronco.

"Maybe," Ty answered seriously. "When the Ravens lose you can find any number of drunken people wandering the streets, looking for mindless physical comfort. And the two times the Os won last year were pretty exciting."

"Are you a Ravens fan?" Zane asked as he opened the passenger-side door. He paused as he looked at the passenger seat and the door that he held onto, stilled by a spark of irrational fear that caught him every time. It was why he rode the bike almost exclusively now. Logic be damned, the motorcycle felt safer than a car. "I mean, are you a . . . a f-football fan?" he forced out, unconsciously rubbing at his right arm as he made himself get in the truck.

Ty glanced over as he heard the stutter. "The Ravens were named for the story by Poe, you know," he said as he watched Zane. They both had their scars, inside and outside. He could see that now.

Zane met his eyes and slowly relaxed. "No," he said quietly. "I didn't know that."

"I bet there's a lot you don't know," Ty told him with a small, teasing smile.

The corners of Zane's mouth turned up. "Yeah. There is," he agreed.

Once they were out on the road, Ty reached over and slid his fingers through Zane's tentatively. His thumb rubbed absently over the wedding ring Zane still wore, then he squeezed his hand and kept his eyes on the busy road, not mentioning the ring or all the complications their new partnership might entail. Ty took his eyes off the road long enough to look over at Zane and smile crookedly. "It should be easier to sleep tonight," he said softly instead.

"Yeah. It will."

Explore more of the *Cut & Run* series at:
riptidepublishing.com/collections/cut-run

Cut & Run

THE SERIES

Abigail Roux

Dear Reader,

Thank you for reading Abigail Roux's *Cut & Run*!

We know your time is precious and you have many, many entertainment options, so it means a lot that you've chosen to spend your time reading. We really hope you enjoyed it.

We'd be honored if you'd consider posting a review—good or bad—on sites like **Amazon, Barnes & Noble, Kobo, Goodreads, Twitter, Facebook, Tumblr,** and your blog or website. We'd also be honored if you told your friends and family about this book. Word of mouth is a book's lifeblood!

For more information on upcoming releases, author interviews, blog tours, contests, giveaways, and more, please sign up for our weekly, spam-free newsletter and visit us around the web:

Newsletter: riptidepublishing.com/newsletter
Twitter: twitter.com/RiptideBooks
Facebook: facebook.com/RiptidePublishing
Goodreads: tinyurl.com/RiptideOnGoodreads
Tumblr: riptidepublishing.tumblr.com

Thank you so much for Reading the Rainbow!

RiptidePublishing.com

RIPTIDE PUBLISHING

ALSO BY ABIGAIL ROUX

Cut & Run series
Sticks & Stones (with Madeleine Urban)
Fish & Chips (with Madeleine Urban)
Divide & Conquer (with Madeleine Urban)
Armed & Dangerous
Stars & Stripes
Touch & Geaux
Ball & Chain
Crash & Burn

Sidewinder series
Shock & Awe
Cross & Crown
Part & Parcel

Novels
According to Hoyle
The Gravedigger's Brawl
The Archer

Novellas
The Bone Orchard
A Tale from de Rode
My Brother's Keeper
Seeing Is Believing
Unrequited

With Madeleine Urban
Caught Running
Love Ahead
Warrior's Cross

About the Author

Abigail Roux was born and raised in North Carolina. A past volleyball star who specializes in sarcasm and painful historical accuracy, she currently spends her time coaching high school volleyball and investigating the mysteries of single motherhood. Any spare time is spent living and dying with every Atlanta Braves and Carolina Panthers game of the year. Abigail has a daughter, Little Roux, who is the light of her life, a boxer, four rescued cats who play an ongoing live-action variation of Call of Duty throughout the house, one evil Ragdoll, a certifiable extended family down the road, and a cast of thousands in her head.

Enjoy more stories like
Cut & Run
at RiptidePublishing.com!

Kill Game

The deck is not stacked in their favor with this game-playing killer.

ISBN: 978-1-62649-620-0

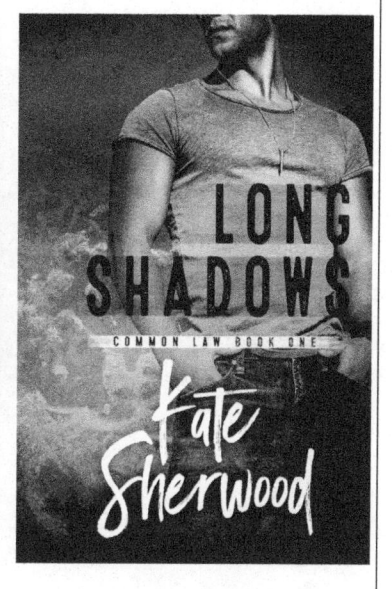

Long Shadows

Sometimes a bad decision is so much better than a good one.

ISBN: 978-1-62649-526-5

RIPTIDE PUBLISHING

Made in United States
North Haven, CT
04 July 2024